NIGHTMARE HUNT

Nightmare Hunt

ILEEN MARTIN

E.L.I.
PUBLISHING
& LITERARY SERVICES

Published by E.L.I. Publishing & Literary Services, 2024
NIGHTMARE HUNT
Second Edition. January 19, 2024.
Written by Ileen Martin.
ISBN: 979-8-9911956-1-4

To my husband, Leo. I love you more.

CONTENTS

PREFACE

There was an eerie quiet outside. And then the doors cracked open.

Belle slammed them back shut and a great bellow of rage shook the room. The strength in her legs left her and she collapsed, just barely keeping her strong grip on the doors. The wardrobe began to shake violently, and she screamed in terror.

The electricity erupted in her hands. "No." She didn't want to kill him. "No powers." She tried to do what she'd learned, imagine her hands free of the blue energy.

It worked.

One of the doors ripped off. She flattened herself against the back of the wardrobe. "No powers, no powers," she chanted in a ragged whisper.

But the energy, not finding an outlet in her hands, began building beneath her skin, all over her body.

"No, no, no, no." It was like the moment before she killed the three Hammerson brothers. If the power exploded out of her now, Liam was a dead man. And Ernesto, too.

The other door ripped off. The terrifying Beast framed her view now. She crouched down into the farthest corner, trying to make herself as small as possible.

No powers, no powers.

The Beast roared into the closeted space, the very sound assaulting her every fiber. She squeezed her eyes shut, tears streaming out.

Belle had made up her mind. She'd die before she killed her loved ones.

She heard the click-clack of the claws entering the wardrobe.

Energy roiled beneath her skin, prickling outward, on the verge of bursting out of her. Soon, she would pass out, and then awaken to the carnage.

A rippling growl filled her ears and hot breath fanned her face. She could feel her strength leaving her.

This was it.

Her eyes peeled open, and she found herself looking into minty green, yellow-flecked eyes devoid of emotion, framed by blonde fur.

"Hurry," she whispered.

Just like in her nightmare, he opened his razor-teethed mouth wide and latched onto her throat.

Darkness consumed her.

| 1 |

Beastly Nightmare

Liam Rawlins had been dreaming of Belle Montague again. Finishing that night they'd started three weeks ago, cuddled up in each other's arms on the living room couch watching a Batman movie.

But they hadn't really been paying much attention to the television in the dream, what with all the lip-locking and carnal exploration they were absorbed in. Something his gentleman side had promised not to dive into with her so soon.

But dream-Belle had made the first move, so who was he to deny his girl?

He knew the real Belle, or even he himself, would never have let things progress so soon to where they had. Clothing landing on the floor, a shoe tugged off and hitting the TV, and two heated bodies collapsing on the couch together. Impossible, he knew from Belle's character, but thankfully it had still been *his* dream.

1

Only, it'd turned into a nightmare. The same nightmare every dream of Belle always turned into.

He cupped her face as he kissed her neck, his other hand roaming down the soft skin of her back.

"Ow," she winced. "That hurts."

He loosened his grip on her and concentrated on keeping his cursed fingernails from sharpening into claws.

But, dammit, he was losing control. Again.

He could feel the hot passion coursing through his blood, morphing into a boiling rage that felt like it was taking hold of his very bones, twisting and pulling at them until the only relief was to allow himself to succumb to the animal within.

"Ow, Liam!" She scuttled away to the far end of the couch and felt her neck. "You bit me." Her horror-stricken eyes met his, at the warm blood seeping through her fingers.

He opened his mouth to beg for her forgiveness and to try and explain, but the searing rip inside his belly wrenched the words from his mouth. He collapsed to the floor, writhing and clutching his stomach.

"Liam!" She tried holding him as convulsions wracked his body. "What's wrong? Please, talk to me!"

One strangled word was all he could manage before he lost human speech. "Run."

"What? No, let me help you!"

He meant to say the word again, but what erupted from his throat was an unnatural snarl that made her recoil.

The transformation happened quickly now, a familiar physiological process his body had memorized. The blonde fur sprouted out of every pore of his skin as his joints snapped, bones lengthened, and jaw stretched.

It was excruciating. Every. Single. Time. Like his body was undergoing every medieval torture at once. Even in these nightmares, his subconscious writhed with the agony.

His human form never remembered what he did as Violet Wickeby's cursed canine beast. But in these dreams, his mind felt conscious during the whole ordeal, so he knew what would come next.

He was the beast now, and it pinned Belle with a feral stare, growling its warnings.

She clambered to her feet, her face frozen in terror. Palms up as she backtracked slowly.

The sight of such easy prey made the hairs arch on his back and his claws elongate with anticipation, and with a snapping bark, he rushed at her. He sank his sharp canines into her throat, until her screams died off in the night.

Liam pinched the bridge of his nose and squeezed his eyes shut. He waited for the painful white spots to flash, the only thing that worked in clearing the remnants of the nightmare from his thoughts.

He'd dwelled achingly on the first part of the dream, raking in his lower lip at the memory. But the ending—Belle's bloody and lifeless body—always served to remind him why he'd made the decision to cut her out of his life.

For her own safety. He wasn't going to give his nightmares a chance to become reality.

He looked down at the feminine hand bedecked in expensive rings and bracelets trailing up his inner thigh. With a grunt of disgust, he snatched the hand and cast it back towards its owner. "Don't *ever* touch me, witch."

Violet Wickeby laughed as she let herself fall back against the limo seat perpendicular to his. "I can't help myself when it comes to a Rawlins man." Her eyes trailed over him. "And that suit you're wearing makes you extra delectable."

He grimaced. Violet and her twin minions had ambushed him on the balcony outside his bedroom three weeks ago. Her wannabe thugs hadn't been a problem, but she'd bent him to his knees with her threats to possess Belle. She'd cast a spell on him then: a beast at her beck and call. But he'd never given her his permission, so he'd kept his free will.

Only problem was she used threats to break him, manipulate him into obedience.

When he'd refused to obey her first order—accompany her on a business trip to Europe to intimidate wealthy elites into fattening her bank account—she'd made good on her first threat: she killed Jacques. The family butler who'd been there for him for as long as he could remember.

And now he was dead, cast in the deepest dungeon cell of the castle.

Then, she'd threatened Belle's family and friends. She would pick them off one by one until she'd gotten what she wanted from him. All he had to do was obey, and no one would get hurt.

Which was why he was currently wearing an Armani business suit, his blonde hair cut short with the sides shaved, top gelled slick back, and sitting in a stretch limo—next to the smug, demon-possessed immortal woman who'd killed his parents and his butler, and separated him from the girl of his dreams—on the way to the next business executive's office soon to be suckered out of millions of dollars.

As current owner of his late father's multinational corporation, Rawlins Enterprises, his business proposals would attempt to persuade the targeted CEO first, and when that wouldn't work, Violet made sure the Beast came out to intimidate.

"Mr. Rawlins," Violet cooed in a way that churned his stomach. "You're *so* sensitive."

He glared at her with every ounce of hatred he could muster.

She didn't look like Belle's mother, Abigail, anymore, the body that the demon witch had possessed. Violet had taken to wearing stage make-up and facial prosthetics to change her appearance and cover up the scars Abigail had torn into her own face.

She dressed like a powerhouse businesswoman and wore a convincing brown wig, blue eye contacts, and a nose piece that hid her identity from Ernesto Panzinski, Belle's uncle, who they knew was using all of his police force's resources to search for Violet.

Liam had once left Ernesto a clue in the last hotel they'd stayed at, hoping the Elmridge sheriff would eventually catch up to them, but Violet had caught the note and punished him by making him watch as she broke the maid's leg in three places.

He never tried something like that again.

Many times, he felt himself close to snapping and outright strangling her. But he knew Violet could simply call a lightning bolt down from the sky or zap him with one from her own hand. It would be suicide to physically attack her.

"Oh, don't look so melancholy," she purred, scooting a little closer. He looked sharply at her in warning. She smirked. "How about I make you a promise? You know I always keep my promises."

True. But it was always the kind that felt like making a deal with the devil.

She still had his attention, which signaled her to continue. "This is the second-to-last deal we're going to tie up together."

"What's the last deal?"

"And then a *favor* after the last deal."

He ground his teeth at her stalling to answer his question. He didn't like to waste words, breath, or even attention on her.

Knowing this, Violet sighed and leaned back in her seat again, analyzing her long, blood-red nails. Stalling. "I do need to take care of these again."

Liam launched a champagne glass at her. The instant it smashed by her head, an electrified bolt shot from her hand, stopping just a hairsbreadth away from his chest.

If he breathed, the bolt would kill him.

"Temper, temper," she sneered. With her free hand, she dabbed a napkin at the champagne that sprayed her face and blouse and shook the glass shards loose from her hair. "And you'll pay for that starting now."

He stared down at the end of the bright white bolt, fizzing and crackling. Just one deep breath, one sigh, and he could end it all now.

As if reading his thoughts, Violet curled her hand in, and the bolt lazily retreated into her palm and vanished. She smiled, a delightfully wicked idea just occurring to her. "You will pay...by listening to the information I am going to give you. How is it they say these days? Good news and bad news."

Liam merely shifted in his seat away from her and gazed out the window. He could see in the window's reflection the dead look in his green eyes. It was the only way to stay sane: mentally disconnect himself in her presence.

"Good news first. After this particular job, you will help me get my hands on the next gem I need in Elmridge, and then you will transfer all of your wealth to me."

He couldn't help it; he snorted.

"Oh dear, you're right. I guess it was good news for *me*."

He let one corner of his mouth curl into a half-smile as he continued staring out the window, the front façades of the Amsterdam business buildings rolling by.

The witch didn't know it yet, but as soon as she started using him to blackmail and intimidate other wealthy people into handing her a hefty slice of their fortune, he immediately transferred all of his wealth in secret to Mr. Gregory Ellerson in Elmridge, his father's former business partner and a trusted family friend while he was growing up. In fact, Mr. Ellerson and his daughter, Cindy, were supposed to be moving into the castle by now.

At least Liam had one-upped the witch on one score.

"When you've finished both tasks, I will release you from my spell."

His breath stilled.

"See, there is a bright spot for you."

"What's the bad news?" he asked, his voice monotone. Bright spot or not, he didn't trust her.

When she didn't answer right away and he heard rustling, he looked over at her just as she pulled out a large, thick book from her Hermès Birkin bag. She tossed it onto the seat next to him.

The Elmridge Book of Fairy Tales by A.E.P. He'd seen a copy in Belle's museum collection, but this copy looked very old with its moth-bitten corners and yellowed pages sticking out unevenly.

"I swiped it on my last visit to the Prynn home from Abigail's secret drawer," Violet said, all smug. "It's the original. It has stories that the widely circulated edition doesn't have. Did you know these legends and fairy tales that the Prynn sisters recorded in this book are all true?"

Liam's lips twitched with doubt.

She murmured a strange word as she flicked her index finger toward the book.

He flinched as it snapped open. He watched, transfixed, as the pages flew past on their own, finally settling on a large, colorful illustration of a grassy field under a blue sky dotted with white, puffy clouds.

Two characters occupied the hazy Monet-styled picture: a shadowy figure with gem-like eyes and a glowing blade in its hand, stalked a beautiful, unsuspecting young woman holding a bundle of wildflowers to her chest. Tiny, fat Valentine cherubs watched the two from their perch on the clouds.

But it was the girl's hands that drew Liam's focus: they were covered in blood.

"Remember what I told you about your Belle and her deadly secret?" Violet asked. "Well, listen to this and tell me what you think."

She closed her eyes and began reciting a poem.

Liam realized it was the curly-scripted poem on the adjacent page. He read along silently, his stomach hollowing out more with each stanza:

> *For those gifted and empowered*
> *From the immortal Fae's bower,*
> *Let no human blood spill from your kill.*
> *Let no human life be cost of your strife.*

For soon as their blood seeps into the Earth,
Your Jäger—your death—will be given birth.
But the Fae love twists and polar opposites,
The cure for the death then is a love truly pure.

The Jäger, the hunted—one match of true love,
Passionate soul symmetry ordained from Above.
Only one switched prophecy in Jäger history.
Only one doomed kiss for Dommedag bliss.

Fury fired up in him. "You promised Belle wouldn't be hurt if I obeyed you. Now you're telling me that a Jäger is going to try to kill her? You *lied* to me." He pounded his fist on the armrest, which was met with a crunching sound. "You should have left me behind to protect her."

She rolled her eyes. "Were you not listening, you hothead? Belle's Jäger *is* her true love, so he won't hurt her."

He opened his mouth to counter, but hesitated, until all he could say with a touch of uncertainty was, "You don't know what you're talking about."

She flicked her wrist and the book snapped shut, startling him. The book zoomed straight into her waiting hand.

He wet his lips nervously. He never could get used to the magic tricks.

"Oh, but I do know it's about Belle." She stashed the book back in her purse. "I have a very reliable source from the Jäger Temple. I happen to know who Belle's Jäger is." She flicked a glass shard off her sleeve.

He was about to ask how she could possibly receive help from the Jäger, sworn enemies of murderous monsters like her, but he didn't get the chance.

"Are you ready for the bad news now?" She leaned forward in her seat, a wicked glint in her eyes. "If you are not her true love, and my spell's proviso is that you won't be able to hurt your true love, whatever in the world is going to keep you from hurting Belle?"

She smirked as she watched it sink in his mind. With a glance at her watch and out the window, assessing how far they were from their destination, she said somewhat absently, "It is going to be quite the entertainment when we get back to Elmridge. You'll be my eyes and ears, of course."

Shaken to his core, he finally ground out, "I will never hurt Belle, and I will never spy for you."

A small, mysterious smile spread on her blood-red lips. "Oh, you will, my dear Rawlins man, you will."

| 2 |

Ghosted

"One?" Jan, the waitress at Ridge Rats Bar and Grill, asked hopefully.

Belle Montague glared at her. "Two. My friend's meeting me here."

Jan's prejudice against Liam Rawlins was obvious from the last time the two had eaten there. Or *tried* to eat there.

That is until the cook, Miguel, decided to leave a particularly organic you're-not-welcome-here sauce on Liam's grilled chicken.

She hugged the latest novel she was reading to her chest as Jan led her to a corner booth of the restaurant, far away from the busy section of innocents the waitress didn't want Liam to murder.

Jan wiped down the table. "Would you like to order now, or wait for your guest?"

"I'll wait. Just a glass of water for now, please."

The waitress left behind two menus, and just as Belle was feeling grateful that the Timbuktu-section of the restaurant was perfect for some quiet reading, she reappeared with her water.

"Thanks, Jan."

The waitress perched her hands on her hips with a concerned big-sister look on her face. "Do you know what you're doing, sweetheart?"

"Um, reading a book?"

"I mean about Liam Rawlins."

"Oh."

Before Belle could summon a defense on his behalf, Jan started ticking off on her fingers. "He's known for three things in this town: football god, millionaire playboy, and," she whispered loudly, "killing his family."

"He's innocent."

"Maybe." Jan raised her palms. "Maybe it's possible he's not a murderer, and the news reports weren't totally accurate. But, from one female to another, that playboy business? You can write a country song album off the number of hearts he's broken."

Belle felt her temper simmering beneath her skin and knew where that heat would fire up next. She clenched her fists in her lap. "I'd like the grilled cheese, please."

Jan glanced at the empty seat in front of Belle before looking back at her as if she was going to be the next track number on Liam's *Achy Breaky Heart* album. She shrugged her shoulders. "Sure thing. White or wheat?"

After Jan left, Belle re-checked the text message Liam had sent her that morning:

Meet me at Ridge Rats. 1:00. Come alone.

Three weeks. An eternity since she'd seen him and enjoyed his barrage of kisses. It seemed like the universe had ushered them into each other's arms.

She'd moved there to Elmridge, town of the uber-rich and exclusive, from her one-room life with her father in Littleton, just after he'd died in her arms. Meanwhile, Liam had secluded himself for a year after being blamed for his parents' murders, when in fact, they had been killed by her own mother.

Well, her possessed mother, who was hundreds of years old and could shoot lightning from her hands.

And that dose of deadly and weird is what had woven Liam and Belle's lives together. Hunting for the truth together. And occasionally tripping and falling onto each other's lips.

Belle blushed thinking of the last night she'd seen him. Those kisses and embraces had been so full of promise.

So much so, they'd made her forget the hellish hours just before. Her mother, Abigail Prynn, possessed by a centuries-old vengeful spirit, Violet Wickeby, had tried to kill her uncle and then had made off with the golden pixie dust. All for some ridiculous endgame of crowning herself queen of the world.

Then, after having been locked in a dungeon of his castle by Aunt Emily for his own safety, Liam had shown up later that night, spilling his soul to her and sealing his words with kisses.

Oh, and he'd used Shakespeare as his wingman. What Elizabethan-loving girl could resist that? And then, before leaving her swooning on the front porch, Liam had promised to return within half-an-hour.

It was now three weeks.

Unreturned phone calls had her thinking the worst. Had Violet gotten to him and made good on her threat to hurt him?

Her uncle, Ernesto, had stopped her from marching over to his castle after a few days of non-replies, and he'd gone in her stead. He'd returned with the news that he'd had to stick his gun in Jacques's face to get the butler to take him to Liam, who'd claimed he didn't want any visitors.

Ernesto had found Liam living in a pigsty in his bedroom, as if he hadn't left the place in a week. All her uncle would say then with his stoic ex-KGB or CIA demeanor (she still didn't know who he used to work for) was that Liam needed time to "process everything." Soon after, Ernesto found out Liam had crossed the Atlantic Ocean on a business trip to Europe, where he's been ever since.

And time to process everything?! That was euphemism for *I need to stay the heck away from you for a while.* Even she understood that, and her experience with real-life boys was sadly lacking compared with the book-boyfriend ones that thrived in her head.

She was just so confused.

How does a guy go from making you feel like you're the most special thing in existence to *Hey, let's take a break because you're a weirdo who can spit electricity from your hands. And, oh yeah, your mom killed mine.*

The only rationalizing Belle could do was that once Liam had gone home after their snuggle/smooch-fest, reality had hit him, and he realized he had to get off the crazy train he'd boarded when he got himself involved with her.

If she really thought about it, *really* put herself in his shoes, then she guessed she could respect that. She wouldn't want to be involved with herself either.

An incoming text-chime startled her.

Check in.

She slumped against her seat. Just Ernesto and his random daily check-ins.

Belle: **Having lunch at Ridge Rats.**

Ernesto: **With who?**

Belle: **By myself.**

Ernesto: **Why?**

She let a few seconds pass, her uncle probably watching her text-bubble "thinking." She shrugged as she hit send, **Why not?**

Ernesto: **Ok.**

Typical. No frills, to the point.

These days, Ernesto was holed up at the Wall, the militaristic fortress that enclosed the town. He'd learned through some secret intelligence that Violet Wickeby was spotted in Europe, and so with the main threat on another continent for now, Ernesto didn't hesitate to leave Belle behind at home on most days so he could chase Wickeby's virtual trail.

After all, the Jäeger, fabled hunters who eliminated dangerous supernatural targets, wouldn't bother with Belle, especially since she hadn't killed anyone. So Ernesto didn't need to worry so much about his niece's safety since no hunters would have been "activated" to her presence.

Or so he thought.

Belle hadn't the heart nor the guts to tell her uncle that she'd already killed three men. Albeit, in self-defense. But still. Was it enough to draw a hunter to her? Wickeby had sure taunted her with the idea, and assured her, quite gleefully, that it was only a matter of time until she met the end of a hunter's blade.

Belle wrinkled her nose. A crisp burning smell came from the pages of the book gripped tightly in her hands. Her eyes widened as she lifted her fingers, each one leaving behind a charcoaled spot on the pages.

She closed her eyes, trying to keep her breathing steady. *Think happy thoughts.*

An ostensibly silly piece of advice given by Aunt Emily. Surprisingly useful for getting her raging firecracker hands under control. This—and blood on her hands—was why the Jäger, no doubt, would be after her.

Her hands were sparking now like live electrical wires.

She glanced around to see if Jan or anyone else was close enough to notice. A waiter was wiping down a table in the next aisle.

"Happy thoughts, happy thoughts, happy thoughts," she chanted, panicking.

Liam came to mind. With his golden skin and hair and mint green eyes, the feel of his strength beneath her hands as he held her...and how long it's been since she'd seen the jerk.

The sparks in her hands erupted into fire.

"Aaack!" She waved them around frantically beneath the table and squeezed her eyes shut, trying to grasp like straws at any memory that brought her happiness:

Papa's crinkly smile. My two best friends, Candy and Millie. Aunt Emily finally reuniting with her long, lost son, Peter, before he took her away.

The crackling noise was dying down, so she held onto that last memory.

Emily, eyes shining with pure joy as her prodigal son held her hand and guided her to the open window. Then, Emily turning her head to spare Belle—who was seated, watching, from a dark corner of the room—a tearful wink and a smile of *thank you.*

The fire finally dissipated, leaving behind a strong, smoky odor that was sure to arouse Jan's suspicion when she returned.

Belle collected her things and moved three booths over.

Looking down again at the soot fingerprints on the book, she sighed. It wasn't even her book. It was her new friend's book, Eddie Helsing, a newbie at the school who'd recently joined her and her friends, Cindy and Q, in the cafeteria at their table. He'd had to earn his seat by passing Q's rapid-fire round of fantasy and sci-fi trivia.

Eddie, the friend who'd finally made her feel *something* after being numb for weeks. Given her a miraculous kick out of her emotional hidey-hole with just one smile.

At first, she'd treated his arrival like a passing breeze: she'd acknowledged it, and then forgotten about it.

All she knew was that he was tall, had dark hair, and sat a few seats away from her at lunch. And if he had ever addressed any questions her way, she'd grunted in response and continued pushing the food around on her tray.

At the time, everything had been filtered through her Liam-abandoned-me goggles, leaving her world a dismal gray.

Eddie had sat at their lunch table every day, and after quietly answering Cindy's polite questions, had withdrawn into himself. Once more, the routine of perpetual silence had settled at the table.

The lunch table had already emanated a society-rejects-sit-here vibe, and so it seemed as if the new-arrival had naturally gravitated to his "people."

He was probably a kindred spirit, if Belle just gave him a real chance.

Whatever the case, she still knew in her mind the right thing to do would be to show him the same kindness she'd received at the lunch table when she'd first been the newbie. But whenever she tried to think of friendly openers, the gray fog in her brain crowded them out.

That is, until one day, Eddie so happened to have the conversation piece that had rebooted Belle's brain. A book. A real live book in his hands. Outside of Liam's castle library and her family's small collection in the museum, all literature in Elmridge was digitized. Tragically so.

So how did Eddie get his hands on an actual book? Just maybe, he had his own stash. So as a book-addict, Belle's mind sharpened up rather quickly at the prospect of scoring a new book to read.

And that meant making Eddie her new friend.

Only she hadn't been prepared for the total onslaught of finally looking him in the face.

"What are you reading?" she asked, a sporkful of spaghetti paused midway to her mouth.

Eddie, sitting two seats away, ignored her. He was busy slurping up a noodle while his eyes remained glued to the page. His wire-rimmed glasses sat precariously at the edge of his nose.

Belle looked to Cindy Ellerson, sitting across from her, for support.

"Welcome back," was all Cindy said to her.

For the past two weeks, their roles had been reversed. Before, her utterly beautiful blonde friend had been a silent shell of a person due to the abuse she'd suffered at her stepmother's hands, who'd also happened to be the principal of the school.

But with the wicked stepmom out of the picture now, her father fully recovering from a coma, and the new, fun-loving Dr. Earheart as principal now, Cindy was slowly returning to her old, slightly more outgoing self.

With her hood continually drawn up and her hands stuffed into its long sleeves, Cindy still walled herself from others, but she was smiling more and meeting people's eyes now. "Baby steps," she'd said.

Now, Belle was the quiet, sullen one at the table.

"Um, Eddie? Belle's talking to you," Cindy said.

With one finger, he slid the glasses back up his nose and brought the book closer to his face, so only his messy black hair peeked over the edge.

Frowning in annoyance, Cindy picked a grape out of her fruit cup and launched it towards the book.

Like lightning, Eddie snatched the projectile fruit out of the air and popped it into his mouth.

Slack-jawed, Belle mirrored Cindy's shock.

Even Q, who'd been typing away at his laptop the whole time, paused long enough to state, "The likelihood of that happening was 1 in 1,132."

Eddie still hadn't responded. He chewed slowly, his eyes roaming the page more quickly now before turning it.

As Belle watched him, waiting for him to acknowledge their existence, she realized she was really seeing him for the first time. And not like the quiet, fuzzy figure through her peripheral vision these past three weeks.

Call it a serving of cold karma, but after pretty much ignoring him this whole time, now that she wanted to talk to him, he was ignoring her. Feeling she deserved that, she was about to retreat into her shell again, when he suddenly snapped the book shut, causing her to bounce on her chair.

"Hunger Games," he said, looking straight at Belle. He turned to Q, who merely raised an eyebrow at him, "And with enough LARPing, making that sort of catch becomes very possible."

"What is LAR-" The girls were cut off by Q, "You Live-Action-Role-Play?"

Eddie nodded. "I'm the Highlander Samurai."

The girls exchanged incredulous glances. They'd never seen stone-cold, logical make-a-Vulcan-proud Q this excited—the only indicators being his wide eyes and laser-focus on Eddie and not his laptop.

Q shook the ruddy hair out of his eyes and adjusted his tortoise-shell glasses. "It would not be illogical to presume that you are also familiar with Dungeons & Dragons?"

Eddie nodded. "I've never lost a quest."

"Yet." And Q actually smiled. A disturbing Cheshire Cat smile. "You have never served at my table."

"You're on, Dungeon Master."

And then, Eddie smiled. Just a small side-smile that tugged up his left cheek.

Belle couldn't tear her eyes away.

"You've never asked me to play?" Cindy whispered at Q, her voice gaining strength as she spoke. "It's always work, work, work at your store."

"You would not talk before." He retreated behind his laptop again and muttered, "Now you talk too much."

Cindy glared and chucked a handful of lettuce at him.

Belle laughed at the large piece that landed on his hair like a little hat.

Q frowned and flicked the offending lettuce off. "You are fortunate you top my Friends List."

Belle stifled a guffaw, and when she caught Eddie's eye, her laughter dissipated.

He was staring at her intently with his glasses in one hand and one of its temple-arms caught between his teeth.

Oh Mylanta. He was...stunning. Like he must have fairy and vampire blood mixed together because the beauty was ethereal. And not of the good-fairy, tame-vampire kind. But the kind your mother warned you about and your father wouldn't let you leave the house with.

The kind that ruined a girl.

He had the chiseled jaw and lush lips that struck an uncanny resemblance to Liam's. But Eddie's thick, black eyebrows were permanently angled in a way that gave him a resting smolder-look. And without his glasses as a buffer, that look had just been unleashed on poor, unsuspecting Belle. Those caramel-colored eyes made his allure even more unnatural. Even if those eyes did look angry. Glaring, in fact.

Wait, why was he glaring at her?

"What?" Belle asked.

He slid the book over to her. "You like to read?"

Did she like to breathe?

Cindy answered for her with a giggle, "Like a fat man likes cake."

"That was size-ist of you," Q said drily.

Belle gazed longingly at the book. She missed books. And Liam's library. And Liam.

She sighed gloomily.

Eddie leaned forward again, ensnaring her in his gaze. "Take it. Take the book." He stared intently, unblinking, and even narrowed his eyes as if concentrating.

"I think he's challenging you to a staring contest, Belle," Cindy said. Oddly enough, she added, "You should take the book, though."

"Go ahead and borrow it," Eddie said, not once relinquishing his stare. "I insist."

Ok, now she could feel a creepy-stalker vibe clutching at her like a tentacle. She shivered and shifted uncomfortably in her seat. "Um, no thanks."

He blinked.

She returned to her plate and twirled up another bite of spaghetti. A gorgeous creepy dude was still a creepy dude.

His eyebrows flew up in surprise. "That's not...supposed to happen," he mumbled to himself.

Belle gave him a sideways look as Cindy took the words out of her mouth, "You mean like you've never lost a staring contest?"

He slid his glasses back on. "Uh, something like that." But that fierce façade he'd been projecting for some reason shattered. He looked as if his center had been thrown off kilter. "I-I have to go." He stood and slung his arms through his backpack, his black sweater displaying an anime character that her friend Millie also sported as a patch on her bookbag.

He turned to go, but Belle held up his forgotten book. "Wait, what about this?"

He faced her, his expression gentler than before. "You should read it."

She turned it over and looked at its cover. "What's it about?"

"Hunters."

The word sent a chill through her.

He held her gaze as he continued, his tone dead-serious, "Ordinary citizens selected and primed to hunt others."

She had to look away. He was striking too close to home. She noticed the bookmark stuck halfway through the book. "But, um, you're not even done." She offered the book back.

"It's fine. She's just deciding whether the guy she thought was a friend is really trying to kill her or not."

"I'll bet the guy's just in love with her," Cindy said. "That's how it always turns out."

Eddie blanched. "Yeah, um, that's not always the case. Later." He turned abruptly and hurried away.

"What was that about?" Belle asked as she carefully stowed away her new prized possession into her bag.

"He's weird," Cindy replied, biting into a baby carrot. "Insanely hot, but weird."

And now, sitting in her lonely booth at the Ridge Rats restaurant, Belle almost laughed out loud at how alarmed she'd been over his talk of hunters. Having reached the point where Eddie's bookmark still stuck, she knew now it really was just book-talk.

Frowning as she scraped at the charcoaled fingerprints on the page, she wondered how she was going to explain this away, when another text chimed in.

I'm here. Meet me behind the restaurant.

Liam. Her heart lodged itself in her throat. She couldn't text back. Her fingers trembled too much.

She looked toward the entrance, wondering if perhaps Liam had tried to enter, and Jan greeted him and pissed him off with her "warm" welcome.

Instead, what she saw made her sink lower into her seat.

The Princess Posse from school had arrived. All gorgeous eight of them. Bearing gifts and balloons as if they'd each stepped off a photo shoot for Teen Vogue's "Birthday Brunch" spread.

Maybe that was why Liam wanted to meet out back.

Belle peeked around. She couldn't use the front entrance now without being seen. Back exit through the kitchen? It always worked as a quick get-away for the movie heroes.

Before she lost her nerve, she dashed into the kitchen, responded with a sheepish grin and an innocent "Where's-the-bathroom?" to an outraged waiter's questions, and then cringed as she ducked past an unkempt cook—probably Miguel—who'd just finished wiping a snotty nose before grabbing a pair of hamburger buns.

Ugh! Note to self: Find a new burger joint.

She paused as she touched the Emergency Exit bar and took a moment to re-arrange her facial expression. She was not going to be greeting Liam with that lit-up Christmas grin she no doubt wore right now.

Remember, he kissed you, teamed up with you against a possessed witch, snogged you some more, and then abandoned you. What was the term nowadays? As Candy would say, "You got ghosted, girl!"

Belle was fuming.

Okay, now she was ready. She pushed against the bar and slipped outside, the door slamming shut behind her.

Dangerous Encounters

It was an alley. If she took five long steps forward, she'd run into the adjacent building's wall. A dumpster stood to her left, and to her right, blocking the shortest exit to the public boardwalk was a sight that felt like an ice shower: Goth Twin, one of Violet's faithful minions. His dark shaggy hair just about covered his coal-rimmed eyes, and he was dressed like an extra on the set of *The Crow*.

"What do you want?" Belle's eyes darted past him, looking for his preppy look-alike.

"Just to play," he rasped, his voice sounding like broken glass. He flexed his hands at his sides, and she spied the glint of brass knuckles.

Her internal alarm system blared, setting off her flight response. She turned back to the door without taking her eyes off him and tried to pull it open, but it wouldn't budge. She banged her fists against it. "Open the door!"

Goth Twin started slinking toward her, and since he was blocking the only clear escape, she darted in the direction of the dumpster, praying that it wasn't a dead-end.

Where was Liam? He was supposed to be here!

But it *was* a dead-end. Only it wasn't a wall, but the heavily cologned body of Preppy Twin. He'd caught her, encircling her in his arms.

She shoved against him with all her might, ripping herself away from him and crashing down onto the gravel floor. She cried out as pain shot up her arms.

"Whoa. Anxious for a meet-and-greet, are we?" Preppy, in his linen slacks and polo shirt with the collar popped up, flashed her a megawatt grin, the kind that only the friendly neighborhood serial killer could sport. "I don't think we've ever been properly introduced: I'm Elias and this is Toby. And you must be Belle. See? We're all friends now." He clasped his hands together and leaned down as if he were speaking to a toddler.

Belle scooted back. "Stay away from me." Something glinted in his shirt pocket, and her eyes widened when she recognized the sleek, silver device. "Why do you have Liam's phone?"

"A little breaking-and-entering cured some of our boredom. Right, Toby?"

The brother growled out, "Let's do this already."

"Do what?" Belle's voice wavered as she tried to scramble to her feet.

Elias's foot came down on hers like a cinder block. Her screams and the sounds of bone crunching as he ground his heel resonated in the alley. When he finally took a step back, she collapsed into a fetal position, cradling her foot.

"Win back Violet's respect, of course." Elias tucked his thumbs into the belt loops of his pants, all casual as if hadn't just brutally crushed a human limb. "We let her down after that last fiasco with her new pet. So, if we do her a huge favor now and get rid of a thorn in her side—that's you—then maybe she'll take us back. I mean, I don't know about you, Toby," he glanced over at his brother, who merely grunted, "but I need her back. I *need* Vi."

Belle uncurled herself and forced herself to sit up, grimacing at the streaks of pain bolting up her leg. "She's just using you two," she winced. "You're both under her spell."

Elias kneeled down to her level now.

"Careful," Toby muttered.

Elias only smiled up at him before facing Belle again. The desperation that shone in his eyes was the only real emotion behind that cool mask. "That's the thing. We *want* her to use us." He reached out and squeezed Belle's broken foot.

She screamed. She wanted to summon the lightning in her hands, but the blinding pain chased away all thought.

"I need to be close to her. Now. I should be with her in Europe, not that animal. If we kill you," Belle tried to tug away, but Elias squeezed harder, "then, we'll earn back the privilege of being with her again."

Kill them, she rasped in her mind. *Summon the lightning. Destroy them.*

"You're crazy. Both of you!" She kicked Elias hard in the face with her good foot. He let go of her as his head snapped back.

She scrambled upright onto her feet as best she could, but upon touching down with the injured foot, she was surprised to find that the pain was only a dull throb. In fact, she stepped on it now and found that she could bear weight on it. She couldn't stop to think about what that meant when only a second ago, that foot was mangled, and now, it felt merely bruised.

Momentarily stunned, Elias cradled his bright red jaw, the look in his eyes murderous when he climbed to his feet.

Belle glanced behind her as she backed away. There was an exit! She could see the grass beyond.

The twins advanced on her. Toby took the lead, punching the brass-knuckled fist into his other hand, a preview of what waited for her. She turned and ran just as he lunged for her.

Belle dashed down the narrow alley, jumping over crates and narrowly clipping each dumpster. Far behind her, she heard "What the—!" followed by sounds of grunts and thuds and clangs fading away as she ran.

Her lungs on fire at the end of the alley's opening, she had to pause for a breath. She was about to take off again, but when she realized there were no sounds of pursuit, she dared a look behind her.

Her jaw unhinged. "How in tarnation?"

The twins were in the middle of the alley, suspended in the air together, swaying, bound back-to-back by their middle, and hanging from a side pole jutting out of the roof. They were out cold.

How in the world did they get up there? Who—?

A blur of black pinned her to the wall. A black gloved hand clamped down on her mouth, muffling her cries, as the other large hand pinned both of her wrists together high above her head. Before she could even kick out, he'd immobilized her legs with his own by pressing heavily against her bottom half.

"Don't move. Don't make a sound," he spoke low in her ear, a gravelly voice with a distinctly British accent. "And I will release you." His grip on her tightened as he drew in a slow, deep inhale along her cheek.

Was he *smelling* her? She bristled at the unwelcome and seemingly intimate gesture. Still pinning her, he leaned away, and for the first time, she got a clear look at him.

A ninja. A frickin' ninja, dressed head to toe in black. She would have laughed out loud had she not been viciously immobilized beneath his weight. He was a head taller than her and broad-shouldered.

And those eyes.

She stilled as she stared at the small golden orbs glowing unnaturally from behind the shadowy mask. Her heart hammered at the thought; she knew this encounter could only mean one thing....

He was here to kill her.

Of their own will, her hands flared to life, crackling with electricity.

"Stop that," he warned, his hand trailing down from her mouth and gripping her throat instead.

"You're Jäger," she bit out.

"So you know." There was a touch of surprise in his tone.

Hearing his confirmation though, sent panic roiling beneath her skin, magnifying the electrical orbs surrounding her hands. She began struggling against the weight of his body crushing her against the wall.

"Behave," he growled out, and smacked the back of her head against the wall, eliciting a cry from her. "Why were those two chasing you?"

"Th-They said they wanted to kill me."

"Why?" he asked sharply.

"I don't know." She wasn't about to set a Jäger on her mother's trail, evil possession and all.

"Maybe you were trying to kill them, and you slipped up so they started chasing you." He started squeezing her throat again as he leaned in close to her face. "But those three Hammerson blokes weren't so lucky, yeah? They didn't stand a bloody chance after you torched them."

The electricity in her hands fizzled out as the numbness spread down her arms from his ironlike grip on her wrists. He was cutting off the circulation in her arms, as if he knew that would disable her from using the power in her hands.

"It was self-defense," she croaked out.

He made a scoffing sound, but she noticed he loosened her aching throat and slid his hand over to grip her collarbone instead.

Belle swallowed painfully. "They had killed a bunch of girls, and I was going to be next." She repeated weakly, "It was self-defense...and I didn't even mean for it to happen. I had no idea about this power before that day."

The golden glow of his eyes became more pronounced, and he became very still, as if he were turning over this new piece of information in his mind.

And Belle didn't know why she did what she did next. Perhaps, the oppressive weight of his leg anchoring her in place was becoming too much. Or, the maddening indignity of having this strange man so entrenched in her very personal and private space was all pushing her over the edge of submission into defiance.

She'd had enough.

"But that doesn't matter, doesn't it?" she challenged, feeling her temper rise. "*You're* a killer. Not me. Isn't that why you're here? To kill me?"

"Yes," he said, and her courage flailed.

Before she could try to muster the heat in her hands again, he pulled off of her and the refreshing coolness of *space* rushed over her. Her arms fell to her sides like dead weight, and she slackened against the wall. Even though she was relieved of his crushing weight, he still remained just a foot in front of her, an impassable wall.

"But," he said, his voice softer, "I find that I don't *want* to end you. At least, not yet."

She straightened up, rubbing her sore wrists and eyeing him. "Okay...then kindly move aside, and I'll be on my merry way." She took a step as if to bypass him, but he blocked her path.

He pointed at the twins, who were starting to groan and twist about in the air. "Who are they? They reek of enchantment. Pure bloody evil. That was your doing, wasn't it?"

"No." She glanced at the wide open exit of green grass and the parking lot beyond, wanting more than anything to make her escape, especially before the Jäger decided he *did* want to kill her after all.

The twins could be heard cursing now and arguing about how to get down. One of them shouted, "I'm going to kill that girl!"

The Jäger ninja clenched his fists.

Belle looked at him as if saying, *See?*

Whatever response the Jäger was about to make was silenced by an unnatural breeze that brushed past them. They watched as it streamed down the alley, swirling the street litter, in the direction of the twins. The wintry chill of the wind, inexplicable on a mildly warm afternoon, raised goosebumps along Belle's skin, her insides twisting at the familiar sense of evil she'd only experienced in a particular person's presence: Violet Wickeby's.

"Witchcraft," the Jäger muttered, stiffening and casting an accusing glare at Belle.

She threw her hands up. "Not me, I swear."

Violet's laugh rippled along the breeze, raising the hair along the back of Belle's neck. A melodic enchantment in a foreign language followed, echoing louder as the strength of the wind picked up.

"She's casting a spell." Alarmed, he ordered Belle, "Cover your ears."

"But what about you?"

He blinked once. Twice. As if thrown off by this unmerited concern from her. "I'll be fine."

She dipped her chin and clamped her hands over her ears.

Debris flew now, ping-ponging around the alleyway, a wooden crate smashing into the Jäger's back, who instinctively backed Belle into the wall and shielded her with his body. The scent of herbs, the kind a fakir may use to ward off evil, engulfed her. And something else. Of fresh cedar and spice. Unable to stop herself, she leaned into the crook of his hooded neck and inhaled deeply.

Memories flooded her. Papa's belly laugh at a good chemistry pun she'd told him. The children of Littleton hanging on to her every word at story-time. The sunlight streaming through the canopy of the woods by her house and warming her upturned face. Sharing breakfast at the kitchen table with Emily and Ernesto.

The Jäger cocked his head toward her, and she diverted her face as color filled her cheeks and the memory-lane connection severed.

Before she could dwell on how *that* had even happened, her gaze landed on the twins, mouths wide open as if screaming in terror, swaying like a pendulum while a torrent of wind engulfed them. The enchantment must have grown louder because she could hear it now, and she felt her body grow weaker and her eyes glaze over.

The Jäger, seeing this, pressed his own hands firmly over hers, muting the world around them.

As they weathered this freak storm in the alley, her mind raced on: why was he helping her? She'd been warned by her father's dying words to stay away from these assassins. And even Violet had warned her once.

But here this one was. Protecting her.

Belle's hair quit whipping around her face as the wind ceased, and the Jäger stepped away from her. "It's over," he said.

They both looked toward the twins, still hanging in midair, but a change had come over them. They were yelling out in French, and although Belle didn't know what they were saying, their tones seemed anguished now.

The Jäger translated. "They don't know how they ended up here. They're crying out for help." Amusement colored his tone now. "One's crying out for his mother."

He faced her again, his golden eyes glittering brighter. "The spell that had bound them is broken. The sorceress somehow knew they were compromised." He let out a frustrated breath. "They're useless now, having no memories of anything that happened during their enchantment. They will be like recovering drug-addicts with amnesia." He looked down the alley again, and said more to himself, "Why wasn't I assigned the sorceress? I'm the only Jäger capable of destroying her."

Belle lurched forward with her words. "No! She's my mother."

The Jäger looked sharply at her, the golden orbs at their widest. And then she wished her mouth were sewn shut.

Those golden eyes narrowed. "Someone's coming."

A side door burst open, and Miguel emerged into the alley, throwing his apron over his shoulder.

"I am not finished with you, Belle Montague," the Jäger whispered darkly. And when she turned to look at him again, he was gone.

"What the hell's going on here?!" Miguel shouted, looking from the hysterical twins dangling before him to a wide-eyed Belle frozen silent at the end of the alley.

~~*~~

"Speak." Ernesto had picked up on the first ring, and when he answered this way, it meant this wasn't a good time. As usual.

"Hi, Uncle. Um, I'll be quick." She drew in a breath and hugged her leather brown messenger bag across her chest. "I need something from the grocery store." Code for she had information about the Wickeby case.

They had worked it all out before, in case they ever needed to discuss "the grocery store" over the phone or in front of others. As Sheriff in town, Ernesto knew personally that any call or video could be pulled for surveillance.

"I can't get it for you right now but tell me what you need." *I'm not alone but tell me anyway.*

"Twinkies." Violet's minion twins. "I saw some behind the Bar and Grill's alley, and it made me want some. Um, Miguel the cook is, er, watching both Twinkies now."

She was figuring out how to code-splain that they were still hanging in mid-air, disenchanted and clueless, when Ernesto said sharply, "Go straight home. I'll get the Twinkies."

"Okay, but I need to go to Candy's." And before he could object, she quickly added, "Mama Jo's home."

A pause. "Fine. But be back for dinner." Another pause. "If Jo—"

"Makes any gumbo, bring some home," she finished for him. "I know. But listen, I won't be home for dinner; there's a small party tonight I'm supposed to-" *Click.* "-go to," she finished into the dead air.

He'd snapped his phone shut.

She sighed out her irritation. Papa would have simply said, *"No, end of story,"* but she wasn't the clueless caged little bird of Littleton anymore. And Ernesto understood this. So if she wanted to do something, and there was nothing she knew would be morally reprehensible about it, she'd inform Ernesto of her plans. Not ask permission. He wasn't her father after all. Then again, she wasn't a rebellious brat, either; she deeply considered her uncle's advice and opinions.

But tonight was a Saturday night, and while she was most certainly not in the mood to socialize, she owed her dearest friend, Candace Laveu-Brennan. Owed her big time. Candy had given up a potential first date with her long-time crush, Dmitri, to let Belle cry on her shoulder over Liam.

And while Candy never said that Belle owed her, Millie Kwan-Yin, their other best friend, had pulled her aside at school yesterday and explained how Candy needed their support now. So, nothing, not Ernesto's silent disapproval, or even a near-death experience at the twins' and Jäger's hands, was going to stop her from being Candy's wingman tonight. She was locking up all that trauma of the past half-hour in the back of her mind. Padlocked and dumped into the deepest mental ocean of oblivion.

Her bosom friend needed her.

"Well?" An irritated Miguel huffed out from behind.

Belle jumped. She'd forgotten for a moment about the cook and the cursing, French twins still swinging in the air. She waved her phone at him. "I got the sheriff coming."

"Why were you whispering on the phone?" He pointed at the twins. "How do I know it wasn't you who did this, huh?"

"I already told you; I didn't do that. I just found them like that." She started backing away.

"Where do you think you're going? You gotta stay and talk to the cops." He jutted his thumb toward his chest. "*I* gotta get back to the kitchen."

And she did the only thing she could think of: she turned and high-tailed it out of there.

| 4 |

Bus Buddies

Belle shivered against the crisp Fall breeze that started up as she hurried toward the jitney stop at the end of the long boardwalk. The crowd was thicker now in the early afternoon, and she could feel eyes on her, and when she heard someone call out her name (a classmate from school?), she retrieved her earbuds from her bag and jammed them in, syncing with the playlist on her phone.

For the few weeks she'd been in Elmridge, she'd learned that while she didn't miss the isolation she'd experienced in Littleton, she did value her solitude and privacy. Seemed she was an introvert after all. And music, she discovered, was a new escape. It soothed the chaotic rage that had filled her in the wake of Emily and Liam's disappearance. Emily, she was happy for, but Liam, she wanted to slap. Cold, hard smack right across his *GQ*-model face.

But today, it wasn't the absent Liam who churned that storm inside her. She had this Jäger to thank for that and everything that had just happened in that alley.

She couldn't stop the questions overtaking one another like the Indy 500: what task did the twins mess up that enraged Violet enough to leave them behind? She knew from Ernesto's intel that she was in Europe, but the twins seemed jealous of the "animal" that was with her. Who or what was it?

And the Jäger. He hadn't killed her because he didn't want to *yet?* He'd even turned bodyguard and kept her safe from Violet's spell. And those memories that surfaced when she inhaled his scent…all happy memories.

But *that* she knew she could blame on her flighty focus. Her mind did have an embarrassing habit of wandering off on its own and hi-jacking her along for the ride.

She wasn't the only one randomly sniffing people—the Jäger had done it. Goosebumps erupted along her skin at the memory. It seemed intimate. She knew the Jäger wasn't an old man from his voice and build. But, still. These goosebumps had to be creepy crawlies and not…anything else. Especially with the freaky, glowy eyes he had.

There was also that voice buried deep in her mind that had reared its ugly head in the alley. It didn't sound like Violet's. It was a raspy, rumbling voice that terrified her when it emerged. It rarely happened; only speaking in her most frantic, disturbing moments. Since Liam had left, it spoke in her moments of rage, whispering of revenge. It felt like the little cartoon devil on her shoulder, only the creature resided in some deep, remote part of her mind.

She couldn't deal with the idea that she was possibly losing her sanity, so she coped through distractions—school, her friends, music, books—and by completely pretending the whispering *thing* didn't ex-ist altogether.

But a new question plagued her: how in blooming heck had her foot healed so quickly? She knew she hadn't imagined the blinding pain of her crushed foot. She looked down at the blue Keds-clad foot and wiggled it.

Nope. Not even a flinch of pain.

"Young lady, you gettin' on?"

Belle's focus clicked in place, and she saw the bus driver hunched over his steering wheel, watching her expectantly.

"Sorry." She quickly found her place on the crowded electric bus, standing and sharing a grip on the pole with another passenger.

The bus pulled forward, and she turned the volume up on her music, drowning out the plague of questions. She gazed out the window as Merry Lake, crowded with beachgoers, disappeared, and beyond that, laid the imposing iron gates that guarded the entrance to Manor Hill, a.k.a. Rich Row, a neighborhood of mansions where the wealthiest families resided.

Belle's stomach dipped as she stared at the turrets of the Gothic-like castle further beyond, home of the second wealthiest family, well, now just one person: Liam Rawlins.

She blinked and wiped her hoodie sleeve across her eyes. Jerk.

Belle stared back out the window, willing herself to stay off that particularly painful memory lane. Her home, the Historical Society of Elmridge with its Southern-style, wrap-around porch and second-story balconies cruised by next. The first floor was a museum dedicated to Elmridge's history, and the second floor was where she lived with Uncle Ernesto and Aunt Emily. No one else knew it but them, but Emily and her sister Abigail had personally collected the artifacts in the museum for over 300 years now. They literally preserved and built Elmridge into what it was today.

But she didn't have her mother or aunt anymore. It was just her and Ernesto in that big, lonely house, an uncanny reminder of how it used to be with just her and Papa in Littleton, Kentucky. Which was why she found herself more often at Candy's nowadays, and why she was gladly heading there now. The walls would start to close in on her if she had to wait alone at home now with her thoughts and replays until her uncle returned hours later.

She sighed and skipped to the next song on her phone. Celine Dion's "All By Myself" wasn't helping her current state of mind. Dido's "Thank You" cued up.

Much better.

Life really was better here in Elmridge, Rhode Island. She'd made some friends, started attending a school, met more family, had a crush that turned into a weekend boyfriend....

She huffed out another sigh. *Ok, I desperately need to get out of my head. Turn and chat with the nearest stranger. Go.*

Finally looking directly at the person with whom she was sharing the pole, her eyes popped. "Eddie?"

"Hi." He raised an eyebrow at her. "Took you long enough."

He was wearing dark blue jeans, a loose-fitting gray thermal that she noticed was inside out with the long sleeves pushed up to the elbows, revealing a black leather wrap around one wrist, and a black beaded chain that disappeared beneath the neck collar. His black hair was short along the sides, but medium-length and tousled on top, as if he left it up to the wind to comb it for him. He stood just a foot from her, and now she could see she came up to his chin. Those full lips were curved into a slight frown.

Once again, being confronted by a full-faced look from Eddie just about knocked the wind out of her. Jeez, was he even aware of the effect he has? And why wasn't he already recruited by the Princess Posse to sit at their table at lunch? Oh, right, he chose to sit at Q's table. Automatic nullification as a *Bold and the Beautiful* candidate.

Feeling sheepish, she tugged her earbuds out. "I'm sorry, I've just been totally lost in thought. You must think I'm horribly rude." He pursed his lips as if considering, but she rambled on, "I mean, we've sat at the same lunch table for a few weeks now, and I've barely spoken to you. I'm really sorry about that, by the way. I have a lot of, er, stuff, I guess, on my mind."

His lips twitched into the barest hint of a smile. "We've all got *stuff* on our minds. I, uh, like to escape through books."

Oh dear, a man after my own heart. "Me, too." She flushed pink with book-talk excitement. "Only, I've already read everything I could get my hands on. I still can't really focus on a screen for reading so the e-books are a lost cause for me. Which is why..." she pulled the *Hunger Games* book from her bag, "I'm absolutely over the moon that you let me borrow this."

She stood grinning ear to ear at him, waiting for a response. But he was just staring at her, his mouth slightly agape and his thick brows furrowed, as if conflicted over something.

"Um," she pressed on, "I just reached the part where you left off." She opened the book to show him, but then realized those pages had the fingerprints charred onto them, so she snapped it shut and slid it back into her bag. Hopefully, he hadn't noticed.

He was *still* staring, but his expression had grown darker.

She glanced away, out the window. This was going to be a long bus ride if all he was going to do was glare at her like he'd done at lunch. But he'd let her borrow the book, and she was really grateful for that. Maybe he was bi-polar or something. That would help explain his lunch-table choice. Guess he was a kindred spirit after all. Like called to like, what with the issues that plagued her own mind and all.

"Do you think Peeta's actually trying to hunt down Katniss?"

He'd spoken softly, in an octave that would've made her knees go weak, if she wasn't so hung up on Liam. And was that an accent she detected? Or did he just articulate his words really well? He wasn't glaring at her anymore. It was more reserved, like he was studying her. Why? Not a clue.

Cindy was right. Really hot, but weird.

"No way," she responded. "He's definitely a friendly. Probably even likes her." She sighed, feeling herself transported to her very favorite place, inside a novel. "He's very brave putting himself in danger for her sake. I think the story's really just a romance at heart."

"Hmm." A light shone in his amber eyes. "What about Katniss? Think she'll feel the same way?"

"Katniss, I'm not sure about. I don't think she'd recognize true love if it stared her in the face."

He reacted so quickly, she almost missed it. His eyebrows arched and his jaw dropped a fraction, but just as quickly he schooled his features. "So," he cleared his throat, "where are you headed now?"

It took her a second to recover from his whiplash change of subject. "Oh, um, my friend Candy's place. We're going to a party later. I don't know where actually, but you can come with us if you want. I know you're new here. I was the last newbie, so I have some idea of what it might feel like in your shoes here."

Something dark crossed his features and his face became stone. He looked away, and if it hadn't been for her uncannily superb hearing lately, she would have missed him barely murmuring, "You have no idea."

Before she had a chance to wonder at that, the bus swerved abruptly, landing her right smack against his chest. He'd quickly shifted his feet to balance himself, at the same time reflexively wrapping an arm around her so she was flush against him.

Holy smokes, Eddie works out!

He exhaled roughly and muttered something under his breath that sounded to Belle like, "Bloody hell." But she had to have heard wrong because Eddie wasn't British.

When she was finally able to right herself and put some distance between them, her cheeks were flaming and she couldn't look him in the eye.

"Sorry, folks," the driver announced. "Had to avoid a peacock jaywalker."

Belle mumbled her apologies and her thanks to Eddie, while he grunted in response. When they finally looked each other in the face, the absurdity of the moment struck them at the same time, and Belle erupted into giggles while Eddie tried very hard not to smile, despite the mirth glowing in his eyes.

In her giddiness, she prodded him, "It's okay, you can do it. Go ahead and smile. See?" She gave him a dazzling grin. "Like this."

But that had the opposite effect on him. He looked taken aback.

Confused again by his reaction, she rolled her eyes. "You're hopeless."

"Indeed," he said on an exhale.

She noticed a brown shopping bag by his foot. The outside read Annie's Antiques. "What do you have there?"

"This?" He lifted three objects from the bag, one of them exciting her. "The Beatles vinyl record—my original broke. *Bleach* anime DVDs and Charles Dickens' *Great Expectations.*"

Belle reached for the book as if it were a puppy. "This is the only Dickens book Papa never brought me." She touched the worn hard copy cover. She was definitely going to have to check out Annie's Antiques.

"Let's do something then. Let's switch books. You get Dickens, and I get *Hunger Games* back."

This was a rare show of amiability from him, and she counted that as headway in making him her friend. A friend with books. "Alright then."

"But let's make this more interesting. We'll each write our thoughts in the margins of the books as we read."

"Oh, I like that."

"And then we'll switch books again."

"You are *on*, mister." Belle grinned with nerdy excitement. As they made the switch, she noticed as he dropped the book in the paper bag that there had been another thicker book in there. He noticed her craning her neck to see, so she straightened quickly. "Sorry, I was being nosy."

"No, it's fine." He retrieved the heavy book and laid it in her hands. "I figured I'd get to know the mythology of this place, if I'm going to be living here."

"*The Elmridge Book of Fairy Tales,*" she read aloud. "By A.E.P." She swallowed. Abigail and Emily Prynn. Her mother and aunt had written the book hundreds of years ago as a way to record the new knowledge and stories that were imprinted into their brains when their transformation was initiated by touching the golden meteor they'd found in the forest. It was a family secret.

And because she felt so comfortable in her new friend's company, it wasn't so difficult to say, "I have the first edition at home."

Eddie stilled. "You do?"

"Since I am officially declaring you my Book Buddy," she touched each of his shoulders with the book, as if knighting him, "I welcome you to my personal library of books." She had also realized with relish that literature seemed to be the thing to get him talking.

And then he grinned. A natural, lopsided grin.

She gasped comically, pointing. "*There* it is."

He shook his head at her. "Silly creature," he murmured. But all the same, his grin widened as the left corner of his smile climbed higher.

"Quite lovely, sir," she gushed, ignoring his last comment. "You should do it more often."

While she could still feel the frightful weight of the terrors she'd just experienced a little more than an hour ago nagging at her in the back of her mind, along with the mild relief that the vicious Minion Twins were no longer a threat to her and were probably bound in Ernesto's interrogation room wishing they'd never been born, she was in this moment blissfully distracted and wanted to keep it that way for as long as possible.

So when his smile slipped away as he studied her, the same dark cloud overtaking his features, she continued talking, trying to hold on to this camaraderie with him until she at least got off the bus.

"But I warn you," she continued, "my little library's not much. Just dusty old history books about Elmridge. If you decide to read them, they'd have to *stay* in the museum. There's an old rocking chair you could sit in. See, I live right above the museum on the second floor."

"I know."

Belle blinked. "You know?" A mental alarm bell went off.

"Well," he drew in a breath, "it's common knowledge. Said so in my 'Welcome to Elmridge' pamphlet."

"Are you sure it's not from all the absurd rumors circulating the school about me? Which you shouldn't believe, by the way."

"I'm the new kid who decided to sit at Q's table. I'm sure there are a few rumors about me, too."

She nodded, smiling. "Well, since you know where I live, it would feel less stalker-ish if you told me where you live. Fair is fair."

"But I *am* stalking you."

Her smile faltered, unsure if he was joking or not.

"I mean," he continued, his caramel eyes glittering, "we're lunch buddies, book buddies, and now," he gestured around them, "bus buddies." He let loose another rare lopsided grin, effectively distracting her from her concerns. "Can I ask you about one rumor though? Did you really tase those girls?" He watched her closely.

"No." She bit her lip.

He waited to see if she'd volunteer more information, but instead, she looked away and gazed out the window. The flock of peafowls roamed the field in the distance, right next to the Elmridge K-12 school complex. The Home of the Peacocks.

"I believe you," he said finally, and with a firmness that made her lock eyes with him. "Was it Kat and her neon clones?"

She nodded. Katerina Sirtis, the self-declared Queen B of the tenth grade, and her henchwomen had cornered her in the hallway at school, taunting her. Kat had viciously circulated rumors about her and flaunted them in her face.

The most disconcerting lie had to do with the very first weekend she'd arrived in Elmridge. It was true she had spent some totally platonic time with Jared Prince, the hottie international pop star sensation, who also happened to be her chemistry lab partner. He'd given her a ride to the mall and then taught her to swim at a lake party, but that was the gist of it. Liam Rawlins was another matter that would have made front-cover tabloids if Elmridge had one. He'd been the one to take her to the lake party and then on a dinner date afterwards on the boardwalk.

And they'd kissed that night for the first time. It was her first kiss.

But Kat had spun all this into the new girl being the Urban Dictionary version of "a lady of the night." So when Kat and her clones had cornered her, Belle placed her hand on the lockers they were leaning against and released an electric current from her hand. The shock had flung Kat and her posse onto their butts, and so the taser-rumor had been born.

"Well, then," Eddie said, "I only wish I'd been there to see it."

"You know," she began, a smile spreading on her lips, "I call them 'neon clones' too."

"Really?"

"I've imagined them at the roller-skating rink pumping to—"

"—80's music," he said at the same time she did.

"How'd you know I was going to say that?" she asked.

Eddie had only stilled, in shock himself, staring at her. "I...don't know," he said. His eyes tracked off to the side as if deep in thought.

Belle frowned and then tried to laugh it off. "Jinx, then."

She knew anything out of the ordinary would be most likely her fault. This morning, her foot had healed itself, and now, maybe, she was manifesting some sort of mind-influence power. At this rate, maybe her appearance would mutate too, and she'll truly become known as the Thing from Littleton.

She found herself leaning her forehead against the pole. She really missed Emily. Her aunt was the only one who she could talk to about anything supernatural or super-weird. But Emily was M.I.A. So who could she even talk to? Ernesto? He was a walking storm cloud over Emily's absence and hellbent on tracking Violet. Belle wasn't about to burden him further with her personal "mutant" issues.

She squeezed her eyes shut against the migraine that threatened to sink its hooks into her temples.

"So, what's it like in there?"

Belle blinked up at Eddie. "Where?"

He touched her temple. "There. Your hide-out."

She blushed at his recognition of her flaw, but mostly at the point of contact he'd made with her skin. "Messy. Frustrating."

Hmm. This venting felt good, and she had an attentive friendly listener. What was that saying? It's sometimes easier to open up to a stranger than your best friend?

So she didn't stop the words that tumbled forth. "Like...my sanctuary is an outrageous mess, and I *want* to clean it up and put everything in order, but I just..." she shook her head, "end up staring hopelessly at the chaos."

Eddie nodded. "I've had a few ravaged Mind Palaces in my lifetime."

"That's actually what I call it, too," she said, barely above a whisper.

"Or Fortress of Solitude."

Her eyebrows went up. "And that."

He was staring at her intently, and then the corners of his mouth kicked up. "Let's see how good I am. Think of a number from one through twenty."

"Seriously? Ok, um, go." She closed her eyes and concentrated on the number sixteen, her age.

"I need to see your pretty eyes."

She opened them in a flash, pink coloring her cheeks, and found his amber gaze locked on hers in a way that made her body warm. "Y-You aren't wearing your glasses, I just noticed."

"I only wear them when I need to. Have you got the number clearly in your mind?"

"Yes."

"Sixteen."

She gasped. "That's not normal."

"I have a confession to make. I dabbled in magic shows once upon a time. Had the beautiful assistant and everything." His eyes twinkled. "You were thinking of your age, weren't you?"

"Is that like a statistical thing you knew would happen?"

"Guilty as charged."

"Can I try?"

"Well, now, it won't be so easy as me thinking of my age."

"313," Belle blurted out.

Eddie blanched.

She scoffed at herself. "Sorry, that was random. I kind of just threw that number out there because I was going to give you the same one through twenty range."

His Adam's apple bobbed visibly as he ran his hand through his hair.

Truth was she saw the number clearly in his mind: *313* made of white smoke against blackness. She'd called it out before the number dissipated.

This had to be a new power of hers emerging.

She needed to sidetrack him before he became suspicious. "Can I try again?" she asked in a small voice. "One through twenty. Pick a number." If she did see a number in his mind again, she was going to lie and tell him a different one.

He shook his head, his lips pressing into a thin line, and his eyes narrowing slightly on her as if trying to make sense of something important.

Belle's smile faltered under his scrutinizing gaze. "No?" she asked weakly.

Was he figuring out she was a freak of nature?!

At that moment, the bus stopped in front of the townhomes complex, right behind the grandiose Peacock Plaza Mall. As the people in the front made their way out, a young man exclaimed from the back of the bus, "Thiago, bro, wake up. We're here."

Some cursing from the presumed Thiago followed, in a distinctly rough, Hispanic-accented voice.

Belle waited with Eddie as she allowed the people to pass before she followed out. A gap opened and when Belle stepped in, it had unfortunately been right in front of what could only be Thiago because he stopped and opened his mouth upon seeing her.

"Daaamn, mamacita, where you been all my life?" He was biting his lip and looking her up from head to toe. He was tan and just a little taller than her, but with wide shoulders, a dark shaved head, and dark eyes to match.

Thiago and his friend looked sweaty in their gym clothes, and the tall friend, about Eddie's height, with short dark hair that had been frosted at the tips in blonde, had a basketball under one arm. He was staring wolfishly at Belle, too.

A nervous laugh escaped her, and she instinctively retreated a step back toward Eddie. "Around."

Thiago rubbed his hands together. "Then let me get your digits, honey, and we can go around together."

"Yeah, um…" She glanced at Eddie, whose steely gaze was fixed on her, while his real attention was completely bent toward the guys like a viper poised to strike. "I don't think so."

Thiago frowned, and then finally looked at her hulking shadow. He jutted his thumb toward Eddie as if he were nobody. "Why? You with him?"

This time, Eddie did see her. He raised his eyebrows as if also waiting for her answer, leaving the decision entirely up to her for how to proceed with the situation. She thought she saw a glint of amusement in his eyes, too. As much as she wasn't here to amuse Eddie, it was the far better option than encouraging Thiago and his sketchy friend to stick around.

"Yes," she said decidedly. "I'm with him."

Eddie looked back at the two. "She's with me." His tone was clear: it was time for them to leave.

The bus driver yelled out, glaring at them through his huge rearview mirror, "On or off?"

"A'ight," Thiago conceded. He gave Belle one last, long look. "But if you ever need a real man, look me up." He frowned once more at Eddie, and then lightly elbowed his friend behind him. "Let's go, G." But when his friend didn't move, he repeated, "Yo, G?"

Belle realized with alarm that G was too busy locked in an epic stare-down with Eddie. G had his hand in his pocket, and she could hear a clicking noise coming from there. The sound filled her belly with dread. A switchblade?

Eddie, with his thick, dark brows drawn tightly together over hard amber eyes, said in a firm, frosty voice, "Keep walking."

Expecting a fight, Belle was surprised when G turned and nudged Thiago to start walking. She and Eddie listened to their fading conversation as the boys stepped off the bus.

"That girl's the sheriff's niece," G said.

Thiago spun the basketball on one finger. "So what?"

"He locked my brother up for something petty. Cost him his college scholarship."

Thiago planted the ball in his friend's chest. "Assault-and-battery's not petty, cabrón."

When the bus driver slammed the door shut, Belle jumped and called out, "Wait, please! I'm getting off here."

Before she could say goodbye to Eddie, he spoke up, "Me, too. I'll walk you."

| 5 |

Maple Tree Trail

On the sidewalk, Belle and Eddie watched Thiago and G's retreating backs before they followed on the same path toward the townhouses. The walkway was an extension of a much longer walking trail that wrapped around the entire townhouse complex and also branched off toward the mall.

She had walked it once. It was a beautiful sight: lined on both sides with maple trees turning different shades of burnt orange and reds, welcoming wooden benches and concession carts were dotted along the path, beckoning pedestrians. There was even a little wooden bridge over a waterway where Belle liked to pause and watch the ducks and fish swim by. A rowboat service offered customers a lazy cruise down the picturesque canal, something she was eager to try out in the future.

"Um..." She didn't want this time with Eddie to end so soon, and the Maple Tree Trail to their right sure did beckon prettily. And there was also the matter of Thiago and G still straight up ahead. She knew she could ultimately defend herself if she had to, but she was terrified of revealing her powers, not to mention committing outright murder. Again. "Are you okay with taking the scenic route back to the complex?"

He shrugged. "Sure."

"Thank you."

"For?"

"For backing me up on the bus and accompanying me now."

He shrugged a shoulder. "It's part of the Bus Buddies contract."

She laughed and gave him a friendly bump with her hip as they walked. After a spell of silence, she started reflecting on the bus showdown. "You know, you were brave back there. I thought G was going to fight you for sure. I'm shocked he just left when you told him to."

He made a dismissive snort. "That wasn't bravery. *You* are brave for having to deal with those hounds." He gave her a rueful look. "My apologies on behalf of the male species. It seems that the art of treasuring women has been lost these days."

Belle touched his upper arm, bringing him to a stop alongside her. "Well spoken, sir, like a true gentleman."

Amusement pulled at the corners of his mouth. "Tell me," he said, as they started walking again. "Jane Austen or J.K. Rowling?"

"Jane Austen."

"*Star Trek* or *Star Wars*?"

"Neither. Give me Jules Verne or H.G. Wells."

He smiled indulgently at her response, and the light in his eyes seemed to glow brighter with each of her answers.

"Steven Spielberg or James Cameron?"

"Who?"

He chuckled. "Beach or camping?"

"Beach is boring. I'd like to go camping or hiking in Wychblack Forest. That's more my kind of nature scene."

He nodded and pursed his lips as if considering. "Genesis or Darwin?"

"Both."

He gave her an approving look. "Classical masters or the Beatles?"

She closed her eyes and extended her arms as if being held by an imaginary ballroom partner. "I wish that age of proper ballroom dance still existed. I would love to learn the waltz and those fancy choreographies."

He smirked at her, his gaze like melted caramel.

"What?" she asked. "I know." She twirled her finger in the air. "I'm weird."

He shook his head. "You, my dear, are an old soul."

"I guess. But you most definitely are one, too."

"How do you figure?"

"You just called me 'my dear' and you mentioned 'the art of treasuring women'."

"And you called me 'sir' twice today."

"Fair enough." She tipped her chin as her mind drifted elsewhere. "I think I would be happy getting a job in the future in one of those historical re-enactment towns. Maybe an old Western town that has a ghost story behind it. I could be the tough innkeeper who spies for the sheriff, or the magistrate's wife that gets kidnapped by the outlaw." Before she got carried away with her own fantasy and forgot about Eddie, she asked him, "What character would you play in our old Western town?"

He pursed his lips and thought for a second before answering. "I'm the debonair ghost the wife falls in love with."

"Ooh, how intriguing," she gushed, clasping her hands together beneath her chin and adding this new spin to the fantasy playing out in her head.

Eddie watched her as they walked. Little did she know how irresistibly intriguing he was finding *her*. She wasn't even aware of the effect she had on everyone who lay eyes on her. Looks of awe, appreciation, envy, and lust.... The last one he banished from any man's stare with the menacing glare he shot their way, each one quickly diverting their attention.

And Belle was too wrapped up in her idyllic cares to even notice.

"Okay, my turn to ask questions," she announced.

"Nope. I have one more." He stopped and gestured with his chin toward the concession stands. "Ice-cream or soft pretzel?"

A slow, sinful smile spread on her face, and he found himself smiling much too easily along with her now.

"Ice-cream."

They soon sat across from each other at a bistro set, Belle gleefully scooping a bite out of her banana boat sundae, and Eddie watching her with an arched brow over his one-scoop, rum raisin ice-cream.

They'd had a stand-off in front of the vendor, with both of them insisting on paying, Eddie claiming he was "old-fashioned that way" and Belle telling him that she'd "called it first and that 'first dibs' rule trumped any etiquette, old-fashioned or not."

Belle paid, and Eddie stubbornly dropped the same amount as tip.

"It's my turn," she said, pointing at herself with her spoon.

"For what?"

"My questions."

He made an annoyed grunt. She took that as a go-ahead.

"So what's your story?"

"My parents died, and I ended up with my uncle."

Belle frowned. He'd said it so mechanically, it seemed rehearsed.

"Are you sure you're going to eat all that?" he asked, finishing his last bite and nudging his empty cup aside.

"Yes," she countered, drawing her bowl in closer and forming a protective barrier with her hands. "But I will graciously leave you a substantial serving if you tell me a bit more."

He pursed his lips and stared at his splayed hand on the table. There was a ring on his right index finger. It looked like steel with an engraved black band that was scroll-worked with intricate swirls. It was indeed eye-catching, and she wondered why she hadn't noticed it before. She wanted to ask him about it and look more closely at it, but she thought it better not to distract him from the story she was still waiting for.

"I joined my uncle, you know, Dr. James Helsing, your English teacher, quite some time ago in Nepal. His work as a writer took us traveling all over the world. And Elmridge was our next stop."

His purposeful lack of details did not escape Belle. Clearly, he didn't want to divulge his past. And she wasn't one to pry. Maybe it was too painful for him. So instead of his family life, she asked about the exotic places he'd been, and his face and hands grew animated recounting those experiences.

She became completely enthralled. This Eddie was so different from the quiet, withdrawn one she first got to know. Admittedly, she also became entranced by all the subtle shifts in his handsome features as he talked at length. And he had such a smooth, dulcet voice....

Belle felt herself sit up inside. *What am I thinking? This is just Eddie. Get a grip, woman.*

He paused at her reaction, giving her a questioning look. When she shook her head and smiled for him to continue, he did. "So James researches and writes about the legends and folklore of each place, and we, uh, investigate them."

"That sounds so thrilling. I wish I could've swapped places with you for a bit." The next thought slammed into her like a block of ice. "Wait, so what's there in Elmridge to investigate?"

He spooned up the last few bites of her banana boat left-overs. "Well," he said around a mouthful, "there is the Elmridge Fairy Legend with the Prynn sisters." He pointed the spoon at her. "Your ancestors."

How quickly she regretted inviting him to her family's book collection.

"Do you think your aunt would be willing to sit down with James for an interview?"

Her heartbeat sped up. "Uh, she's, um, out of town for a while on a business trip."

"So we heard." He wiped his mouth with a napkin and tossed it in the bowl. "Ready?"

They ambled the rest of the way in companionable silence. Belle feeling grateful for the reprieve Eddie offered her from her troubles and at making another friend, and for the fine, cool Fall weather that had just settled over the Kinkade painting-like vista that the trail offered.

She sighed, content, if only for the moment.

"Mademoiselle, what beauty!"

A thick, French-accented older man had called out to Belle. He was thin, balding and looked unkempt and darkened by the sun, as if he were homeless, but the professional camera and racks of elegant scarves and hats behind him proved him a vendor. He was stationed before a magnificent maple tree and a rustic wooden bench at its feet.

"Come! Pretty scarf, for a pretty lady." He brandished a lovely scarf indeed, but it was the one on the rack patterned with the Eiffel Tower and an old map of Paris that drew her attention.

Eddie groaned as she moved toward it, but followed, nonetheless.

"How much would you like for this one?" she asked, fingering the silk embroidery of the edges.

"Interesting choice," Eddie remarked at her shoulder.

"I was born there." She rubbed her thumb over the word Paris. "Papa brought me to the States when I was a baby."

"Ah, very nice, mademoiselle, a sentimental touch. I, Vigo, would very much like to take your picture with the scarf, and I give you 25% off price. Good deal, yes?"

"Why do you need her picture?" Eddie asked, sounding very much like Ernesto.

"I am professional photographer. See?" He produced a large black photo album and flipped through some of the pages. "Once upon a time, I'm famous. But life is a fickle lady, and so now, here we are."

"It's settled then," Belle said. "Where do you want me?"

With Eddie managing to look both interested and annoyed at the same time, Vigo had her sit on the bench before the maple tree with the scarf around her shoulders and ordered her to hold one end of the scarf to her face "with soft fingers, like holding cloud," which earned a snort from Eddie.

Vigo stepped back and positioned both hands before him as if framing her. He frowned. "My apologies, mademoiselle, but could you please remove your jacket and let down your hair?"

Her face warmed at the act of undressing under watchful eyes, even if it was just removing her hoodie. She had taken care that morning with her appearance, thinking that she would be seeing Liam. She wore denim skinny jeans and a fitted green, long-sleeved shirt that she was once told made her hazel eyes more green than brown. The sweetheart neckline she knew accented her "assets" while still providing decent coverage. But after getting assaulted in the alley that morning, she hadn't been in the mood to feel pretty anymore, so she'd zipped her Peacock High hoodie all the way up and spun her copious hair into a tight bun.

She shrugged out of the hoodie and tossed it into Vigo's beckoning hand. He immediately handed it off to Eddie next to him, who absently grabbed it and tossed it onto his shoulder while standing as still as a statue. She blushed deeply under his stare.

"Lovely, absolutely lovely, mademoiselle. Now the hair."

"You can just call me Belle," she said. "I feel real silly..." She reached up to unpin the clip from her hair. "But at least I can cross professional photograph off my bucket list." And then her chestnut curls cascaded down her back.

"Oh, Belle," Vigo gasped, clutching his chest. "If only you'd been in Paris ten years ago, I'd be rich today."

"And she a mere child," Eddie growled. "Take your picture already."

"Of course, monsieur." He snapped a photo. "You are the boyfriend, yes?"

"No," the two responded at the same time.

"Ah, I see."

Belle was rather confused by Eddie's change in mood. He was staring stonily at her now, one hand gripping the shopping bag he'd lugged from the bus, and the other jammed in his pocket. She gave him a questioning smile, but he only sucked in his bottom lip and looked away.

She shrugged off her concern. Guess she'd have to take his mood swings along with the new friendship.

"Could you please stand, mon chéri? Yes, perfect! So statuesque, lovely figure! But you mustn't blush too much, Belle." He approached her and gestured toward her hair. "May I?"

She nodded.

He arranged her long hair over one shoulder and swept the hair off the other shoulder. "If you don't mind…" He grabbed the scarf from her and plucked a long fake red rose with an exaggerated bloom out of a bucket of props. "Here. Hold it just under your chin there." He stepped away and readied his camera again. "Now, smile into the camera like you have a delightful secret." He snapped away. "Perfect, mon chéri! You are a true Botticelli's Venus."

Belle felt mortified and pleased at once, but when she caught Eddie's eye, the smile slipped off her face. Was that a trick of the sunlight? His eyes had to be reflecting the yellow autumn sunlight because they were glowing like two dazzling gold spheres.

She dropped the rose. "Eddie?"

He slammed his eyes shut.

"Are you well, monsieur?"

Eddie retrieved his glasses from his back pocket and slid them on. The lenses slowly transitioned to black. "My eyes are sensitive," was all he said. And then to Belle's surprise, he turned to Vigo and spoke quickly in French, in a low voice so she wouldn't hear, "Que comptez-vous faire de ces images?"

Vigo too looked taken aback. "Je dois gagner un revenu, monsieur."

He nodded his understanding.

Side-eyeing Eddie now, Belle thanked Vigo and paid for her scarf. As they resumed their stroll, she pounced, "I heard you say something in French to him."

"I asked him what he planned to do with the pictures."

"And?"

"He said he needed to make an income."

"That's all?"

"That's all."

"I didn't know you spoke French."

"You don't know much about me."

She planted herself in his path. "Take off your glasses."

He arched an eyebrow.

"Please."

Exasperated, he sighed and promptly removed them. "I didn't know you were so bossy."

Normal. Perfectly normal human eyes. Eddie had the lightest brown eyes, almost yellow. But they weren't the glowy Jäger ones.

She narrowed her eyes at him and used his own line against him. "You don't know much about *me*."

They locked eyes, each wondering about the other.

Finally, Eddie said, "You're absolutely right." He started backing away. "I've got somewhere to be. Have fun tonight."

Belle blinked, startled by this about-face between them. "Eddie, wait...."

But he turned away and walked on, returning in the direction they'd come from.

| 6 |

Party Your Body

"Hi, Mama Jo!" Belle called out as she entered the Laveau-Brennan household.

They'd left their front door unlocked for her. She followed the warm, spicy smell of her cooking and found her stirring a large pot on the kitchen stove. While Candy had the black corkscrew afro curls that brushed her shoulders, her grandmother had her own gray curls cropped close to the scalp. Jo was the older and rounder version of her granddaughter, and she gave the best hugs.

She drew Belle in for one now. "How's my third baby girl today?"

"Third?" she replied, scrunching her nose at the insult.

Jo gestured towards the upstairs. "Millie's already here."

"Oh." Belle peeked expectantly into the pot.

"Ernie want some gumbo? Don't even answer that. I'll have a dish set aside for him. Just mind you bring the Tupperware back next time you come."

Belle beamed at her and gave her a peck on the cheek. "Thanks, Jo."

"Hold on, child." She lay the big wooden spoon on the counter and wiped her hands on her front apron.

Belle's concern spiked when Jo pressed her lips into a grim line. "Is everything okay?"

"Wait here."

Belle watched, increasingly baffled, as Jo walked past her, looked up the stairs, waited and listened there, and then nodded before returning to Belle in the kitchen.

"You're kind of freaking me out here, Jo."

"Nonsense, child." But she spoke in a hushed voice, nonetheless. "The girls are getting ready, and just to give you a heads up, they've got a surprise for you. But that's not what I need to tell you."

She gripped Belle's upper arms and looked earnestly into her face. "I know about your auntie." Belle's eyes widened. "Emily. She was my best friend in high school, and then after that...well, even I could tell she wasn't aging right. Now, I know that *you* know." Jo waited for a confirmation from her. When Belle gave her a small nod, she continued, "That's what I thought. And now I also know your uncle's history. See, Emily needed a confidant once upon a time, and I just so happened to have gained her trust."

"How'd you do that?" she asked in a small voice.

Jo dropped her voice to a whisper. "I never told a soul, until now, that I saw her disappear before my very eyes. Poofed right out of existence. There had been some trouble with Peter." She swallowed visibly and paused again to check if the girls were still talking upstairs. They were.

She lowered her voice even more, until she was almost mouthing the words. "I know the fairies took him." Then, tears welled up in her eyes.

Feeling as if this moment was made out of crystal and could shatter with a wrong word uttered, Belle whispered, "Go on."

"I know why Emily takes these extended 'business trips,' which must be leaving you without much of anyone besides Ernie to talk to about any of *this*. And I know he's not much of a talker or sometimes even a listener. He's so busy all the time."

Belle's eyes filled with tears, and she felt her lower lip tremble.

"So, what I'd like for you to understand is…that if you ever need a confidant, I'm here for you. About anything."

The tears exploded out of Belle.

"Oh no, baby girl, come here." And Jo wrapped her warm arms around her, and for the first time, Belle experienced some semblance of a healing embrace that only a mother could provide.

"Th-th-thank you," Belle blubbered into her shoulder.

"Oh now, you let it out. Mama Jo's here for you."

And she did. Big, ugly sobs that wracked her shoulders against Jo's soothing hand rubbing her back. She cried over Papa again; the mockery of her own mother very much alive, but so unreachable she may well be dead to her; Emily and Peter's happiness; Ernesto's anger and loneliness; her own loneliness under the crippling burden of such dark secrets to keep hidden….

She remembered that shooting star she'd wished upon her first night in Elmridge. She'd wished for a confidant. Someone to share her burden with and help her through this utterly strange tale she'd been mandated to live out. That, she thought, would make the journey bearable. And she thought she'd found it in Liam, but his callous ghosting had proved her wrong.

Heartbrokenly wrong.

Footsteps clambering down the stairs had them drawing apart.

Candy and Millie were framed in the entryway of the kitchen, the picture of surprise. Both were in tight jeans and sparkly sequined tank shirts: Millie's was silver, Candy's was bronze, and they wore heels, long, dangly earrings, and metallic eyeshadow that matched their shirts. They reminded Belle of sexy mirror balls, and she had the sneaking suspicion she was about to be whisked upstairs and coordinated into one, too.

"Oh, honey, you crying about Liam again?" Candy asked, dismayed.

What could she do but nod?

"We are so going to help you forget that twit tonight," Millie said, determination etched on her face.

With a sniffle, Belle tipped her chin up. "You know what? That sounds like a plan." And then she winked at Candy. "And Dmitri's going to take one look at you and say 'Kat, who?'"

Candy beamed, Millie rolled her eyes, and Jo announced, "That meathead? I agree with Millie on this one. Baby, you can do better than him! Bring me home a cultured boy with some sense, not a primate."

Belle's eyes popped while Millie collapsed into snorts and giggles. "Mama!" Candy yelled.

"You know it's true." She waved them off with the wooden spoon. "Go on now. Hurry on out. I got company comin' over soon."

As the girls made their way upstairs for what was surely Belle's turn for a glow-up, Candy called over her shoulder. "I hope it's not Mr. Sanford. 'Cause you know how I feel about *him*."

"You hush now, I'm a grown woman!"

Candy slammed her door shut.

~~*~~

The "surprise" the girls had for her had been what Belle suspected: a gold version of their mirrorball outfits. She kept her dark skinny jeans on and traded her green shirt for the gold sequined tank top. She had to confess: she felt like a model with her hair swept up into a high ponytail, her messy curls tamed with mousse into loose swirls, and light make-up consisting of lip gloss and gold cat-eye liner with black mascara. She felt extra fancy with her long, dangly gold earrings and three-inch heels.

Candy had tried to persuade her to wear the five-inch ones, but Belle convinced her that for her very first time wearing heels at her very first house party, she did not want to end up in the emergency room with broken ankles. She doubted in her mind though, if she'd even need the E.R. given the emergence of her freaky, speedy healing power.

When Candy turned Jo's 1990 Cadillac Deville (her fourth baby) into the massive security gate of Manor Hill, Belle squeaked, "The party's in here?"

"Of course," Millie said, lowering the pop music that had been blasting from the radio. "Where else would Jared's party be?"

"*Jared's* party?!"

Candy grinned at her through the rearview mirror. "Jared's celebrating the release of his new single. It just dropped today." She slid her window down and handed the security guard her driver's license. "Guess what it's called?" She exchanged a gleeful look with Millie next to her.

"What?"

"'The New Girl'!" They both shouted at once.

"You don't mean—?"

"Yes!" Candy cut in. She accepted her license back from the guard and drove the car forward after the gate slowly slid open, revealing a long, wide road hedged on either side with more walls covered in climbing ivy. No one could get a peek at any of the mansions unless they drove into the actual driveways of the properties.

Privacy wasn't just valued by only the Prynn family, it seemed.

"Surprise!" Millie said.

"The *song* is the surprise? I thought it was this outfit."

"No, girl, *this* is definitely the surprise," Candy said. "You haven't heard the song yet?"

Belle could only shake her head, feeling immobilized by the horrific implications if this song were truly about her.

"Let me play it for you." Millie synced her phone's music app with the car's radio.

You showed up at school one day
Your eyes, your hips, blew me away.
Brushing elbows in Chemistry,
Girl, you know the rest is history.
Oooooh, that new girl!
She came into my world.

Candy and Millie stopped singing along when they caught Belle's expression in the rearview mirror. Millie turned around in her seat to face her. "Are you okay? You look like you're gonna be sick."

Belle clutched her stomach and put one hand over her mouth as she felt the vomit hit her throat. "I *am* going to be sick."

"Ooh, not in my mama's car." Candy pulled the car over to the curb, and Belle practically leaped out. She lurched to her knees on the grass just as she threw up. Millie was at her side in an instant, rubbing her back and holding her hair.

"What's wrong, hon'? Talk to us!" Candy called through the car window.

Belle climbed back into the back seat, and Millie scooted in next to her, her mood glasses a light shade of blue with worry.

"You guys," Belle began, "you know I don't want any attention like that on me. My aunt had the reporters gagged, so they wouldn't talk about me in the press. How am I supposed to avoid being mentioned, if a world-famous singer writes a song about me? Plus, I don't even *like* him like that," she wailed. "I barely answer his calls and texts, or even talk to him in Chemistry. Jeez, can't he take a hint?"

Candy shook her head in disbelief. "Honey, that is exactly why he's chasing you. You are the one girl he can't have."

Belle let out a long, frustrated sigh.

Millie was staring at Belle, a gleam in her eyes.

"Oh no. I know that look," Candy said. "What are you planning, girl?"

"What if," Millie said, as if she were hatching an evil plot, "you act like those girls he's afraid of?"

"Meaning?"

"You go fan-girl on him!"

"She's not gonna do it," Candy said.

"Do what?"

Millie answered, "Throw yourself at him when you get there. Don't leave his side, and demand that he dance every song with you.

He'll be calling for his security guards to remove you from his presence by the end of the night."

Belle's quick shake of the head signaled her *nope* reaction.

"I didn't know you had such a flair for the dramatics, Mills," Candy said. She shook an index finger at her. "Hmm, something's up with you. This isn't your style."

"Oh, whatever," Millie said, throwing her hands up. "I'm just trying to help."

Candy had started the car forward again, while Belle grabbed her friend's hand and gave it a squeeze. "I appreciate it, Millie, really. But I think I just want to hang out with you two tonight, and then when Candy finally abandons us for Dmitri, like we know is going to happen, then we can cheer her on, or make fun of her, whichever you prefer."

They both laughed when Candy stuck her tongue out at them in the mirror.

"Oh my God!" Candy's eyes lit up in a Eureka-moment. "I know what's up with you, Millie! You've been playing your old Backstreet Boys songs, re-watching that romantic anime series—the one that has Snow White with red hair—and you won't stop texting someone, and you're lying about who it is when I ask."

"How do you know I'm lying?" Millie threw out.

"I know you, girl. C'mon, 'fess up. Who's the new guy?"

Belle gushed, "Oh my gosh, Millie, how exciting! You have a crush?"

"Why does it have to be a *crush*?" she said, as if the last word tasted sour. "I'll have you both know, my life is more than just about a boy and a hobby."

"Meaning?" Belle said, at the same time Candy said, "Girl, what you tryin' to say?"

Millie looked pointedly between both of them. "Meaning, Liam and books, and Dmitri and cupcakes."

"Girl, what is the man's name before I knock you off your high horse."

Millie exhaled and sunk back into her seat. "Eddie Helsing. He's in my art class, and we both love anime."

"See? You about a boy and a hobby, too," Candy returned. "But tell us about him. It's been a while since you've liked a guy that wasn't a cartoon character."

Millie visibly resisted the urge to correct Candy. "We just talk in class sometimes. He looks and walks like a jock, but he's got that emo, keep-ten-feet-away-from-me vibe."

"So, naturally…" Candy said.

"I was attracted," Millie finished. "The Dragon Ball sweater he was wearing was the convo-starter for me. You know what I found out? He's done ghost hunts, you know, paranormal investigations? So when I told him that I write for the school's Peacock Press, and that I could find out if there are any hauntings in Elmridge, he was super interested. So I text him when I have info about a house reporting a haunting. An alarming amount have reported, by the way. It's scary." And then she pouted. "But he won't let me join him on a ghost hunt."

"Oh, Mills," Candy complained. "Sounds like this guy would take you to a séance on a first date."

"And that would be awesome," Millie said. "He helps his uncle research for his books. They, uh—what was it exactly he said that they research?" she muttered to herself.

"They travel the world and research the supernatural legends of each place they visit."

They both turned to look at Belle. She'd been listening quietly this whole time, trying to understand the initial shock at Millie's confession and how small the world was, and then whether she was feeling jealous that Eddie was possibly interested in Millie or angry that he was possibly dragging Millie into supernatural activities.

And what was Eddie doing involving himself in these kinds of things? She knew he researched legends, but ghosts?

"You know this guy, hon'?" Candy asked.

She glanced warily at Millie. "I do. He sits at my lunch table. He likes to read and not be bothered. Um, he's nice, too. He was on the bus this morning, and he walked me to the complex after some guy was bugging me on the bus." She didn't want to rub in just exactly how nice he was dallying with her on Maple Tree Trail and sharing ice-cream with her. She'd credited the fine weather for his extra show of kindness.

Candy and Millie exchanged a look that didn't sit well with Belle. "What? We're just friends."

Millie crossed her arms over her chest and gave her a tight smile. "We're just friends, too."

But something felt strained between her and Millie now, and she hated it.

"Okay, then," Candy said, putting a period on that discussion. "Here's the plan: we are partying our boo-tays off tonight!"

They finally arrived at a huge mansion that looked like it was plucked out of Malibu. It was like a party scene straight out of the TV show she watched with Candy at her house, *Teen Hearts in Paradise*, minus the tropical beachfront. Rows of valet-parked cars spilled out onto the street, and there was a long line of people at the door, waiting to be screened for entrance.

As soon as Belle and the girls started heading for the back of the line, a Secret Service-looking bouncer waved them to the front and then ushered them right through the front doors.

"Excuse me, people, Jared's 'New Girl' coming through!" Millie called out.

"Stop that," Belle hissed.

"Please sign here." A tired-looking woman in a suit presented an electronic tablet with what looked like a tiny-font document that filled the entire screen. A line marked with an X was highlighted at the bottom.

"What's this?" Belle asked.

"Just your standard NDA," she replied.

She watched as both Millie and Candy signed using their finger. "Just sign," Candy said. "Every party in Elmridge has one. What happens at the party, stays at the party."

Millie elaborated. "You're agreeing to not publish any pictures or gossip to any tabloids about anything Jared-related, or you get sued for your soul."

"Oh, okay then," she replied weakly and signed.

Anything else Belle was going to say died on her lips when they emerged into the foyer. "Oh my...."

Liam had a Gothic castle, but Jared's family had an Art Deco palace. The three-story high foyer looked more like an atrium. It was big enough to contain the entire party, which spilled through the open doors of the back wall made up of floor-to-ceiling windows, and into the backyard, with its five-star resort swimming pool encircled by posh cabanas. And was that a helicopter just sitting there in the distance?

She'd only seen places like this once in a travel catalogue she'd flipped through on the train to Elmridge.

The place was filled with people from school and elsewhere, but she barely recognized anyone since they were all dressed to the nines in true fashion-show spirit. She was certainly glad she'd let her friends dress her for tonight.

The main sight was a large dance pit packed with gyrating bodies at the foot of a small stage occupied by a DJ, and swirling neon lights morphing into different patterns as if also dancing to the beat of the music, which was so loud, she felt the thumping bass drumming on all her organs. Elsewhere, people lounged, talked, played some games involving red cups and darts, and disappeared into the various corridors that branched away from the foyer.

Candy led the way through, craning her neck for a certain tall, muscular redhead.

Seeing the growing disappointment on her friend's face, Millie yelled over the music, "Let's just dance! It's better if he finds *you!*"

Belle soon discovered a new kind of freedom. The exhilaration of drowning herself in the music as she let the notes and beats dictate her body's movements. She'd never had her face hurt so much from grinning and laughing as she and her two best friends danced their cares away.

During a particularly ear-popping hip-hop song filled with dance instructions, Belle and the girls were in the midst of following the rapper's orders to "jump around," when she saw Dmitri slinking up behind Candy with a shush-finger to his lips meant for Belle not to give him away. She smiled broadly at Candy, and just as her friend gave her a questioning look, Dmitri wrapped an arm around Candy's waist and hauled her back to him.

"Found you, boo!" He grinned down at a very surprised and ecstatic Candy. She turned and threw her arms around him, and then they started bopping closely together to the music, completely lost in each other's presence.

Millie gave Belle an alarmed look, and before she could react, an arm snaked around her own waist and Belle felt herself pulled back against a solid, very male body. She screeched as she spun around to look.

"Jared!"

Grinning down at her was the face with baby blue eyes and deep dimples that made countless girls swoon. Jared's black hair was artfully swirled up; he wore a short-sleeved, black button-down shirt that was sheer, the lines of a finely tuned chest just visible.

A glance in Millie's direction revealed that Hans had snuck up on her and was just about to pull the same shenanigan, but when Millie turned and met him with a death-glare, he backed off with both hands in the air.

Jared grabbed Belle's hand and twirled her slowly. "You look incredible."

She didn't think she could ever get used to these kinds of compliments. "Uh, thanks?"

"Let's dance."

Millie spoke in her ear, "I'm going to check out the food."

"Do you want me to come?"

"No, you stay." Her eyes flicked over to Jared and back to her. "Enjoy," she said firmly.

In other words, forget Liam and have fun.

And boy did she. Before she even knew it, several songs had passed. She and Jared fell into a game of mimicking each other's moves with sometimes hilarious results. She didn't even notice that a wide berth was given them by the other dancers, with some watching approvingly.

A sultry slow song came on, and without giving her time to react, Jared wrapped his arms around her waist and drew her close to him. She could only curl her arms behind his shoulders and turn her face against his chest. Their bodies were warm and their clothing damp with sweat. The pressure of his arms around her felt soothing. After all that bouncing around, this was a welcome change of pace. She rested her cheek against him, and she didn't resist when he squeezed her in tighter.

This felt...incredibly nice.

She let her eyes flutter closed and just focused on keeping out of her mind and in the moment with the physical sensations that the pressure of his body and the lulling notes of the music wrought.

Belle soon felt him pull away slightly, and just as she opened her eyes, she saw a pair of lips looming toward her own. She jerked back as her eyes widened. "Um, Jared?"

He straightened and blinked rapidly, embarrassment dampening his normally confident grin. "Sorry. I, uh, thought we were having a moment."

"Listen, Jared, I just want to be fr—" An audible gasp wrung off her next words at what caught her eye.

"What? What is it?" A concerned Jared turned to look behind him, trying to follow her line of sight.

She pointed at a corner of the stage light trusses, raised high above them, but the shadowy figure with the glowing golden eyes was already gone.

The Jäger. He'd been shoulder-leaning against the metallic frame, arms crossed over his chest, foot crossed over the other, as if casually surveying the scene below him, except those two golden points had been boring straight into her.

"I-I think I need some water," Belle gasped out.

"Yeah, yeah sure. Come with me." He led her out of the dance area by the hand, into one of those corridors, and then into a massive den-like gaming room.

If Belle had known what she had been walking into before-hand...if she had known who the occupants of this room were, she would've stayed on that dance floor and whistled for that Jäger to come over and put her out of her misery.

| 7 |

Viper Pit

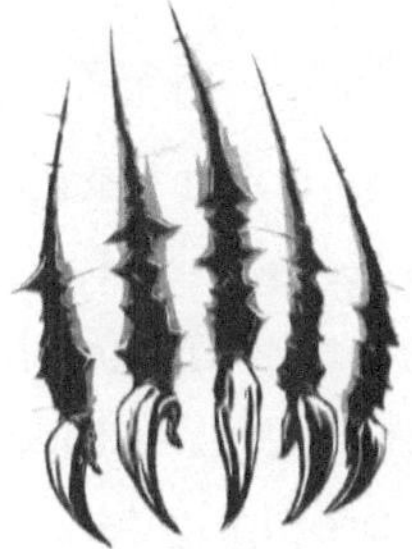

Belle read *A Worst-Case Scenarios Survival Handbook* once. Thrilling reading, indeed. The long afternoons in Littleton imagining herself in each predicament had been some of her best fantasy-adventures.

So when she suddenly found herself fallen into a viper pit, in this case, a room full of the high school's most notoriously venomous creatures, Chapter 6 came to mind as her survival instinct kicked in.

Step 1: Do not move while you immediately assess the threat. Are the snakes venomous? How far are you from striking distance?

Belle froze inside the doorway as her eyes swept the room.

Four Princess Posse models.

Two venomous: Vasilisa Shveya a.k.a. Lisa (Senior Queen B and Liam's ex-girlfriend) and Fatimah Abdallah (wears intimidating resting sneer-face and Vasilisa's #2).

Two non-venomous: Nieves Blanco (sweetheart, but notorious gossip) and Marissa "Mari" Havfrue (most beautiful and the nicest, but in love with her own best friend, Jared, so she must secretly hate Belle).

Vasilisa and Marissa were playing pool with two college-aged guys. Nieves and Fatimah sat in chairs with one other guy hovering nearby. And at the second pool table, was the King Cobra—Kat—and two of her friends. Even worse, Thiago and G were with them at the table.

Step 2: Back away slowly.

Just as Belle was about to do so (escape seemed like an excellent idea right now), Jared dragged her forward by the hand.

"'Sup, peeps! I've got Beauty with me!" he announced, beaming.

All heads snapped toward them. At the wicked collection of smugs all around, Belle's stomach promptly deposited itself into her shoes.

Kat flipped her long, red ponytail over her shoulder. "Ugh, seriously?"

Jared planted a big kiss on Belle's cheek, causing her to instinctively drop his hand. She'd been holding it in a frightening death-grip.

Nieves waved her over and patted the empty chair between herself and Fatimah.

Belle beelined for the empty seat, while Jared headed for Marissa. He told the guy closest to her to take a hike, and then promptly dropped a kiss on her head. Mari spun her wheelchair around to face him, her wide sky-blue eyes made brighter by their sharp contrast with her wine-red hair, and chastised him in a low voice for dismissing "John."

"No *John's* stealing you away from me," Jared snorted, touching the same knob on her chair to wheel her back to face the pool table. He bent over her shoulder and encircled his arms over hers, encouraging her to line up the pool stick. "Now, show me how you're whipping Lisa at this."

"Sooo obvious, right?" Nieves whispered in Belle's ear.

"What's obvious?" she whispered back.

Nieves pouted her apple-red lips and looked meaningfully towards Jared and Marissa.

Belle wasn't feeling gossipy, so she raised her shoulders in ignorance.

Nieves shook her head, her black Texas hair curls bouncing from side to side. "Jared just won't admit he's in love with Mari, too. I mean, he chases any guy away who shows her the slightest bit of interest. How is she supposed to get a Homecoming date then?"

Belle was about to suggest that Mari ask Jared to the dance, when Fatimah's voice slid in like a knife, "Maybe if Jared wasn't being led on by the 'new girl' he'd notice Mari."

"I'm not leading him on," Belle countered in an indignant whisper.

Fatimah only adjusted her silk Shayla scarf, tossing one end stitched with beads over her shoulder, which promptly smacked Belle in the face. With a smirk, she sauntered over to Vasilisa.

The whispers between them and sly glances toward Belle confirmed her suspicions. They were talking about her.

A hot itching in her palms made her squeeze her hands into fists.

Kat's obnoxious laughter sounded through the room. Belle could hear Thiago and G relating to Kat the incident that'd happened on the bus. Falsehoods thrown into the mix, such as Belle feeling up Eddie's chest, had Kat responding snidely, "Of course. It's what she's known for around school."

Step 3: If a venomous snake bites you, remain calm. Do not panic or rush as this speeds up your metabolism and spreads the poison faster.

She had to get out of there, or her hands were going to send up some fireworks, and then she'll become known for something far worse. She shot to her feet. "I-I need water. Where can I get some?"

Nieves gave her a quizzical look, but Jared was already headed her way with a cup of water and a mega-watt grin. "I haven't forgotten, Beauty."

"It's Belle, Jared, not Beauty. Please."

He placed his arm lightly around her shoulders. "Beauty with humility. Hmm, that's a good line in my next song."

Something snapped inside her. She shrugged off his arm. "Jared, I like you as a friend. That's it. Nothing more."

The smack of billiard balls was deafening against the silence that followed.

She bit her lip. "I'm sorry, Jared. I-I didn't mean to say it like that. I *like* being your friend."

But the hurt in his deep blue eyes was done, and the disappearance of his famously permanent dimples made her eyes water. To make those disappear was rare, he was so cheerful all the time.

And Belle had done it. She'd managed to do to him what the mean kids were doing to her: humiliation. She'd sunk to their level.

Shame gutted her.

It took him a moment, but he said, "Yeah, Belle...I like being your friend, too."

He was only a foot away, but the space felt immense. Only a few minutes ago, she'd been happily in his arms, dancing the night away, and now here she was, shoving him away.

Jared looked toward Marissa. "Feel like a swim, Mari?"

"Sure." Mari's round eyes had been fixed on them. Sympathy for Jared, but as she made eye contact with Belle, she smiled, just a little.

Gratitude, Belle realized.

Holding her chin up just a bit higher and swallowing her guilt, Belle smiled back. She had done the right thing. Maybe not with that tone, but it'd been necessary for everybody to understand, and Mari had just confirmed that for her.

Jared turned to Nieves. "Can you grab the mermaid-suit from the pool house and meet us in my room?"

"Sure thing." She bounced out of her chair.

Jared gave Belle a longing look, and then leaned in and whispered, "Thank you for 'New Girl.'" And then he followed Mari out of the room.

Belle was still standing. With all the friendlies gone, she took it as her cue to exit, too. And fast.

She had just reached the open door, when something Fatimah said to Vasilisa made her stop in her tracks. "Did Liam call you again?"

What. Did. She. Say?

Belle felt her body turn around and remain transfixed as she watched Vasilisa reply, whipping out her phone and tapping on it. "Shoot, he did. I missed his call. See?" Vasilisa showed Fatimah the phone, clear enough so that Belle couldn't miss it.

She could see the missed call from Liam.

Her feet moved her body closer. She felt numb, as if she was having an out-of-body experience. Somewhere in the back of her mind, the doubt insisted that some other Liam, not Rawlins, was the name on that phone.

"I guess I'll just call him then," Vasilisa said. "He's been busy with those business meetings in Europe."

Her heart felt like it had frozen over. She knew she should leave; she knew it was going to get worse, but like watching a train wreck, she couldn't tear her eyes away. She watched as Vasilisa tapped her phone again, held it to her ear, and Belle, with her cursed hearing, listened as it rang three times.

A male voice answered. "Hey, Lisa, it's not a good time right now. I'll call you later."

It's Liam. My Liam.

Vasilisa, with a gleam of triumph in her eye, held Belle's stare. "Alright, sweetie. You know you can call me anytime."

Belle's feet had already brought her within arm's reach of Vasilisa. Everyone in the room must have been staring at her like she'd gone off her rocker, but she didn't care. She didn't see anyone, except that phone at that—to use Kat's term—that *skank's* ear and the smooth male voice coming out of it. The same voice that had whispered sweet nothings in her own ear and promised three weeks ago to be back in half an hour.

Doubt suggested that maybe that was a saved voicemail that Vasilisa was playing for Belle's torment.

There was only one way to find out.

Slowly, Belle reached her hand out for the phone. Vasilisa smirked and handed it to her.

He was still speaking. "Hello? Alright, I'm gonna go. I don't have time for this."

"Liam?" She asked in a ragged whisper, her vision blurring with tears.

A pause. "Belle? Is, Is that you?"

She tried to swallow the huge lump in her throat. All she could manage was, "Why?"

Now, Belle didn't know it then, but she had said "Why?" exactly the same way she had countless times in Liam's nightmares, just before he'd ripped out her throat. So she didn't understand when all he said was, "Because...I can't, Belle. I'm so sorry."

And then the line went dead.

She stared at the phone, the tears falling freely now, and when the screen saver on the device lit up with a past school homecoming dance picture of a devilishly handsome Liam in a crown and tuxedo with his arms around a similarly crowned Vasilisa, she dropped the phone as if it were a real snake.

"You should know the truth," Vasilisa said, no trace of smugness in her face, only pity. "Liam and I never stopped talking."

The implication struck her like a blow in the chest, making her rail back a few steps.

Kill them, kill them all, the voice rasped from its cage.

"Aww, boo-hoo," Kat taunted from the other side of the room. "The little orphan got dumped. I bet he was her *first*, know what I mean?"

G laughed, and Thiago thumped him a reprimand on the chest.

A quick death is too merciful. Electrify them...slowly...until the flesh melts from their bones.

"Shut up, Kat," Fatimah said, while Vasilisa had said, "That wasn't necessary, Kat."

Belle's out-of-body experience was complete now because she hadn't processed anything after Kat's insult.

Only that demon voice. And she couldn't control what was happening next.

Someone gasped in horror. "Oh my *God!*"

"Belle?" That was Vasilisa. "H-How are you doing that?"

Electricity encased Belle's hands up to her elbows, snapping and crackling up and down, her forearms live wires. Her mind screamed, *Get out of there!* But her body wouldn't comply. Unseeing, she shook violently from head to toe, feeling the current building up beneath her skin, the outer edges of her vision going white.

Screams punctuated the air as all the electronics and lights popped, and the room was cast into darkness.

No, not again, her own mind cried. She was going to kill everyone. The Hammerson brothers' crime scene was going to look like child's play compared to what was about to happen here.

Belle could only manage one word, "Run."

And right before she exploded, a dark figure, blacker than the shadows the room was engulfed in, dropped down in front of her and swept her into his arms, bringing them both into a crouch so that his whole body covered hers, as she curled into a fetal position in his lap.

The sound of a thousand lightning bolts striking filled the air. The windows blew out in a symphonic explosion, but her killer blast had been completely absorbed by this hulking mass enveloping her.

A pregnant pause followed, like the one of survivors emerging from a shelter and witnessing the destruction of a catastrophe before them.

"Are you okay?" a gruff British voice asked in her ear.

When she made no response, he tipped her chin up. Golden orbs stared back at her.

Cries of terror and shouts of confusion shattered the silence.

Belle blinked, tears leaking out of the corners. She hadn't killed everyone, but had anyone been hurt? Her common sense was returning, and with it, a full panic mode.

"How did you—? Ev-Everyone saw," she whispered, her voice climbing with anxiety. "Is everyone okay?"

"Everyone's alive. At least, until the next time you lose your temper again." There was a scolding in that tone. His voice a deadly whisper now, he pressed his masked mouth directly to her ear, "You have ten seconds to find somewhere we can finish our business in private, while I clean up your mess here."

He dropped her roughly, and she clambered to her knees. She watched as the shadow stood to its full height, and the golden eyes turned away from her. She could hear the people asking, wondering, about her hands filled with electricity, blaming her for what happened. The word *freak* pricked at her ears.

"Eight seconds," the Jäger murmured darkly over his shoulder.

She got to her feet, but almost collapsed again at the sound of the Jäger roaring at the group before him, "Look at me!"

In the darkness, the whites of eyes turned toward him as if hypnotized.

She backtracked until she smacked into a wall. She slid along it, feeling for the open doorway. Just as she slipped out, she heard him command in a godlike voice, "Forget what you saw and heard in the past five minutes. Lightning struck the windows...."

Whatever else the Jäger said had been swallowed up by the dance music pounding in Belle's ears. She ran, pushing blindly past couples in the dark corridor and out through a side door, trying to outrun Death itself.

For surely, what other business could the Jäger have with her now?

| 8 |

Killing Me Softly

Belle was running through a House of Mirrors, a maze of dark corridors, crashing into people instead of glass walls, her frenetic hands leaving a trail of yelps and cries in their wake.

"What the—! Someone's got a taser!"

"Hey, where'd you get those sparkler fireworks?"

"Owww!"

In her panicked flight, she ignored them, but she couldn't shut out the questions about Liam and the Jäger that flashed in her mind. One question stood out above the rest and drove her to move faster: how long did she have to live before the Jäger found her like he'd promised?

She burst out a side door of a small kitchen and felt the instant shock of the frosty night air against her heated skin. She was standing in an area that appeared to be under construction and cordoned off with a *Do Not Trespass* sign.

Perfect. That's where she'd go.

She slipped beneath the thin orange rope and ventured carefully past the unfinished framework of what looked like an enormous shed. Just beyond, she could make out another longer building, its walls somehow reflecting the moonlight.

A greenhouse! She rushed toward it, drawn by the idea of having only plants for company. She bet she could hide in there long enough to call Ernesto before the Jäger got to her. It was already way past the countdown, and he still hadn't found her. She knew it was a wafer-thin hope, but she had to get her mind on happy thinking or her fire-cracker hands would never quit.

The glass door eased open without a sound, and a rush of wet warmth washed over her chilled skin as she stepped in. The sides were stacked high with shelves of flowering plants, as was a long narrow table that ran down the middle of the entire length of the building.

She closed the door behind her. Walking down the right side of the room, the subtle taps of her heels sounded against the earthen-tiled floor. The only light came from the moon's filtered glow through the glass panes and the crackling sparks that erupted at intervals from her hands like frayed live wires.

She reached the end of the room and decided to hide in a corner, behind a cluster of tall potted plants and stacks of soil bags. Sitting on an overturned pot, she huddled into herself, her palms outstretched as if in divine petition, and let her head fall into the crooks of her elbows.

The heat in the greenhouse felt oppressive now. It settled over her skin like a heavy blanket. Perspiration dripped over her, and her hair clung to her neck and shoulders like cobwebs.

"Think happy thoughts, think happy thoughts," she chanted to herself.

"Because...I can't, Belle."

The air smelled like it was burning. The power in her hands alternating between electricity and fire.

"Happy thoughts, happy thoughts," she said desperately.

"Alright, sweetie. You know you can call me anytime."

Fire erupted in her hands.

She tumbled back from her seat, huddling further into the dark, dank corner, trying to distance herself from her own raging hands while keeping them away from the plants.

Nothing would call more attention to her like burning down a building.

They all deserved to die. The Jäger got in the way.

"No!" she shouted. She had to clear her head, empty it out. One way she knew how was by counting, a relaxation exercise Papa had taught her as a little girl to control her tantrums.

One.

Two.

Three.

Four.

Five.

At forty-two, she stopped. She'd heard a noise. A click.

She held her breath and waited, watched on a nearby plant's frond as a black beetle scurried toward a quivering helpless cocoon and sunk its pincers into it, tearing at it, ensuring that moth or butterfly never saw the light of day.

She tore her eyes away, the symbolism not lost on her.

There had been no other sound since, except the pounding of her heart and the thumping base of the house music in the distance. She let herself draw in a long, damp breath, the tumult in her hands finally easing.

Next step in her plan: she dragged her phone out from her back pocket.

"Fudge," she cried in a whisper. The lifeless, cracked screen stared back at her. She'd zapped her own phone to death.

And then, Belle heard it. Soft footfalls. If she hadn't developed freakishly sensitive hearing lately, she would have missed it.

Only one person could tread in cat-like silence.

The realization turned her insides into ice, petrifying her like a gazelle caught in a tiger's path. This was it. She could flee or hide like a frightened coward and be caught, or she could take a stand somehow and fight back.

So then, she'd have to stand. Literally. She couldn't let herself be caught helplessly balled up in a mucky corner.

She scrambled onto her wooden legs, peeling off her gold high heels first, and edged around the potted plant. She clenched each heel in her hand like a weapon, not sure how she'd wield them exactly, but maybe those glowing eyes could serve as two bullseyes for the pointy ends of these shoes.

Shame pinched her conscience at the violence she'd just pictured. This wasn't her.

But what could she do? The Jäger hadn't been hurt by her electrical blast, so she couldn't use that power to defend herself with.

Her eyes swept the greenhouse, made eerily monochrome by the moonlight, searching for any inspiration for a defense plan.

I like your plan. Plunge the heels into his eyes.

The Jäger stepped into her line of sight.

Time slowed as he stalked the length of the aisle towards her, his unnatural eyes burning with malicious intent.

Terror wracked her body. Her skin was ice cold, yet sweating bullets.

What can I do? What can I do?!

What she knew of this Jäger flashed in her mind: he'd saved her from the twins in the alley, and then hadn't kill her; he'd stopped her from zapping a room full of people, and then commanded them to *forget* what had just happened....

The realization slammed into her. Could he control people's minds? He'd needed them to look at him. Oh, geez, this was going to be like fighting Medusa—she'd have to close her eyes!

She ordered her eyes to shut, but they disobeyed and remained peeled wide open, trained on the Jäger, who'd paused with half the distance of the greenhouse still stretching between them.

He opened his hand at his side, and Belle's knees almost buckled as she watched a golden shimmer issue from his hand and materialize into a dagger. He wrapped his fingers over the handle as it solidified.

Yep, that was real. And he was definitely here to kill her.

Now would be a good time to get her hands to spark some defense. She gave her hands a shake, mentally commanding her powers to work, but she only managed to make her palms sweat even more, and she wasn't sure if that response came from her or the sight of the Jäger twirling the dagger in his hand. She couldn't even get her sandpaper throat to gulp in fear.

It was so quick, just a mere flicker of his wrist. The Jäger's dagger sliced the air by her ear, and she jumped at the sound of the blade sticking in the wall behind her.

Her breaths came out in short bursts as she stared at him in horror.

He opened his hand, and the dagger behind her dematerialized into a golden shimmer. She watched, transfixed, as the trail of shimmer flowed past her into his waiting palm. He closed his hand again as it reformed into a solid dagger.

Holy crap. He could have an arsenal at his disposal if that's how he wielded weapons.

He gestured toward her hands. "Your turn, luv."

Right. The *British* Jäger.

Her hands flared with electricity, and she sucked in a breath of relief. They'd decided to work after all. Good timing.

Finally able to swallow and loosen her throat, she found her voice. "Y-You want me to attack you?"

"Don't you want to?"

"I don't want to die."

"Siren..." he cooed. "You know you have to try a little harder to stop me from completing my mission."

"Siren?"

"You know, *siren*—a devastatingly gorgeous and enchanting creature who lures men away from their missions to their doom. It's the only explanation for what you do to me. Or are you unfamiliar with the so-called mythological monsters of our world?"

Thunderstruck by both the compliment and the insult, she tripped over her words as she spoke, "I am not a *siren* doing anything to you. I'm just me." She showed her trembling hands, still grasping the heels. "With a few quirks, give or take. And I just want to be left alone. I don't mean anybody any harm or trouble. I'm not a m-monster; they're not even real. They're just what you said: mythological."

"Oh, siren. They're *all* real."

"Liar."

"I don't lie, luv. Can't."

A vision cropped up of a hairy monstrous hand reaching up from underneath her bed and wrapping clawed fingers around her ankle. "Well, then," she said in a small voice, "I'll never sleep at night now."

He let out a soft chuckle and straightened. "Let's have it, luv. Blast me. You get the first crack."

"Just let me go." She stepped to her right, and his eyes followed. She tensed.

He wasn't letting her out of his sight.

"I see you need some triggering. How about we call that boyfriend of yours, yeah? Find out why he's stopped talking to you. Does he know your secret?"

"Stop. Please."

"Scared him off, did you?" Anger shook his voice now. "How many people has he told about you? How far does your mess really spread?"

"Stop it!" She threw her hands up and a bolt of electricity, followed by a pair of heels, flew at him.

The shoes bounced pitifully off his chest. But the bolt...he'd caught it. Like something out of a movie, he'd caught the thing. With his hand open, the bolt curled in on itself like a lazy cat spinning in its spot, receding into him as if he were a giant, black sponge.

Belle's jaw dropped. This guy defied the laws of physics.

"That's all you've got?" he taunted.

She wasn't even *trying* to hit him. The bolt had just shot out on its own. But he didn't need to know that.

"I've got more," she threw out lamely.

"Why don't you come at me with the lightning storm you unleashed on those kids back there, yeah? You know, the ones you almost slaughtered."

"I-I didn't want to do that. I lost control."

"You lost control," he repeated, his tone making her feel small. "A few schoolyard bullies poke at you, and you almost level the entire compound."

"What? I-That was not—"

"Not going to happen? I know exactly the magnitude of that blast. You would have taken out every person in that house. Your friends? All dead."

His words speared her. He didn't need a glittering dagger to bring her down. His cruel truth was doing it all on its own. She pictured Candy and Millie's charred, dead bodies littered among blackened corpses.

Don't listen to the cretin.

The Jäger cocked his head and whispered ominously, "There it is."

"Kill me," Belle whimpered. "I'm...I'm a menace to everyone around me." Her whole body trembled as the electricity sparked into orbs that encased her hands. "Papa kept me locked up in the house, my aunt didn't claim me until she had to, three people are dead because of me...." A sob caught in her throat. "It all makes sense now."

Kill him! Blast him with everything you have!

"Let it out, luv." His tone was softer.

"If it wasn't for you, my friends and all those people would be dead just because, just because I can't control myself." The wetness that had gathered in her eyes spilled over.

Pathetic weakling.... Let me out. I'll take him.

She paused as understanding dawned on her. "Oh."

Belle thought the Jäger was encouraging her to let her emotions out, rile herself up for a fight. But he wanted her to let *it* out. The voice. The creature that writhed now against the back of her mind, restless in its cage.

Through blurry eyes, she peered down at her hands, the electricity running the length of her arms now. She asked in an agonized whisper, "What's wrong with me?"

"Nothing I can't fix, siren." And there was no malice in those words, only a lifeline.

He'll fix nothing! Let. Me. OUT!

"Help me," Belle mouthed. The electricity crawled over her shoulders now and down her body like a freshly escaped entity exploring its new surroundings.

The Jäger stood less than ten feet away, an imposing sentinel of darkness with a fierce, unwavering glow in his golden eyes. She was ensnared in that penetrating stare, as if he was seeing right through her, pinning the creature in place.

He gave a small nod of encouragement. "Close your eyes."

Putting her faith in her assassin, Belle closed her eyes.

The Jäger said something in a foreign language, and like a light switch being flipped, her mind went dark. Something—her spirit, her conscience—was still awake, but she felt the creature push past it and open her eyes for her.

She sucked in a breath as if it were her first. She zeroed in on the Jäger and glared, her mouth curling up into a sneer. "How did you know, Jäger?" It spoke in Belle's voice but slurred the ends of the words like a snake.

"I heard you inside the girl's mind, goading her to kill the others. Now, tell me your name, demon." The Jäger's tone brooked no room for refusal.

"I have no name." She slinked toward him. "I am just a shadow of my master."

"Not a step further, or you will taste the end of this blade."

She hissed at him but remained rooted to her spot.

"Tell me your master's name."

She struggled to keep her mouth shut, but the more she resisted, the more a painful burn spread beneath her skin. The only relief was in obeying him. "Infernal Jäger." She spat at him. "Violet Wickeby."

He recoiled in surprise. "Violet Wickeby? Tell me what she wants with the girl."

"To wear her, of course."

"Why this girl?"

The demon was silent.

"Tell me."

She gave a mock-sigh. "Isn't it obvious?" She ran her hands along her sides to her hips. "Young, beautiful, powerful...."

"Remove your hands, you fiend," he snarled.

A raucous cackle filled the air. "You want her for yourself. Who's the fiend now?"

He was in her face in an instant, dragging the tip of the dagger down her cheek, leaving a trail that felt like fire.

She screamed.

"Tell me how you ended up inside Belle."

She breathed hard now, recovering from the acidic sting of the magical blade. When she didn't answer, he pressed the tip against her chin. Feeling the flesh was going to melt off there, she jerked her chin away and gasped out, "The girl. She doesn't know it. Not even Violet knows." The Jäger stepped back, giving her more breathing room. "But *I* know."

"Go on."

She gritted her teeth before continuing, "Weeks ago, the girl lost control in front of Violet. Killed everyone in her family. Violet took possession of her then, and then those odious creatures—"

"*What* creatures? Tell me."

She grimaced. "The Fae."

"What did the Fae do?"

She paused. Knowing the Jäger was hooked, one side of her lips curled. "Let's make a bargain, and I will tell you anything you want to know."

The Jäger moved in one strike, and she screamed again, crumpling to the floor.

He'd stabbed her in the thigh.

"You are in no position to bargain, demon. On your feet. Now."

She scrambled clumsily to her feet, leaning on her good leg as she stood. The pain in her injured thigh was blinding. "You don't care that you're hurting the girl? Where is the famous Jäger compassion for these pitiful humans?"

"I am not hurting her, I'm hurting you. Stop stalling and tell me what the Fae did to Belle."

The need to obey burned hotter than her thigh now. "They re-wound time. She was warned not to reveal her powers to Violet, and the memory of the Fae's intervention was sealed away in her mind." Her tone took on a taunting edge. "You know how to access that memory, Jäger, but you'd have to break your prophecy to do it."

He ignored the bait. "Tell me why you're still inside her."

"They couldn't get *all* of Violet out for their do-over."

"Tell me why the Fae intervened for Belle."

"I'll only say this: Dommedag won't happen without her."

"What do you mean? Explain."

"No. We *want* Dommedag, and you can't stop it." She bared her teeth, and the electricity snaking all over her body ballooned out into a sphere that encased her and the Jäger. "Maybe you won't damage this body, but *I* will!"

The Jäger lunged for her, dagger ready, and she let out an ear-splitting shriek as she threw her arms out. The giant electrical orb inflated until it blasted out of the greenhouse. Glass shattered all around them, raining down a tinkling storm of jagged shards.

The Jäger held Belle's body cradled against his own, her head tucked into the crook of his neck and shoulder, shielding her from the glass rain. He cursed under his breath when a two-inch piece of glass stuck into her exposed left forearm. He picked out the glass and wrapped his hand tightly over the wound to staunch the flow of blood.

Belle opened her eyes and gasped at the yellow orbs glowing mere inches from her face. Holding her against him, the Jäger had one arm wrapped around her waist. His other hand held something cold and heavy against her chest, right over her heart.

Looking down at herself, her eyes widened.

His hand was wrapped around the handle of the dagger, its blade buried in her chest. She felt the solid cold mass inside her, but there was no pain, no blood.

Swiftly, he pulled the dagger out and her chest contracted.

"Easy, siren. You're alright now."

Her eyes found his. "Is the creature…gone?"

He nodded slowly.

"I'm so tired," she whispered, her eyelids suddenly weighing a ton.

She felt herself sinking into his arms, one still around her waist, and the other hand cradling the side of her neck, his thumb stroking her cheek. She leaned her face into that warm hand and felt herself fade away into the black abyss of unconsciousness.

The Eye of the Beast

Belle padded on all fours, turning in circles, matching the frantic pace of her incoherent mind. Emotion and instinct were all she knew. In desperation, she lunged herself against the cage, over and over, the biting pain radiating throughout her body, but to no avail.

Snarls of frustration escaped her throat. She stared at the glint of the bars, the only visible sight in the pitch blackness, until her hot rage slowly spiraled into helplessness, and she sunk down onto her belly, her head coming to rest pitifully between her shaggy, blonde front paws.

After what felt like an eternity of slumber, her ears perked up as her head lifted groggily. She heard sounds of an outside door unlocking, followed by the voices of two females growing louder as they neared.

Her shoulders tensed. A low, long snarl of warning ripped out of her.

The voices paused before the unfamiliar one asked, "Is that...the *beast* you were talking about earlier?"

A sugary voice that was all too familiar, drawled out, "Oh, yes. Come, Hagar, I'll show you." There was a pause. "It's perfectly safe. He's somewhat docile."

"Somewhat?"

Bright light flooded her vision as a door was thrown open, revealing a floor-to-ceiling cage, the kind that could contain a lion at a zoo. And she was inside it. As her vision adjusted, she took in the lavish apartment and the two women, who couldn't be more opposite from each other, standing before wall-sized windows showcasing the Amsterdam skyline.

The tall, thin woman, Violet Wickeby, wore a navy business suit, and chin-length, sleek black hair framed her true face. Without the prosthetics, it was a face that looked very much like Belle's own, except this one was scarred on one side like jagged puzzle pieces roughly connected.

The other woman, Hagar, was all Gypsy-Bohemian style in dress, with flowy, multicolored layers, bangles that ran up her forearms, gaudy rings on every finger, wide hoop earrings, and a scarf that wrapped all her brown her into a pile on top of her head. Her most distinct feature was her wickedly long nose with a dark, hairy mole. The only thing missing was a crystal ball in her hands.

Violet stood smugly admiring the impressive reaction her *pet* had on others. Beside her, the cowering, squat woman's eyes grew wider and wider as they followed the beast's human-like rise onto his back legs until he stood towering over them at well over six feet tall.

"Good God..." Hagar gasped out, gripping the edge of a desk she had backed into.

"*Good* God'?" Violet crossed her arms over her chest. "And from *your* lips?"

"H-How did you manage such a spell?"

"A bloody, red-rosed dream catcher. Made in Elmridge, you know, the hub of Fae magic." Violet flicked a wayward hair back. "I had to sacrifice two of my pets for this one. A keen momentary loss, but the payoff has been quite lucrative." Hagar gave her a questioning look. "Let's just say he's been persuasive in helping certain business partners see things my way. Even if the beast's efforts are only half-hearted."

"What do you mean?" Hagar inched toward the cage, horror and admiration mingled on her face.

The beast, still partially steeped in shadows, reached out with its powerful forearms and wrapped its taloned, fur-matted hands around the bars of the cage.

"Meaning the creature never gave me full submission, so the spell is only half as effective. Which brings us to why you're here. I need his total obedience if he is to be useful when we travel back to Elm-ridge soon."

The beast extended its long snout through the bars and stilled as it waited. Belle felt the constant simmering anger beneath its skin tempered by the predatory anticipation of this foolish woman drawing ever closer.

"Careful now," Violet drawled. "He can be quite...moody."

"Imagine now." Hagar murmured, hooked by the icy green eyes that reeled her in even closer. "Total control over this magnificent creature." A scream tore from her as its paw whipped out, slashing across her chest and tearing through layers of her dress.

Hagar crashed back onto her bottom, her face bleached with fright and gaping at the colorful layers of fabric that fluttered to the ground. The beast released a roar that shook the room and sent her whimpering and scampering back like a crab.

Violet leveled an icy stare at the beast. "Do you need another lesson in manners?"

From inside her blazer's pocket, she withdrew a small cylinder. With a flick, it elongated into a thin metal rod. A click of a button at its handle and the other end crackled with a burst of electricity.

Belle felt herself relent with a loud grunt and retreated to the farthest corner of her cage. She dropped back onto her haunches. Ears perked for listening, she watched them silently.

Hagar tore her eyes away from the bright green ones in the shadowy corner of that cage and clambered to her feet. She shook her skirts out and said to Violet, "Let us resume our business."

Violet stashed the metal rod back in her jacket. "By all means."

Hagar reached into a deep pocket within the folds of her dress, withdrew three corked vials the length of her hand, and laid them on the desktop. "I have what you ordered."

Violet's eyes gleamed, but when she reached for them, Hagar blocked her hand.

Violet gave her a murderous sneer.

But Hagar was not to be trifled with. Her pupils expanded until her eyes were a solid black. "Payment. First."

Violet straightened. "Of course." She retrieved a basketball-sized burlap sack from the other room. "I'm always good for business."

She lifted the sack onto the table. The sides and bottom were coated in dark stains that looked suspiciously like blood. There were jerky movements within the bag, a slithering and prodding that pushed at the sides. "It's all there. Your special order of very rare potion ingredients."

They each reached for their prizes at the same time and cradled them close.

Hagar made the sack disappear into another deep pocket of her dress. She pointed a gnarled finger at the red vial in Violet's hand. "That one's for the beast. He'll be eating out of the palm of your hand in no time. The potion's injectable, and it's one shot. I can't make another one of those. Take care if he resists while it's being administered. He'll need every drop if you want 100% obedience."

She pointed at the green vial. "That one has the opposite effect. It breaks anyone's unnatural hold on them. Mix it into a bottle of wine—red is best—and then it must be drunk at one shot a day, until it's all gone."

Violet held the purple vial up to the light. "And this one must be for masking the smell of magic."

"The potion must be given in small doses. It's good for one year." She frowned. "That one was the most painful to make. I won't attempt to boil a live leprechaun ever again. The creature nearly scratched my eyes out in the attempt."

"Yes, well, I can't have that Jäger in Elmridge interfering with my plans."

Hagar crossed herself (in the opposite order) at the mention of the Jäger, as if warding him off.

Violet led Hagar to the door. By way of small talk, the latter asked, "So, who is this relative that you said the green potion is for?"

Still inflated with the triumph of acquiring her prized potions, Violet answered a bit too candidly, "Oh, just the son of a…friend. He needs to escape his captor before he can be of any use to me."

And just like that, Violet froze in her tracks. Against her will.

Hagar peered sideways at her. "Whatever is the matter?"

Violet stared straight ahead, unseeing. She trembled with the effort to move, only managing to grit out, "Back. To. Sleep, Abigail."

A change came over Violet. Her features melted into an expression of alarmed grief, and she wailed out in a tone that was not her own, "Violet, no! You'll get him killed! You promised—my family would not be harmed!" Her breathing ragged, Abigail lowered her voice, "I *will* kill you this time. I will end myself, and—"

Violet cut her off, "You are already dead, and you know it. *I'm* the one keeping this carcass alive now. And when I leave you, all that's left of you will rot." Her voice rose into a fevered pitch as she spoke, "As for James, I am doing you a favor—freeing him from the clutches of that hunter. And when I have finally made my wish with the Jade Blade, I will rule this planet, and your children will serve by my side!"

Abigail slapped her in the face.

"Demented," Hagar murmured, backing away slowly.

Ignoring her, Violet reached up and touched the stinging flesh of her scarred cheek. "You ungrateful wretch," she seethed. "You will pay dearly for that. Do you know what I will soon be able to order my beast to do to Belle? Keep pressing your luck, Abigail."

Her posture slackened as the tension of Abigail's presence instantly faded away.

"Now," Violet straightened the lapels of her blazer, "that's more like it. Hagar, dear, where were we?"

She was answered by the front door slamming shut.

She rolled her eyes and turned back to the cage. "Well, Beast," she held up the red and purple vials, "I daresay, it's time for your medicines."

A roar of desperation was her answer.

| 10 |

What Are Friends For?

Belle awoke in the middle of the night, desperately kicking at the vise of sheets wrapped tightly around her body. Truth be told, she thought she was still inside the beast and was thrashing around, trying to free herself from the prison of its body.

She dropped into a free-fall for a nanosecond, and the solid smack against the floor jolted her out of her semi-dreamstate. She froze. The filtered moonlight through the blinds, not the greenhouse panes, let her see that she was in a bedroom, not her own, but it did look vaguely familiar.

She scrambled to a sitting position on the floor, the blankets wrapped protectively around her shoulders, her back against the bed. Once she spotted the small square poster frames on the wall of various New Orleans landmarks, it finally registered in her brain that she was in Candy's spare bedroom. A glance down at her outfit proved she was still in her party clothes, and the Louis Armstrong mini-statue clock on the nightstand showed the hands at 3:45-ish in the morning, which all meant that…

Holy bluebells, this night really happened!

Her mind zeroed in on the most immediate shock: that dream.

She reached over to the nightstand's drawer but only found candy wrappers from the last time she'd stayed over. She needed pen and paper; she needed to write down this dream.

Keeping one of the blankets wrapped around herself, she ventured out into the hall toward the catch-all drawer in the kitchen she knew would have what she needed.

"Belle."

The scream she bit back came out as a gurgled gasp.

"Hey," Candy whispered, gripping her pallid friend by the shoulders. "It's just me. I heard a noise from your room."

Belle struggled to steady her breathing. "How, how did I end up at your place? I don't remember."

They shuffled back into the guest room. Perched on the bed facing each other, Candy pinned Belle with her classic let-me-*tell*-you expression. "Honey, you must've had a wild night. Millie and I found you curled up, sleeping on a lounger at the far edge of the back patio. You even had a big beach towel around you, which some kind soul must've covered you with because you looked as snug as a bug. And then, we couldn't get you to fully wake up, and you were mumbling something about Jäger, so we figured you passed out drinking Jägermeister." She clucked her tongue in disapproval. "Only you didn't smell drunk, and you were clutching a ketchup bottle, which, by the way," her tone sharpened, "you got all over my gold Gucci shirt." She paused and squeezed Belle's arm. "Long story short, we need to build up your partying stamina. And it was rough-going between Millie and me trying to get you out of that lounge chair, but then guess who showed up?"

"Who?" Her head was spinning. Let them think she was drunk-buzzed into sleep on a ketchup cocktail. That worked for her. The

Jäger in the greenhouse-incident was real. He must've been the one to set her down where her friends could find her.

"That boy Millie likes and who you know from lunch. And let me *tell* you, he is fine with a capital F. He asked what the trouble was, we told him, and he said 'Never fear, help is here'—so you see, he *is* fine, but he is a dork, so I get why Millie likes him—and then he scooped you up in his arms like you was just a feather, and, girl, the people parted like the Red Sea when he walked through with you. You should've seen Jared's face, poor guy…and poor Mari! Jared was flirting with some blonde right in front of her before he saw you being carried off."

"I told Jared that I only like him as a friend."

"You did? Well, good for you. But listen, I'm not finished. Our resident hero, Eddie, followed us in his Jeep since he said he was staying at this complex, too. I dropped Millie off at home, drove us here, and then he *carried* your cute Sleeping Beauty behind up the stairs—we tried the elevator, but it wouldn't come—all the way to this bed. Never complained once. And you were just clutching at his shirt and burying your face in it, mumbling something about '*You smell so nice*' and '*Happy thoughts.*'"

"You're lying."

"Nope."

"You're exaggerating."

"Not one bit. And then he sure charmed Mama with his, '*Pleasure to meet you, m'am,*' and his, '*Is that some delicious gumbo I smell?*' I could tell she wanted to feed him a bowl and adopt him, but I had to get rid of him."

"Why?" Belle's cheeks were on fire, but her heart had been doing cartwheels this whole time, imagining herself being shepherded in Eddie's arms as her rescuer. Forget the life-or-death stuff, this was a total Willoughby-&-Marianne moment. And, jeez, her damsel-in-distress fantasies were a bit antiquated, but they were her guilty pleasures.

"Three reasons. One, your uncle was on his way—"

"What?!" she whisper-screeched.

"Mama called him. Told him you were staying over because you weren't feeling well. He did come by, but Eddie was long gone by then, and your uncle checked on you. I guess he was satisfied you really were just sleeping and not passed out drunk. Mama sent him packing with some leftovers. Hmm, now I wonder if he really did just want the gumbo and used you as an excuse."

"That *is* highly probable."

Belle had a *lot* to tell Ernesto. She'd have to tell him everything that happened just this whole day. Had it really just been one day, today, that the twins and the Jäger attacked her, and then she was somehow exorcised by the Jäger after she almost committed mass murder? And what was that bit of crazy-talk the demon had mentioned about her killing her family and getting a do-over?

That was just a lie. Had to be.

This was all too much. Just too much. She couldn't even process all that right now. Not to mention the dream she'd just awakened from, seeing through that Beast's eyes. The details of the dream were growing fuzzy already. She needed to wrap up this conversation with Candy and write it down already.

"And two?" Belle prompted.

Candy pursed her lips. "Millie. Don't even tell her how accommodating Eddie was for you. Her glasses will turn a permanent shade of green."

"It's not like I was encouraging him," she said defensively. "I was unconscious."

"Still. Even unconscious, you swept that man off his feet."

"What are you talking about?"

"And three, Eddie *likes* you, girl."

"He was, um, just being a gentleman." Belle thought of the way she and Eddie had parted on Maple Tree Trail. Not very amicably. "Yes, he was just being nice. Maybe he was helping me for *Millie's* sake, huh, did you think about that?"

"So you're not interested in Eddie? Not even the littlest bit?" Belle must've taken too long to answer because Candy added, "And now we officially have drama. My advice? Let Millie have this one."

Belle could only sputter as she stared. "Eddie is not mine to give. Plus, I don't want to worry about boys. I'm still trying to get my mind off one as it is. I have too many other more important things to worry about."

"Such as?"

Catching a witch. Freeing my mom. Surviving a Jäger. Or, how about even forming a plan for all of that?

"Such as?" Candy repeated.

"School and homework."

Once she got home, she and Ernesto were going to form a plan that included her. No more of his *"You worry about school and being a teenager, and my Mission Impossible team and I will nab Violet."* She needed to be involved. She needed to make herself useful. This was *her* life, and she had to start taking the reins and stop being a passive observer. Yes, her life was the script to a *Twilight Zone* episode, but she was still the star and so she had to play her part.

She was still working out the *how* part, though.

Candy yawned loudly and rubbed her eyes. "Okay, girl, goodnight. I left you some fresh PJs in the bathroom. Oh, we're having a pool day tomorrow. I invited Eddie."

Her jaw dropped. "Did he say he was coming?"

Candy didn't even turn around as she walked out, teasing, "'School and homework,' huh?"

Belle threw a pillow at her backside, but Candy only laughed before closing the door behind her.

~~*~~

The next morning was *not* a pool day. Belle had slept in all the way to noon to the sounds of thundering rain outside. As soon as the sleepy frog was out of her voice, she called Ernesto on Mama Jo's phone.

"I dreamt of a flower."

A pause. "*The* flower?"

"Uh-huh. The flower is in Amsterdam."

"What else?"

"Uh, the flower would go well with a navy business suit and a brown-haired wig. This flower was there with a different flower. It looked like it would, um, go well with a Bohemian outfit and a head wrap. And potions." She felt the code-splaining getting ridiculous now. "Um…a wolf-type animal is sniffing around these two flowers. They're all in a hotel room with the Amsterdam skyline visible through a window."

Unfortunately, that was all she had remembered from the dream. She hadn't been able to find anything with which to write it down, so she'd lain in bed trying to replay the dream in her mind, and before she knew it, sleep had claimed her.

"I'll get the ball rolling toward Amsterdam right now," Ernesto said. "When will you be home?"

"Soon. I need to buy a new cell phone at the mall first."

"What happened to your phone?"

"It broke."

She could tell he resisted asking about it further. "Okay. Bueno, are you feeling better?"

"Yes, thank you."

He waited for her to elaborate, probably explain how she was ill in the first place, but she didn't want to concoct a lie, so she remained silent.

"I'll see you at the house then."

"See you soon, Uncle."

So in borrowed navy jogger pants and a fitted black strappy tank top from Candy, she zipped up in her gray school hoodie, applied cotton candy-flavored lip gloss, and wrapped her bird-nest hair into a low bun.

While tucking yesterday's clothing into her messenger bag, she noticed the dark brown patch on the gold sequined party shirt. The pattern tracked down the left side of the shirt, and it was bright red, not brown. She licked the spot. Metallic, coppery, and definitely not ketchup.

That was blood.

Belle unzipped her hoodie and pulled the front of her tank top down a tad. She stared at the spot where the Jäger's magical dagger had been embedded. If the dagger was supposed to kill the demon and not her, then why was there blood all over the shirt?

Was it possible...the Jäger *meant* to kill her, and she'd healed after he left her for dead?

Her perfectly unstabbed heart hammered in her chest. That could only mean that the Jäger would try to kill her again. He probably knew now that she healed fast, and she didn't even want to think about how he would make sure that she stayed dead.

When the rain died down, she and Candy headed to Peacock Plaza. First stop, Candy's bakery. Belle parted ways with her best friend after scarfing down her favorite cupcake and an iced mocha latte. The world could be ending—doomsday fireball comet right outside her window—but that heavenly chocolate ganache could keep her blissfully occupied.

Properly caffeinated now and her sweet tooth appeased, she headed for Q's electronics store, Q-Tech.

The Elmridge high school was known as one of the best and most exclusive in the nation. They were really hands-on about educating the students in their future career choice, especially when it came to making money, which was why some of the high school students already had a business or income of their own. Candy had her bakery; Q, his electronics store; Vasilisa, a clothing store; Hans, an event planning business; Jared's a singer, and Liam runs an international shipping company.

Even Belle was supposed to be in charge of the Historical Elmridge Society Museum on the first floor of her home. Except it'd been closed this whole time, plagued by rumors of being haunted, courtesy of Peter's shadow. But that was a non-issue now since the shadow had followed Peter and Emily out the window that night.

Maybe she should start focusing on running the museum and making it accessible to the public. After all, it was part of her Work Study grade, her last class of the day, only the teacher responsible hardly ever kept tabs on her.

But, still. Emily had wanted her to take charge of the museum. It would probably be a productive diversion for her.

Belle caught sight of Cindy just inside Q-Tech, working the check-out station. As she drew closer, she could see something was boldly different about her shy friend. Cindy's sandy blonde hair was up in a high ponytail. Her bangs were artfully cut, the center covered her forehead, and the sides remained long enough to frame her face. Her lips were glossed pink, and her cornflower blue eyes really popped. Make-up! Cindy was wearing make-up and no hoodie. Her black employee t-shirt had the signature electronic banner running across her chest, *Q-Tech, Your best bet for the best tech!*

"Hi, Belle!" Cindy called out.

"Hi yourself!"

As she waited for Cindy to finish ringing up a customer, Belle glanced around at a sight that would make Tony Stark proud. Robotic arms and self-serve touch screens protruded from the ceiling over counters of electronic merchandise. Q, with his infamous dislike of people, employed robots as sales agents, and Cindy, the only human he appeared to like.

Belle felt like Q just tolerated her presence for Cindy's sake, but it was apparently enough to land her on his very short list of friends.

Cindy waved her over, and they hugged. "Q's in the back, so we have a few minutes to chat. How was the party last night?"

"It was fun, I guess. I called you beforehand and left you a message to see if you wanted to go."

"I know. I was just *really* busy." She bit her lip and couldn't quite meet Belle's eyes. "Um, I have something to tell you."

Belle's alarms went off. "Okay."

"So, my dad and I spent the last week moving into a new place because he got a new job."

"That sounds great. Right?"

"Yes, it's amazing actually. Daddy's well enough now that he's on his feet with the help of a cane, and he's almost completely back to normal, physically and mentally. Enough that he's ready to hold down a job."

"Seems this news keeps getting better and better. I'm so happy for you. So, what's wrong then? Are you moving out of Elmridge?"

"No." Here she paused and nervously tucked the longer sides of her bangs behind her ears. "Daddy and I moved into Rawlins Castle."

Belles eyes widened and her breath stilled in her chest, but Cindy rushed on, "Daddy used to work with Liam's father in the business. They were partners or something. Liam called Daddy up a week ago and told him he'd heard how he was out of the hospital and improving so quickly. Liam asked him if he could resume his old post, you know, partners, and with the Europe-angle eating up so much of his time, Liam wanted Daddy to run the North American division. Well, Daddy accepted, and, um, Liam g-gave him the castle, and told him to staff it and run it however he wanted to because it was his now."

The silence stretched between them as Cindy looked anywhere but at Belle's stricken face.

Looking down at her shoes, Cindy finally moaned, "I'm so sorry, Belle. I didn't want this to be hurtful to you in any way."

That snapped Belle out of her inward spiral toward the mental toilet. "No. No, you have nothing to be sorry about. This, this is the best news I've heard all day. I mean it. Are you happy about this change?" Cindy nodded, a weak smile beginning to spread. "See? And you look happier. You're absolutely glowing."

"Daddy insisted on re-hiring Arturo. He used to be our live-in nanny, well, *manny*, before…the drowning accident. He did my make-up and hair, and, um, yeah, I guess my therapist would approve of all this."

"Well, I definitely approve." Belle gave her a watery smile. "Did you, um, did you talk to Liam?" She flushed with shame at even asking.

"Oh, no. No. He didn't speak with me, but—"

"Yes?"

"I wasn't sure if I should tell you or not, you know, because of how you were feeling about, well, you know…" Belle nodded vigorously for her to go on. "But Liam told Daddy to tell me that if any of my friends wanted to use the library or the rose garden that they were welcome to either. I think, I think he was talking about you."

Hot tears welled up and a golf ball formed in her throat as she nodded her thanks.

So, on some teeny-tiny scale, Liam still cares about me.

"You *do* have a line, Cindy." Q's robotic voice made both girls jump.

Cindy thumped her finger against the small monitor attached to the register. Q's face stared back at them.

"Why isn't this turning off?" she demanded.

"I removed that option after you refused to turn the screen back on yesterday."

"Can you blame me? You're spying on me."

"I am spying on the store," he corrected. "And when I spy that a line has grown at the register because you are chit-chatting with a friend, then I must intervene."

Cindy whipped out a small plastic bag and covered the whole monitor with it.

"I did not anticipate that," came Q's voice.

"Hah!" Cindy patted the bagged monitor triumphantly.

Belle giggled.

Bagged-Q spoke up again. "I overheard you talking about inviting friends to the castle."

Cindy gave an annoyed huff through her nose. "Yes, you may host your next Dungeons & Dragons game at the castle."

"In the dungeon."

"Nope. We were told that level is strictly off-limits to anyone, including ourselves. And how did you even know about the dungeon? No one knew about it."

"I hacked the castle's blueprints."

Belle's jaw dropped along with Cindy's.

Someone from the line answered, "That's messed up." The other two customers in line nodded their agreement.

Cindy yanked the bag off the monitor. "Okay, now I am officially rescinding the invitation."

Q's eyes widened. "No, no, no, wait. I will go away now. Watch." The screen went black.

"That's not enough," Cindy called out.

The other screens in the store all changed into a live feed of Q's face.

"Aack!" Someone on the floor dropped the screen with the tutorial that had been playing a second ago.

"I will give you a raise," Q said from all over the store.

"And an hour lunch break?"

"Forty-five-minute break, and I can host all the D&D game nights I want at the castle."

"A raise, one-hour break, weekends off, and only one D&D—"

"Per week."

"—per month!"

"Deal."

"Okay, deal. Now go away." Cindy made shooing motions with her hands at the monitors. "All of you!"

The monitors all returned to their previous screen displays.

"Wow," Belle quipped. "I should come by more often, huh?"

"Yes," Cindy grinned. "Then maybe I'll end up getting paid vacation time."

After Cindy helped Belle obtain her new cell phone and watch a twenty-minute tutorial on how to set up and use her new device, she left the store.

| 11 |

Annie's Antiques

Belle's mind was such a flustered mess going over everything Cindy had said that she missed her stop to get off the bus at her house. It would be an hour now before the bus would loop around back to her place. She got off at the next stop, the boardwalk, figuring that walking back now would be quicker at this point.

She waded through the light Sunday crowd and stopped at Treats and Eats for a bottle of water to take back with her on the trek. Realizing she'd never ventured to the far end of the boardwalk, curiosity got the better of her and she decided a quick stroll to the end and back wouldn't hurt.

Ernesto was usually never home before dinner and, really, the only reason she was antsy to get home was to have that very long overdue chat with her uncle about the state of supernatural affairs in their lives.

She passed one quirky store after another, thinking that each store's uniqueness enabled them to survive outside the all-consuming retail mall, Peacock Plaza. She practically ran by a joke shop where a worker stood outside in suspenders, checkered pants, and the fake Groucho glasses/mustache combo, offering to spray passersby with a mystery fragrance. Someone shrieked close behind her, and Belle caught a whiff of sweaty sock.

A window display case of last-century items made her stop in her tracks. There was a 1990s boombox sitting next to a gramophone and two mannequins wearing clothing from different eras, '60s hippie and '80s rocker.

"Annie's Antiques!" she said under her breath.

Okay, this boardwalk officially felt like Diagon Alley to her. She shivered with excitement as she pulled open the heavy glass door. The musty, glorious scent of dusty, old things hit her nostrils, and an Elvis Presley jam filled her ears.

From what Eddie had said on the bus, real books awaited her here.

She walked in and resisted the urge to rub her palms together like a greedy bank goblin. The store was a long, narrow room with wood-paneled walls lined with shelves of blast-from-the-past artifacts. Eclectic light fixtures and different chandelier styles hung from the ceiling. Racks of decade-clothing peppered the central floor space.

It was a literal house of horrors for the OCD-inclined.

But for Belle, well, she was in love. She stared rapturously around the room, imagining herself in period outfits and the many stories she could play out. She didn't care that the store wasn't empty. Three other customers cast odd glances her way as she stood transfixed before a grand suit of armor displayed on a wall.

A high-stakes Arthurian joust against another knight cued up in her mind, completely oblivious to someone calling out her name in the store.

Just as she knocked Sir Lancelot off his horse, a too familiar, too male voice suddenly spoke by her ear, "That's sixteenth century armor."

Startled, she bumped into a rack of wooden staffs and swords.

Strong hands caught her by the arms, steadying her. Her eyes connected with a set of amber ones. "Oh, wow! Hi, um, Eddie."

The *wow*-part couldn't be helped. Again, that face up-close, unannounced, was like accidentally smacking into a gorgeous stained-glass window and not even being mad about it. She had to just step back and marvel at the artwork.

And that's what Belle did. She took in his soft tousled black hair that beckoned her fingers to run through it; the thick, dark eyebrows, usually tensely furrowed, now relaxed and slightly raised as if surprised to see her, too. His wide lush lips and stone-cut jaw made her wonder for a wild moment if he and Liam could possibly be related. He wore a black t-shirt with a bald-anime guy that Millie'd probably recognize, but Belle's gaze was a bit snagged on how the front of the shirt stretched across his chest and how the short sleeves hugged his biceps. Her gaze stalled there, so she didn't get to notice the rest of his wardrobe at the moment.

"And this," Eddie palmed his chest, "is modern-day armor." He was teasing her, making it clear that he knew she was outright staring at him.

And she was. She totally was. Her mouth responded on its own, "Right." And that's when she remembered Candy saying, *"And you were just clutching at his shirt and burying your face in it."*

She squeezed her eyes shut at the wave of embarrassment that rushed over her. "Last night," she murmured.

He reached out and squeezed her left forearm while studying her face. "Looks like you're all better now," he said, frowning.

"What is it?"

"That was blood on your shirt last night, Belle, not ketchup."

So someone *had* noticed. She blinked a few times at the accusation in his tone. "There was," she said bluntly. "And I was hoping someone could explain that to me."

"Did you ask Candy or Millie?"

"No. They probably thought it was just ketchup, and I didn't want to worry them."

"Are you hurt anywhere?"

Her hands flew to her chest, right over her heart. When he narrowed his eyes, she dropped her hands. "I don't think so. I checked."

Her heart was beating so loud on this topic of conversation, it was a wonder he didn't hear. The blood on the shirt had to have been her own, she hoped, but that was definitely none of his business.

And what was with the angry face?

"Are you mad at me?" she blurted out. "Did I do something to offend you last night?" He looked taken aback. She rushed on, "If I did, then I'm sorry. Truly. I was out of it, and, in fact..." Maybe she could use kindness to throw some cold water on his sour attitude. "I-I actually want to thank you for, um, helping my friends last night with me. I mean, it mustn't have been easy lugging me around. I'm not exactly a sack of feathers."

It must've worked because the hardness in his eyes melted, and he slowly closed the distance between them, as if he was going to say something. Something moody probably.

But he didn't open his mouth, and his focus on her lingered. She noticed the limbal rings of his eyes were a thick black, making his irises look almost yellow by contrast. The bright store lights must be having some sort of effect on them because his eyes were luminous now, especially when his gaze dropped lower and rested on her mouth.

The air in her lungs stalled. *Was he, was he going to—?*

He lifted a hand to her face, and the pad of his thumb swiped gently over her bottom lip.

A small gasp escaped her, and his eyes widened as they met hers. He retracted his hand. "Forgive me," he said gruffly. He turned away, facing the shelves of merchandise.

Still rooted in her spot, she watched his face through a mirror angled downward from the top shelf. He didn't seem to be aware of it. He lifted a small porcelain figure to inspect it, and then casually brought the wandering thumb to his mouth and sucked on the pad. A look of pain crossed his features and his eyes fluttered shut. He whispered a curse and then, "Just like candy."

Elvis Presley's song *Only Fools Rush In* crooning from the store's hidden speakers should have drowned out Eddie's words, but Belle's keen ears heard every syllable.

And she was no fool. This was proof Eddie liked her.

And what was she to do with this information? Her inner life coach reminded her, *No boys. You already have too much life-drama.*

But her silly heart was too busy doing cartwheels, and her body was a useless ball of flame still reeling from the fact he'd touched her mouth and snuck a taste of her lip gloss.

"What are you doing here, Belle?" The edge was back in his voice.

Great. The good old Jekyll and Hyde switcharoo. Classic mood-killer.

She followed him as he turned his attention to the racks of clothing, sliding hangers aside. "Distracting myself. What are you doing here?" she asked. "Looking for something in particular?"

"I am. It's Q's birthday this week."

"Oh, I'll get him something too then." A pleasant warmth invaded her at Eddie's thoughtfulness for their friend. "That's really nice of you."

"You wouldn't say that if you knew my motive."

"'Fess up then."

"I'm buttering him up for our D&D campaign next weekend. I've never lost, he's never lost, so I'm…" he threw her a cautionary glance, "prepping my victim."

"Quite devious of you then, Mr. Helsing."

He couldn't help smiling and decided to humor her. "I am of the mind, Ms. Montague, that the red Dungeon Master cloak will be perfect for our mutual friend."

Clap-happy pleased he was playing along, her grin spread from ear to ear. She asked in her best British accent, "And pray tell, my dear Mr. Helsing, what gift do you suggest I buy for Q?"

But he was staring at her now, his facial features flickering with a vulnerability that confused her. He cleared his throat, and after a moment of trying to decide something, he pivoted and left her standing there.

How rude. She watched, mouth agape, as he strode to the back of the store. Two female customers' heads turned to watch him pass, no doubt admiring the view.

Eddie exchanged words with the store attendant, a "Melanie" in a Renaissance-peasant dress, who then nodded and disappeared through an Employees Only door.

Well, forget him then, Belle huffed. She moved on to her primary objective: books. When she finally found one solitary shelf of eight books, her shoulders slumped after reading the titles.

"Read all of them?" Eddie said by her ear.

She jumped and stopped short of swatting him on the arm. "Jeez, you're like a ninja. A little warning next time?" She turned back to the books and pouted. "And, yes, I've read all of them. I might come back for *Wuthering Heights* for a re-read, though. I kind of miss Heathcliff."

She turned for his response but found herself talking to nobody. He'd drifted away again.

This guy just doesn't know how to stick around properly for a conversation.

She marched over to him to explain the etiquette he was sorely lacking but found herself giggling instead at the shirt he was inspecting that read, *"Don't trust atoms, they make up everything."*

She joined him at the t-shirt rack. "Papa would've loved this one." She pulled the shirt out. *"I'd tell you a chemistry joke, but all the good ones Argon."*

He showed her another one and gave her an exaggerated smolder. *"Are you made of Copper and Tellerium because you're Cu Te."*

Belle laughed. She came back with a shirt of William Shakespeare in dark sunglasses. *"I'd challenge you to a duel of wits, but I see you are unarmed."*

He clutched his chest like he'd been hit. "Oof, shots fired."

And so a battle of comebacks began with the shirts, with the loser having to buy a shirt for the other.

Eddie surrendered when she attacked with a famous snarky line by Winston Churchill. "Alright, you win," he said. "Take your pick of the spoils."

Feeling mighty pleased with herself, she chose a Jane Austen shirt, which he slung over his shoulder to purchase later.

After they wandered over to a medieval times section, Eddie plucked up a purple wizard's hat with silver stars on it. "I suggest you buy this for Q. It might earn you an invitation to the D&D table."

"If it involves costumes, sign me up." She tried the hat on, but her massive hair bun was in the way. She unraveled it and shook out her hair before tugging the hat back on.

"You won't be much of a wizard without this." He held out a wooden staff as tall as he was. The top end branched out and closed back in on itself as if it could encase a small sphere.

"Alas, my brave knight," she said in deep character-voice, "my staff is missing the Arkenstone. I have need of it, if I am to work my magic."

"You just can't help yourself, can you?"

She poked him in the shoulder with the staff. "You started it this time. Besides, this place is like a toy store to me."

There was a spark in his eye now. "Then, let's play."

He strode over to a nearby wall with famous replica swords displayed. A sign above it read, *Do Not Touch. Ask for Assistance.* After ensuring Melanie wasn't looking, he pulled Andúril from *The Lord of the Rings* off the wall.

He pointed the sword at Belle, and promptly laughed.

Belle was sporting a long, gray beard she'd plucked off a nearby rack of facial disguises. She twirled the end of the beard and arched an eyebrow. In her deepest voice, she said, "You are a fool if you think you can defeat the great Saruman."

"But you look more like Gandalf."

She muttered, "You're ruining it." Thumping her staff once against the floor, she boomed, "What say you, Aragorn? Strike, if you dare."

With one flash of his sword, he smacked the staff out of her hands. Belle blinked. "Awkward."

He smirked. "Want me to teach you, oh mighty Saruman?"

"Yes, please."

For the next few minutes, she mirrored his moves on how to wield the staff and parry his strikes. It was incredibly difficult at first to concentrate on his directions because she kept getting hung up on the outline of his muscles moving and twisting beneath his shirt in distracting ways. At one point, when she couldn't get a particular stance and grip right, he moved in closer and repositioned her fingers on the staff for her. His touch sent a bolt of heat through her that ended as a spark in her palms.

At that, he paused, promptly letting go of her fingers and stepping away.

Holy canoli, he noticed, Belle thought. She let out a nervous laugh. "I think this wool beard is turning me into a static electricity conductor." She blushed at her lame excuse as she tore off the beard and hung it back in place.

Eddie took up a sword stance and pointed the weapon at her. "En garde, electro-wizard."

"Okay then." She readied her grip on the staff and spread her feet into the new stance she'd just learned. Her palms still tickled with heat. "You know what? I'd rather—" Eddie struck by her ear, and she quickly parried. "Hey," she protested. "I wasn't ready."

"Hmm," he said, sounding impressed.

He came at her again with three short, consecutive swings, but she blocked them all. They were clumsy blocks, but they stopped his sword, nonetheless.

"You're fast, Belle."

There was something in his tone that made her worry, as if he was really asking, *Why are you so fast?* She wasn't sure herself, but she knew she could add speed to her growing list of powers on her personal magical "Belle" trading card.

"I had a great teacher." She scrunched up her face, as if changing her mind. "Eh, to be perfectly honest, he was only sub-par."

Better to use banter to keep him distracted from her freaky quirks, she thought.

He stilled as his eyes flashed, his smile turning dangerous. "You're right. I haven't been giving my best." He started moving, forcing them to circle each other.

The steel look in his eyes made her question, "W-We're just playing, right, Eddie?"

Without warning, he came at her in a flurry of thrusts. She could only block some of them; the other blows never landed, but she felt the wind of each one against her skin.

Feeling like this play-fight was starting to get too real, she let the staff clatter to the ground and raised both hands. "Okay, okay, you win!" If he thought she was fast, then he moved like lightning. "How do you move like that?" she gasped, her hands on her hips as she tried to catch her breath.

Eddie squared his shoulders. "Practice." He casually lay the flat of the long sword behind his neck, across his broad shoulders. "So, since I'm the champion, what's my prize?"

But before she could wonder at the possible insinuation behind that smug tone, the smirk on his lips faded into concern as his eyes zeroed in on something on her face. Aware now of a stinging sensation on her cheek, she touched the spot. Her fingers came away with blood.

He'd cut her. Accidentally or not, he'd drawn blood.

Sword tossed aside, Eddie was already before her, the tips of his fingers cradling her face. "I'm so sorry, siren. I didn't mean to hurt you."

"It's just a scratch," she replied. "I'll be—" Her eyes popped open. "*What* did you call me?"

Eddie's eyes were wide. He'd recognized his error before she did. He stepped away slowly, his hands up in the universal *please stay calm* gesture. "I was going to tell you."

"It's *you*." She pointed at him. "You're the J—!"

"Don't. Don't say it out loud."

She palmed her forehead, the wizard hat toppling off her head. "'Jeez, you're like a ninja'?" she repeated, not believing her own earlier admission. "God, I feel so stupid! How could I have not known?"

"I wouldn't be good at what I do if you knew."

Hot tears stung her eyes. "Good at what you do, huh? At assassinations?"

But he'd raised his voice and was talking over her, "But I slipped up just now. That's never happened before." His voice strangled with emotion when he said, "I'm always slipping around you."

She shut her mouth at that last part.

All the clues to the Jäger's identity flashed before her. So obvious, but she never put it together. He was *Eddie*. Her new friend who, like her, appreciated books and solitude and play-fighting in the middle of a store. But also the Eddie who showed up on the bus right after the Jäger-attack in the alley. No wonder Eddie had beelined for her lunch table—he didn't really fit in with them, he was just scoping out his target. It was like that illusion drawing of either a rabbit or a duck, depending on how the viewer looked at it.

Only she always saw Eddie, and never the Jäger. Until now.

Keep your friends close, but your enemies closer, Belle thought, feeling bile rise up in her throat. *This must be his creed.*

"Talk to me, siren," Eddie said, looking worried.

She inhaled deeply through her nose before exhaling slowly through her mouth. He waited patiently while she did it again.

She felt the urge to throw up pass. She had a million questions, a million thoughts to process right now, but the most important question remained. "Are you going to kill me?"

A beat passed before he responded, just above a whisper, "I don't know."

She knew she shouldn't ask. It was probably counterproductive to her staying alive, but she was barely maintaining her sanity at the moment. "What's stopped you so far then? You say you keep 'slipping' around me. Are you trying to say you can't do it because you have a crush on me?"

She'd meant that last question as a jab, but her cheeks blazed with regret at the way it sounded out loud.

Eddie scoffed in a low voice, "A crush?"

She tilted her chin up to show she meant it, even though her insides felt like quivering Jello. She opened and closed her hands at her sides, the electricity dancing in them.

"You think what this is, is a *crush?*" He took a step toward her and she locked up, so he stayed put. "Don't you know what happens when someone like me finally gets activated? September 19, 2020. That was the day I started dreaming about you, and your face hasn't left me since. Every night, every daydream, every bloody thought." His British accent was seeping in. "It is physically painful for me to be away from you. So, no, siren, this isn't a crush. It's bloody torture, is what it is."

"That's not my fault," she said weakly.

His eyes flashed a brilliant gold. "You want to know now how this is going to end up?"

"It would be nice."

"This is how it's going to be: I'm either going to kill you, or I'm going to keep you." She inhaled sharply, and he erased the space between them. He brought his face so close to hers, she had to tilt her head back to look at him. "Either way, siren, you're *mine.*"

Neither of them moved as they assessed each other, their mouths just mere inches away, already lined up.

She didn't know what emotion he was seeing in her face. His words had rocked her to her core. The depths of his words frightened her, and she was ashamed to admit it, but at some obscure, primal level, they also thrilled her.

She felt his breath on her lips, and a sudden, extremely forbidden, irrational need to *feel* more pulsed through her.

Eddie's heated gaze shifted to her cheek. His brows furrowed in confusion. "Looks like your wound has completely healed."

Belle backed away, sucking in a breath to clear her romance-junkie thoughts. She needed therapy. All those love novels she ate up must have warped her mind. Jäger-Eddie did not belong in the swoon-category.

She wiped her cheek with her hand. It didn't sting this time when she touched it.

"May I?" he asked softly. "You still have blood on your cheek."

She should say, *"No, never. Don't touch me."* She should run from him. Scream for him to stay away from her. That liar, that deceiver—assassin!

Her mouth said, "Yes."

His eyes were liquid gold as he reclaimed the space between them again. He withdrew a small white square cloth from his back jean pocket and unfolded it with a flick of his wrist.

Belle couldn't help it. Even while her hands were jumping with electricity, and her mind was a rollercoaster she desperately wanted to get off of, a smile tugged at the corners of her mouth. "You carry a handkerchief?"

A small smile crossed his lips, too. He gently dragged the cloth across her cheek. "An old habit I could never break." He pocketed it. "You know, you were right about my age. On the bus."

Just as that extra truth bomb exploded in Belle's brain, a woman's voice called out, and they sprang apart. "Eddie-boy, you know better. No playing with the merchandise. Are you trying to get me in trouble here?" Melanie showed up with a red cloak over one arm.

"I'm sorry—" he began.

"I need this job," Melanie continued, shaking her finger at him. "Annie will have a stroke if she sees any of her precious swords missing from that wall." She turned to Belle and pointed at the wizard hat by her feet. "And are you going to pay for that, missy?" But before she could answer, Melanie gasped, "What's wrong with your hands?"

Shoot. She'd forgotten to hide the fireworks show behind her back. "Uh..."

"I got this, siren." He tilted his head toward the exit. "Go."

Still reeling from shock, she held his gaze for a moment longer. "This isn't over," she said sternly. "I have questions."

"So do I." His eyes suddenly blazed like the Jäger's, and Belle watched spellbound as he turned them on the poor, befuddled Melanie. "Stay quiet, and do not move from your spot until I tell you to."

Belle gasped as the woman's eyes glazed over.

"Belle?" he said, without breaking eye-contact with his target.

"Yes?" she squeaked.

"Do not tell anyone about me."

She didn't answer.

He waited.

A burning question made it out of her mouth instead. "Have you ever done that to me?"

"Compel you? I tried, once."

"That day in lunch, right? When you told me to take the book."

"Right. It didn't work."

"Why not?"

"That's the same question I have."

Another pause.

"Siren?"

"What? And stop calling me that."

"Leave, before Melanie's brains turn to mush here."

Her breath caught in horror.

He chuckled. "I'm just kidding. She's perfectly safe. Go. Please."

"Fine. Only because you said *please*. But remember, we're not done."

"Indeed."

| 12 |

Misery Loves Company

Belle blasted music on her cell phone while she dragged herself around the kitchen, reheating leftovers for dinner on the electric stove. Her Linkin Park playlist was doing its job to keep her distracted from the melee in her mind.

She yawned and rubbed her eyes, but she knew she couldn't hit the sack until an all-important update with Ernesto, who was going to be home from work any minute now.

She'd showered, wrapped her damp hair in a towel turban, and pulled on a fitted, pink PJ shirt that read *"Never Give Up on Your Dreams, Keep Sleeping,"* paired with gray, ultra-soft lounger pants, and fluffy, yellow grip socks covered with flamingos. Freshened up but feeling like an untethered anchor at the bottom of an ocean, she sagged into the kitchen chair and rested her head in the cradle of her arms.

The problems and questions in her life swirled in her mind like a dark kaleidoscope. The more she tried to focus the pieces into place, the faster they swirled. The questions turned into faces: Eddie's, Liam's, Violet's, until they all morphed together into one monstrous beastly mask. Its maw yawned wide open, lips curling back over bone-white, razor-teeth, the mouth stretching wider and wider, until the darkness of the throat's opening consumed her whole view.

"Belle!"

She awoke with a start, heart hammering in her chest.

Ernesto rushed past her, dropping his briefcase on the kitchen table and turning off the stove. Black smoke poured out from beneath the pot lid. "Get the window open, now!"

She jumped out of her chair. "I'm so sorry! I fell asleep!" She threw open the kitchen window and backed away.

"Where are the oven mitts?!"

She snatched them off the sink and tossed them to him.

Muttering a string of curses in Spanish, he carried the pot outside and set it on the aluminum ledge, the pot smoking like a chimney.

She fanned the over-sized dish towel at the window, trying to blow back some of the smoke. A coughing fit wracked her.

He turned on the overhead oven fan and faced her with a haggard look, his arms falling to his sides. "That was the gumbo, wasn't it?"

She cringed. "I'm sorry."

"It's okay." It wasn't. The poor, hungry man stared despondently at the empty table.

When Belle first met her newfound uncle just about a month ago, she thought he could've easily played the part of James Bond twenty years ago. Hailing from Russia, but having spent most of his life in Cuba, the copper-haired, cool and classy detective with the Spanish accent was now grey-streaked and weathered with the massive burden of keeping this town safe. As well as running secret surveillance and pursuing a powerful supernatural creature, all while his wife and son were missing.

Her cell phone started ringing from the living room, but she ignored it. She pulled open the fridge and peered in. "We still have Chinese takeout from the other day."

Ernesto sighed and settled into the kitchen seat. "It'll do, thank you."

She set the white takeout cartons on the counter. "Don't thank me. It was my turn to prep dinner, and I ruined it." She shook her head in self-disgust. She poured the contents of the takeout into their individual bowls before organizing them into the microwave and setting the timer.

"Belle," he said pointedly. "It's fine. Really." Her cell phone rang again. "Are you going to get that?"

"Nope." She'll call Candy or Millie later. She sat across from her uncle and propped her elbows on the table, perching her chin on her fists. "Please, tell me what happened with Violet's twins."

"And then you're going to tell me more about that Amsterdam dream. I already sent a team up ahead. I'm joining them soon. I have a red-eye flight in a few hours."

"Oh."

"I'd rather you not stay alone here, Belle. There's been an uptick in crime. More of the petty kind like graffiti, shopliftings…but now we have these violent outbursts and assaults from people you'd never expect them from." He exhaled gruffly.

"My goodness. Why do you think there's an uptick?" The microwave dinged. She set about bringing the food and cutlery to the table.

"I can't really explain it, but I think it may have something to do with complaints of hauntings that we're getting. Police show up to check it out, and there's nothing, just highly agitated individuals screeching about seeing shadows knocking things over, hearing voices…." He lifted from his chair and crossed over to the refrigerator and withdrew a beer from it. "If Em were here, I think she'd understand it." He sank back into his chair and took a swig from the bottle. "My theory is it has something to do with that witch, even though she's not in Elmridge right now."

His eyebrows scrunched together in thought as he pressed the bottle to his lips again. She eyed him as he set it back down on the table, twirling the neck between his fingers. Since Emily left, he'd picked up the habit of having one beer every evening at dinner. He said it helped him "take the load off a bit," but it made her anxious, knowing her uncle was taking a step on a seemingly harmless path that could eventually turn and twist into a devastating vice.

Belle sat and picked up her fork. "What about Violet's twins?"

The doorbell sounded at the front door.

They locked eyes. "Are you expecting anyone?" he asked.

"No, but I'll get it," she said, already getting up.

"No, no, no. *I'll* get it." He moved past her and called out over his shoulder. "Uptick, remember?"

Guessing it was someone from his job at the door, she went to her room to check her phone. It was a number she didn't recognize, and there were no recent voicemails. Shrugging her shoulders, she spent a few minutes responding to Candy and Millie's text messages. There was one from Jared asking about the chemistry homework, which she politely replied to.

Her fingers froze over the phone's keyboard at the sound of a *double* set of footsteps coming up the stairs. When she heard Ernesto chatting with what sounded like another male, a very familiar male, Belle dropped her phone and hurried out into the hall.

She felt as if she'd just collided with a brick wall. Ernesto was beaming as he emerged from the stairs, and coming in behind him was—

"Eddie?"

"Ah, you two know each other already," Ernesto said, smiling. He wrapped his arm around Eddie's shoulders as if they were best buddies.

"Hi, Belle," Eddie said. And was he blushing? Embarrassed? His hair was the most disheveled she'd ever seen, and he looked like he'd thrown on clothes in a hurry. Black basketball shorts, a white t-shirt that was inside out and backward with the tag showing in the front, and he was barefoot.

"Why are you here?!" she thundered.

"Belle," Ernesto chided, "that's no way to treat my longtime friend."

Flabbergasted, she sputtered, "Your longtime—" Her head whipped to Eddie, who was busy looking anywhere but at her. "My bedroom, now."

Eddie smiled at his old friend. "It'll just be a moment, Ernie. We already know each other from school."

He clapped him on the shoulder. "No problem, Ed. We've got take-out in the kitchen. You can join us."

Belle didn't think her blood could boil any hotter. There was only one reason why her safety-paranoid uncle was acting like Eddie was his best friend.

She whirled on Eddie when she shut the bedroom door behind her. "You mindwiped him!"

"Mindfluenced," he corrected, palms up. His eyes traveled the length of her from her towel turban down to her fuzzy socks. He smirked. "Flamingos?"

But Belle was seeing red. "I don't care *what* you call your mind manipulations," she seethed. "How dare you!" She came at him, to push him, punch him, but he grabbed her fists and whirled her about so her arms were crossed tight in front of her chest and her back pressed against his front.

"I had to, siren," he said against her ear. "I thought your house was on fire, and when you wouldn't answer your phone—"

"That was *you?* And what? You're a fireman now?"

"I've been many things in my life, siren." He paused. "If I let you go, will you behave?"

In response, she thrashed around in his arms. He drew her in tighter, his arms forming steel bands around her chest and waist. The towel tumbled off her head, and her loose, damp hair fanned over the side of her face and his arms.

She stilled, breathing heavily. "What did you tell my uncle?"

"That I'm a friend he can trust. That we've known each other a long time, and he can tell me anything."

"I thought you couldn't lie," she gritted out.

"I haven't."

"Then, I don't understand."

A beat passed, as if he were considering how to explain. But in that pause, she became very aware of the way their bodies were lined up and pressed together. Her body betrayed her and relaxed a fraction into his hold. It wasn't long before she felt the tip of his nose touch her hair and she heard the slow inhale. Lightning zipped through her. Not the kind that found release through her hands, but the kind that made something low in her stomach curl.

She clenched her teeth. This was all so wrong. "Let me go."

He opened his arms, and she sprang away.

"Tell me. How have you *not* lied to my uncle?"

He drew in a deep breath and exhaled slowly, a hint of pain written on his face.

Her brows furrowed. "What is it?"

"You."

She shook her head. "I don't care. Answer my question."

His eyes were luminous. "You know he is a Jäger, right?" She nodded. "I'm the one who delivered him to the Jäger Father when he was an infant." The color leeched from her face. "I was also tasked with placing him with a family in Russia. Once we knew he was flourishing in their care, I was ordered to stay out of his life."

"So then...what are you doing here, with him?"

"Pure chance encounter. Perfectly allowable. He so happens to be *your* uncle. Small world, huh?"

"So you really mean it then? You're his friend, and he can trust you?"

"Yes."

"Well, *I* don't trust you. I want you to leave."

"You're right not to trust me, but I'm not leaving. This goes beyond your feelings. I'm here for a reason, mainly you, but there's a bigger picture here that I'm learning I need to address, starting with Violet Wickeby. So, I need to know what you and Ernesto know, so I can form a plan."

"We."

"Pardon?"

"So *we* can form a plan."

"Of course."

"Fine." She walked up to him and got in his face. "If you insist on staying, I'm going to make you miserable while you're here."

He lowered his face even closer to hers. "Do your worst."

He snapped his teeth within an inch of her mouth, and she jolted. He straightened, smiling devilishly at her shocked expression. He prowled past her toward the door, and she looked after him, wide-eyed, and stupid heart all a-flutter.

Great Scott, I'm in trouble.

At the kitchen table, Eddie pulled up a chair across from Ernesto, who was already on his second bowl of fried rice. Belle sat at the short end of the table, between both men.

"So, Ernie—" Eddie cut off when Belle kicked his chair under the table.

Both men looked at her, one quizzical and the other with narrowed eyes.

"Oops," she said, innocently, batting her eyelashes for effect. "My leg spasmed."

She didn't like how Eddie was calling her uncle "Ernie" as if he'd earned that closeness—not even Belle called her uncle that—when she knew that under normal circumstances, non-mindwarping circumstances, Ernesto would *never* let this Jäger set foot in the house. There would've been a rumble outside the front door first.

She felt it her duty now to make Eddie pay for his inexcusable violation of her uncle's free will.

"It's Ernesto to you, *friend*," she told Eddie.

He rolled his eyes and gave a slight shake of his head before turning back to Ernesto. "So, like I was saying, what—"

"Would you like some miso soup?" she asked sweetly.

He ground his teeth. "No, I'm—"

"I'll get it for you." She jumped up and grabbed a bowl from the cabinet.

Eddie heaved a sigh as Belle started ladling soup into the bowl. "What do you know about Violet Wick—" He scooted back in his chair when the hot soup sloshed onto his chest at Belle's "mis-step."

"Belle," Ernesto chastised.

"Oh, I'm so sorry." She bit her bottom lip and put on her best apologetic face. "I'm such a klutz." She grabbed the dish towel by the sink and launched it at Eddie's face. "Here, this should help."

Eddie slowly dragged the towel down his face with both hands. For a second, Belle feared his reaction; he was lethal after all, and her assassination was still on the table. As his face emerged behind the towel, his eyes glowed golden, but there was that same sinful smile from before. He tossed the towel onto the table, and with his eyes locked on Belle's, he reached behind his neck and dragged the soaked shirt off.

That single action had magically happened in slow-mo for Belle. She'd been struck dumb as her eyes tracked the length of him. A long, black beaded rosary chain hung around his neck, resting down his chest and abs. She felt the corners of her jaw unhinge as she marveled at the incredibly defined lines and cuts of his muscles. It was like looking at Liam again, but Eddie wasn't as bulky, and his abs were so sharp and jagged they seemed unreal. She could scrub her laundry the old-fashioned way on that thing.

"Here, Ed," Ernesto got up, "I'll get you a shirt."

When she met Eddie's gaze again, it seemed an eternity passed before his smoky eyes would release hers. Then the corner of his mouth pulled up into a smirk, and that was just enough for a wicked idea to knock at her stunned brain.

"No, wait, *I'll* get it." She hastily moved towards her room before Ernesto could finish his protest and returned with a purple t-shirt. "Here, *Ed*." She tossed it in his lap. "That should fit. Might be a bit snug, though."

She tried not to ogle as he pulled the shirt on, but her deviant hormones were rebellious.

Eddie glanced down at the front of the shirt and grinned. Beneath what read *"Girl Power"* in lightning bolts, there were three women's portraits exaggerated into comic book-style heroines: Mary Wollstonecraft, Sojourner Truth, and Susan B. Anthony.

"This is badass. I'm keeping it." He looked at her, obviously pleased with himself. He knew her plan to embarrass him had backfired.

Her jaw dropped. She wanted to be mad, but his genuine approval of the shirt's message softened her ire. Not to mention, that shirt was hugging him in all the right places...*she* was the one being punished now.

Ernesto looked from one teen to the other. "You two sure you're just friends? Is there something I should know about, Belle?"

Eddie didn't dare reply while her eyes flashed. "Whatever do you mean, Uncle? And how are you even best buds with Eddie, huh?"

There. Maybe that'll help her uncle wake up to Eddie's hold on him.

When Eddie opened his mouth to interrupt, Belle delivered a vicious kick to his chair, but this time, he caught her foot and held it firmly in his lap. She tried to tug it away, but he peeled off her fuzzy sock and his warm, strong hands branded her ankle and foot.

There was a pause in her futile attempts to tear her foot away, especially with Ernesto looking curiously at them, wondering what exactly was going on underneath that table. In that pause, Eddie squeezed and drew his thumb up the underside of her foot in a way that sent a shock of pleasure through her. She swallowed back a moan.

"I know Ed," Ernesto said. "We go way back."

"How so?" she asked, her voice unnaturally high.

Eddie cleared his throat. "The Jäger Temple."

Belle gasped at his admission and turned to gauge her uncle's reaction. She could see the implications of what Eddie had said playing out across her uncle's features.

"So then, *you* must be a Jäger," Ernesto concluded. He reached a hand behind his lower back.

Eddie's hands stilled on her foot—she reigned in a pout—while his eyes flashed like two yellow suns. "I am your friend. Put your hands on the table."

"Stop doing that," she hissed.

Ernesto complied, and when the glow in Eddie's eyes faded, Ernesto relaxed.

She tried to tug her foot away this time—he'd just bamboozled her uncle again—but Eddie slid her pant leg up her calf, along with that torturous hand. Her eyes widened and a small noise got lost in her throat as he glided that hand back down her calf in a searing burn.

A ragged exhale escaped him and when he glanced at her, those eyes were a glittering citrine behind a thick fringe of lashes, and something deep inside her purred in response.

He abruptly withdrew his hands from her leg.

It took her brain a moment to command her leg to leave his lap. She briefly wondered for a sinful second if she should kick him with her other foot to see if it would get the same delicious treatment.

Eddie leaned back in his chair, rubbing the back of his neck. He finally settled his gaze on Ernesto. "Owen found you as an abandoned infant outside the Jäger Temple doors."

"Owen," Ernesto repeated slowly, as if trying to remember something. "The meta-Jäger? The one who could change his form?"

"Yes. It was March 1892 when he found you."

Because it was more shocking than the meta-Jäger bit, Belle blurted out to her uncle, "But that would make you more than 100 years old!" She looked between him and Eddie, even more confused. "But how come you've aged, and Eddie hasn't?"

"Em and I had a theory," Ernesto said, swirling his spoon absently in his soup. "When we fell in love and came together, instead of me killing her like I'd been activated to do, my Jägerhood began fading away, and I started aging slowly."

A spell of silence fell upon them.

Eddie, deep in thought with his arms crossed over his chest, spoke again. "You are the only Jäger to have this happen to."

"What, exactly? Fall in love?" Belle asked.

"No. Owen fell in love with his target, but she was killed."

"He killed her after all?" she asked, just above a whisper.

He met her eyes, and said softly, as if it pained him, "No. I did."

Her breath hitched. "Why?"

"Leah was a vampire with a bloodlust that she couldn't control."

There was a pause from Belle, and then, "I'm sorry, she was a what?"

"Vampire."

"Those are real?"

"As real as beautiful electricity-wielding women."

She blushed, and then squeaked, "Great. Something else to keep me up at night."

Her own powers, lightning bolts shooting uncontrollably out of her hand, electrifying the roomful of classmates at that party. That is what could've happened if Eddie hadn't been there. He'd saved all those people in the room, in the whole compound, according to him. And he'd saved her from his own hand.

Belle understood now, his ultimatum. If she didn't want Eddie to kill her like he'd killed Leah when she lost control, then Belle had to keep her powers in check and not hurt others.

She ignored the other option he'd mentioned in Annie's Antiques, the "keeping her" part, if he didn't kill her.

In his wildest dreams, she thought with a huff.

Ernesto turned to Belle, "To answer your first question, I think what Eddie means is that I am the first Jäger to fade away."

"Once a Jäger, always a Jäger, unless you're killed in battle." Eddie thrummed his fingers on the table. "All the Jäger know each other's prophecies because the Jäger Father told us that one pair of prophecies had been switched." At Belle's confusion, he clarified, "The Fae are infamous for their obsession with twists. Some might even call them pranks. So, as a Fae twist, two of the Jäger, in fact, have the other's prophecy. So far, the switched pair hasn't been revealed, but with only a handful of Jäger left in the world and the command from the Jäger Father to stay out of," he pointed at Ernesto, "your life unless Fate intervened, I am going to go out on a limb here, Ernesto, and say that you and I have the switched prophecies. Come to think of it, my prophecy may even make more sense for you than for me...."

"What does your prophecy say?" Belle asked.

Eddie slid the silver ring off his index finger and read aloud the Fae inscription carved inside the band. *"You are the Secret Ehrenjäger. Do not give a kiss, or you will be stripped of your powers, forsaking the Jäger-hood, and ultimately fading away into everlasting obscurity."*

She gasped. "You've never kissed anyone in 300 years?"

Eddie's face was inscrutable.

"I kissed Emily on the RMS Titanic," Ernesto said.

Belle slammed her hands on the table. "What?! Holy icebergs, I need all the details!"

"Another time, Belle. With her gone, retelling that story would take me back to a place I can't handle right now."

She wanted to reach over and give her uncle's hand a heartfelt squeeze, but she was still motionless with shock at Eddie's apparent never-been-kissed status and Ernesto's cameo on that fated ship.

"After this encounter with Emily," Eddie began, "your Jägerhood faded away over time." Ernesto nodded. "As did your strøm?"

"What's a strøm?" she asked.

"A Jäger's unique strength or power," Eddie answered before turning back to Ernesto. "What was yours?"

"I never had one."

"Every Jäger has one. Mine is the ability to influence the mind."

"Mm-hmm," Belle said in an attitude that would've made Candy proud.

"I never had one," Ernesto repeated. "I was only trained to fight by Khabib Shlemenko in Kronštadt."

"So, you never trained in the Jäger temple, and you never had a strøm." He crossed his arms and touched his chin. "Hmm. Secret EhrenJäger."

"What does that mean?" Belle asked.

"Honorary hunter. I thought the 'honorary' part was because I had to be honorable, but now I wonder...."

"'Honorary' usually means having the title, but not the full responsibilities that go with the title," Belle said.

Eddie nodded. "That sounds like your Jäger status, Ernesto."

"It does. I was never shown much of the supernatural world we were supposed to hunt. I did feel like I was being kept in the dark."

"The Jäger were kept in the dark about you; we were ordered not to inquire after you. *You* were the Jäger Father's secret." Eddie leaned forward. "You are the Secret EhrenJäger, Ernesto. You must be. Our prophecies have to be the switched ones. What is your prophecy? Please, say you got one."

Ernesto scratched his head. "I did, but I don't remember it. That, too, faded from my mind. All I remember about it is something about 'true love' and 'ending Dommedag.'"

"What's—?" Belle began.

"I don't know," Ernesto said, at the same time Eddie mumbled, "Fae Armageddon on Earth."

Ernesto and Belle's heads whipped toward Eddie, who looked like he'd seen a ghost.

"What *kind* of Armageddon?" Belle asked, leaning closer to him.

"The Fae-kind...and the humans will be collateral damage." Before Belle could press him further, Eddie turned on Ernesto. "The ring. Your ring should have the prophecy inscribed in it." His eyes searched Ernesto's hands. "Where is it?"

"I-I gave it to Emily as a promise ring. She wore it around her neck on a chain. I wanted to give her a diamond ring, but she insisted on the Jäger ring. Said it truly meant I was giving all of myself to her."

"And where is Emily now?"

Ernesto and Belle exchanged looks.

"We should probably start at the beginning," Belle said. "But before we tell you anything else, you need to give us assurance first that you won't use this information to hurt us."

"Why would he hurt us?" Ernesto asked. "He's my—"

"*Friend*, I know." She resisted the urge to roll her eyes. "But just in case his Jäger-side itches to complete his real mission here—"

"Who's your mission, Ed? Who have you been activated to hunt?"

Eddie's eyes flamed golden, ensnaring Ernesto's. "Don't move."

Ernesto stilled, his face locked in confusion.

"No!" Belle shot toward Eddie, but he was faster and dodged her. She stood behind Ernesto now, with Eddie on the other side of the table. She grabbed the wooden apple from the decorative fruit bowl on the table and launched it at his head.

He ducked, the apple just narrowly missing the living room lamp.

"Why are you doing this?" she yelled. "Leave him be!"

"I'm not going to hurt him." He dodged a wooden pear. Something crashed to the floor somewhere behind him. "I don't want to tell him that you're my mission. I'm going to get him to focus on what I need to know instead."

She lifted the wooden bunch of grapes and found that each grape could be plucked out individually. She gave him an evil smile, and he gave her a *don't-you-dare* face.

"All. I. Asked..." she launched each grape one by one, "was for *assurance* from you that you wouldn't hurt us before we told you anything else! And you go and hypnotize my uncle again!"

By this time, Eddie had grabbed a large metal ornamental plate off the wall and was blocking each grape.

"I'm not going to lie to you, siren, especially when I already explained my position to you."

Ping.

"Get out! And don't come near us again!"

Ping.

"I'll get out but let me finish with your uncle. I can't leave him like that."

Ernesto was still staring straight ahead at Eddie's empty chair.

"What are you going to say to him?" she demanded, already taking aim with another grape.

He ignored her question. "You're behaving like a child."

She launched the whole bunch at him. He blocked most of them, but a few had gone low, and he dropped out of sight behind the table with a loud "Oof!"

"Ha!" she exclaimed.

A moment passed, and with her uncle still immovable, she figured it was about time Eddie released him from that trance.

She peeked over the table but didn't see him.

"Eddie?" She walked around the table and a hand shot out, grabbing her ankle. She was suddenly on her back, staring at the ceiling. "Oww," she groaned.

While she lay momentarily stunned and recovering, Eddie appeared, leaning over the table and telling Ernesto, "When you hear Belle say, 'Eddie is awesome,' you will forget everything from the time I rang the doorbell until now."

"Ernesto's never coming out of that trance then," Belle muttered from the floor.

Eddie chuckled as he headed toward the door.

"I hate you," she called out.

There was a pause, and then, "Good." The door opened and shut.

Eddie was gone.

| 13 |

Venus Flytraps

Belle sat in lunch on Monday as she had sat in each class before that, with a book in her face to hide her shellshock over the weekend's events.

After Eddie left Sunday night, and she'd finally calmed down enough to utter the hateful words, "Eddie is awesome," Ernesto had emerged from his trance claiming he didn't remember eating two bowls of fried rice, and why the devil were the wooden fruits strewn about everywhere? After she claimed he'd simply been preoccupied and hadn't noticed her drop the bowl of wooden fruits, Ernesto had turned back to his miso soup and to the original topic that Eddie's arrival had interrupted.

"Toby and Elias Tomás. After 2 hours of interrogation, tears, and soiling themselves, they could tell me nothing of their time with Violet Wickeby. The last they remembered was preaching door-to-door for their church, and then hanging off the side of Ridge Rats until I got them down. They are en route to France, back to their family, who did not even know that the boys were missing in the first place. Violet was thorough in her spellwork, I'll give her that. She covered their tracks so nothing could lead back to her."

"And they don't remember anything about her?" she'd asked.

"No. They seemed genuinely confused and terrified. One of them, Toby, I think, wanted to know how he'd gotten so many piercings. Anyways, to make a long story short, they're convinced the government kidnapped and drugged them, and performed experiments on them. They were actually sweating and shaking like a pair of junkies in withdrawal, so I let them believe their own theories."

Belle had remembered what Elias had said to her in the alley, that they'd *needed* Violet. And Jäger Eddie had said that the twins would be like "recovering drug addicts with amnesia." Apparently, being under one of Violet's spells was like a powerfully addictive drug.

She'd then told Ernesto every detail of the Beast nightmare, and what was crucial was that now they knew exactly where Violet was in Europe, and with the details Belle had provided about the interior of the room and the angle from which she'd seen the Amsterdam skyline, the authorities would be able to actually pinpoint her location.

Even more important, Belle dreamed of real-life events before they actually happened. They'd found this out when she'd dreamed of Violet killing Ernesto, and then she and Liam had arrived at the house with plenty of time beforehand to stop it from happening.

So, now, Ernesto was prepared to take advantage of this fact. Which was why he'd already taken that red-eye flight out to Amsterdam to spearhead the mission himself for a week, leaving Belle with the promise he'd send Sergio, his trusted lieutenant, to check up on her each day, despite her protests that she didn't need that.

Last night's episode had been running through her mind, when the weight of the lunch table shifted, and someone sat near her. She'd been vaguely aware of Cindy sitting directly in front of her, Q two seats away typing away on his laptop, with the usual silence of camaraderie eating away at the half-hour lunch period.

But with her eyes on her page and her mind on her problems, it didn't register that her biggest personal threat had just arrived.

Thunk.

Belle jumped in her chair. A large gift bag now sat on the table in front of her. It had *"Happy Birthday"* splashed on the side in balloon letters.

She wrinkled her nose. *It's not my birthday.*

"Hey, Ed," Cindy said.

Belle sat up ramrod straight. How could she have forgotten? With her nightmare preoccupation, she'd let her guard down and allowed herself to be exposed to her Jäger. Sitting just two seats to her left now. And how dare he sit near her? Hadn't she demanded last night that he stay away from her?

As if in response to her own question, Eddie's strangled words from before floated back to her. *"It is physically painful to be away from you...."*

"Hi, Belle," he said.

She chewed her food slowly, still refusing to look at him. His voice sounded...normal. Friendly, even. But of course it would. He couldn't lie, apparently, but he knew how to pretend like everything was fine and like he didn't somewhat want to kill her.

He cleared his throat.

Ok, now she was just being rude, and Cindy would grill her later if she didn't act normal. She swallowed her mouthful and turned a fake smile on him.

Big mistake. She got hit with the full-face frontal again and those sigh-inducing, smoldering eyes. He was leaning towards her, his elbows on his knees, glasses on, and his hair doing that customary beckoning again that make her fingers itch.

I am...losing my marbles.

But then she caught his scent, and a barrage of happy memories hit her like before when he'd had her pinned against the wall in the alley.

What *was* this devilry? A Jäger ploy for putting their prey at ease? Making them easier to catch?

She pressed her faraway smile into a grim line. "Mud," she blurted.

"Pardon?" Eddie's brows quirked.

"Bad body odor," she continued, trying to banish those feel-good memories. "Rusty green trucks."

"Are you okay, Belle?" Cindy asked, while Eddie snuck a whiff of his armpit.

Belle brought her broccoli cup to her nose but ended up gagging, so she settled for moving a seat further away from Eddie.

After a beat of her friends staring at her, Cindy, with her voice rising to a higher pitch, turned to Eddie, "So, who's the present for?"

"That one's actually for our body-snatched friend here." He gave a pointed look at Belle. "She forgot it somewhere."

Right. At Annie Antique's. She glared at him. *Right after you blew your cover.*

But apparently Eddie didn't need to hear her thoughts to know what she was thinking. When that caramel gaze ensnared hers, making her feel like a canary in a cat's paw, she knew he was waiting on her next move. Knowing his identity now, how would she react in front of their friends?

How *would* she react? He'd stalked her, hurt her in the alley, barged into her personal life, and still threatened her with a half-chance he'd kill her. No matter he'd saved her from Violet's twins, spared her from killing her own friends at the party, de-possessed her from a demon, and no matter that she'd *really* liked his company on a few occasions, gotten physically close enough to ignite an electric chemistry that rivaled her own power.

Eddie had made it clear that he didn't want to kill her. But that didn't mean that he wouldn't. What had Ernesto told her once about the Jäger? Once a Jäger acquired a target, they became unnaturally obsessed with it until they killed it. But he'd said there was another way to prevent that. Love.

And as soon as she thought it, she rejected it, blushing from head to toe. A reaction not unnoticed by Eddie, who immediately arced a brow at her, the side of his mouth tipping up. But she ignored this and a baffled Cindy wondering at the epic stare-down between the two.

An idea finally came to her. What if she exposed him to everyone else? Wouldn't he *have* to go away then? Wouldn't the Jäger Father have to recall him if his cover was publicly blown, and he failed to "complete" his assignment?

She narrowed her eyes at him. She *would* act normal, stay within the safety of numbers at school, and avoid him in all other circumstances. But if he wanted to stick around, she would actively sabotage his secret identity.

It was about to get really uncomfortable for him in Elmridge.

Eddie was the first to break the spell between them. He plunked another gift bag on the table and slid it toward Q. "Happy birthday, Q-Master," Eddie said, grinning.

For a second, her heart did this weird, erratic flip at that lopsided smile.

When Q lifted the red wizard cloak out of the gift bag, he blushed, smiled, and stammered his thanks. It was a lunchroom miracle that would've touched any Grinch's heart.

"I emailed you a gift card," Cindy said, her eyes twinkling as she smiled. "Go ahead, check it out."

A quick flurry of tapping at his keyboard, and his lips pressed together into another rare smile. "And you chose the best store for anyone to shop at for all their superior electronic needs."

"Q-Tech," Cindy announced proudly.

"You bought him a gift card to his own store?" Belle asked, perplexed.

"It's the thought that counts," Eddie said, briefly meeting her eyes before smiling approvingly at Cindy.

"I shopped at the best store since I only want the best for my bestest friend," Cindy grinned at Q, and when she did, it was like a light that dazzled whoever witnessed it.

Q smiled sheepishly, and then sat erect as if alarmed. "You cannot flirt with me, Cindy. Becky would not approve."

Cindy's jaw dropped. Eddie stifled a laugh.

"Who's Becky?" Belle asked.

"My girlfriend," Q replied matter-of-factly.

"She lives on the other side of the country in Portland," Cindy explained. "But distance is no match for true love, right, Q?"

"Indeed," Eddie commented quietly.

Belle avoided the keen temptation to look inquiringly at him about that.

"Actually, the distance is ideal," Q said. "I find that I do not like Becky so much in person as I do online."

Belle exchanged a look with Cindy, who merely shrugged a shoulder.

"What did you get Q?" Cindy asked her, eyes on the untouched gift bag.

"Oh…" Belle spied a purple cone tip peeking out the top of the bag. The wizard hat!

She turned to look at Eddie, but he was already watching her. Watching this new understanding dawn in her eyes. He'd done this for her, for Q. If it wasn't for him, she would've been wallowing in shame right now at being the only one at the table who'd forgotten Q's birthday. He'd just helped her save face and showered Q with specialness.

Why? Wouldn't it have made more sense to let her be humiliated? Why even help at all? Maybe this goes back to that predator tactic of luring the prey into a false sense of security, before snapping its jaws over the unsuspecting victim. Classic Venus flytrap.

Well, *this* little lightning bug wasn't going to fall for it.

She pressed her lips into a grim line and whipped her attention back to Q, his eyes a-lit like a child's on Christmas morning. He was rubbing the velvety fabric of the red cloak.

She nudged her gift toward him. "I believe this will pair well with that."

Speechless, Q surveyed his whole new wizard outfit.

Not beneath showing gratitude where it was due, even if it reeked of ulterior motive, Belle looked over her shoulder at Eddie, and mouthed, *Thank you.*

He held her gaze for a minute, his features revealing nothing, but when he looked back to Q, he smirked.

Belle huffed silently. What was he thinking? What was *she* thinking even thanking him?

Eddie spoke up. "So, Q, you think Belle is worthy of joining our table now?"

Outraged, Belle launched into Eddie, "I was sitting here before you!"

He didn't answer her. His eyes dancing with laughter, he waited for Q's response.

Q dropped the outfit in his lap and sat up even straighter, startling Belle when he zeroed in on her. "Lisselle 'Belle' Montague of Littleton, Kentucky, originally hailing from Paris, France—" *Did Q hack into my personal life story? I never told him any of that!*"—you are hereby granted a formal invitation to join our D&D campaign at the Questing Table. Should you accept, you will receive a secret summons when the time comes to embark on this adventure. What is your answer?"

Besides that disturbing bit of digging Q must have done to her, Belle…was…enthralled. She saw herself escaping into that world of fantasy that could carry her so far away from this long nightmare in Elmridge with its all-too-brief meager periods of respite. Maybe, just maybe, role-playing in D&D would re-fuel the imagination that had helped her survive her isolation in Littleton. She needed that now. She could reclaim the peaceful Mind Palace that constant worry had evicted her from.

Belle bowed her head and placed her right hand over her heart, "Sir Q-Master, I humbly accept thy most gracious invitation."

Q inclined his head, and then returned to his laptop, as if he hadn't been interrupted in the first place by all this birthday-attention.

Pure pity etched into her features, Cindy whispered, "Are you sure you want to do this?"

"Why?"

"They get *really* intense."

"Are you part of the table?" Belle asked hopefully.

"No thanks. But Q pays me to get the costumes together."

"Costumes?" She perked up even more.

"I'll bring you some choices the night of. You choose your character then." She winked.

Belle turned to Eddie and paused. He was reading the *Hunger Games* now. Doing what he said they'd agreed to do on that bus yesterday. And now he was writing a note in the margin. She resisted her curiosity to peek at what he'd written. She'd get the book back eventually enough. That meant she'd have to hold up her end of the deal and write her thoughts in the margins of *Great Expectations*, before they switched books and read each other's notes.

She blushed. Was that not intimate? Sharing each other's thoughts this way? It had been his idea. Probably a way to figure out her thinking patterns, so he could use them against her somehow. Hmm, another Venus flytrap. She could use his own strategy against him. He'd be sharing his own thoughts as well in the book. She could create her own criminal profile of him. She did already have the very same Dickens book open before her, so why not start the act now?

Deciding she'd use their agreement to her own advantage then, she retrieved a pen from her messenger bag, and wrote in the margin, towards the end of Chapter 1: *Why this scoundrel popping up out of nowhere and giving poor Pip a fright certainly rings a familiar bell.*

When she peeked over at Eddie, she smirked when she found that he'd also been peeking and had quickly diverted his attention back to his book.

"What character do you play at this Questing Table?" she asked him conversationally.

When he didn't answer and kept his eyes glued to the page, Cindy spoke up for him, "He's the Highlander Cleric."

"Oh," Belle replied, sounding even more interested. She turned to him again, "Villain or hero?"

This time, Eddie dragged his gaze from the book and sat back in his chair, his broad shoulders and chest announcing their presence.

He fixed her with a lazy look. "What do *you* think?" His golden eyes behind his glasses a brighter hue than usual, he poised the capped end of the pen between his molars as he waited for her answer.

Admittedly, she got hung up for a second on his mouth. She brushed the hair off her shoulder and said somewhat loudly, "Villain, definitely." She snatched her chance at some sabotage now. "Probably some ninja assassin with a secret mission to kill one of the members of the table."

There was a slight tremor in her voice on that last part. She knew she was being recklessly bold.

He stared at her, the corner of his mouth tipped high in amusement, but there was an unmistakable steely glint in his eyes. He twirled the pen artfully between his fingers for a minute before he replied, not as loudly as she had, "Perhaps, for *your* character, you should choose the Siren Mage—you know, irresistibly alluring, but lethal."

Eyes wide, cheeks flaming, she hid her face behind the pretense of taking a long draw from her chocolate milk carton. But he wasn't finished. "The mage part comes in because she possibly reads minds, and most definitely wields electricity from her hands."

Belle nearly choked on her milk. In her split-second effort to save Cindy from a milk-shower, the cold, brown liquid spurted out of her nose.

"That is disgusting," Q said dryly.

She froze in utter humiliation, while Cindy fumbled around for fresh napkins to hand her. She heard a dark chuckle from her left and then the bell signaling the end of lunch.

Eddie snapped his book shut and rose from his chair. She bristled as he leaned in close to her ear, "Two can play this game." He tossed her a clean napkin and left.

"Wow, Belle," Cindy said, as she wiped at the table, while Belle dabbed angrily at her nose and her wet button-down shirt, which was unfortunately white and now sporting the brown cow-patch pattern. "*That* was intense. You'll be able to hold your own at the Questing Table." She dropped her voice and searched Belle's face, "Do you...like him?"

"What? No! Of course not. What would make you say such a thing?"

Cindy backtracked. "S-sorry. I just thought—"

Pained by any ounce of anger she'd deflected Cindy's way, Belle cut in, "No, I'm so sorry. Please, forgive me. That's no excuse for my outburst."

Cindy smiled and shouldered her bag. Q was already gone. "Well, if you don't mind a friend's opinion, I think he likes you."

Belle bit her tongue. She didn't want any of her outrage aimed in Cindy's direction.

"See you tomorrow?"

Belle nodded. She watched as Cindy joined the osmosis of students leaving and entering the lunchroom.

Looking at the spot Eddie had vacated, her blood warmed traitorously. *Irresistibly alluring?*

She blinked hard and gave herself a good internal shake. "Venus flytraps," she gritted, slapping sense into her Jane Austen side. "His words are nothing more than that."

| 14 |

Team Belle

Tuesday through Sunday dragged by with the entire student body poring over their school-issued tablets and laptops, studying for the quarterly exams that were to take place that following week. Even Belle put her life-drama on pause to focus on preparing for these much-hyped exams that the teachers claimed their futures depended on.

The days were uneventful for Belle. Eddie ignored her, his face hidden behind the book, writing and doodling in the margins (did he not care to pass his exams?), and Cindy and Belle quizzed each other over their notes at lunch each day.

Sergio was true to Ernesto's word and checked in on her at 8:00 on the dot, every night, always with a covered dish of his wife's home-made meal, and each time refusing to be dissuaded from bringing her dinner. She was a big girl, she could feed herself, she'd argued, but Sergio's wife, apparently, wouldn't hear any of it. Or so Sergio said.

While the food warmed her belly, a chill had entered her heart. The emptiness of the house without Ernesto's presence felt oppressive and steeped in shadows. His phone calls were all too brief, and he never divulged information about Violet over the phone. She could sit and have a powwow with herself and analyze why she was feeling down in the dumps, but she'd rather not. That was a downward spiral that led straight to excessive napping cocooned from the world in her ultra-plush comforter.

Exams beckoned.

So she threw herself into her homework and discovered a semi-placating satisfaction in earning top marks at school. Her teachers nodded their approval at her, her peers started paying less attention to her, and the only contact she had lately with Millie and Candy were the brief three-way nightly updates they had over the phone.

And even then, Belle's heart wasn't into the girl-talk, particularly when Millie gushed about Eddie and his prowess with the paintbrush, and how close he sits next to her in class when they're talking, and how he keeps finding ways to "accidentally" touch her like when he handed her a pen and he made sure to touch her pinkie.

Belle was a horrible friend then, tuning out and ignoring Millie entirely, while her two friends had sympathetically chalked up her behavior to the Liam-heartbreak syndrome.

In reality, Belle had been fuming and biting her tongue from letting a Kat-worthy comment slip out towards Millie. And she definitely avoided the psychoanalysis of why she was even reacting that way.

On this particular Monday of the following week, Kat's nasty shoulder bump in the hallway on her way to lunch didn't even phase Belle.

But at lunch, something even more humiliating happened that made her want to crawl beneath a rock and live there.

"Belle Montague?"

A voice like exotic silk made her turn and look up at the olive-skinned, almond-eyed Arabic princess, Fatimah. Her demure face framed by a purple shawl embroidered with tiny jewels, and her mahogany lips drawn in a smile that seemed to hold a secret.

"Um, yes?" Belle smiled back and warily eyed her business-like tablet and fancy stylus pen with oversized jewel on top. She bet it was real.

Fatimah's smile stretched wider at her and the other three at the table, but her gaze lingered on Eddie. "I'm here on behalf of the Homecoming committee, and as you must already know, Belle, you're competing against Katerina Sirtis for the tenth-grade princess spot on the Homecoming Court. Not to sound like a Debbie Downer, but because you didn't respond to any of my emails or messages—"

"What messages?" Belle cut in, icy dread sinking in.

"Your Peacock Profile messages."

"Oh." She hadn't checked her school's online social media profile in weeks. And she didn't even know she had an email account.

"All the basic talent categories have been filled, like singing, dancing, acting, etc. So, I need to know what talent you'll be performing."

"Um, can I...recite a poem?"

Fatimah scrunched up her nose. "Ew, no. Boring. And I also need to know your designer's name since no two evening gowns can be the same."

It took a moment for Belle to reign in her stupefaction. Eddie was at least peering at them over his book now, an amused twinkle in his eye, Cindy was listening a bit too eagerly, and Q had already lost interest and retreated to his laptop.

Belle turned in her seat to fully face Fatimah, who was impatiently tapping her stylus against the edge of the tablet. "Ok, I'm going to make this easy-peasy for you and Kat. One, the only other talent I have is attracting horrible luck. Two, I don't own a dress, and three, Kat can have the spot on the Court." She clapped her hands once. "There. Everyone's happy."

"Right, then," Fatimah said, as if Belle was passing up on the biggest opportunity of her life. "This has never happened in our school's Homecoming history, but if that's how you feel...." She raised her stylus as if to strike out Belle's name.

"Wait!" They all turned to Cindy. This was the loudest Belle had ever heard her speak. Even a few others at nearby tables were glancing over at Cindy now. "Um," she began, lowering her voice once again so they all had to lean in to listen. Her blue eyes bright, she looked straight at Belle. "I could...design your dress."

"That's really kind of you, but—"

"I would love, really love, to do it," Cindy pressed quietly.

It clicked then for Belle. She had once overheard Cindy tell her wicked stepmother that she'd designed a ballgown for a contest and won. Cindy had fashion skills, and she was eager to put them on display.

Baby steps.

"Of course!" Belle said, unable to deny her sweet friend. "I'm in. *So in.*" She added weakly, "Pffft, Kat doesn't stand a chance."

She mentally swatted aside the barrage of mortifying moments that her kind of luck guaranteed awaited her along this ridiculous path to Homecoming Princess. She could already see herself trying to sashay across the stage in the evening gown, tripping over high heels she'd never worn before, and then as she gathered her dress to stand up, her jittery nervous hands lighting the dress on fire.

Something struck her temple. "Ow!"

A plump grape bounced onto the floor, and she scowled at the person whose direction it'd been flicked from. Eddie was grinning his famous half-smile, and his caramel eyes had a softness in them that melted her indignant expression into a question.

Fatimah, apparently, had been trying to talk to her while she'd zoned out in her day-mare. "I was asking you, Belle, if you agree."

"Agree to what?"

Cindy piped up, "Ed here volunteered to teach you a magic act."

"What?!" Oh no. This was going too far. *He* was going too far. "No! No way."

"I think the audience would love it," Fatimah said.

"It won't kill you to learn," Eddie said pointedly, but that little smile of his oozed with conniving pleasure. *What* was he playing at? And just the word "kill" coming out of his mouth sent a cold bolt through her. He added, "I already have a costume and everything for you. A bodysuit, no pants." The curl of his lip was sinful.

She narrowed her eyes at him and just before she opened her mouth to smack down his offer, Fatimah tsked and smiled. "Excellent." She scribbled on her tablet, articulating each syllable as she wrote, "Se-xy ma-gi-cian."

"No!" Belle impulsively reached out to snatch the stylus, but Fatimah turned out of reach and frowned down at her.

Surprising all of them, Q spoke up, "I can design your lighting and sound effects."

Fatimah replied, "Oh, we already have someone for that." When Q stared stonily at her, she added hastily, "But I'm sure Dennis won't mind taking a break during Belle's act."

Smart girl. Q was notorious for using digital means of retaliation against people on his Enemies List. Just a few months ago, he'd threatened to erase someone's identity for bothering Cindy at lunch.

Belle took a moment to process what was going on. These three were *helping* her. Cindy and Q wanted her to succeed, and she guessed they also wanted a chance to put their own skills on display for the event. Make their own contribution. But Eddie? His eyes were catlike in the way he watched her now. Helping her this way had nothing to do with what he was *supposed* to be doing here in Elmridge. Right? He probably just enjoyed watching the torment she was squirming under.

Fatimah turned her bejeweled stylus in Cindy's direction. "And you, take notes of what I'm about to say because I have a feeling Ms. Zone-Out-A-Lot here won't remember any of this."

Belle covered her face with her hands. *Jeez, is it that obvious?*

Cindy dove into her backpack for her cell phone and opened the *Notes* app.

Fatimah took a deep breath. "The competition begins on October 31st. You have to make an appearance at my annual Halloween masked ball," Cindy groaned, "where you'll be judged on costume and social mingling skills. Your pageant team is, of course, invited. The final contestants will be announced after that night. Then, right before Thanksgiving break, *if* you're one of the finalists, you'll answer one question during halftime at the Homecoming football game, you know, to prove you have brains. The next evening is the beauty and talent pageant during the Homecoming dance, where the queen will be announced and crowned."

Belle grimaced. "All this public humiliation sounds like a lot of work. Um, what's the payoff exactly for the winner?"

Fatimah stared at her as if she was an unidentified species, which might actually be true. "Well, let's see, uh, high school glory? Bragging rights that never expire? Validation as a serious contender in the Miss America pageant? A feature in *Teen Vogue*?"

Horror, just sheer, utter horror. A spotlight the size of the moon. "Gee, sounds like everything a girl could ever want," she said weakly.

"Oh, and this year," Fatimah's voice pitched with excitement, "some fabulously wealthy European socialite donated the pageant crown. The centerpiece is a huge, rare mauve, pear-cut taaffeite" She sighed. "I only have the lavender one in my collection, so whoever wins this crown will be the envy of us all."

"Us all" meaning the Princess Posse, Belle figured. *Oh God, another reason not to compete.*

Sensing Belle's growing anxiety, Cindy reached across the table and touched her hand. "I'll help you. We'll all help you through it. I bet Millie and Candy would love to help out, too. Maybe with promoting. I think you're really going to have fun with this." She smiled, and it was the first time Belle had seen the luster of anticipation in it.

Belle squeezed back. "Definitely."

For my friends, she affirmed, feeling her outrage at the whole situation losing its steam. *Not including Eddie, of course.*

The bell signaled the end of lunch.

"I assume you'll be Belle's assistant in the act?" Fatimah asked Eddie.

Eddie looked to Belle for confirmation. So he *was* asking her permission. He wasn't just forcing this whole magic act on her. She looked over at Cindy, who smiled back encouragingly.

With a relenting eye-roll, she sighed. "Yes."

Eddie rewarded her with a genuine smile that didn't belong on the face of a maybe-assassin.

"Full name, please?" Fatimah let her eyes trail approvingly over him. He'd stood to his full height next to her—she reached his shoulder—and was slinging his arms through his book bag with the book still in his hand. He gave her that charming smile that bordered on predatory, and for some reason it made Belle want to kick him.

"Edward Helsing."

"Right then." She double-clicked her stylus and an ink-tip emerged from its end. She reached for Eddie's hand and scribbled something on it. "You'll need my number, you know, for this Homecoming business." She smiled demurely at him and then walked off, sashaying her hips.

Belle fully expected Eddie to do the guy-thing and watch Fatimah walk away, so when his eyes crashed with hers instead, and his lips spread into a knowing smile at the irritation etched on her face, she snapped her attention away and stabbed at a grape in her fruit cup.

"Repeat that part again, please." Cindy was on her cell phone, ashen-faced, staring straight at Belle as she listened to the caller on the other end.

Eddie was drawn to his seat again, mirroring Belle's concern. Even Q had paused packing up his things, wondering what words were leeching the color from their friend's face.

At the same time, Belle's phone started vibrating, and just about everyone in the lunchroom also reached for their phones. Mouths dropped, wicked grins spread, and a firestorm of exchanges erupted. The gossip mill was running at full blast now, and the worst part: everyone kept looking Belle's way.

"What's going on, Cindy?" Eddie asked, glaring back at the gawkers.

"Daddy, are you sure?" Cindy whispered into the phone.

Belle's keen ears picked up everything.

"He told me so himself. We're all having dinner tonight in the formal dining room. He also said he'll be bringing his girlfriend. I think formal attire will be best. What do you think?"

"Of course. Sounds fine. I have to go." Cindy's eyes never left Belle's as she slid her phone back into her pocket.

"Cindy?" Eddie tried again. "Who is your father talking about?"

"How did you—?" she began, but Belle answered Eddie, "Liam's back. And he has a girlfriend."

| 15 |

A Jäger Thing

"**I**'m sorry, Belle," Cindy's eyes watered for her friend.

"Would you like me to add Liam Rawlins to the Feds Most Wanted List?" Q offered. "He'll be promptly removed from our presence. For a *long* time."

Floored, Belle could only give a slight shake of her head as she stared at her half-eaten ravioli, barely processing what her friends were saying around her.

"Wait a minute, Liam Rawlins *Jr.,* not Sr.?" Eddie asked.

"Don't you know?" Cindy whispered back. "Liam's parents are dead."

"I knew the Rawlins family had been killed, but I thought that the *father* was the survivor and was conducting his business in Europe now."

"Liam Rawlins *Jr.* was accused of murdering his parents," Q said factually. "The evidence points to his guilt. He killed his parents in the

157

West Wing with what I surmise can only be a Tesla coil gun, and then overdosed in the bathtub in a failed suicide attempt."

"Q!" Cindy admonished. "That's not something you talk about like you're giving a weather report."

"How do you know all this?" Belle asked in a tightly coiled voice. "Only my uncle and the police know this."

"I retrieved the report online."

"It's a public report? No wait, of course, not. You hacked it." Belle was disgusted.

"Affirmative."

"Gosh, Q," Cindy said. "*Not* cool."

"I use primary sources for facts," Q replied unapologetically. "Not news media and hearsay."

"You want facts," Belle said, balling her hands beneath the table, "I'll give you facts: Liam is innocent because a lightning witch murdered his parents!"

A hush fell over the new lunch crowd of students that had just filled the cafeteria. Many stole glances Belle's way and whispered in similar fashion as the last crowd.

She drew a sharp intake of breath as Eddie's warm hand covered hers under the table and squeezed. He slid closer to her and reached for her other hand. Looking down, she saw that electricity was fritzing from both her hands. As he covered them with his own, her eyes locked with his. There was a wealth of words in that sharp amber gaze, but the most pronounced seemed to be, *Calm down.*

"For what it's worth, Belle," Cindy said, "I believe Liam's innocent, too."

After some eye-goading from Cindy, Q joined in, a hint of an apology in his tone, "And I *respect* that you believe he is innocent."

Belle nodded her thanks.

The truth of his innocence was important to her, but it didn't override the knowledge that Liam was turning out to be a supreme douchelord. With a *girlfriend.*

The late bell rang, interrupting the last thought that had sparked a new electric frenzy in her hands.

Q left in a rush, while Cindy lingered, "Will you be okay, Belle?"

She nodded vigorously, still not moving from her spot or relinquishing her death grip of Eddie's hands. She suspected he was somehow absorbing the electrical show from her palms.

Cindy turned to Eddie. "Will you help her, Ed? I'd stay, but if I miss this next exam, I'll fail history for the year."

Belle shot up, the chair flinging back into the next table. "Oh no, Helsing's exam. I'm late!"

Cindy departed, promising to call later. Belle slung her bag over her shoulder as she cut through the crowd on the way out. Eddie followed close behind. Her cursed hearing picked up on snippets of different conversations as she passed through:

"That's her. The last girl Rawlins was with. He's back today, you heard? Have you seen him, yet?"

"Yeah, I'm voting for her over Kat. She went out with Jared and Liam in the same weekend. My life-long dream!"

"Have you seen Beast's new girl? She's from the Netherlands."

The last bit made Belle pause in step, sending a short, red-haired boy pirouetting to avoid crashing. Eddie reached out and steadied him before the flustered boy scurried away.

Without looking back at Eddie, she reached behind her, frantically searching for his hand.

Understanding, he grabbed her hand and laced his fingers through hers. He gave it a squeeze that squashed the electric charge there. He loosened his hand to release hers, but she held on and continued walking forward, half-dragging him behind her.

She knew holding hands with Eddie in the hallway was going to blow open a new channel in the rumor mill, but this time, she didn't care. Eddie's magical sponge presence was soaking up her dangerous anxiety and keeping her from barbecuing the school.

On autopilot, she headed in the direction of her literature class with Eddie in tow.

"Siren?" he whispered, knowing only she would hear him.

"Hm?"

The hallways were mostly clear, but the stragglers were eyeballing the new piece of gossip.

"How long has Violet Wickeby possessed your mother?"

She swallowed. "Since October 31, 2004."

"Do you know if Violet is collecting certain gems through certain nefarious means?"

"She is."

"Excellent," he sniped. "Violet is the Lightning Witch you mentioned, isn't she? Using your mother's powers?"

"Yes."

"And she killed Liam's parents?"

She paused. "Yes."

"Do you happen to know which gems she still needs to complete the Jade Blade Wish Spell?"

"Last time Ernesto and I checked, she still needs the taaffeite, fire opal, and the jade blade itself." They were about to turn the corner into the aisle of her lit. class, when a horrifying thought struck her.

She ground to a halt. "Liam might be in there."

Eddie took the lead this time and diverted her toward the dark, open space beneath the stairs nearby. But a couple was already in there.

"Get out," Eddie growled at them. He led Belle into the newly vacated space and faced her, lacing his hands with both of hers.

"What are we doing here?"

"Listen to me, siren. You're stronger than you give yourself credit for."

She scoffed. "I thought you said you couldn't lie."

"I can't."

"Is that a Jäger-thing?"

"No, it's a me-thing."

"You can't, or you won't?"

He sighed. "Stay focused here, siren."

"On the pep talk you're trying to give me?"

"Yes, actually. I'm trying to prevent the mass slaughter of school children at your hands, and your consequent death on mine."

"Oh."

"Oh, indeed. So we *all* need you to remain in control and not lose it."

She drew in a long breath through her nose and exhaled slowly through her mouth. "That demon you eliminated in me—it said you knew how to retrieve the blocked memory I have."

"It would involve a certain level of intimacy I am not prepared to...*allow* myself."

"Meaning?"

"Siren, that is not what's important right now."

"Not important? Allegedly, I lost control, killed my family, Violet possessed me, and then the fairies re-wound time and gave me a do-over. I'd like to know exactly what happened, especially since I am, like you said, a walking time bomb set to mass m—"

She was cut off by Eddie's hand smothering the rest of her words. "We don't have total privacy here," he reminded her, dropping his hand.

"I am out of control," she whimpered. "I can't even emote without sparking these puppies." She raised her excited hands, lighting up the space.

He instantly backed her further into the darker recesses of the nook and grabbed her hands, bringing them to his chest and shielding her from any prying eyes. "There are surveillance cameras out there."

Belle leaned back against the wall, and with Eddie forming another wall in front of her, she was completely hedged in.

Under normal circumstances, she'd like to think she would kick her way out of there and put a mile between herself and the Jäger, but his scent permeated the space now, and when she inhaled, her eyes fluttered closed, and she let her head fall back against the wall.

"What is it?" Eddie asked.

"Your smell." He began to apologize, but she cut him off. "Your scent makes every happy memory I have come to mind. Why is that?" She opened her eyes, and his were glowing in the darkness. "Is that a Jäger-thing?"

He was quiet for a moment. The light of his eyes illuminated his cheekbones and contrasted sharply with the dark fringe of eyelashes that lifted to meet her questioning gaze. In the barely-there lighting as of dying candlelight, his beauty was unearthly.

"That's not supposed to happen," he said softly. As he spoke, he pressed her hands open against his firm chest in a way that drew her in even closer and made her whole body feel quite warm. "A Jäger smells like something *wrong* to his target. A subtle scent, but pervasive. A hint of sulfur or spoilage. It's the only warning the target gets before a Jäger closes in."

It took her a moment to respond. She wasn't even sure she heard him correctly because not only was she overwhelmed by his fragrant presence, but he had her hands pressed against his pecs and was absentmindedly massaging the top of her hands with his own.

She tipped her head back to look at him. "Maybe...I'm not a target then."

He had her so close; the back of her forearms were also pressed against his muscular torso. The thin material of the school-issued white button-down shirt did not do much to buffer the heat that was radiating from his skin at her touch.

But propriety knocked at her senses, and she slowly pulled away, her hands sliding downward in the act, and the small space between them converted into a sauna.

He drew in a ragged inhale. "Maybe."

"I know it's nuts that I'm asking *you* this, but what can I do? I don't want to hurt anyone. I-I don't want to end up like Leah."

He nodded, deep in thought. When he finally spoke, he reached out and took one of her long curls in his fingers. "Is this Liam the wanker that disappointed you?" She nodded. "Does he *know* about you?" She nodded again. "And he disappeared to Europe, when?"

"Violet had threatened to kill Ernesto if I didn't give her the pixie dust." His fingers stilled on her curl. "Emily had advised me to hand it over before she disappeared with Liam, taking him back to his castle."

"Violet would've finished him," he stated knowingly.

She nodded. "Violet hurt Emily. And then my mother emerged and attacked her own body until Violet left. I haven't seen her since, except in this nightmare I had recently. You see, I don't dream every night like everyone else does. Emily said my mother was, I mean is, a dream-catcher, and I'm a dream-seer. My mother was sending me visions as dreams of Violet's plans. And I-I somehow see the events *before* they happen. So, the last time I saw Violet was in this dream where I was seeing through some creature's eyes—Violet called it a beast—some sort of giant canine that she controlled."

"And you didn't see Liam in this dream?"

She shook her head. "H-He just cut me off after that night, and it was just so confusing because that was totally *not* the trajectory we were on, even after he found out about my...unnatural side. I-It had seemed very promising." She blushed remembering just how promising Liam's kisses had felt.

"That you would be his girlfriend and he your boyfriend."

She dipped her chin. The gloom she'd wallowed in for so many weeks resurfaced, but somehow it felt more manageable just now, like she'd been thrown a buoy named Eddie to keep her afloat in the depths of this despair. She wasn't dense. She recognized that in some ironic turn of Fate—or maybe the Fae's love for twists was orchestrating all this somehow—that her would-be assassin was behaving like an unexpected savior.

If the Fae were somehow watching all this, she bet they were busy passing buckets of popcorn amongst themselves.

Eddie shouldered the wall while he listened to her, one hand twirling with the edge of one long piece of her hair while she stood within his space, their feet just inches from each other.

"So," Belle continued, "if I walk into that classroom, and Liam is there...I honestly can't say how I'm going to react. What's to stop me from going supernova?"

"Hmm. You know the Fae adage, 'Think happy thoughts'?"

"Yes?" She drew the word out.

"Just think: Eddie is awesome."

She gaped at him. "You're joking. I can't believe you're joking right now."

There was a glimmer in his eye, and she could just vaguely make out a smirk in the semi-darkness. "I can't lie, remember?"

"Are you going to help me or not? I need to retrieve my missing memory, and I need to know how to maintain control."

There was a pause, and then he heaved a deep sigh. "I am going to help you."

Relief crashed through her. "Thank you, Eddie." Something he said before surged in her mind, and she bit down on her lip, worrying it. "Um, so that intimacy-thing you mentioned about retrieving the memory, what exactly does that entail?"

A soft chuckle escaped him. "We'll come back to that one. First, know that I am going to be leaving for a bit—"

"Leaving? What do you mean?" Why, oh, why was she feeling a jolt of separation anxiety?

"Because," he continued, as if she hadn't interrupted, "in order to help you, I have to let you borrow this." He removed the long, black beaded rosary from around his neck and gripped it in his hand so that the cross hung from his closed fist.

"How did you get that?"

"Another story for another day. But this, this is what tames me."

"Tames you?"

"If I don't have this on, the Jäger and I are one."

She opened her mouth to ask a question, but he put a finger to her lips to shush her. She frowned, but then heat invaded her senses when he pinched her chin and dragged his thumb gently across her lips.

His voice dropped to a husky whisper. "See, right now, this is all I'd do, but without my rosary, I'd have kissed you a *long* time ago."

"Forcibly?" she whispered.

"Never. I'm always still me, but the Jäger has low inhibitions, which is why I'm faster, deadlier, in that form. Without the rosary, I'm still in control of all my decisions, but definitely more impulsive, which can lead to all sorts of trouble I can't afford to have. So, step one of Operation Help Belle is you wear this rosary, and it should tame you, your powers."

She held her palm out expectantly.

"Not yet. Step two, I take a leave of absence from you and investigate to see if Liam has been bewitched—"

She gasped, covering her mouth with her hand. "You don't think Violet's actually gotten to him? How would you be able to tell anyway?"

"I can smell enchantments. Remember in the alley with the twins?"

"Yes, I remember." Her stomach sunk at the idea of Violet harming Liam all this time, while her heart leaped with hope that Liam may not have willingly forsaken her that night after all.

"And I also need to catch up with Ernesto in Amsterdam. A potions witch aiding Violet is bad, very bad."

"Ok. What can *I* do? I don't want to just stand on the sidelines here."

"That's another thing, siren. You are the riddle in all this. Everything about you, it just doesn't make sense."

"That's. Not. Helping."

"I think you may have something to do with the final prophecies and Dommedag. I'm going to pay a visit to the Jäger Father and get some answers, but, uh, to do so, I need something from you."

"Like what?"

"A memento that reflects you. The Jäger Father is a High Fae, and in exchange for mementos—meaningful souvenirs—a Jäger can enter his presence. The Fae are extraordinarily odd," he said rather affectionately. "I'll tell you more about them another time."

"Okay then. What can I give? Um, my favorite hoodie?" she hugged herself, rubbing the sleeves like her beloved security blanket was about to be ripped away.

"How about a lock of hair?" He held up his index finger with the curl wound loosely around it.

"Sure?"

He gripped the cross in his hand so that the longer point stuck out. There was a click, and then a short, thin blade snapped out of its end.

She jumped. "Oh my."

He swiftly sliced the curl off and pocketed it. Another click, and the blade retreated. "Step three is…help you get that memory back."

Jitters immediately erupted over her skin. Her hands started trembling with the electricity again. *How* exactly did he plan to help her with that?

As if understanding what she was thinking, he reached for her hands again. "Relax. What I'm talking about is a hug."

"Oh." Her relief was comical. "Wait, so you've never kissed or hugged before?"

"Are you ready or not, siren?"

"So we're just going to hug, and the memory will come back to me?"

"It's not as simple as that." He toyed with the rosary in his hand, and she was surprised to find he was nervous.

"What's the catch then?" she asked.

"It-It's me. You already know how I feel about you."

"You've been activated toward me, so…."

"Let's go with that," he said offhandedly, perplexing her.

Surely, he didn't mean when he'd supposedly staked a claim on her like a Neanderthal in Annie's Antiques store. *"Either way, siren, you're mine."* All that was left for him to do was grab her by the hair and tow her into a cave. The feminist in her may have been outraged but remembering the heat behind those words had sent her heart into a stutter.

Eddie rubbed his palms together as if trying to ward off a sudden chill.

"You're nervous, aren't you?" She was befuddled by this unexpected loss of composure from the stoic Jäger but found it endearing at the same time. "What's so scary about a hug?"

"I am a little scared," he confessed.

"Why?" She wanted to laugh at how silly that was but stopped herself. This must be a big deal for Eddie.

"I'm not going to have the rosary on when I hug you."

"So? It's just a hug."

"Siren," exasperation marked his voice, "just do me a favor, please. While I've got my arms around you, don't move or do anything to tempt or encourage me. In fact, I'm putting a timer on my phone, and when that thing goes off, you're going to put that rosary in my hand again."

"Gosh. Well then maybe we shouldn't do this."

"No. It's-It's important. So this is what we're going to do: you're going to put this rosary in your pocket, we'll hug for one minute—"

"One minute? You think that's enough time for the memory to—"

"One minute." And he set the timer on his phone. He looked into her eyes, and she could see a slight panic in them. "I can*not* kiss you. When I'm holding you, and that becomes even a remote possibility—and I apologize in advance if it does—then I need you to touch my skin with the rosary."

"So then I should have it ready in my hand, not my pocket."

"No, it can't touch your skin yet either because we both have to be at our most open, and, um, *receptive*, to each other if we're to draw this memory out. Understood?"

"Yes. No smooching, timer goes off, and I touch you with the rosary."

"I'm counting on you, siren."

"Of course. Let's hug already. It's only for a minute anyways, then we'll know what happened with Violet and my family. And I'm totally missing Helsing's exam right now."

He brushed off her concern. "He'll let you make it up." And then he pinned her with those golden eyes. "Come here."

With those words, the situation got real. "It's just a hug," she reminded herself. She rested her hands on his shoulders as his left hand lightly touched her waist. "Nice, friendly hug."

"That's the plan, siren," he said a bit hoarsely. He lifted the cell phone in his right hand, the timer's red start button just beneath his thumb. "Remember, just try to relax and let your mind clear, and I-I'll try to do the same." He touched the rosary to his forehead and whispered, "Dominus mihi auxilium."

"You sound like a priest," she said by his ear.

"I am a priest." He pressed start and dropped the rosary into her hoodie pocket.

| 16 |

Wrecking Ball

Belle almost reached for the rosary right away. Almost.

Eddie's eyes flashed a brilliant gold, and he drew in a sharp breath as his left hand splayed on her hip and squeezed her in toward him.

"Bloody hell," he muttered, full British now. "I feel like I've dropped the weight of a Kevlar suit." Sliding his phone back into his pocket, he dragged his right palm up along her back, bringing her in tighter.

Her body temperature decided to climb all on its own.

"Friendly hug," she reminded him in a whisper.

"Of course, anything you want, siren."

Whoa. "What were those words you said in another language?"

"God help me."

Oh. "Y-You said you're a priest."

"I am."

"Care to explain?"

"No."

Well then.

Her next question evaporated on her tongue when she felt his hand glide up over her shoulder, her neck, until he cradled the corner of her jaw with his fingers nestled in her hair. He gently squeezed her in even tighter against him with his other arm around her waist.

"What I care to explain, luv, is what *your* scent does to me." He rested his forehead against hers and closed his eyes as he inhaled deeply. "It is heaven for my soul and hell for my body. Your presence is an utterly exquisite torture."

That accent in that deep timbre spouting off words like that.... Belle was melting like heated candle wax, becoming putty in his hands.

Grasping at her last shred of propriety, she asked, "Is the memory retrieval working?" She'd meant to sound practical and diffuse some of the invisible fire that was lighting up the tiny space, but with Eddie's breath mingling with her own and the rise and fall of his chest pushing against hers, her words came out all breathy, and she was sure she was going to feel mortified over it much, much later.

But she was drowning in the sensations. His very scent and presence seemed magnified, transformed into a seductive force that lured her in, and she felt powerless to resist in a way that was unnatural. She'd never felt such a pull before. It was pure magnetism.

He grazed his parted lips along the line of her jaw, and her fingers found their way to the hair at the nape of his neck. His nose brushed against her own, and he angled his head.

An alarm finally went off inside her. Her brain screamed he wasn't allowed to kiss her, but her body was singing *carpe diem.* She felt the lightest touch of Eddie's lips against hers.

His earlier plea cut through the haze. *"I'm counting on you, siren."*

Belle withdrew a fraction, even though it pained her to resist letting herself tumble over this forbidden edge with Eddie. With great effort, she turned her face, wrapping her arms tightly around his neck so she was cheek-to-cheek with him, and he wouldn't have room to kiss her. Immersed in the heady swirl of this mysterious passion, she was suddenly falling, slipping into a waking dream, only this felt more like remembering, like she was re-living.

Violet's dark spirit hovered before her, staring eerily at her while her mouth moved as if speaking, but no sound came out. Belle looked around and found herself standing on the second floor of her Elmridge home, with the walls and roof blown out and the open, blue sky overhead. In her chest, she felt the oppressive weight of terror and regret and-and...death. Three familiar bodies lay in the distance with thin columns of smoke issuing from their immobile forms. Her chest constricted painfully when she realized who the dead were.

Violet's spirit hovered closer, her mouth a sneer, her lips moving, but in this living memory, all sound was muted. Then, Belle's own mouth must have opened in a scream because Violet shot toward her and engulfed her from the inside.

She awoke—but not really—on a cold, metal surface with glittering, golden bodies flitting about. The strange room struck her as a type of hospital setting. A handsome man, whose black hair, square jaw, and light green eyes all looked familiar, moved beside her with alarm. Again, words were exchanged between himself and...did that second, reed-like man beside him have giant fairy wings fluttering from his back? But no sound was heard. William Rawlins. That was the beautiful man's name. His green eyes, the same as Liam's, grew rounder with concern as his mouth formed silent, urgent words. Just before her eyes fluttered shut, she saw the glint of a golden, shimmering liquid in a syringe, which William primed once in the air, before plunging its needle deep into her chest.

The timer on Eddie's cell phone rang and they broke apart with a gasp. Her face wet with tears.

"The rosary, Belle," he said roughly, the tears on his face mirroring her own.

She drew it from her pocket and deposited it into his waiting hand. He exhaled deeply after clenching it tightly in his fist and touching his forehead with it.

"Did you see what I saw?" she whispered, still shaking.

He nodded. "And felt what you felt." He wiped one hand down his face.

"I-I killed my family. And the Fae...they gave me another chance."

His eyes held hers in understanding. He reached out and touched her cheek with the tips of his fingers, and then with sudden urgency, said, "The man in your memory. He is—"

"You two lovebirds! Out of there, now!"

The school's newly minted principal stood next to the staircase, hands planted on her hips and glowering at the two shadowy forms huddled in the darkness. Her wild mane of crimpy, curly red hair made Belle's own curls look like a sleek curtain. Her thick square-framed glasses and immaculate pencil skirt suit shouted *boss*, but her lapel pin of a little schoolhouse hinted at a sincere I-love-my-students side. Plus, her reputation with the students as the yes-woman for fun school spirit activities, and with the school patrons as a gifted admin-istrator, made her an all-around popular figure.

But at the moment, her next word looked like it might be, *"Deten-tion!"*

"Dr. Earheart!" Belle cried out, stepping into the light.

"Ms. Montague," she said sternly, "shouldn't you be in class right now taking an exam?"

"It's my fault, Dr. Earheart," Eddie said, joining Belle. He grabbed her fingers with the rosary, so they were both touching it. Smart move. "I wanted to talk to Belle in private about something."

"Oh," Dr. Earheart suddenly looked flummoxed. "Mr. Helsing." She pulled at the bottom of her jacket to straighten it and patted one side of her hair. "You're James's nephew."

Eddie exchanged a brief side glance with Belle. "I am," he replied, suspicion leaking into his tone.

The principal's lips split open in a dazzling grin. "Well," she clapped her hands once together, "there is still some time left of class, so if you both hurry, we'll file this one under no harm, no foul."

"Thank you so much Dr. Earheart," Belle said.

"Oh, just a second there," the principal said to Eddie. "How soon will you see Dr. Helsing again?"

"I...do not know."

"I'm seeing Dr. Helsing now," Belle volunteered with a smile. "I have him now for Lit." It seemed to be taking Eddie a minute longer to catch up to what Belle was already figuring out about the principal and his uncle.

The principal's eyes lit up. "Will you be an absolute dear and tell him just one word from me, please?"

"Sure."

"Eyepatch."

"Eyepatch?"

"Eyepatch."

Seconds later, Eddie walked Belle to class, holding her hand. *It's only so that we'll both be touching the rosary until he leaves me with it,* she told herself, but the stupid butterflies in her stomach wouldn't listen.

They stopped outside Dr. Helsing's door and those butterflies turned into bats. "Liam's probably not even in there," she said, failing miserably to sound nonchalant. Eddie held her gaze as she rambled on, "And even if he is, he's-he's not worth my time. Unless, maybe, if he was bewitched by Violet like you suggested, then he would need my help, or *our* help, if-if this is something you would concern your-self with."

He raised an eyebrow. "I would. I have. In fact, if Liam is in there, I need you to get my uncle to send him out here on some errand, so I can smell if he has been bewitched. I'll text you what I learn."

"What excuse could I use to send him out?"

"You'll think of something." He squeezed her hand and inched closer. "That memory of yours...changes everything."

"How?"

"It—"

He was interrupted by Dr. Helsing's muted announcement from within the classroom. "There are ten minutes left of testing."

"I'll tell you another time. Go in, siren. You've got this."

She nodded. Slowly, he released her hand, leaving the rosary in it as he stepped away from her, still facing her. With his other hand, he retrieved his glasses from his pocket and slid them on just as soon as his fingertips left hers. A flash of gold disappeared behind the glasses, and with a sharp inhale, he turned abruptly away and leaned against the wall, forcing himself to not watch her as she turned the handle of the classroom door and walked in.

Do not look towards the back, she commanded herself. She kept her eyes forward on Dr. Helsing who was seated behind the teacher's desk facing the classroom. She felt the weight of everyone's stare and the heavy hush of a testing environment, as she came to a stop directly in front of him so that her back was to the class.

Dr. Helsing took one look at the rosary clenched in her hand and raised an alarmed brow. He had a thin goatee and the Helsing black hair, but while Eddie's was straight, his curled around the edges. He had the face of one who was once handsome, but the skin was now weathered and pockmarked from travels and sun-exposure, not to mention the long, jagged scar that ran down the length of his left cheek. He liked his Hawaiian shirts and linen pants, a testament to where he'd rather be.

Belle whispered so only her teacher could hear. "I'm sorry for being late." He nodded. "Eddie let me borrow this." He nodded again. She noticed a tall, thin, gift bag on the side of his desk. From her angle, she could see what was inside of it: a dark wine bottle with a tiny, square gift tag that read, *"One shot a day."*

He noticed her curious stare and smiled, slightly embarrassed. He whispered, "It's a gift from our *virtual* student."

"So he's here?"

He dipped his chin in response and his eyes motioned subtly towards the back of the room.

Belle felt her heart seize and wondered briefly if maybe this was what a heart attack felt like.

"Belle?" Dr. Helsing whispered, concerned.

Robotically, her mouth moved while the rest of her remained frozen. "Dr. Earheart said to tell you *eyepatch*."

A titter of laughter broke out. She'd forgotten to whisper.

"Are you done, Ms. Montague?" Dr. Helsing asked audibly, his ears turning a strawberry red.

"No," she continued at a normal volume. "L-Liam Rawlins is supposed to go outside and, and greet a member of the Welcome Back Committee." Her cheeks flamed at how lame that sounded to her own ears. Dr. Helsing gave her a questioning stare, and she mouthed, "Eddie."

His confusion cleared up instantly. He called out over her shoulder. "Mr. Rawlins?" There was no verbal response, but she imagined Liam making eye contact with the teacher. "You may step outside. Bring your test materials up here, please."

With her eyes on Dr. Helsing's face, her keen ears tracked Liam's movements. The slide of his body out of the desk, the soft thuds of his footfalls against the tiled floor growing louder until they came to a stop directly behind her. Her heart hammered in her chest while her lungs became inert. Every sense sprung alive exponentially on edge, at once both desiring and dreading his touch, his very presence a palpable force.

She felt the gentle rustle of the whispers of hair at her crown at his slow intake of breath. Her eyes briefly fluttered shut at the realization: he was breathing her in.

No, she thought forcefully. *None of that.*

Belle sucked in a breath and turned sharply away from him, still not looking at him, and headed down the aisle to her seat. She stared down at her desk until he left the room.

"What do you want?" Came Liam's voice from outside the closed door, clearly aggravated.

There was a pause, and then Eddie said, "Welcome back."

A round of chuckles came from some of the students. Belle bit back a smile.

And then she heard Liam say at a volume that she was sure no one else would have picked up, "I know who you are. You're the loser that's been getting too close to my girl."

She heard a scuffle, and then a heavy thud against the wall. Her alarmed expression crashed with Dr. Helsing's own, and the other students reacted similarly. The teacher bolted to his feet, and just then, the bell rang signaling the end of class.

Dr. Helsing paused long enough to shout before heading out the door, "Leave your exams on my desk!"

Belle remained rooted in her chair as the students filed out, buzzing with interest and moving quickly to get a peek at the possible showdown outside. She briefly noticed that Vasilisa wasn't present.

Dr. Helsing's voice boomed, "Edward, get out of here! And you, get back inside!"

Oh no! I'm still inside! she thought panicking.

An incoming text message had her reaching for her phone. It was Eddie.

Your boy has a temper. I almost killed him.

Holy canoli.

Smells like a jackass but not bewitched.

She had just enough time to text back **K**, before the classroom door opened and Liam stepped through. Their eyes collided across the distance, and her very being froze. It was like seeing someone back from the dead. She realized now she'd *mourned* him, and to see him now in the flesh....

Liam was still a vision that stole her breath away like on the very first day of class when he'd walked in, the very picture of Adonis. Her eyes drank him in now. Gone were the blonde locks, his hair trimmed close to the skin on the sides and cut short on top. It made the angles of his face look sharper, the green eyes more penetrating, but his mouth looked as soft as ever. His wide shoulders and powerful chest and arms did not stretch against the fitted uniform shirt like they used to, so he clearly had lost some weight, and his skin was paler than his normally golden color.

The door opened again and Dr. Helsing appeared, coming to an abrupt stop behind Liam. "Oh! Oh dear." He looked between Belle's petrified posture and Liam's rigid stance. "My apologies." He looked at Belle when he said this, making it known that he was aware of the drama between the two teens. "Erm, Mr. Rawlins, if you would excuse us, please, I need to speak with Ms. Montague about her make-up exam."

"I'm not going anywhere," he replied, his searing stare never wavering from her face. "Belle and I need to talk."

"But—" Dr. Helsing tried again.

"It's okay," Belle said, finally finding her voice. "I'll talk to him."

"Right, then," Dr. Helsing inched around Liam and moved toward his desk. He started stacking the exams and packing his briefcase. "I am going now on my lunch break, so you two can have the room for thirty minutes." He quickly added, "For talking. Only talking." His ears reddened at what he knew he was implying, which made Belle blush as well. Liam, however, let a tiny smile escape.

After the door clicked shut behind Dr. Helsing, the seconds of silence that followed were profound. The sound of a pin drop would've rivaled a cannon shot.

Liam finally spoke, "I've missed you."

The feeling behind those words cut to her, right through her heart, but the effect disintegrated against the spine of steel she'd grown at his abandonment.

She narrowed her eyes at him as she slowly lifted out of her chair and stood. "You've *missed* me?" she repeated, incredulous. "You liar."

He walked slowly towards her. "I couldn't communicate with you this whole time."

"Why?"

"It's complicated."

"Complicated." She nodded dramatically and crossed her arms over her chest. "Complicated is you knowing my deepest, darkest secret, helping me save Ernesto from a monster, kissing me on my front porch, and then disappearing for a month after promising to be back in half an hour!" She was shouting now. Sparks of electricity flickered around her hands, and she knew that if it wasn't for Eddie's rosary around her neck, safely tucked beneath her shirt, she'd look like a human plasma globe right now.

"Like I said, complicated."

"You are a royal jerk, you know that?"

He was standing just a foot away now. She fought against the temptation to touch him to see if he was real, but also zap him and cause him pain. She knew both options would make her feel better.

Liam lifted a hand toward her face, but she stepped away. "And what about your girlfriend, huh? From the Netherlands? Cindy said you're introducing her at dinner tonight."

"That's still happening."

His words were like a smack in the face. Tears stung her eyes, but before she could react any further, he said, "*You're* my girlfriend. My new *assistant* is from the Netherlands."

The words must have just slipped on out the other ear because she said, "Come again?"

He smiled and claimed the last bit of space between them. "I'm bringing *you* to dinner tonight."

Still in shock, she let him grip her forearms as he brought his face closer to look her in the eyes. Her mind was reeling with this new information. The only thing she managed to say was, "That makes no sense." She shook off his hands. "Why would you ignore me this whole time, and then suddenly think that you're my boyfriend? How could you even—?"

Liam's lips silenced her. Her eyes remained wide open as his lips moved gently against her unresponsive ones. And then her brain slid into the backseat as her body took the wheel, especially when Liam drew his fingers across her cheeks and through her hair, bringing her closer. With that, her lips finally sprung to life and her eyes closed. When the kiss deepened, she was transported back to her front porch, and now this was another one of those long kisses goodbye etched with the promise of that I'll-see-you-later she had missed so much.

Her hands found their way around his waist, and he immediately flinched upon the contact. She tore away from him, looking down at her hands. Thin ribbons of electricity snaked across her palms. She hated to think what her unhampered touch could've done to him.

Liam tilted her chin up and landed a soft kiss. "I'll pick you up at 6:00."

She could do nothing but stare at him, mouth slightly agape, as he turned and walked out of the classroom, like the receding swing of a wrecking ball, all done causing its sweet, sweet damage.

| **17** |

The One With the Shadow Man

That night, Belle sat at home, not in the Rawlins Castle's fabulous dining room where Cindy and her father were exchanging glances over a lavish spread of dinner at the table, and a sullen Liam sat thrumming his fingers, staring stonily at his untouched dish. Cindy's tentative question of whether everything was alright, had him growling in response, pushing away from the dinner table, and stomping out of the room, the door's thunderous slam echoing throughout the castle.

Cindy texted Belle: **His girlfriend didn't show.**

Belle: **He thinks I'M his girlfriend.**

Cindy: **WHAT???**

Belle: **And I'm definitely not.**

Belle promised to tell her everything tomorrow. She was tired out from her emergency two-hour session she'd had after school with Millie and Candy, camped out in her living room with popcorn and gelatos, and an old *Saved by the Bell* TV marathon running in the background. They'd dissected every aspect of Liam's absolutely outrageous, but totally awesome, entrance back into Belle's life.

She'd wavered in a sea of bitterness, excitement, indignation...a sweet and sour mix that boiled down to the three BFF's conclusion: Liam wasn't allowed to just waltz back into her life, sweep her off her feet with a mind-blowing kiss, and then expect everything to be fine and dandy, especially without any explanation or apology for his deep transgression. Which was why, with Millie and Candy looking over her shoulder, she'd texted Liam that she wouldn't be making it to dinner and that they were *not* in a relationship as he had so claimed. His response had been to ignore her text, which spawned another half-hour of righteous girl talk before her best friends finally departed.

But at 6:00 p.m., Liam had rung her front doorbell anyways.

Belle opened the door, and when she saw him standing there on her porch as if he'd just stepped off a magazine cover—silver aviator glasses, dark jeans, a black short-sleeved button-down shirt with the top few buttons undone, allowing a peek at a defined chest—she almost lost her resolve. Almost. Because when he said with an air of nonchalance, "Ready?" She snapped.

"Did you not get my text?"

"I did."

"So then?"

He raised the glasses. His crystal green eyes were so alluring. He gave her a sheepish smile that knocked at her heart. "I still want you to have dinner with me."

She paused then, disbelieving that it didn't matter to him that she didn't. But, this was Liam. They had history, albeit, very short, but very significant. She could count the number of people on one hand who really knew her. And Liam was one of them. He was deserving of some ounce of mercy, and truth be told, she still liked him a crazy lot.

Belle would allow herself on one condition.

"Fine," she said, crossing her arms over her chest. "Only if you explain to me what was so complicated that you had to suddenly ignore me all this time."

He heaved a frustrated sigh. "I can't."

"Have a nice life." She backtracked into the house and closed the door on his protests.

"C'mon, Belle, I'm sorry!" he shouted through the door. "I just...it's a busi-ness-thing I can't talk about."

She yelled back, "And you can't explain any of that to me after I told you and showed you stuff about myself that could get me strapped down in a government laboratory?!"

A pause, and then, "No."

"Go away, Liam!"

He protested and with a final blow that sounded like he landed a heavy fist against the door, he departed, but only after telling her, "This isn't over, Belle. You're my girl."

So now, in an utterly sour mood, she lay wrapped in the sherpa blanket with her head on the living room couch's arm, staring blankly at the TV, vaguely following Zack and Kelly's escapades in Las Vegas.

She was wearing the Jane Austen shirt she'd won in her t-shirt comebacks battle with Eddie in Annie's Antiques. She had completely forgotten about it. She'd discovered it in her backpack in class after Q's birthday lunch. Eddie must have snuck it in there when she wasn't looking. She paired the shirt now with comfy black pajama shorts imprinted with silver constellations of the night sky, and with fuzzy black ankle socks sporting little green aliens and silver spaceships. Her hair was comfortably loose, cascading in all its soft twists and curls down her back.

While her eyes were trained on the TV, her mind was a chaotic whirlwind that she tried to ignore. Liam popping back into her life without explanation. Literally. That confounding relationship status he'd claimed, and then that kiss.

She sighed deeply just thinking about it.

But then another embrace replayed itself, and that one plagued her even more. Eddie hadn't even kissed her, and just being in his arms had set her very molecules aflame in a way she'd never experienced before. It felt unnatural. Was it because of that Jäger pull he feels toward her? He'd said he felt what she felt when they...did whatever that was that they did. Did that go both ways? Had *she* felt what he felt? It would explain that tsunami of desire that had bowled her over until she fell into that lost memory.

She squeezed her eyes shut against the tears that still managed to leak out. She'd killed her family. Lost control somehow, until Violet herself took possession of her. The whole scenario was her worst nightmare.

Gratitude for the Fae welled up inside her. They'd given her another chance to get it right. Even her killer-turned-savior was helping her.

She pulled the rosary out of her shirt and held it in both hands, her fingers tracing over the intricate swirls etched into the cross. There was a tiny inscription on one of the edges: *1 Corinthians 13.*

She blinked. She remembered that chapter in the Bible. It was one of the most renowned for its message about love and truth. Eddie was a walking contradiction. A trained assassin, yet also a priest bearing a token symbolic of pure love.

She suddenly hoped that Eddie hadn't taken that leave of absence he said he was going to take. She still had so many questions. He was starting to feel like a necessary part of any solution she could come up with for freeing her mother and stopping Violet.

Her doorbell interrupted her thoughts. For a fleeting second, she hoped it was Eddie. *I've got unfinished business with the man,* she stoically reminded her fluttering heart, but a quick glance at the clock told her it was Sergio with the usual.

She went to the door with her blanket wrapped around her shoulders. When she opened it, a gust of cold wind blew in, and she shivered deeper into her blanket. The temperatures had been dropping lately.

"Hi, Sergio."

Sergio stood there in the black Elmridge police uniform, which looked more Special Forces than cop. He gave her a tight smile, not the usual wide grin, as he presented her with the covered dish, "Beef stroganoff, and please don't say again it's not necessary. It's always a pleasure."

Belle thanked him and took the dish. "I owe you and your wonderful wife a week's worth of amazing dinners." When he only frowned as if preoccupied with something else, she asked, "Sergio, what is it?"

"An incident in the peacock field. Just happened. I'm on my way there now."

"What happened?" Her heart pounded in alarm.

"So far, what's coming in over the radio is that there's a bear or a large mountain lion that's gotten over the eastern wall somehow by Wychblack Forest. There are some peafowls slaughtered out there on the field."

"Oh my goodness!"

"So the word's going out tonight to all Elmridge residents to stay indoors until the animal's caught or we give the all-clear. So, please, do not step outside the house tonight."

"Of course."

After he left, she retreated to the couch again in a daze. Sergio's dish sat untouched on the side table.

Could things get any weirder in Elmridge?

It wasn't until a *Friends* marathon began running from its very first episode that she started paying attention to the TV. Soon enough, a God-sent distraction of bellyfuls of laughter and rooting for Ross made her forget her worries.

It was just after midnight, Belle had just finished wiping away tears of laughter when Joey was fired for over-acting his role as Al Pacino's butt double, when she heard a laugh. It was a high, unnatural laugh, and it very clearly came from somewhere off in the formal dining room.

She turned her head to look, but the room was steeped in shadows from her view in the living room. She stared towards the area, waiting.

Cold sweat dotted her skin. The adrenaline coursing through her body pounded loudly in her ears. She held completely still. Only the laugh track of the TV show could be heard.

"Eddie?" she called out timidly. Maybe he'd taken his stalker-level up a notch. If that was true, she was going to zap him until his Teflon skin finally cracked.

But still. She hoped it was him, and not some unknown intruder. Or a ghost.

"Not Eddie," came a hoarse whisper. The shadow of a thin man stepped into the light from the dining room.

Belle screeched as she flew off the couch. She raced to her bedroom, her blanket fluttering like a cape behind her. She slammed the door shut, locked it, and dove for her phone. With trembling hands, she dialed the only person who she knew could help her.

After one ring, he answered.

"Eddie!" she whisper-shouted.

"Siren? I'm on my way, luv. Stay on the phone." He was in British-mode. She heard what sounded like feet pounding heavily and quickly against the ground. And the rush of wind. "Talk to me."

"It's a sh-shadow man. In my dining room." She shivered again and anxiously watched her bedroom door. "It laughed."

"Cheeky bugger," he muttered. "They're called Shadow Spawn."

"Shadow-what?!"

"I'm at your front door."

Whoa, that was inhumanly fast.

"I-I'm too scared to leave my room," she admitted, embarrassed.

"No worries, luv. Open your window then. I'll let myself up."

She threw her window open and stepped back, wrapping the blanket tightly around her shoulders as the biting cold whooshed in. Eddie's form soon crawled in through the window.

"Why are you dressed like that?" she asked, eyes wide, assessing him from head to toe as he closed the window and faced her. He had on black boots and gloves, black camouflage tactical pants and jacket, a black beanie, and his face was covered in black camouflage paint.

The only bright color were his eyes, a fierce gold that pinned her where she stood.

The intensity of his focus on her shattered all thought as she simply waited for his next move. But the seconds ticked by, and he continued to hold her in his predatory gaze. The room suddenly felt like it was too small for them. With a tremor in her voice, she asked, "Eddie? Why are you just standing there?"

Slowly, he lifted his hand toward her and opened his palm, as if asking for something.

The rosary. He needed it back.

She slipped the beaded necklace off and approached him slowly, feeling like she was under a lion's feral stare set to pounce on a hairtrigger. Her eyes never leaving his, she dropped the rosary into his waiting palm.

As his fingers closed over it, the light in his eyes dulled, and the tension in the room retreated as well.

Slipping the rosary over his head, he answered her first question as if they were having a lunchroom conversation and he hadn't just been staring at her like she was dinner. "I'm assuming you heard about the wild animal on the loose?" She nodded. "I was doing some tracking in that peacock field before the police showed up. I thought it was a bear at first because the prints were so large, but it has the fifth digit of a wolf, so it must be an abnormally giant wolf. I tracked it into Wychblack Forest. I have to go back there and finish tracking it when I'm done here." He pulled off his beanie and gloves and started unzipping his jacket. "May I?"

"Be my guest."

He continued talking, without the accent now, something about finding other small animals' mutilated carcasses, more pawprints, and not finding the wolf, and then warning some campers he'd run into in the mountains beyond the wall.

She heard but didn't really listen. Not when the jacket slid off revealing a tight black tank that did nothing to disguise the cuts and swells of his muscles. His very manly presence in her room felt forbidden, and her whole body flushed under the weight of that sensation.

He draped the clothing over her desk chair, which creaked under its new load, and looked around her room.

"You look like Rambo," she said. *But hotter, waaay hotter.*

He laughed. "I bet he smelled better than me, though." He plucked the front of his shirt for emphasis. "I hope you will forgive my...presentation tonight."

What an old, proper thing to say, she thought, pleased. And he *did* smell. But his scent held an inexplicable attraction for her and seemed amplified now with his sweat. She inhaled deeply.

He smells mouthwatering.

"Mouthwatering?"

Her eyes snapped open. Curse her fanciful brain and unfiltered mouth. He was staring at her, his eyes glowing, and his mouth slightly agape, as if he couldn't quite believe what she'd said.

There was no recovering from that, so she reached for a distraction. "W-Why are you not hunting in your Jäger form?"

But he was not going to be deterred. He approached her slowly, his eyes never leaving hers, the temperature rising substantially in the room. He reached out and touched the blanket she still had tightly wrapped around herself. "What are *you* wearing, siren? I hope it's more than just those ridiculous socks, or the most dangerous creature in this house is going to be you."

He was so close. She had to tilt her head back now to look at him. Without thinking, she reached out and touched the black paint on his face. A silly idea came to her, and she went with it. Her index finger traced a happy face on his cheek. She smiled up mischievously at him when she finished.

His heated gaze had softened into amusement. "Did you just draw on my face?"

"What are you going to do about it?" she challenged playfully.

He stared at her, all sorts of ideas running through his mind that tilted one side of his smile all the way up. Then with one finger, he rubbed some paint off one of his cheeks and dragged the smudge down her nose.

"Fair enough," she said, her smile matching his now. "Why did you say I'd be the most dangerous creature in the house?"

A slight blush colored his cheeks at whatever he was thinking. He exhaled and took a long step back. His voice was deeper when he spoke again, "Because when I go Jäger, he'll come for *you*, not the Shadow Spawn."

"And do what to me?"

"Break my prophecy."

A beat passed as a rush of warmth swept through her. She turned away and sat on the bed. "You never answered my question. Why didn't you hunt the wolf in Jäger form?"

"Jäger is only for supernatural hunts. If I'm hunting an animal in the wild at night, then…" He gestured to his outfit to finish the statement for him.

A thump was heard outside the bedroom.

Belle squeaked as Eddie's head swiveled in the direction of the noise.

"And now it's a cocky bugger." He turned to Belle. "Stay here." She nodded vigorously. He let himself out of the room, locking the door before closing it behind him.

She stood stock still. Listening.

After a good ten minutes that felt like an hour of imagining all sorts of silent Jäger-Shadow battles—because there was no sound out there—she heard a soft knock on her door. "It's me."

She rushed him in. "Did you get it?"

He walked past her and sank into the desk chair, worried. "No." She waited for him to explain. "It hid. And there are two of them."

A pause as she tapped her chin. "I think I can convince Ernesto it's time to move out of this house."

"I can tell how long the Shadow Spawn have been lurking by how deeply they can hide from me." He rubbed his jaw, thinking. "These two have been here for over a month. I can still sense them, but I can't fish them out."

"Definitely moving out."

"We'll have to trick them to draw them out."

"We?"

"Yes, *we*." He rose from the chair and approached her. "I'm going to need your help on this one, siren."

"Really?" She definitely hadn't expected that. "Why?"

"It only took me a minute to assess the situation outside."

She frowned. "So then what took the other nine minutes?"

"I-I couldn't get rid of my Jäger form. I stood outside your door, and…it wouldn't go away when it should've."

"Why not?" she asked softly, but she suspected she already knew why.

"It *wants* you, siren. Remember, inhibitions are almost non-existent with the Jäger."

"Would it hurt me?"

"No," he said quickly, assuring her. He huffed out a breath before speaking again. "But it'll hurt *me*."

"Because of your prophecy?"

He nodded, his eyes trained on her face.

"Would that be so bad?" she asked in a small voice.

He caught the confession behind that question. Her face warmed as she realized she'd just admitted she wanted him to kiss her. His eyes became hooded as he slowly closed the distance between them. Swallowing visibly, he raised a hand toward her lips, and with two fingers, traced the contour of her mouth. When her lips parted on their own, he pressed against them, and she planted a soft kiss on his fingers.

He sucked in a breath and stepped away, facing the window. With the ragged rise and fall of his shoulders, he looked as if he was struggling to control his breathing.

"I'm sorry," she said.

After a minute, he seemed steadier. "Don't be, siren. You've done nothing wrong." He turned to her again, his eyes still glowing like two suns. "I just hope you can understand. If my prophecy is my own, and it's not switched with your uncle's, I don't want to fade away. My instinct tells me I have an important part to play in Dommedag and a lot of lives will depend on me. So I *can't* allow my prophecy to come true until Dommedag passes."

She nodded. A heavy, sad weight settled in her chest, mixed with an ounce of pride at her noble friend's self-sacrificing nature. Did she really consider Eddie an actual friend now?

"Now, back to the most pressing concern: I'd like to avoid using the Jäger tonight."

"But then, how will you—"

"I have a theory that I'd like to test. I think because your dream-seeing ability is a type of telepathy, you're able to see into my mind sometimes, which leaves you open to me being able to draw on your electrical powers."

"And this helps us with the Shadow Spawn, how?"

"I'm going to use you to zap them."

She was quiet for a moment. "So, I'll be like a supernatural weapon in your hands."

"It sounds bad when you put it that way, but yes."

"You think my electrical power can take them out?"

"It's worth a shot."

"And if this works, then I can actually be, like, a Shadow Spawn hunter?"

He nodded as if considering that for the first time. "Yes, you could. I'll even train you, if you like."

Something sparked to life inside her. "Then, let's go zap those suckers!" She threw her blanket on the bed and propped her hands on her hips, Super Girl style.

His eyebrows flew up. "Hold on, siren," he said with a wide grin. "Before you get all gung-ho—and I like this, by the way—I said it was just a theory that I wanted to test. I'm *hoping* it works. If it doesn't, and I have to go Jäger again, you lock yourself in your room until I give you the all-clear."

Right. Because the Jäger might try to kiss her senseless.

She liked this Jäger.

He focused on her shirt and smiled. "You wore the shirt." And then his smile faded, and his eyes widened as he noticed something else. He dragged a hand down his face as he turned away and groaned, "You're *killing* me, siren. At least, put on a brassiere, please."

She hid a laugh behind her hand.

He cocked his head. "And what is so funny?"

"You said *brassiere*."

He rolled his eyes. "Very mature."

She brushed past him as she headed for her walk-in closet. "Well, my apologies if I'm not as mature as you," and just before she shut the door, she stuck her head out and added, "old man."

She heard him mutter, "Lord, help me."

He washed the black paint off his face in her bathroom, and when they finally stepped out of the bedroom into the hall, she found herself pressing close to his side.

They moved into the living room. "They're hidden right now." He pointed toward the TV, the *Friends* marathon still running. "Is this what you were doing when you heard the laugh?"

"Yes. What exactly is a Shadow Spawn, and how did they get in here?" Answers. She needed answers.

He prompted for her to sit on the couch, while he moved to a spot by the door that led to the ground floor. He looked down at the spot, as if deep in thought.

"What are you doing?" she asked.

"These shadows spawn from dark supernatural events. You have two of them in this house. The first one, the smaller one, spawned here." He looked to her for explanation.

"That's where Violet stood throwing her lightning bolts at us and demanding the pixie dust." She frowned at him. "How did you know it happened right there?"

"Jäger can sense imprints in time." Her befuddled look prompted him to elaborate. "We can sense when a powerful supernatural event occurred, in the spot that it occurred."

He crossed over a few paces until he stood before the archway that led into the hallway. "The second one spawned here. The imprint is so strong…" He locked eyes with her. "This spot must be where you lost control and—"

"Killed my family," she said softly.

He nodded. "And where your do-over started. The shadow this event spawned is massive. I bet it uses the whole house to hide itself." A cold shiver worked its way down her spine. "The Shadow Spawn release negative energy, and when the human soaks it in—depression, pessimism, laziness—it feeds off that in turn. They're parasites. I'm sure you've been feeling their effects this whole time."

"I must have been. I thought it was just because of the drama in my life, though." No wonder Ernesto seemed to never want to be in the house. She always just wanted to nap in the comfort of her bed, or else she would mope about most of the time. Her only distraction had been homework. She hadn't even wanted to socialize over the phone or on the internet much when she was home. Yes, Liam leaving had made her sad, but after a while, her natural love for life should have kicked in and motivated her to experience her new life in Elmridge with relish.

"Then these Shadow Spawn have been feasting on you." He sounded like he was ready to take these shadows outside and smack them around.

She bit her lip. "So, whenever a dark supernatural event happens, these shadows are spawned?" He nodded as he slowly approached her. "And that night in the greenhouse, were any shadows spawned then?"

He sat on the coffee table facing her so that her legs were between his. "I already took care of them." He scooted up until he could comfortably wrap his hands behind the crooks of her knees. He squeezed, searing her bare skin, and her eyes widened. He held her surprised gaze with unflinching intensity, and said softly, "I know you have questions. And I promise you, I will answer every single one. But to be able to answer you as truthfully as possible, I need to see the Jäger Father first."

It took her a moment to respond. His face from this angle was turning her brain to mush. "How long will that take?" she finally asked.

"I will try to be back in time to teach you that magic act." He smirked. "I really do need to see you in that costume."

She swatted his hands away, the thumbs of which had been absently grazing the sides of her knees. "That costume's not happening." She huddled back into the cushions while he took the spot beside her, spreading his arm over the back of the couch. "So you're going to go away for about a month then?" She couldn't keep the pout out of her voice. "The Jäger Father doesn't have a cell phone you could reach him at?"

That smile crept up his cheek and a light danced in his eyes. "You gonna miss me, siren?"

"No," she replied a bit too quickly.

"Useful trick that, lying."

She glared at him, but before a retort could leave her mouth, her stomach let loose an ungodly rumble.

Eddie gave her a pointed look. "You need to eat, luv."

Belle lifted off the couch, grabbed the beef stroganoff dish, reheated it in the microwave, and then returned with two glasses of water and two forks. She set the glasses on the coffee table and the dish between them on a throw pillow and handed Eddie a fork. "Bon appetit."

He blinked twice. "You want to share your plate with me?"

She paused mid-bite. "You make it sound like it's a big deal." She turned her own loaded fork in his direction. "Here. Try some. Sergio's wife, Trina, is a culinary genius."

She kept talking as he leaned forward, and she touched the bottom of his chin with her other hand to guide the fork into his mouth. His eyes latched onto hers, and something about the way he slowly dragged his mouth down the fork made her shut her mouth mid-sentence. He leaned back, chewing, and nodded his approval.

After he refused any more, stating that his stomach wasn't the one whining like a house cat, she shoveled the next bite into her mouth, ignoring the tiny shock that she'd just hand-fed her Jäger, like hand-feeding a tiger, only this one seemed to behave like a kitten around her.

Remembering how he'd just called her *luv*, she asked, "Why do you keep using your American accent around me? I already know it's fake. Just a part of your cover."

"It is a part of my cover, which goes with wearing the rosary, but I've lived in this country long enough to properly claim an American accent. I've just lived much longer in England."

"Then what makes you, you know, slip up and go British sometimes?" She had an inkling already—slipping when he was in Jäger form, without his rosary, and when he was alone with her sometimes—but she wanted to hear him confirm it.

"Nice try, siren, you already got one question in. It's my turn. How'd it go with the prodigal boyfriend today?"

He'd asked too casually, as if he was taking great care to *be* casual.

She returned her eyes to her food. "Oh, um, we had a misunderstanding." Her cheeks tinged pink remembering the lip-locking part of the disagreement.

"Just to be clear," he said, again too casual, "any *misunderstanding* on his part that causes you any physical harm will cost him a body part." He flashed her a fake smile.

"There's the stalker-Eddie I know." She took a sip of water. "Save your threats, Jäger. You said he wasn't bewitched, and until Liam fully explains himself to me, I am not giving him the time of day."

"Even though he knows your secret?"

She shifted uncomfortably. "I...trust him with it." She looked over at him, and he was staring stonily at her.

"Well, *I* don't. Anyone who tries to attack a member of the Welcome Back Committee can't be trusted."

The corner of his mouth quirked, and Belle laughed. "That was the only thing I could think of on the spot." But he was suddenly staring at her, eyes wide, with a vulnerability that made her immediately shift closer to him and ask with concern, "What's wrong?"

He blinked. "Oh, no, it's just, uh—"

"What is it?" Seeing him so flustered all of a sudden was odd.

He stilled. Those dark lashes lifted, and the black-ringed gold of his eyes were incandescent as they rested on her face. "It wouldn't be prudent of me to answer…just yet."

"Because you have to see the Jäger Father first." He nodded, his eyes never leaving her face. "About me and my demon-possessed mom."

"That's part of it, yes," he said cryptically. "But I also need you to tell me what happened with Emily."

"You know, this information-sharing seems a bit one-sided."

She waited to see if he would open up and offer something, but when he didn't, she lifted off the couch with a disappointed sigh. She returned the half-empty plate to the kitchen and sank back down on the opposite end of the couch, as far as possible from him. She crossed her arms over her chest and faced the TV.

From her peripheral vision, he hung his head for a second and made an exasperated noise before he said, "What do you want from me, siren?"

"Oh, nothing. Everything's perfect. I have a million questions that I'm not allowed to get answers for, but somehow, it's okay for you to get answers. And I want to physically help and do something about Violet, but it's not needed because you and my uncle are taking care of everything. So I get to live my life like a regular teenager, go to school, dream about beasts, hang out with my friends, and hopefully not lose my temper and fry everyone within a mile radius. Just normal teen stuff, you know?"

He scooted closer. "What did you say again?"

"Are you kidding? You weren't even listening?"

"No, about you dreaming of beasts. You mentioned it before under the staircase, but we, um, got sidetracked before you fully explained."

"Oh, yeah, I told my uncle about it. That's why he's in Amsterdam. I actually wrote down what I could remember from the dream. Wait here." She disappeared into her room and emerged with the *Great Expectations* novel he'd let her borrow.

She settled next to him on the couch and tucked her legs underneath her, holding the book to her chest. "Sorry. I wrote on one of the blank pages in the back. I wanted to write down the details of the dream as soon as I could, and I got my chance the next day at school, so I unfortunately didn't remember everything." She was about to hand him the book but hesitated. "I, um, didn't finish my annotations. I'm at the part where Pip just learned the true identity of his benefactor. I still have some interesting things to write about *that*."

"Indeed." The real-life similarity to their own situation wasn't lost on him. "You can rip out that page you wrote on and hang on to the book until you're done. I do want all your thoughts."

The intensity behind that last sentence rubbed her the wrong way.

"Now, see, that just reminds me that I don't get to have any of *your* thoughts. Like any information about your world, or even the crazy part of my world."

"How about this," Eddie reached for one of her hands and held it in both of his. "Tomorrow, during lunch, meet me at the Peacock Fountain behind the Art building. Come alone."

"Won't I just see you in the lunchroom though?"

"No. I won't have the rosary, so I won't be attending classes. I'll just meet you at the fountain during lunch, and then you put that rosary in my hand."

"Okay, and then what?"

"And then...we ditch school." Her eyes popped with alarm, and he chuckled. "Have you been to the planetarium yet?"

"No." She drew the word out as a smile spread on her face. She liked where this was going.

He tucked a wayward curl behind her ear. "I'll take you there and tell you all about the Fae and where they come from. I just can't explain the current situation that's going on now until I return from the Jäger Father. Deal?"

"Deal." She stuck her hand out so they could shake on it.

A realization dawned on her. She chewed the inside of her cheek as she thought it over.

"What is it, siren?" He touched her cheek. "You do that when you're worrying."

"This is a very open and honest moment we're having."

"I'm always honest."

"I'm not. With myself, I mean." She swallowed and felt the pounding increase in her chest. "I...like you, Eddie. I'm not scared of you anymore. I-I feel safe with you." She shrugged a shoulder. "And I'm sorry if that's not what you intended, but there it is. If I'm truly honest with myself, I actually consider you a friend now. I mean, I wouldn't be sitting here with you alone in this house at 2 a.m. if that weren't the case."

A tiny smile pulled at the edges of his mouth as he watched her intently. He opened his mouth to say something, but Belle put a finger to his lips. "I'm not finished." Her eyes zeroed in on his lips. *Gee, those are soft.* She ran her index finger across his bottom lip.

He nipped the tip of her finger, and she snatched her hand back.

"Focus, siren." His eyes were liquid gold.

"Right." Her breathing was embarrassingly erratic. "So, um, the last thing I want to tell you is that I believe you are really trying to do the right thing and protect as many innocent people as you can, even if...it's from me. If you have to, um, end me because I'm a threat, I'm telling you now that I-I guess I understand if you have to, eventually. And...I forgive you, ahead of time." She rambled to a close, "Although, I *do* want to live; I'm not suicidal."

He still hadn't moved, but his breathing had deepened. Slowly like a panther, he leaned toward her and laced his fingers with hers. "Then, I need to confess something to you, *friend*. I'd like your permission to kiss you." Her breathing stalled. "In the future." A smile played on his lips. "You see, as soon as I am able to, only a resounding *no* from you now will be able to hold me back when the time comes."

A kiss from Eddie. She wondered what that would be like. If that hug they shared earlier under the staircase was a preview, then, "Yes, you may."

He rewarded her by wetting his lips as he looked at hers. Then, those dark lashes lifted, meeting her eyes, and he gave her that famous haphazard grin.

She may have sighed, but she wasn't sure. She was a bit bedazzled at the moment.

"So, show me what you wrote down about the dream." He pointed at the book in her lap.

"Oh, right." She slowly tore the page from the back, feeling criminal for mutilating such a classic.

She started explaining the dream as he read the paper, but his growing alarm made her pause until he stood to his feet with the paper in hand. She stood too. "What is it?"

He swallowed and grabbed a fistful of his hair as he stared at the paper. "I-I need to go to the Jäger Father with this." He moved toward the door.

"Wait!" She followed him. "What about the Shadow Spawn in this house? A-And the planetarium tomorrow?"

He came up short and turned to face her. "Right." He held up the note. "Can I keep this?"

"Sure."

He pocketed it and scratched at his scalp. "Right after the planetarium tomorrow, I'll go."

She pouted. "While you're gone, what can *I* do? I can't just sit around while my uncle is off in Europe chasing Violet, you're meeting with the Jäger Father, and I'm stuck here pretending to live a normal life. I just-I just don't know what to do though." She was surprised to feel the hot tears well up. She walked back to the sofa and sat with her elbows on her knees, palming her cheeks. "I feel so inadequate, like a failure." Her voice caught on the last word.

Eddie joined her again on the couch. His thigh pressed against hers as he also sat with his elbows on his knees. "What exactly do you feel that you've failed at?"

"My mother. I feel like I've let her down. She sent me these images of Violet and what she was up to, clearly asking me for help. And all I've managed to do was give Violet what she wanted."

"When was the last time your mother sent you a vision?"

She paused. "It was that beast vision. Only this time, I wasn't watching from Violet and my mom's perspective, it was from the beast's. So this was really different. It didn't feel like it came from my mom, but how else would I have had that vision? She's the dream-catcher, and I'm the dream-seer. I see what she catches and gives me. Anyways, that's how I understand it."

"What if...what if *you* tried contacting her through a dream? Maybe you could glean more information about what Violet is up to."

"I don't know how to do that."

"Perhaps it's similar to what we were able to do, you know, under the staircase earlier today."

She blushed. "Go on."

He took a deep breath before continuing. "You have a type of tele-pathic power. Have you been able to see into anyone's else mind, other than mine and your mother's?"

She thought about it. "No. But with you, it's different than with my mom. She reached me, while I was able to reach you."

"And how did you do that?"

"Well, on the bus, when I guessed your age, you had the answer in your mind, and, I don't know, I just saw the number. White smokey numbers against blackness, and then the numbers faded."

"And under the stairs..." he prompted.

"I did what you suggested. I relaxed in your arms and then..."

"We both saw what we wanted. The lost memory."

She nodded. "So then, to reach my mom, I should relax, focus on her, and—"

"Think happy thoughts."

"What is it with that creed? Is that really a Fae-thing?"

"Yes, and it works. So when you think of your mom, you need to focus on happy memories with her."

"But I never knew her."

"Did your father ever tell you stories about her? Or did your aunt?"

"No. It was a taboo topic." Like the ding of a bell, she remembered something important. "But I do have her diary."

"That should work. Pick happy memories that she shared in the diary and focus on them."

She blinked and straightened as she looked at him. He arched a brow in response. A slow smile spread on her face. It mirrored that feeling that started unfurling inside her like wings that hadn't seen flight in a while and were finally stretching out their cricks. "Edward Helsing, how can I ever thank you? You've helped me find the purpose that was eluding me."

"Siren," he said, all serious as if she had said something wrong. "Stop making me feel like a savior. I'm the one that still has to hold you under the guillotine."

The smile fled her face, but as she looked into his eyes, she only saw sadness and regret there, not threats. "I know that," she said softly. "And you'll only let that blade come down if I'm too dangerous to be kept alive. I told you, I already understand."

After a thoughtful moment of silence, he reached over and squeezed her knee, the right side of his mouth tipping up. "I thought we had Shadow Spawn to hunt here."

"Yes. We do." She clapped her hands once, surprised at her own enthusiasm and how fast she dropped all other concerns.

He grinned and leaned back against the couch cushions. "Well, step one is we watch Monica here make her dozen lasagnas." She gave him a questioning stare, as she settled back into the couch. "If you're enjoying yourself for too long," he explained, "there will be no negative energy to feed from, so then the Shadow Spawn eventually gets hungry. It'll usually do something subtle to frighten you so that it can feed again."

She shivered. "That is so creepy."

He stretched his arm along the back of the couch. "So, in the meantime, we enjoy the show, and they'll make their presence known soon."

"A little hard to enjoy myself now after hearing that, but I'll try." She scooted away a bit since her cushion was sinking into his side.

It only took one more episode to cry with laughter and forget about shadow hauntings. Many times, Belle caught Eddie staring at her as she laughed. When she finally asked him if she had drool on her chin or something, he merely looked away, the tips of his ears flaming. But afterward, he made a conscientious effort not to stare and then got sucked into the show as well.

She liked his laugh.

"You're the one staring now, siren." His eyes glowed softly when they locked with hers.

"Was not." And she turned to watch Paolo make a pass at Phoebe in the massage parlor. "Oh no, he didn't," she commented as Candy would have. "Phoebe needs to tell Rachel."

A clanging sound came from the kitchen, and they both stiffened.

Eddie took her hand in his. "Follow my lead, okay?"

She nodded, her heart starting to race. He led her off the couch, and she followed close behind, almost completely pressed against his back as he headed toward the kitchen. He paused at the breakfast table.

A shadowy movement flickered in the corner, and then the refrigerator rattled.

She squeezed the hand at his side, and she pressed tighter into his back, gripping a fistful of his shirt in her other hand.

He held their clasped right hands out before them, pointing in the direction of the disturbance. "Can you call your power forth at will?" he asked over his shoulder.

She whispered back, "It only works when I think I'm in danger, I'm really scared, or..."

"Or?"

"It's too embarrassing."

There was a pause, and then, "Oh, I see." He cleared his throat. "And you're not frightened or threatened enough because I'm here, so...that leaves the third option." Before she realized what was happening, he quickly shifted so that he was behind her now.

"What are you doing?" she whisper-screeched.

"Activating our nuclear option." He splayed a hand on her hip and gently hauled her back against him. A heat in her chest flared at the full-body contact, but he wasn't done. "Remember at Annie's Antiques, when I got close to you," he whispered through her hair, "and touched you to help you grip the wizard staff properly?" At those words, a fire had started beneath her skin. "You zapped me. I suppose you were...feeling a certain way." He loosened his grip on their clasped hands and caressed the tips of her fingers.

"This nuclear option is so humiliating," she groaned half-heartedly.

"But fun." She could hear the sinful smile in his voice. As he swept her hair aside, goosebumps broke along the trail his touch had left from her scalp to her neck. "Beautiful," he murmured. He grazed his lips like a whisper along her exposed neck, from her ear to her clavicle.

"You are behaving scandalously, Mr. Helsing," she breathed out. But she drew his arm tighter around herself as if snuggling deeper into his embrace.

Soon, a popping and crackling was heard, and she felt a familiar heat in the hand that Eddie was holding. He held out their joined hands before them. It was encased in an electrical orb.

"And *you* are perfectly divine, Ms. Montague."

That sent a delicious tingle down her spine, but before she could swoon, the refrigerator doors burst open, and the electric orb flew from their hands and struck the Shadow Spawn that flitted out squarely in the chest. It looked down at itself as the orb spread out like an electrified net over its body, crackling brighter until the shadow dissipated along with the charge.

A beat of shock passed as they stared at the now empty spot of air. And then, "We did it! We got the shadow man!" Belle bounced on the balls of her feet and clapped her hands.

"Bullseye, siren. You're a natural." He grinned down at her with something like pride. Elated, she held her hands up for double high-fives which he promptly met with resounding slaps. "We've got one left. The big one, the Stay Puft Marshmallow Man."

She stared at him. "I think you may have fried your brain when you borrowed my power."

He chuckled. "Never mind."

"Are we going to have to, you know, get up close and personal again? Because that wouldn't be, um, *efficient* for any time I need to call upon my power."

"Agreed. We'll reserve that as last resort." And then with a wicked smile, he added, "Unless you ever feel like it's our best option."

She faked an impatient sigh. "How are we going to get marshmallow man then?"

He glanced at the clock on the oven. "It's three in the morning. You should really get to sleep."

She looked taken aback. "I can't sleep knowing I'm in the belly of some house-sized shadow monster!"

"I'll take care of this one. You need to go to sleep in your room, with your door locked."

"Yes, Dad."

"I'm serious."

"Lock my door because you're going to use the Jäger, right?"

"Correct."

"And I should be afraid of you–I mean, the Jäger–coming into my room?"

He gritted his teeth. "Yes."

"Because he might kiss me to death?"

He growled. "This is not a joke, siren."

"Okay, okay, sorry. But there's no way I'm falling asleep. I'm too pumped. I wanna hunt again—can I say that now?—and I'm still too frightened to be left alone." She was jittery with energy like she'd just knocked back two espresso shots.

"*I'm* hunting this one. Alone. You'll have more opportunities to hunt other Shadow Spawn, especially after I've trained you."

She started bouncing from one foot to another. "Okay, now I'm just *too* excited."

"Do I need to use a pressure point to render you unconscious?"

"I don't know, maybe. Can you really do that?" She gasped as he reached for a spot between her shoulder and neck. "You wouldn't!"

He pinched, and she was out cold.

Crouching Beast, Hidden Jäger

Belle's ears perked up as drunken laughter reached them. She spit out the last of the rabbit's bones and stalked toward the sound, keeping her head low to the ground. In the pitch blackness of the forest, she easily spied the glow of the crackling campfire through the trees. Several tents were pitched and a group of young adults, college-aged, were spread out sitting on logs about the campfire. They knocked back beers and roared with laughter at what looked like someone performing in a game of Charades.

They would be oblivious to her approach. They were trespassing in *her* territory. The mistress didn't allow her to kill humans, it would draw too much attention, but she was surely allowed to frighten them, and she couldn't be blamed if one of them found their way into her jaws, and she crunched down and had just a taste.

She lapped her tongue over her lips at the thought.

"Craving a 4 a.m. snack? Peacock just not doing it for you any-more?" A British man's chiding voice came from somewhere off to her side.

Instinctively, she swiveled her whole body to face him and growled. She felt her claws elongate, puncturing the packed dirt.

A shadow emerged from behind a tree. Its eyes glowing bright yellow like a cat's in the darkness. "You're not a wolf at all, are you?"

The hairs along her back stood as she arched in warning and sent a ripple of snarls into the cold night air.

"And you're no bear either." A light wind swirled leaves around. The shadow made a sniffing sound. "Curious…no unnatural scent."

A flurry of leaves smacked into the shadow. It was man then, flesh and blood, something Belle could sink her teeth into. Salivating, she let out a bark as she rushed at the stranger.

In a flash she barely registered, the man dashed two steps *toward* her, and just as she reached him with her maw wide open, he leapt to the side, spring-boarded off a nearby tree and side-kicked her in the ribs. She let out a yelp as she crashed into an opposite tree.

But just as quickly, she scrambled to her feet and faced him.

He stood in a swathe of moonlight that had broken through the canopy, revealing that he was dressed like a military operative on a nighttime mission. Ignoring her growls as she primed to strike again, he cocked his head. "Your eyes. They're human." He sounded shocked, but untouched by fear.

She would give him something to fear. She reared back on her haunches.

He reflexively moved into a defensive stance.

She continued to rise, rise as his eyes followed and those yellow orbs grew wider, until she reached her full height and stared down across the way at the man.

"Werewolf," he whispered. As if the word were a trigger, ribbons of black smoke snaked out from his right wristband and curled up his arm toward his shoulder, over his entire body. The smoke solidified like a second skin, and now he truly resembled a shadow.

A distant memory of a word, a warning, brushed against her mind. *Jäger.*

And she could feel it now, the cowardly human in her telling her to run. But the Beast was in play now, and it would be against her predator instinct to turn tail and become prey. She rolled her shoulders back and cracked her neck from side to side, as the boxer side of her human would.

Sensing an attack coming, the Jäger's golden eyes flashed and he cooed with a steely edge to his voice, "Steady now, mate. I don't want to kill you. You're clearly under a curse. I can help you."

The Beast snapped her hands open at her sides so that her claws flashed, and with her massive chest puffed out, took one step forward and let out a bone-rattling, "*Roooaaarr!*"

The forest erupted with the frantic flight of birds from the canopy and the wild pitter-patter of creatures escaping through the brush. The revelry of the campers in the distance fell silent.

The Jäger flexed open his right hand at his side. "Now that you've gotten that off your chest..." Wisps of shimmery golden glitter emanated from his hand, elongating and solidifying into a golden thick chain. He closed his hand over it as the other end of the chain landed with a heavy thud on the ground. He twisted his wrist, the chain coiling around his fist. "It's time for your obedience lessons." He patted his thigh and whistled. "Here, boy."

With a roar of rage, the Beast blitzed toward him, but her talons tore through air because the Jäger had leapt over her in a flip and lassoed the heavy chain around her neck. He landed nimbly on his feet behind her some yards away and yanked the chain. She choked as it tightened around her neck like a vise.

He dug his heels into the ground and pulled the chain toward him, one hand over the other. "C'mon, mate," he grunted. "Just roll *over.*"

She struggled against him—he was strong!—but she was strong, too. Just as black spots were appearing in her vision, she gripped the chain and gave a giant tug. The Jäger went sailing past her, crashing deep into the shrubbery. She loosened the chain from her neck and cast it aside, but it disappeared in a shower of gold before it hit the ground.

She dashed into the shrubs, pawing and swiping. She could almost taste his flesh now. But the minutes dragged on, and she came up empty.

A cellular ringtone of a Beatles song came from the tree, right above her head. A sigh followed, and then, "Siren, I thought I left you asleep."

The Beast leapt onto the trunk, sinking her claws into the bark, and climbed toward the voice.

"You're rambling. Slow down."

She pounced on the spot, but not before the Jäger leapt down to the forest floor. Her eyes followed as he dashed into the line of trees.

"I'm playing hide-and-seek with it right now. Don't worry, siren, I've got this. Just tell me one thing, are you still wearing those little shorts with stars on them?"

She stalked on all fours now and kept her belly low to the ground. She tuned her sensitive ears to the hysterical girl's voice from the phone.

"Are you listening?! You're not going to be able to compel it! And then there's that stupid rock you trip over, and the beast bites you! Over and over!"

She launched herself, jaws wide and talons out, expecting the Jäger to lash back, but hoping she was faster than him. Instead, she found herself staring at a lone cellphone sitting on the ground, its screen lit up with the picture of a girl that jolted her with a painful sense of deja vu. She snarled at it.

The voice in the phone screamed. *"What was that?!"*

She swiped it away from her as if it were a poisonous snake in her path. It sailed wide and the Jäger caught it.

He stood in a small clearing, lit by a beam of moonlight. He raised the phone to his ear. "I'll see you tomorrow, siren. Wear the alien socks." He slid the phone into a pocket, which was more like black smoke swallowing the device.

The Beast entered the clearing, and the two slowly circled each other. "Did Violet Wickeby do this to you?" She paused with her paw mid-step at the utterance of her mistress's name. "Poor bloke. I'll take that as a yes. Think you can be a good boy and lead me back to your master?"

The Beast charged.

The Jäger's eyes flashed a brilliant yellow. "Stay," he commanded, one hand out indicating *Stop*.

She did pause, but she kept pawing at the ground, wanting to spring at him.

"Sit."

She sat back on her haunches, growling savagely and frothing at the mouth.

He relaxed his hand and straightened. "Lead me to Violet Wickeby."

Like a rubber band stretched too far, she felt the Jäger's control over her snap, and she lunged at him.

Taken off guard, the Jäger fell back, his heel scraping against a large moss-covered rock, but quickly shifted his balance so his mis-step angled him sideways, just in time to see the Beast's jaws snap at the air where his throat had been a second ago.

"Bloody hell," he whispered, "she was right."

The Beast landed on all fours, reared up quickly on her back two feet, and tackled the Jäger. He only had time to grab the Beast's maw between his two hands and keep it from clamping down on his face. That cost him. She raked her claws across his chest, shredding non-stop, but instead of cloth and blood, tendrils of black smoke billowed out.

In her pause of confusion at this, the Jäger delivered a powerful front kick to her chest, sending her flying back and crashing against a tree trunk. Leaves rained down. Slowly, she stood again and arched her arms out to the side as if stretching the cricks out of her back. Her eyes never leaving the Jäger's.

"You *will* yield. You *will* take me to Violet." He opened his right hand and a cloud of golden shimmer materialized until it formed an enormous collar that he closed his hand around. He raised it and snapped it open. "See this? You'll never be able to hide from me. I'll always know where you are."

Her ears flattened and her tail drooped. It was the first time she'd felt fear as the Beast.

It was the Jäger who went on the offensive this time. He darted at the Beast, side-stepped a swipe from her massive talons, and round-house kicked her in the face. She came back with another swipe, but that was dodged, and she was punished with a painful uppercut to her abdomen. She doubled-over, only for a split-second, but that was all the Jäger needed to close the collar around her neck with a metallic *clink*. He sprung away just as she reared up with a roar, tearing at the collar and trying to wrench her head free from it.

"Tell you what, mate. I'll give you a ten-second head start. I'll even count out loud and everything, and then, I'm going to come find you." He cocked his head. "One."

With a snarling grunt of defeat, she tore off in the direction of the campers, but a slash cut through the air by her ear and then wrapped itself around her ankle, tightening, and jolting her to a crashing halt against the ground.

"Not that way!" he warned. "Two."

She looked down at her ankle. The golden end of a whip was latched on. She wrenched it off and watched wide-eyed as the Jäger snapped the whip back toward him with a great *crack* that evaporated in a shower of gold dust.

"Three!"

She pushed off in a different direction toward a place she knew would give her the extra time she needed to lose him. A plan formed in her mind, and with his countdown sounding farther and farther away, she found the opening to the cave system that she was sure only she knew about. She spotted the familiar boulder squatting against the pine tree, and without stopping, dove through the fronds of a plant growing over the tree's giant, gnarled root that arched above the ground.

She fell in the darkness, tumbling until she popped up on her haunches and clambered to stand on her two feet so her back was against the rock wall. Catching her breath, she tried to focus her feral mind on her anchor. It was the face of an angel, a blonde girl with brilliant blue eyes. It was the only face that worked. She'd tried many other faces, focusing too long without success on one particular brunette's at first, but it was a face she'd already forgotten.

She squeezed her eyes tighter, focusing on the angel, and soon enough, she felt her body shrinking into itself like a balloon losing some of its air. The fur receded into her skin, and she felt the collar hang loosely about her neck. She yanked it off over her head and flung it across the space. It clanged against the rock wall and poofed into a golden mist.

With the coherence of human thoughts starting to form, the rest of Belle's dream slid into a black, meaningless void.

| 19 |

Schoolyard Brawl

Belle: **Are you alive?? You're not answering your phone!**

Eddie: **Sleeping. I'm sleeping.**

Belle: **I'm calling you now.**

.....

Belle: **You're still not answering!**

Eddie: **Woman, I'm trying to sleep.**

Belle: **You were almost dogfood last night. We need to talk about it.**

The next message from Eddie simply said **Me**, attached with a selfie shot that gave her an embarrassing burst of hot tingles everywhere. He looked asleep, face-up in bed, with one arm bent beneath his head. He was shirtless.

Eddie: **Now you.**

And the next text from him was a GIF of a Pomeranian yapping away in its sleeping owner's ear.

Fine, she thought, miffed. *Two can play that game.*

She grabbed her big scissors from her desk and posed as if she were threatening to stab him with it. She snapped a picture but hesitated before sending it. If she really wanted to make him suffer…. She pulled off her pajama shirt revealing a strappy white tank top that was a bit low-cut. She resumed the same pose, scissors in hand like a knife and her *Imma-stab-you* face.

The response was immediate.

Eddie: **Dammit, siren, I hate cold showers.**

After she recovered from her fit of giggles, she texted, **See you later?**

Eddie: **Definitely.**

Before she could analyze the origin of the goofy-grinned sigh that slipped out of her, she hopped off the bed to get ready for school.

Two odd things happened as soon as she stepped out of the house: a black cat zipped past her feet and into the first-floor museum. After ten minutes of not finding the cat, and Candy beeping the car horn at her from the driveway, she gave up and exited the house.

Two, a single, long-stemmed red rose was waiting for her on the porch swing. She held it up to show Candy, who put one hand over her mouth as if gushing. She laid it back down on the swing. Either Eddie or Liam had to be responsible for that rose. The thought filled her belly with butterflies, but she couldn't figure out if it was one or both boys who launched those butterflies.

At school, the red-rose mystery was solved as soon as she set foot in the school. Random guys, some of them in the school's royal blue football jerseys, each handed her a red rose and said, "From Liam."

Even G handed her one, with Kat at his side.

"Oww!" Belle cried out when she closed her hand over the rose. She peered more closely at it. It was laden with thorns. The other roses had clean stems.

G threw her a sinister grin. Kat drawled over her shoulder as they continued past Belle, "Later, loser."

Belle looked at the rose again. It was different from the others. It was a pinkish-red compared to the deep reds of the others. G or Kat must have swapped it out for a thorn-filled one. She tossed the offending flower into the nearest garbage can and washed her bloody palm in the girls bathroom. Thanks to her mutant healing ability, the cuts healed quickly.

In the afternoon, Belle plopped into her seat with her lunch tray. She lay the bundle of roses on the seat next to her.

"Let me guess. From Liam?" Cindy was back in her hoodie, but the silver eyeliner, pink lip gloss, and constant smile on her face happily reminded Belle she was seeing better days now. And Cindy was stunning, without even trying; just her smile was adornment enough.

"That's what each flower-guy said." Belle popped open the chocolate milk carton. "It's a really sweet gesture."

Cindy detected the hesitation in her tone. "But?"

"Well, it's kind of embarrassing. The football team giving me flowers, and everyone's looking and talking about it. I just *really* don't like the attention."

"That's exactly what I told him."

"Wait, so you knew about it beforehand?" Belle tried to ignore the stab of jealousy in her gut. "I mean, I guess maybe you would know since you two live in the same place now."

"I rarely see or talk to him. Yesterday we had an actual conversation when I ran into him in the garden, and it was about you."

Another green needleprick. She missed that garden. "Oh, sorry then. That must have been awkward."

"No, it's okay really. Fair warning though: Liam is set on winning you back."

"I-I know I still like him, I can't help it, but...he won't explain why he left me hanging without a word all this time."

Cindy finished off her fruit cup. "Maybe I can get it out of his assistant, Beatrix."

"What is she like?"

"I try to avoid her like the plague."

"Why?"

Cindy paused, giving it some thought. "She gives me the creepy Stepford-wife vibe."

Belle half-choked on her bite of chicken wrap.

Q looked warily over his laptop at Belle. "Do you require the Heimlich maneuver?"

She shook her head and downed some chocolate milk.

"Good." He looked relieved. "FYI, we have D&D tomorrow at 7:00 p.m. sharp."

Belle perked up. "Where?"

Q and Cindy looked at each other with matching smiles before they both said, "Rawlins Castle."

At her wide-eyed expression, Cindy hurried on. "Liam's not going to be there if that helps."

Belle found that it did help. While Liam's physical presence was titillating, engaging with him at this point made her way too anxious. Yes, Liam was making an effort with the roses, but she couldn't get past his secret for deserting her. That was the wall that Liam would have to knock down between them if he was actually serious about winning her back.

And the several times she'd wanted Eddie to kiss her? For that, she blamed whatever hunter-magnetism he exuded to lure her in as prey. She was sure of it. He was a walking pheromone to her. That resting smolder look, his insanely unnatural good looks, and just his whole being was alluring to her. The perfect predator.

Why was she kidding herself? Eddie wasn't preying on her; he was practically her friend at this point, even though he reminded her sometimes that she was still his Jäger-target. Or more like he kept reminding *himself.* Jeez, she must really have a bad case of Stockholm syndrome if she kept thinking of her potential assassin as a potential bestie.

"Why don't you come over earlier, and we can hang out?" Cindy grew more excited as she spoke. "I can get your measurements for the pageant dress, and I can show you the designs I've been working on. You can tell me which ones you like best."

"That sounds amazing!" Belle could see herself now. Re-visiting Grandmere, the name she'd given the wisteria tree in the rose garden, and sitting in the alcove of the library that she thought in her humble opinion was worthy of a king's palace.

The girls agreed to walk together tomorrow after school directly to the castle. After bagging the rest of her lunch and getting directions from Q for the quickest way to the Peacock Fountain, Belle excused herself from the table.

As she made her final turn around the corner past the boys locker room, excitement began to fill her. She and Eddie were going to ditch class and go to the planetarium where he was going to tell her all about the Fae. All at once, she felt like a rebel and a geek.

The white circular stone fountain was big enough for a children's pool party. A statuesque peacock with its tail feathers fanned out stood in the center, a stream of water arcing from its mouth. Around the fountain was nothing but patchy grass and clay tiles overgrown with weeds. Beyond it in the distance lay the athletics field.

There was one other sight by the fountain that stole Belle's attention. Eddie sat on the fountain's ledge, leaning forward on his elbows, staring pensively at two big red ants duking it out on the ground before him. His midnight hair fell over his forehead. He was out of school uniform and in an army green crewneck sweater and dark jeans. Belle herself was wearing a tan cardigan over her uniform shirt that brought out the light brown color of her hazel eyes.

A crisp chill invaded the air. It was the start of a Rhode Island winter, but according to Candy, not yet cold enough to pull out the Ugg boots.

Before she piped up with a cheery hello, she recalled the way things had last been left between them: flirty text this morning, and before that, Belle dreaming of Eddie battling it out with a beast, a werewolf actually.

Eddie looked like he'd had the upperhand in that fight, but the werewolf had *shredded* his chest. Maybe the Jäger hadn't been hurt by it, but was Eddie hurt and just downplaying the severity of the injury?

"You coming any closer, siren?" He was looking at her, one eyebrow arched in amusement.

Apparently, she had been standing some feet away, lost in thought while staring at him.

"Oh, of course."

He stood as she approached, and she couldn't help the way her eyes tracked him as he did.

The very air between them felt magnetized. She bet if she closed her eyes, she could still find him. No Marco Polo necessary.

That Jäger juju was strong.

"Keep looking at me that way, siren, and you're going to cost me the progress I've made without my rosary." His eyes flashed gold before settling back to their normal caramel.

Right. Tread lightly. No flirting, intentional or not. She didn't want to be accosted by his kiss. Or did she?

"Who's your other admirer?" He was eyeing the roses cradled in her arms.

"Other?"

He raised an eyebrow as if the answer was obvious. Oh, right. Him.

"But you are more stalker than admirer," she corrected, nonetheless blushing from head to toe.

Ignoring that, he asked, "So you *are* giving the Rawlins boy a second chance?"

"Um," she definitely didn't want to have this conversation with him, so she deflected. "I brought you a chicken wrap, in case you still haven't eaten." She handed it to him. "Well, half of one, anyway. I ate the other half."

He gave her his wide, side grin and slipped into a crisp, British accent. "Ah, milady, you come bearing gifts." He unwrapped it and said before biting into it, "Allow me to reciprocate this evening with dinner."

Oh sugar. He can't be milady-ing her in that fancy accent. Didn't he know that was a shortcut to her heart?

She cleared her throat. "I would be delighted, milord." And she curtsied. Actually curtsied. "So you're not leaving right after the planetarium?" Why, oh why, was she feeling something ballooning in her chest?

He polished off his last bite and said in plain old American English, "Not with a werewolf around. Especially one controlled by Violet Wickeby. It's already massacred a slew of peafowls, and it was mighty interested in the campers last night, so I *have* to capture it soon."

"I want to help you."

He balked. "You're helping me by staying with Candy and her grandmother until your uncle returns home. Please, promise me this."

"But Violet's not allowed to harm me. It's a deal she made with my mother. I should be safe in my own home."

He pressed his lips into a thin line. "Crime's up in this town. Shadow Spawn are spreading faster because of the evil magic present with Violet and this werewolf. Yes, you can defend yourself with your electrical power, but if you lose control and kill an innocent? I-I don't want to do what I would have to do, Belle."

He'd said her name. There was a sadness and urgency as he said it, which is why she said, "Fine. I'll ask Candy if I can stay with her. But you know I can still help you. Last night was the second time I dreamt as the werewolf. I was able to see through Violet because it was my mom's body and connection with her mind, but I have absolutely no idea why I'm seeing through this creature now. And Violet didn't seem to be aware of my presence like she had been when I would see through my mom." She reached out and absentmindedly brushed a fuzzy lint off his sleeve. "I wonder if my mother has anything to do with this now. I know that before, my mother used the connection to help me see what Violet was up to, so now, she's letting me see what this creature is up to. So I can stop it. See? This is why I need to help! Isn't the werewolf supposed to be a human? Maybe I can help by dealing with its human counterpart."

Eddie released a deep breath. "Okay, siren, you'll be the Watson to my Sherlock."

She beamed, and he grinned back, so they were both left momentarily bedazzled by the other. Just as he was finally going to say something else, his attention snagged over her shoulder, and he frowned. She turned to look and felt stones drop in her stomach.

The football team had emerged from a backdoor near the boys locker room. She saw Dmitri's red-haired, hulking figure leading the team out to the field. About half of the tail end of the group, led by G, spotted Eddie and Belle, and started heading toward them. The expressions on their faces spelled trouble.

"Siren," Eddie said in a low voice, "whatever happens, try not to lose control." He nodded towards a security camera posted nearby. "In fact, why don't you wait for me by my Jeep in the school parking lot."

"It's a good thing you can't compel me then because I'm not leaving you to face them alone."

He threw her a smirk, but a softness invaded his eyes. "Admirable sentiments, but you might not like what you see, and I don't want to go super saiyan in public if you somehow get hurt."

"Super-*what*?" She shook her head. "Can't you just *tell* him to go away like you did on the bus?"

"I could, but what would be the fun in that?"

G, with his spiky dark hair and frosted tips, stopped in front of Eddie. "Second time I find you trying to put the moves on the Beast's girl."

Eddie's brows snapped together in confusion. "Beast?"

"He means Liam," Belle said. She turned on G, "Did he put you up to this?" Outrage was filling her like a noxious gas.

"All we know," G gestured to the group behind him scowling like a pack of dogs, "if we help Liam with you—like with the flowers and shit—then he said he'd come back as quarterback, starting with the upcoming Homecoming game."

"Unbelievable," she seethed.

"So that means," G stepped close enough so that he was almost nose to nose with Eddie, "back off, punk." At the last word, he shoved his index finger into Eddie's shoulder.

Eddie's lips twitched, containing a smile. He looked past G at the five football players closing in, rubbing their fists, and then at Belle's wide-eyed, *don't-do-it* look. She knew he wanted the fight like a kid wanted a toy, so when he sighed and showed his palms in surrender, she understood he'd done it for her sake.

"You're right," Eddie said, backing away. "I'll go now. See you later, Belle."

"Eddie, wait—" She only got two steps in Eddie's direction before G's hand closed over her arm, hard.

"Where do you think you're going?" G said.

Belle was just about to rip her arm out of his grip and give him a piece of her mind, but Eddie was already by her side, peeling G's hand away from her arm and bending it sideways in a way that made him cry out and sink to his knees.

"The lady goes wherever she wishes," Eddie said, his tone like a blade's edge and the British accent emerging with the last few words.

He was losing control.

She had only enough time to step aside as the other guys lunged for Eddie. Unfortunately, she tripped over her own feet, tumbled backward over the fountain's edge, and landed with a great splash. The frigid iciness of the water shocked her senses like a Russian slapping contest. She scrambled to her feet, thoroughly soaked, her roses fanning out all over the water's surface.

A breathless Eddie was already there, extending a hand. "You okay, luv?"

She wanted to say *yes* as she took his hand and stepped out, but three things robbed her of speech: first, her body was a frozen ice sculpture; next, glancing at her surroundings revealed students now changing classes in the hallways, with some of them venturing towards them with cell phones poised as cameras, so they were officially about to become a *scene*, especially with four football players sprawled on the ground, including G, groaning in pain and cradling various body parts, all thanks to super-ninja Eddie; and finally, the biggest thief, was Eddie's face itself just inches from hers, eyes abnormally luminous with concern, and his strong hands stroking her arms, trying to rub heat into them.

"Are you alright, luv? Talk to me." And full British now.

She shook her head, reaching out a trembling hand toward his yellow, fluorescent eyes.

Understanding, he squeezed them shut. He pulled his glasses from his pocket and slid them on. "We've got to get out of here."

"Hey!"

Belle saw it coming, and she was sure Eddie did too, but when he didn't move to defend himself, only to stand protectively in front of Belle, she knew he was letting it happen, whether it was because his self-control was on a razor's edge, or the spectators with phone-cameras were closing in, or probably both.

As soon as Eddie turned to face the shouter—who turned out to be Shawn from literature class, one of the two remaining football players still standing—a large fist connected with Eddie's jaw, sending his glasses flying off.

Shawn stepped back and shook out his hand. "Dang, dude's got a jaw like Kanye."

"Stop it!" Belle shoved him, and her eyes, and everyone else's, popped open with how far back he flew.

Eddie grabbed her hand and squeezed. "Don't." His lips were pressed into a hard line, but he wouldn't raise his eyes.

She felt her nerves jittering as much as the goosebumps racing over her icy skin. The second football guy—Corey, as he was called by a bystander—was helping Shawn up, while the crowd was starting to take on the frenzied energy of a ringside MMA match, egging on more violence. She also noticed some of the other football players starting to make their way back from the field.

Hastily, she whipped off the rosary, and before Eddie could object, drew it over his head and tucked the cross into his shirt.

Immediately, a deep sigh escaped him and he lifted his eyes. They were still glowing.

She shook her head. "Th-They're still…you need your glasses." She pointed at where they lay, and when Eddie bent down to retrieve them, Corey drove a vicious uppercut into his stomach.

Just as Belle launched herself toward the cretin, Eddie collared her by the stomach. She struggled against his hold, her back to his chest. "Let me at 'em!" she cried.

The crowd roared their approval, but her ears honed in on the crackling sound coming from her hands.

Eddie heard and saw, too. His hands immediately relinquished her hips to cocoon her hands. He put his lips to her ear, "Belle, it's not worth it."

And with his fingers tightly laced through hers, she felt the heated energy in her palms extinguish, and she huffed out a deep breath that had her curving back against him. It was only a second of full body contact. Like the flicker of lights briefly plunging the room into darkness, everyone around them disappeared, and it was just her and the all-consuming, protective male pressed in close behind her.

And the second was gone. The scene unmuted, the din hurt her ears again, the crowd's faces recrystallized, and all those phones pointed at her and Eddie, recording the next juicy piece of gossip, especially considering the romantic-looking position they were in.

She tore from his grasp and ignored the sharp stab of pain that reverberated through her body.

What was that?

She'd have to analyze that later because at that moment the first football player reached them from the field, parting the crowd right behind Eddie. It was Thiago. And from Belle's peripheral vision, another figure shoved through and came running toward them, calling out, "Eddie!"

Was that Millie?

Just as Thiago opened his mouth, "What's going—" Millie tackled him, both hitting the ground with a *thud* and another roar from the crowd. She scrambled off him, and Thiago, still flat on his back, yelled at her, "What the hell?!"

"You were going to attack him from behind!" Millie shouted back. "Your football thugs were already beating him up!"

Thiago slapped Shawn's helping hand away and shot to his feet. "Are you kidding?! Then why are all these other cats on the floor, huh? We were watching from the field—your boy Kung-fu dropped them all in a matter of seconds!"

"Millie," Eddie said softly, "please, stay out of it."

Millie's eyes flashed to Belle. "What happened?"

There was something about her tone that made Belle grimace as if she were really asking, "*Why are you here with my crush?*"

"Excellent question, Millicent Kwan-Yin," Dr. Earheart announced from behind. The crowd parted further as she approached, a red-headed thundercloud, eyes narrowed behind her glasses. She stood in their midst, hands primed on her hips, and glared at every single one of them, including the injured on the ground. "Why don't we *all* have this conversation in my office. Follow me, now!"

While following the principal through the thick of the crowd, Eddie grabbed Belle's hand and they slipped away, oblivious of Millie's incensed stare.

| 20 |

That Juju Feeling

Belle found herself in the passenger seat of Eddie's black Jeep Wrangler heading out of the school parking lot and onto the main road. She toyed with the cross in her hands, the rosary hanging around her neck again at Eddie's insistence.

"W-w-won't we g-g-get in even m-more tr-trouble?" She asked, her jaw practically vibrating. Without the adrenaline rush of the brawl they'd just escaped from, the wet chill had soaked clear through to her bones now.

"Change of plans." He pulled over beneath a cluster of tall trees. "We're not going to make it back to your house for your change of clothes before hypothermia sets in. Come on."

He climbed out and headed towards the back of the Jeep. Belle followed, feeling like a walking accordion.

"It's n-not th-that b-bad," she tried to argue.

The long window of the trunk opened upwards while the bottom half was a door that pulled out sideways. He rummaged around until he found what he was looking for. It was her purple Girl Power t-shirt.

He started peeling off his sweater, but the undershirt started lifting up as well, revealing pristine washboard abs.

Without thinking, she reached out a hand and touched his stomach, amazed that he didn't have a scratch on him after she saw the creature rake its claws into him over and over.

And his skin felt like fire.

He recoiled at her touch, and she jumped back. "S-s-sorry."

"Your fingers are like ice."

She wanted to explain why she'd touched him, but that would require too many words for her useless mouth to form.

He'd already taken his sweater off and tossed it next to the purple shirt. He was left in a black fitted, short-sleeved undershirt.

Hellooo biceps! We meet again.

That's it. Her brain was already fully hypothermic.

He gestured toward the shirt and sweater. "Change," he said gruffly. He turned around and created a space of privacy for her. Hedged into the corner of the open trunk, with the door, dark-tinted windows, and the Eddie-wall, it did seem like she couldn't be seen by any onlookers.

Her wet sweater landed with a slap in the trunk. The buttons on her blouse became troublesome with her trembling fingers. "B-b-buttons," was all she could manage as a complaint.

"Need help?"

"N-no." She blushed. "In your d-dreams."

"Indeed."

She ignored that.

Finally, she had the dry shirt and sweater on, but the wet hair, undergarments, and pants still had her trembling. "D-Done."

He turned around. "You're still shaking."

His eyes were luminous and starting to take on that predatory look. It reminded her of that Eric Carmen song, "Hungry Eyes."

"But not as m-much. Th-Thank you." She bunched the oversized sleeves in her hands and hugged herself. The sweater came down to her knees.

His eyes glowed more intensely as they trailed over her, probably enjoying the sight of her in his clothing.

An icy shiver suddenly convulsed through her. Dagnabbit, she was still freezing. Eddie looked comfortable in his thin t-shirt and exposed skin, as if the cold didn't affect him as much as it did her. Maybe Jäger body temperature naturally ran higher?

She could use some of that right now.

"B-body heat?" she suggested.

He gave her the *Come again?* look.

"Y-You're hot."

He blinked. Like he was trying to figure out how to even respond. Normally, he'd say something snarky like *I know,* but the fact that she'd been half-naked just a minute ago right behind him, was now wearing his sweater, and asking for his body heat? Was she *trying* to break him? He knew her to be sensible, but she knew he was without his rosary, his control teetering on edge.

It'd taken hours of deep meditation and prayer this morning to reach that level of steady self-control he was familiar with when he always had the rosary on. But more than any of that, he realized, he wanted Belle to keep the rosary on until she learned to control her own powers. His fear of having to finish Belle because she killed an innocent was becoming greater than his fear of not being able to stop Dommedag.

She was becoming his kryptonite.

And so he stood dumbstruck for a moment trying to sort this all out and restrain himself from gathering her into his arms all at once.

"Hug?" Belle amended, a noticeable tint coloring her cheeks. "Y-Your sk-skin is warm."

She blushed easily. He loved it. It was a rare quality among women these days.

So she does want to be in my arms. He made his lungs restart. *She's cold, that's all,* he admonished his Jäger-side.

"Come," he finally said. He sat against the Jeep's bumper and held out an arm.

She followed and sat up next to him so her feet dangled, and huddled into his side, keeping her own arms to her chest, while he wrapped both arms around her and rested his chin atop her head.

Soon, a shiver coursed through her, but it wasn't from the cold. His warmth was seeping deep into her skin. She was purring inside.

"Mmm, you're so warm. Can you be my official snuggle buddy?"

"No."

He'd said it so drily, she laughed. "Are Jäger incapable of snuggling? Because you, sir, feel like a pro."

"This is a medical emergency." But she detected a note of humor in his tone.

"Indeed," she said, copying him.

His chest puffed once as if he'd laughed inside. One of his hands began slowly running up and down her arm, rubbing more warmth into her. They stayed this way for a few minutes.

"So…" she began.

"So."

"Sooo, Sherlock, what are we going to do about the werewolf?"

His hand stilled.

"I *am* helping, remember?"

He sighed with resignation. "Only with the research, my dear Watson."

Thoroughly toasty now, she leaned away and straightened so she could see his face.

He also leaned back on his hands and looked thoughtfully at her, long enough that Belle felt like she was being scrutinized.

"What?" she asked.

"How are you not terrified? There's an actual werewolf loose in this town—a massive one—and I get the feeling this is an exciting Nancy Drew case for you."

"I-I am scared. But I'm connected to this, so...I guess my feeling of purpose is greater than my fear." She huffed. "Or so I hope. It's most likely a delayed panic attack. Ask me again tonight after dinner. I think the idea of a real-life werewolf will have thoroughly marinated in my brain by then."

"So, we *are* having dinner tonight," he repeated, a crooked smile splintering his face.

"Or, whenever," she amended, realizing with a blush that she totally ran with the dinner card he'd proposed earlier. Eager much? "So, anyways, I'm researching the werewolf. I can start with the Google," she offered.

"The Google?" he repeated with a laugh.

"Hey, I never had access to the Internet until I got here."

"What else did your father keep from you?"

"Nuh-uh. Focus." She pressed one playful finger against the tip of his nose. "Werewolf," she drew the word out. "We can swap life stories later. Besides, I'm dying to know how you're a priest."

He clapped his hands once and leaned forward. "Right, so werewolf."

She laughed. He obviously didn't want to talk about the priest-part.

"You can come up with a list of suspects for me," he said. "From my run-in with the creature in the forest, the human is male with light green eyes and blonde hair. Given the creature's height when he stood on his hind legs, the man is about 6'3" and would have to be well-built. This guy hits the gym."

Her stomach hollowed out. "That sounds like Liam," she whispered. "Could it be possible? You said he didn't smell enchanted, though."

"He didn't. But neither did the werewolf. I should have easily smelled the magic on the creature. So this can only mean one thing:

Violet used a potions master, as you said in your dream, to concoct a brew for masking the smell of magic."

"Oh no."

"It gets worse. I can't simply magic-stab the evil out of him as I did for you in the greenhouse. I need Violet to break the lycan spell, or…"

"Or, what?"

"I could send the demon back to hell with my blade and all her spells would be broken."

"Great! That's the answer! Stick Violet, and then Liam and my mother will both be free." She tossed out her arms to embrace him, but he caught both wrists.

"The werewolf might not be Liam. You'll help me scout out the potential suspects in this town and keep track of the list." He lowered her hands to her lap and gripped them both in one of his large hands. "You also work on dream-connecting with your mother and see if you can figure out where Violet is." He bit the corner of his bottom lip. "But, um, when it comes to freeing your mother, there's a catch."

The gravity of his tone wiped the hopeful smile off her face. "What is it?"

"At this point, your mother can't physically survive for long without Violet."

"What do you mean? You magic-stabbed me, and I'm fine. Better, actually."

"You said Abigail was possessed on Halloween 2004. That's over fifteen years now. And from the memory I witnessed in your mind of you yourself being possessed by Violet, it almost killed you. Violet died three-hundred years ago and had all that time to fester with bitterness and revenge until she could finally unleash it. She's not a demon that simply possesses a host, she consumes it. She's practically a dybbuk by now."

"But…that injection the Fae gave me. William Rawlins. He injected me with a gold substance and-and it reversed Violet's effects."

"Will wasn't a Fae." His voice dripped with sadness now. "He was the first Jäger who refused to kill his target—his own wife, your mother."

She swallowed hard. She remembered the memory she saw in her mother's or Violet's mind: William standing at the edge of a cliff, drink in hand, tears streaking down his cheeks, before he closed his eyes and let himself fall forward. "He killed himself. He killed himself, so he wouldn't have to kill my mom."

Eddie tucked a wayward curl behind her ear. "Good news: the Fae rescued Will from the water, took him to their world, and revived him."

"Oh, that's wonderful then, I guess, but why did they do that?"

"The Fae love stories. It's their livelihood. They rewarded Will for the grand twist in his story that they never saw coming: the Jäger sacrificing his life for true love."

"That's quite the Hallmark movie," she said quietly.

After a spell of silence, she frowned. "Hold on, from what you said, it sounds like the Fae are always watching us or something." Outrage started to prickle at her. "Are we just entertainment for them?" She threw her hands up. "Is this all like that *Truman Show* movie?"

"Not exactly. It's okay, really. But if you don't mind, we'll talk about that later." He reached over with one hand and reclaimed her hands in his. "The other good news is that if we can get our hands on some pixie dust, we can revive your mother after I exorcise Violet."

She palmed her forehead and moaned, "I gave it to Violet. It was a jar of gold pixie dust that Papa had since forever."

He nodded. "She probably wanted it for strengthening the potions' effects." He rubbed his chin. "Okay, so that complicates matters."

Belle groaned.

"But I do know where I can get more pixie dust."

"You do?" Her eyes lit up, but at the sight of Eddie's face going slightly pale after his last sentence, she asked, "Where will you get it?"

"At a bridge I'll cross when I get there." There was a note of worry in his voice.

Belle laced her fingers with his. "It's going to be okay." She smiled encouragingly when he met her eyes.

He dipped his chin. "You're comforting *me?*"

"Yes." A mischievous grin parted her lips. "Because sometimes in our lives, we all have pain, we all have sorrow, but if we are wise, there's always—"

"To-mor-roow," he finished with a crazy grin. "Really? *Lean on Me,* Bill Withers?"

She shrugged her shoulders. "I thought it was appropriate."

"Why are we so weird?"

"Define weird, mister."

"*We* are the definition of weird."

She thought for a moment. "Okay, you're right. I can wield electricity, and you're a 300-year-old hottie who still watches cartoons."

His eyes flashed, and he looked comically aghast. "Take it back, siren. You know it's called anime."

"Nope," she raised her pointer finger in the air, "I cannot tell a lie." She was mocking him again.

The effect was instantaneous. With a yelp, she was instantly immobilized against his side. She'd already had her arms crossed against herself in a hug, so he simply grabbed both of her hands at her sides from behind so she couldn't un-hug herself. "Last chance," he warned against her ear.

"Or what?" she challenged back. "I'll zap you until you fry."

"I'm immune, remember? At most, you'll give me a tan."

"Weren't we supposed to be talking about werewolves and pixie dust?" she said offhandedly.

"And as usual, our conversation has gone off the beaten path." He squeezed her in tighter against his side and brought his cheek parallel with hers. If she turned her head in his direction, their lips would collide.

She was mighty tempted.

"Focus, siren. We're talking about something very important. I need you to say," he grabbed her chin and squeezed her cheeks at each syllable, "a-ni-me."

But letting go of one of her hands was a mistake. She whipped out of his hold and faced him, but he still had her other wrist. "Cartoons! You watch cartoons!"

A devilish smile spread across his lips. "Oh, you're getting it now."

But as he tugged her back toward him, her palm connected with his chest and delivered an electrical blast. His chest contracted once, and his startled gaze mirrored her own.

She snatched her hand away, and they both looked down at his chest. There was a burn-hole stretching from the collar to the top of his stomach, as if the shirt had been ripped open, Superman-style. The hole framed quite the view. Enough that "Wow" slipped out of Belle's mouth.

"I mean *wow* I did that," she corrected quickly.

He smirked at her and looked back down at himself again. He slowly dragged a hand down the exposed chest area.

Oh. My. Word. She blinked hard, tipping her chin up to force her eyes upward. She wasn't about to be caught shamelessly gaping at him.

"Are you—did I hurt you?" she squeaked.

"That...tickled. Any other person's insides would have been nuked though." He turned back to his trunk and found another shirt.

Belle studiously looked away as he changed.

"I thought this was supposed to suppress my powers." She pulled the rosary out of her shirt and traced the cross pendant.

He turned back to her, wearing a royal blue Elmridge High physical education t-shirt. He gently took the cross from her fingers and slid it back over the edge of her collar so it was hidden under her shirt again. The act sent another round of shivers over her.

"Did you mean to blast me?" he asked.

"Yes, but only because I knew you could take it."

"The rosary helps you control your powers, but it doesn't completely suppress them."

"I-I wasn't really trying to hurt you. I actually like you as a friend, you know."

He cocked his head. "You like me as a friend?" He moved in slowly as she backpedaled at the same pace. "I see. You also think I'm a 'hottie'—your word, not mine—and you undress me with your eyes when you think I'm not looking."

"I do not do that!"

"You objectify me, siren." He said it as if he was offended, but the smirk playing along the edges of his lips more clearly said he was loving it. "And then you try to zap my clothes off?" He tsked at her.

The back of her legs hit the Jeep's bumper, and he stopped close enough for their shoes to touch. He casually gripped the roof edge above with both hands and leaned in enough so that if she didn't sit down, his long body would be just a hairsbreadth away from hers.

But she wasn't backing down. While his sultry approach had rendered her speechless, the least she could do was maintain her footing. Her hands landed on his hard stomach, but rather than pushing him away as she intended, her traitorous fingers curled into his shirt.

A crunching sound came from above. Eddie was gripping the roof even tighter to refrain from grabbing her. His eyes glowed bright enough that she had to look away or they would burn.

His cheek connected with hers in a caress.

"Siren," he whispered raggedly. "Walk away, please."

For all his teasing, it only took one touch from her to have him completely at her mercy. She released his shirt and rested her hands lightly on his hips. "What's the deal with this Jäger juju?"

His face cracked into a wide smile, but the intense smokiness remained in his eyes. "Juju?"

"I think you know what I'm talking about. Your looks, your magnetism, you even read books. I'm your target, right? It's like you were built to be my perfect lure. You're the predator, and I'm your prey. Hence, Jäger juju."

He was so still. His face just mere inches from her upturned one. "You're breaking all the rules, siren," he said softly, his warm breath tickling her face. "You should have been avoiding me the very second you smelled me as something foul. You should have gotten a bad feeling in your gut whenever I was around. But none of that happened, didn't it?"

She couldn't move. She was completely mesmerized, entranced by the lilt of his words falling from that lush mouth, the way those thick, dark lashes hooded golden candlelit eyes, a hue she noticed was reserved only for her.

He brought one hand down and twirled one of her curls around his finger. "At first, when I assumed you were aware of my foul predator scent, I was convinced you just didn't want to hurt my feelings by shunning me because you're an incredibly kind soul. That was the first reason for staying my hand. And then, how could such a nice girl have killed three men? And how could the most beautiful creature I've ever seen choose the most humble group to sit with at lunch?"

He stretched the curl out and released it, watching it spring back into shape. "The next reason was you being immune to my mindfluence. My curiosity was piqued; I needed you alive to solve that one. And then, in the alley behind Ridge Rats, you relished my scent. And ever since, you've been running in the wrong direction. Straight to me." He let one finger trail down her cheek. "And I've been enjoying your company far too much for my own good. The lion playing with the mouse." He lightly pinched her chin with two fingers and ensnared her in his gaze. "You've got me hooked, siren. If anyone's prey here, it's me. You're the one with the juju."

His truth was like poetry feeding her soul. She was lost in the golden warmth churning in his eyes, but all she could say was, "So I take it then…I'm the lion, and you're the mouse."

He tilted his face so their lips were aligned. "That would be an accurate assessment."

His breath was a soft whisper against her lips. The moment weighed heavily with the expectation of what should happen next.

But couldn't.

The sharp sting of restraint emanated from Eddie even as his breathing deepened, and he slid one hand along her jaw and through her hair, cradling the nape of her neck. The other arm remained firmly attached to the mangled edge of the roof above, the muscles bulging in his biceps and forearm as if desperately maintaining his last stronghold of self-control.

Belle reached up and gripped the wrist of his hand at her neck and let her other hand glide around the side of his waist to his lower back. The movement brought them even closer together, just short of their chests pressing together. She closed her eyes and breathed him in. Woodsy spice as potent as magic filled her lungs and invaded her senses.

And then she was free-falling in pitch darkness. Stars appeared in the inky night sky. One star zoomed in until she saw a turquoise blue ocean framing an island with all temperate zones impossibly carved into its landscape. Snow fell from the cotton candy-colored sky on one side of the irregularly shaped island while rain poured on another side, and still the red sun shone down on the center of the island, which looked like a patchwork of desert, jungle, and savannah.

Old-fashioned, *Treasure Island*-type ships dotted the ocean, but then the island zoomed away until she saw the night sky of stars again. The twinkling of the lights grew sharper, and then the very stars began to move as if fluttering about, leaving trails of glitter. They grew larger, until she realized they were, in fact, coming closer to her. Little arms, heads, wings took shape....

Belle gasped.

"What did you see?" Eddie whispered, concerned. He was lightly gripping her upper arms. "I couldn't share the vision with you because you're wearing the rosary."

"Stars, and then an island. The island didn't make sense; it was a jumble of different climates. And then stars again, but they turned into, I think, fairies."

Eddie straightened and smiled, as if highly pleased.

"What?"

"You saw Neverland. It's part of the Fae history I was going to tell you about later."

"Later? You mean now." Unable to contain the excitement bubbling up inside her, she stepped around him and pointed in the direction of the main part of town. "We're heading to that planetarium, and you're going to tell me *all* about it. And then, we're going to have dinner, and then trap a werewolf, and then, when I go to sleep tonight, I'm going to try and connect with my mom and find out where Violet is. And after you get that pixie dust, you're going to magic-stab Violet. We revive my mom, and then we all live happily ever after." She brushed her palms together. "The end."

He crossed his arms over his chest and smirked. "Sounds like you've got it all planned out."

"Big picture's good, but" she did the so-so gesture with her hand, "the details are still fuzzy."

He laughed. "Alright, siren, so we've got Plan A locked in. Let's—" Eddie's gaze locked on something in the distance, and he immediately stood at attention. He looked deeply troubled.

"God, not now, please," he whispered.

The note of anguish in his tone struck a chord of fear in Belle. Eddie was the most-together person she knew. If he was that disturbed….

"What is it, Eddie?" Her pulse thrumming wildly, she turned around, backing into him and trying to spot what he was intently watching.

She heard it first. A tinkling of bells like the keys on a toy xylophone.

His hand splayed on her stomach as he steadied her against himself. He pointed at a glittering spot in the sky. "There."

It was like part of the Neverland vision coming true, but instead of a white, fluttering spark, it was multicolored.

And it was coming closer.

"Is that what I think it is?" she asked.

He whipped her around and held her by the shoulders. "Siren, listen, I don't have much time." Panicked-Eddie made for a very frightened Belle.

She grabbed his wrists. "Eddie, what's going on? You're scaring me."

He touched her cheeks and brought his face closer to hers. "I'm being summoned by the Jäger Father. It's probably another mission, or he knows I need to see him and is expediting my trip, but I-I don't know how long before I can come back to you."

The ground felt like it tilted. "B-But, what about our plan? Plan A?"

Before he could respond, their attention snapped to the shimmer of color that landed on the corner of the open trunk window with what sounded like a crash of tiny cymbals.

Belle's jaw dropped. "That's a fairy. A real one."

"An Iris pixie," Eddie said. "They deliver messages for the High Fae."

The pixie was a tiny half-human, half-dragonfly creature no more than two inches tall. Its upper half had an exposed male torso, arms, and a handsome little face with elfish eyes and ears, but instead of hair, he had the large spherical eyes of the dragonfly covering his head. Besides two humanoid arms, he had six spindly insect legs that protruded from the sides of his torso, and two humanoid legs that he currently stood on. They looked ribbed, so when he joined the two legs together as he flew, it created the long distinctive abdomen part of the dragonfly. The human part of him was golden, while the dragonfly parts, including the four wings twitching at his back, shimmered in ever-changing rainbow colors.

"Don't stare, siren," Eddie warned. "They don't like it."

"How can I not? It's a pixie!" She moved to stick her face closer and analyze its details.

The tiny creature narrowed his eyes. A bow and arrow shimmered into his hands.

"No, don't!" Eddie pulled her back by her elbow, but it was too late. A tiny arrow struck her right on the nose with a tinkling puff of rainbow glitter.

Belle blinked and looked down, cross-eyed, at the inch-long arrow. "Owww." There was a stinging sensation that spread out like a tiny fiery shockwave across her face, making her eyes water.

"What did you do?!" Eddie snatched at the smug pixie but came up with a handful of glitter as he shot away to the top of the Jeep's antennae.

The pixie shook his fist at him in a furious stream of tinkles and rainbow glitter.

"She didn't know!" Eddie said defensively. He grabbed Belle and peered into her scrunched-up face. "Siren, talk to me. What do you feel?"

Numb, but she couldn't mouth the word because something foreign was bubbling up inside her and making its way up her windpipe. She opened her mouth and let loose a great, big belly laugh.

Eddie could only stare as she continued to laugh and laugh, tears spilling down her cheeks. "Belle?" he croaked.

"It hurts," she guffawed, clutching her stomach. It really did. Her sides felt like they were literally going to split wide open.

He turned on the pixie, who was smiling with his arms crossed over his chest, as if mighty pleased with himself.

"Make it stop," Eddie growled.

The pixie shrugged his shoulders and flew into Belle's face. He spit in his hand and lobbed the glitter-split right at her nose.

Belle's laugh stopped abruptly. "Oh," she sighed, relieved.

"Better?" Eddie asked, rubbing her arms.

She gave him a sleepy smile. "Better." Her eyelids fluttered shut, and her head promptly lolled back.

Eddie's eyes widened. He swooped her into his arms before she hit the ground. Her head resting comfortably against his chest now, he gave her a gentle shake. "Siren?"

A loud snore answered him.

His lips set in a firm line, he turned his fiery eyes upon the pixie who was busy fluttering on his back in midair, holding his sides with chimes of laughter. He looked like a colorful, mini-disco ball with the shower of rainbow sparks he was giving off.

"Fix her," Eddie demanded, before turning and laying her in the Jeep's trunk bed. He tucked his gym bag beneath her head like a pillow, his hand lingering on her cheek, thumb grazing across her parted lips.

When he turned back to the pixie, the creature was staring at him with a knowing smile, and a violin appeared in his little arms. With the bowstring, he drew an oversized glittery heart in the air and began stringing a tune that sounded suspiciously like the playground taunt song, *"Eddie and Belle sitting in a tree, K-I-S-S-I-N-G...."*

Black mist swirled up Eddie's arm from his leather wrist wrap until only his arm was covered in the Jäger garb. A large butterfly net shimmered into his waiting hand.

The pixie immediately sobered up and straightened while his wings kept him airborne. A machine gun appeared in each of his little hands, and with a Rambo-style look of warning, he trained both barrels on Eddie.

After a brief stare-down in which Eddie imagined all manner of ways of murdering a pixie, he finally relinquished with a sigh of exasperation. The net faded in a shimmer of gold and the Jäger arm piece snaked back into his wrist wrap.

"Alright, look," Eddie began, "let's just say we got off on the wrong foot. You already know who I am. What's your name?"

The pixie sprayed his chest with a hail of bullets.

Eddie gritted his teeth. It was like being stung by 50 mosquitoes at once.

"It's Drix," the pixie chimed. He blew the smoke off the tips of the gun barrels before they poofed into glitter.

Eddie inhaled a calming breath. With enormous effort at civility, he asked, "Drix, will you kindly awaken Belle?"

The pixie stroked his chin as if he were thinking about it.

"Please," he added through clenched teeth.

"Only if you gift me a story."

"Fine. Once upon a time—"

"No, no, no. Those are taxed out." Drix flew right up to his face. *"I want a personal one."* He waggled his eyebrows. *"Your most embarrassing one."*

"I see you're after gold, you greedy bugger."

Drix shrugged his shoulders. *"Hey, in this economy, a pix has gotta do, what a pix has gotta do."*

Feeling as if he were indeed going to regret this later, Eddie briefly closed his eyes before he began, "It was winter 1956, Oregon. A lonely Sasquatch and me...cooking it dinner...in a dress."

Drix was an explosion of rainbow glitter as he roared with a laughter that sounded like an all-bells orchestra.

"It had already eaten three hikers, and the charade was the only way to get close enough to kill it," Eddie said, his face as red as a beet.

Still hovering before him, Drix wiped his tears away and rolled onto his stomach, still mid-air, propping his hands beneath his chin. *"Details, Mrs. Sasquatch, or your girlfriend will never awaken."*

Belle was being pulled through a dark cloud of cobwebs. Eventually, light filtered through, and her vision was filled with a shockingly handsome face with eyes like golden stars. His thick, black eyebrows were knit together, and those pillowy soft-looking lips were forming the words, "How are you feeling?"

A hand swept her hair back from her face, and then as her arms were tugged forward, the world shifted on its side.

Belle blinked. She'd had a dream! And it wasn't Violet-related! An actual dream, not a vision!

Her focus finally clicked into place. She was sitting up in the Jeep's trunk bed, legs dangling over the edge. Eddie hovered over her, worry lines etched into his forehead as he watched her.

She stood and grabbed his forearms. "Eddie! I had a dream! There was a pixie, a mean one, and he—"

The sound of chimes stole her next word.

The rainbow dragonfly pixie from her dream was fluttering in mid-air just beyond Eddie's shoulder. The pixie sporting an amused smirk, with a large scroll rolled up in one of his hands.

"It was real?" she said haggardly.

"Yes, this is Drix."

The pixie saluted her with two fingers.

Her mind replayed his cruel jokes, and as soon as her mouth opened to tell him off, Eddie's hand covered it. "Not a good idea, siren."

She shook him off. "You don't know what I'm going to say," she challenged.

"I can read your face like a book by now."

She frowned. "What's he doing?"

Drix had unrolled the scroll and was busy folding it into airplane wings.

"He's about to deliver the summons to me, and then I'll be gone."

Her panicked eyes snapped to his. "What do you mean *gone*? For how long? There's a werewolf loose in Elmridge, and we've got to execute Plan A. And what about that magic act you promised to teach me?"

She knew she sounded desperate with that last pitch. In fact, she cringed at how whiny she sounded, especially compared with Eddie's calm demeanor. He just stood gazing at her face, as if trying to memorize it.

"I don't know how long this will take, but I promise, I will return as soon as I can. In the meantime, you can trust James to help you."

She wrinkled her nose. "My English teacher?"

He gave her a small smile. "Yes, my uncle. He knows what I know. And he's like you, a child of a Fae acolyte."

"Ten seconds," Drix announced. He licked the edges of the paper airplane wings and started pinching the nose into shape.

"What did he tinkle or say?" Belle asked.

"Siren." With a sense of urgency, Eddie grabbed her waist and cupped the side of her neck. He pressed his forehead against hers so their noses touched. "Please, don't put yourself in situations where you can get hurt, or..."

"Or hurt others," she finished for him.

He nodded and swept his thumb across her cheek.

"Five seconds, lovebirds."

She closed her eyes as she inhaled him, and an idea came to her. When she opened her eyes, his were glowing like suns and he was staring hungrily at her lips.

"You can't give a kiss, but I can," she whispered.

Just as she closed her eyes and planted a firm kiss on the corner of his mouth, the paper airplane struck his temple, and Eddie disappeared in a shower of shimmering gold dust.

Suddenly left kissing air, her balance was thrown off and she stumbled forward.

"No!" she cried out, swatting the spot Eddie had just been standing in.

She looked for Drix, but the rainbow trail of glitter was already fading from his wake as he darted off into the sky.

One, Two, Freddy's Coming for You

Belle: **Violet's beast is loose in Elmridge.**

Barely a minute passed after sending the text, before her phone rang. She answered on the first ring. "You know, Uncle, it isn't nice to be ignored."

"I was going to call you tonight, Belle. I'm very sorry. This investigation has consumed my time, as well as keeping tabs on the ongoing ones in Elmridge. Did you have another dream about the animal?"

"Yes."

She told him how she dreamt the creature was hanging out in Wychblack Forest. She didn't mention Eddie's involvement; no need to get her uncle on the warpath over a Jäger who he doesn't even remember being brief buds with.

"I'm coming home this Saturday. In the meantime, Sergio reported you still haven't moved to Jo's place. I have to tell you, again, I am not comfortable with you alone in that house."

She cut off the lecture he was building up to. "Tomorrow, I promise. I-I have too much homework to do tonight."

He released a long sigh. Radio garble drew his attention away for a minute. "Belle, I have to let you go."

"Wait, please, give me something! What have you learned about Vi-the flower?"

He paused. She heard shuffling, and then he spoke in a low voice, "Okay, we can talk at liberty now. We had her accomplice, Hagar, but since we found no evidence of an illegal transaction that you dreamt occurred between them, we had to let her go. But we did learn something from a digital trail Violet left uncovered. She used a pseudonym to commission a very expensive tiara with a purple taffeite jewel, and then had it donated to Mayor Markham of Elmridge."

"The Homecoming queen is supposed to win that tiara."

"Markham won't part with it. He threatened legal action if we seized it without a warrant."

"What if, what if I won it? I am on the Homecoming court. That way, she'll be forced to come straight to us."

"Absolutely not. You're not using yourself as bait."

"So then the other girl who wins will be victimized? I'd rather be the one to face Violet. My mother won't allow her to hurt me."

Radio garble interrupted again. "Just a minute," Ernesto replied before turning back to Belle. "If you win the crown, you hand it to me the moment you can."

"Why the elaborate stunt though?" Belle wondered aloud. "Why not just keep the taffeite for herself if she already had it in her hands?"

There was a pause. "Think of that poem about the Jade Blade. What did it say again about each jewel?"

Belle knew it by heart. She recited it aloud, "Red diamond from romantic spice, serendibite from a life's sacrifice, fire opal from vengeful rage, taffeite from one pure and sage."

"You said you had a vision of Violet getting a marriage proposal and a red diamond ring from a Frenchman in Paris. We recently learned the identity of this man. Albert Laurent. He was actually born in Elmridge but lived most of his life in Paris."

Something Violet had said from her vision in the Amsterdam hotel room floated back to her. "Elmridge is the hub of Fae magic," she said aloud.

"What did you say?"

"I just remembered Violet saying that. We know that she got the red diamond through romantic spice, a marriage proposal. She got the serendibite from Liam's mom's sacrificing her life. And they were all native Elmridge residents." The gears in her brain were whirring and clicking faster. "She's going to try to spin this Homecoming court competition so that the winner, someone pure and sage, will somehow gift her the crown. Violet just can't take the jewel. She sets up the scenario and then uses an ultimatum to force the victim to gift her the jewel. She's going to complete the Jade Blade spell in Elmridge because of the Fae magic tied to this place. I bet it has to do with Aunt Em and Abigail being the original Prynn fairies."

"Belle, if you win the crown, she will give *you* an ultimatum. And from what we saw from her last visit, she will threaten to kill someone close to you. I don't think she'd try me again, so you may very well be putting your friends' lives in danger."

"B-But at least we'll be ready for her this time. We can set up a trap or something. If I have the crown, then I could probably be the one to set the time and place. Somewhere my friends won't be exposed."

"I don't like this, Belle. I know Em would never approve."

"It's our only chance to stop her. The Homecoming pageant is the last event, and then the winner is crowned. It's right after Thanksgiving, so we have about a month to prepare a trap for her."

"And for you to win that crown," he added for her. "I've seen how intense these Homecoming competitions can get. You need a solid crew that you trust and can help you win." Radio garble stole his attention again. "I'll see you Saturday, Belle. Be safe."

"Wait!" She stared at the *Call Ended* message and finished dismally, "The creature's a werewolf, and it might be Liam."

~*~

That night, Belle made sure all her doors and windows were locked tight. Except for that one window with the broken latch. She dragged a heavy bookcase in front of that one.

When Sergio visited with another casserole plate, she asked what was being done about the peafowl-massacring beast. He assured her that Sheriff Panzinski had ordered animal control officers posted throughout Elmridge armed with stun guns. She breathed a momentary sigh of relief that Ernesto had heeded her warning and the townspeople were, she hoped, safe for the night from a prowling werewolf.

Which could be Liam. And she couldn't just call him up and ask him, "Hey! Are you a werewolf? Experiencing blackouts? When you open the refrigerator, do you reach for the yogurt or the raw, bloody steak?"

She would have to wait until the next day to see Dr. Helsing and hatch a plan for capturing the werewolf.

She spent some time trying to make a list of suspects. She looked through Peacock Profiles and came up with a handful of names of blonde, green-eyed, fit-looking guys, but then the task became too difficult to tell true eye and hair color from the different lighting in the pictures.

But a list of some names was better than none. At least she had *something* to show Dr. Helsing tomorrow.

Belle then tried calling Eddie, but on the third failed attempt, reached his voicemail again. Instead of just ending the call, she left a message explaining what she and Ernesto had figured out and how she was planning to win the Homecoming crown. Her next step was to call Candy for help with that seemingly impossible task.

"Are you sure, honey? I thought you didn't even want to be on the Homecoming court. What changed?"

Drat. She didn't want to become a pathological liar just to keep her secret. "Um, I guess, I just want to start embracing high school traditions. I shouldn't be shying away from new experiences, right?"

True enough.

Candy made that tongue-clucking sound. "Is Eddie Helsing a new experience?"

Instant mortification. "Candy! Why do you say that? We're just friends. We—"

"Sit together at lunch," Candy finished for her. "I know. But I just got off the phone with Millie, and, honey, she is *not* happy."

Belle couldn't keep the whine out of her voice. "Why? Nothing happened. Eddie and I only met by the Peacock Fountain for lunch."

"And then tag-teamed against Shawn and Corey?" Silence from Belle, so Candy continued, "Girl, you two have gone viral, did you know that?"

"What do you mean?" She did not like the sound of being a contagion.

"Everyone has seen videos of you defending Eddie."

"But...isn't that *good?*"

"Um, yes, but then there's that bit where you two are holding hands, looking very much like you two are *together* together."

Belle groaned.

"And you say you two were meeting there for lunch, like a lunch date?"

"No," she faltered. *Stick as close as possible to the truth.* "Um...I think he likes me," she hurried to tack on, "and I'm just being nice."

Wow, she instantly felt crumby. Like she was throwing Eddie under the bus somehow. But wasn't she telling the truth?

"So, you don't *like him* like him?" Candy pressed.

Belle ignored that dance of shivers all over her body when she thought of his perfect face and perfect form, the warm caramel eyes that could see all the way through to her soul, the crooked smile that could stop traffic, the way he'd crushed her against him in their last embrace. Who was she kidding? She'd dared to defy a Fae prophecy just to semi-kiss him.

But she also didn't want to lose Millie.

"Of course, I like him, but not how he likes me." There. Truth. Eddie was unnaturally obsessed with her; she wasn't obsessed with him.

"How do you know he likes you?"

Sheesh, Candy was relentless. "Well, um, I keep running into him outside school hours, and he insisted on walking me to your place by way of Maple Trail." She could go on, but her chagrin was maxed out.

Candy whistled. "Maple Trail. Did he offer to buy you anything?"

Belle gave an exasperated sigh.

"Did he?" Candy persisted.

"Ice-cream. We had ice-cream."

"Alright, then. Sounds like he's got a thing for you."

"Could you talk to Millie for me, please? I don't want her mad at me."

"Sure thing, honey. And we're gonna need her help if you're going to win Homecoming."

They planned to meet tomorrow after school to kick off Operation Homecoming Queen, after Belle confirmed with Cindy, at Rawlins Castle.

~~*~~

Belle settled into her cushy window nook and read through her mother's diary again. She paid closer attention this time to when she'd given birth to her first child, James, but the only mention of him was on the night Abigail went to visit Zoraya the Seer. The night she was possessed by Violet.

"The only pain that overshadows all for me, though, has been the loss of James. Thirty-three years with my son. The most precious years of my life...before he was ripped from me. But I've numbed that part of my soul so that I can continue on functioning (I won't say 'living')."

And he was mentioned again when Emily took up Abigail's pen in the next entry to explain what had happened that night. In a random moment of conversation with her sister, Emily mentioned her theory about Peter and James being "taken to another world."

Belle knew first-hand from Emily and a poem in the Elmridge fairy tales book, that, in exchange for immortality and powers granted from touching the pixie-laden meteorite, the Fae took the first-born children of these meteorite-touchers a.k.a. acolytes.

So Emily's first-born, Peter, and Abigail's first-born, James, were taken by the Fae to another world. Neverland? Eddie had mentioned it as part of Fae history.

Earlier today, when Eddie informed her that his uncle, James, was a son of an acolyte, it'd crossed her mind that maybe her half-brother and Eddie's uncle were one-and-the-same. But that was impossible because, one, her brother was supposed to be on another planet, and the uncle was here. And two, if Belle's brother was Eddie's uncle, then the family tree wouldn't make sense, especially if Eddie was 300 years old. That would mean uncle/brother James, normally, would have to, at least, be older than 300 years old. So all that was just...no. Nonsense.

James Helsing couldn't possibly be her half-brother.

Once Belle settled on that conclusion, she massaged her temples, grateful that the uncle/brother-James-question wouldn't be nagging at the back of her mind anymore. She turned her attention back to the diary in her lap, but a screeching black mass of fur landed right on it. She screamed, and the demon furball shot across the room with a loud hiss.

"Argh! Stupid cat!"

As soon as she'd gotten home earlier, it had zipped outside past her feet. But a few hours later, it was back at her front door, meowing relentlessly. When she'd opened the door, she was surprised to find it just sitting there, and that's when she'd gotten her first good look at it.

"Goodness, you're huge!"

It was the size and fluff of a three-month-old German Shepard dog. It had a thick black coat, tufted ears, a thicker ruff of hair around its neck that somewhat resembled a bowtie at its chin, and disconcertingly long legs and wide paws. The nose-area looked more tiger than just plain, old cat.

"You are *not* a cat."

It had blinked its dark green eyes, given a loud meow, and begun licking one of its paws.

"Well, I guess you're cat enough. Wait here, I'll see if we have a can of tuna or something."

But before she could shut the door, it'd zoomed inside.

And now, she stood glaring at the hellcat who'd slunk back into her room after unceremoniously pouncing on her, or more specifically, on the diary. Which now lay on the floor, its spine undone with blocks of pages hanging out at odd angles.

"Look at what you did!" She dropped to her knees and began scooping up the pieces.

The cat blinked lazily and hopped onto her bed. It started walking all over one of the pillows. The one Belle used for her head.

Her mouth dropped as the cat curled up on it. "You are *not* sleeping there!"

The cat lowered its head to its paws and closed its eyes.

Angrily, she fell back on her butt and leaned against the wall. The cover and spine of the diary were completely separated from the bound pages, exposing the old twine threaded through them. But when she stacked the pages to align them, she noticed a thin section of pages that had been cut down to where the spine used to hold them together. She checked the dates before and after this section, and the range matched the missing period of time that could account for James's birth. She looked more closely at the ripped edges of these missing pages, ripped so close to the original spine. If this book hadn't fallen apart like it did, Belle would never have seen the edges of these...one, two, three, *four* missing pages. It was like somebody, possibly her mother, didn't want anyone to ever know about this period of time in her life.

What could be so secretive that her mother would not withhold from detailing her exploits in which she describes herself using her powers, but would censor the birth and life of her own beloved son?

She was going to have to ask Ernesto, or maybe even Jo about it.

Or, if Belle tried to connect with her mother in a dream, then maybe she could ask *her* directly.

~~*~~

Belle was running through the grassy peacock field towards her house. She could see her mother, with her long, straight black hair, standing at the second-story window, waving at her from behind the glass as if waiting for her. And this Abigail didn't look possessed by Violet because, although Belle was far from the house, her keen eyesight could tell from the warmth of her smile and eyes that it was indeed her mother waiting for her.

The house looked older, centuries older, and the regular town sights of modern Elmridge were replaced by shanty wooden houses and trees. Lots of them. It looked like the setting of *The Crucible* with the fear factor of a Freddy Krueger movie.

The hairs on the back of Belle's neck stood up. She was being stalked. And by several creatures.

As she ran, a man shot out from behind a tree and snatched her wrist. She whirled about and crashed into his chest-clad, brown leather apron. It was warm and slippery. She pulled away, horrified to find the same substance covering her hands and forearms now. Blood and meaty chunks. She screamed, but there was no sound. She tugged to get away, but his grip on her wrist was like a vise. He had the 1800s look with a dirty blouse and the sleeves rolled up to his elbows. His long black hair was tied back, and he sneered at her from behind a thick curly mustache. He reached into the front pocket of his apron and produced a long butcher knife.

Belle knew in her mind none of this was real, but the pain biting into her wrist from his hold was very real. And she was terrified that if she didn't get away or fight back, she was going to encounter the very real pain of that knife.

But her powers wouldn't work. She was scared enough, so she knew she should have been emitting electricity like a plasma globe by now.

Just as the butcher swung down, a gold beam shot at his arm. The knife fell out of his hand, and he released Belle. She sprinted away and chanced a look behind her. The knife back in his hand, the butcher was staring menacingly at something above him. Whatever it was flew out past the canopy of a tree that had been obscuring it.

Belle gasped. It was a fairy. A man-sized one in a deep blue robe with a long, flowing white beard, and he was flying directly overhead now, trailing gold pixie dust, in the direction of the house. She would have followed his course, if not for the huge pair of fairy wings he clenched in each of his hands. The wings were dripping blood.

She kept running, afraid the butcher would catch up to her. She tried staying out of the flying fairy's sight as well. Something flashed by in her peripheral vision. She halted. Perspiration streaked down her face and body in rivulets. Her heart beat thunderously, but in this Edgar Allen Poe nightmare, there was no sound. She had only her eyes.

There, she saw it. The next monster. It was passing between trees. Its profile was of a tawny, mammoth-sized wolf. Its head was low to the ground, sniffing its way closer to where she stood.

A small rock was thrown onto her path. Her gaze snapped to the direction it came from. There was a girl about her age, half-hidden behind a tree, frantically gesturing for her to come over. The girl had curly blonde ringlets pinned up in a white bonnet, and with the pearl-colored dress she wore, Belle guessed she was also from a past century. The panic in her light blue eyes invoked a trust from Belle, especially as they were both now staring at the wolf that had also noticed them.

But a wolf, it was not. It had the face and color of a lion without the mane but with the shaggy coat of a wolf. Its massive body was a cross between a skinny bear and a giant wolf. It reared its head back and let loose an ear-splitting howl.

Belle tore towards the girl, her mind reeling from the shock of that sound. It was the only sound she'd heard so far. She almost crashed into the girl. Wordlessly, the girl grabbed her hand, and Belle let her lead as they took off.

Belle could hear the pounding of the beast's paws hitting the ground in pursuit of them. She peered ahead for the house, but instead, saw a gathering of pitchfork-carrying townsfolk.

That was never good.

Belle tried to yank her hand away, but the pretty she-devil gave her a serpentine smile and tightened her grip. Belle kept trying to pull away, but the girl dragged her forward with inhuman strength until they reached the waiting crowd.

Two men from the group grabbed her by the arms, and with her kicking and screaming-on-mute, they dragged her through the crowd. She was pelted by rocks, rotten vegetables, and wordless curses. The two men tied her to a stake surrounded by dry brush.

The crowd parted and a heavy-set man in a dark blue robe and powdered wig passed through carrying a large brown leather book in his hands, over his chest. The long length of his nose ended just above a deep scowl. He stopped at the base of the small wooden platform and raised one hand. A lightning bolt tore across the iron sky behind him as if baptizing him with the authority of what he so clearly was about to do. When a torch was placed into his waiting hand, he lowered the book, and Belle gasped with horror at the gaping hole in his chest, the burnt edges rimmed with charcoaled flesh.

The brush at her feet was ignited.

Panicked, she sought for an escape. She tugged at her bonds, her eyes searching for any sign of mercy among the faces in the crowd but found none.

She did see the beast, stalking through the crowd toward her, weaving in and around the unsuspecting folks. She could hear its heavy breathing getting louder as it approached. The fire licked up her legs and *that* she could feel. Her mouth opened in a silent scream of agony.

Through her tear-drenched eyes, she could see the beast climbing up the platform, passing through the fire unharmed. While her body was being consumed, her mind watched as the beast stood on its hind legs, tall like a man. It leaned its face in close to hers. Without warning, it opened its maw wide and struck.

Before the blackness blanketed everything, the last thing that registered in her mind was the familiar set of clear green eyes with yellow flecks, and the emotion in them that she couldn't find among the other faces: mercy.

| 22 |

3 A.M.

Belle awoke to a mouth full of fur. When she shot awake in a pool of sweat, her hair and clothes sticking to her skin, and desperately trying to suck air into her lungs, she thought the cat had been sleeping on her face and trying to suffocate her.

But then she remembered the nightmare she'd just survived.

The cat sat on the edge of the bed blinking its emerald green eyes at her. Either that or the hellcat really had just tried to kill her. As if in response to that thought, the creature sidled up to her and curled up in her lap. Or maybe it really had just snuggled against her throughout her ordeal.

She'll never know.

After rinsing her mouth out and changing into fresh pj's (turns out, the cat stunk to high heaven), she bundled herself in the comforter and sat in the window nook.

3:04 in the morning. There was no way she could sleep now. That dream had scared the pants off her. Before she could fall into analyzing the nightmare, the front doorbell sounded throughout the house. She bolted to her feet and stared out her open bedroom door into the darkness. Even the cat had sat up and was gazing in the same direction.

As the doorbell chimed out its last note, she white-knuckled the edge of her shirt. Who could be visiting at this hour?

She really regretted not being at Candy's right now.

She forced her lungs to work as she moved into the hallway, the cat following at her side. Maybe it was just a prank by some school kids, a doorbell dash. She'd heard of those.

A loud knocking, more urgent, came from the front door now. Maybe it was Sergio and there was some kind of emergency. Maybe something happened to Ernesto!

At that thought, she bolted down the stairs, ignoring the warning pictures flashing in her mind of robbers or possibly the werewolf at her door, but the nightmare must have temporarily fried her internal alarm system because she just swung the front door wide open.

Dr. Helsing stood there. The picture of someone who fell out of bed and rushed over here. He had on mismatched shoes, plaid night pants, and his tweed blazer that he wore to work, an apparent last attempt at professionalism before hightailing it here.

"Ms. Montague, are you alright? Are you in any trouble?" He was panicked and out of breath.

It took her a moment to get over the shock of seeing her literature teacher at her doorstep at three in the morning. "I-I'm fine. I just had a nightmare. How did you know I was in distress?"

Dr. Helsing straightened and sucked in a long, calming breath before releasing it. "A nightmare." At that second, the cat slid past her legs and narrowed its eyes at him. "My, that is...one big cat."

"Yes." She peered down at it. "This is Lady Catherine De Bourg. Lady for short."

Dr. Helsing seemed pink with amusement now. "How decidedly specific."

"Yes, I honestly don't know its gender, and I'm not about to go poking around to find out, so I've decided it's a female for now with an attitude worthy of the duchess's name."

Lady looked up and glared at Belle. Dr. Helsing chuckled, and the cat snarled her displeasure at him.

"If all is well with you, I will tell Edward so. He is most likely beside himself right now. Goodnight, Ms. Montague."

"Wait, please. First, please, just call me Belle. Second, you never answered my question. What prompted you to come over here?"

"Belle, this is not the time for a lengthy discussion. I will see you tomorrow in class, and we can talk about it afterward."

"Please."

After a moment, he exhaled, relenting. "So be it. But no more than five minutes, and we cannot very well conduct our discussion on your front porch."

"Of course." She let him in, but when the cat followed behind, he turned and gave Lady a stare that had her glaring back until she backtracked with a hiss onto the porch. Lady turned and dashed out into the darkness.

"Wow," she said in jest, "you're like a cat whisperer." She shut the door behind her and switched on the first-floor lights.

A wave of awe crossed Dr. Helsing's face as he surveyed the room. "So, this is the history of Elmridge…."

"Yes, but remember you were going to answer my question."

He nodded. "Edward contacted me. Told me you were in trouble and to come to your aid. Immediately."

"How did he know?"

"Ah, well, he felt what you felt. Your distress. His exact words, I believe, were 'fiery agony.' He suspected you may have set your house on fire again."

It took her a moment. Her jaw was presently unhinged. "H-How did he *feel* that?"

"My own personal theory? Soul symmetry." At her blank look, he elaborated further. "I have studied the history of the Fae and of many legends around the world. I'm not sure if Edward has mentioned any of this to you yet, but the Fae deal in stories. It is a sort of lifeline for them."

"He's mentioned it. I don't really understand how stories can be a lifeline to them, though."

"In a nutshell, stories are currency. The highest-paying stories are the ones that are real in one reality, and then become immortalized as tales and legends in other realities."

"What do you mean?"

"Take your Princess Diana fairy tale. Pretty commoner marries the royal prince but dies tragically when pursued by paparazzi. In another reality, it actually happened."

Her jaw unhinged. "That's so tragic."

He pursed his lips thoughtfully. "With Elmridge having a strong draw on Fae magic, I wouldn't be surprised if stories are spinning out right under our noses, only for some watchful Fae to take notice and then take ownership of the stories. Once the story reaches a satisfactory end, the Fae cashes in on it by telling it to the people of another reality and hoping that it catches steam and becomes legend. The more the story is told, the more money that Fae makes. It is how the fairy tales are born."

Mind. Officially. Blown. Belle was speechless. So the fairy tales she so loved—Cinderella, Joan of Arc, El Cid, Mother Teresa—had been real somewhere else? In another reality?

"Over time, these stories naturally become embellished and some of the details are changed. You may have noticed most of these fairy tales are love stories."

She nodded, transfixed on the words coming out of his mouth.

"Well, there's true love, which has of late become quite cliché and therefore not as valuable in the Fae market. And then...there's soul symmetry. The rarest kind, the most highly valued. It is a tale of love that has the Fae spellbound, and that, I believe, is what is transpiring between you and Edward."

She finally found her voice. "What?" she squeaked. "That's-That's just *not* what's happening. Eddie is obsessed with me because he was activated to hunt me but hasn't killed me because I had acted in self-defense against the Hammersons," she rambled. "But, believe me, Eddie has threatened to make good on completing his mission, if I kill any innocent people. He said so himself. So, yeah, that's what's going on here. Not this soul symmetry nonsense."

Because what Dr. Helsing just said was way too dense for her to chew on at this point in her young life.

He sighed. "The fact that Edward felt your keen distress is one such piece of evidence among others that supports my theory. Were you in 'fiery agony,' as he claimed?"

"Yes."

"In this nightmare you had?"

She swallowed. "I was being burned at the stake."

His eyebrows drew together in concern. "Edward told me you don't dream but can rather connect with your mother's mind."

"I hadn't had a chance to dissect that nightmare, since you showed up right after."

"My apologies."

"No, it's Eddie's fault, but the sentiment was noble. Creepy, but noble. Um, but now that I think about it, I was trying to get to her. My mother. She was waiting for me in this very house, but in old Elmridge like 17- or 1800s, I think it was, but I had to get through this field where different monsters kept popping out from behind trees."

She described each terrifying encounter, culminating with the beast giving her the more merciful death.

Dr. Helsing stroked his chin. The other hand remained in his pocket, she realized since he'd arrived on her porch. "I would say that these monsters represent Abigail Prynn's fears."

"That does make sense," she said slowly. "She was burned at the stake before she transformed. And I saw him, the Reverend Judge

Jonas Black. He had the hole in his chest from where Abigail had struck him with lightning. And that beast may well be the werewolf that is skulking around Wychblack Forest. But I don't know who the others are."

"Mm-hmm. It appears you must overcome Abigail's very fears if you are to reach her."

"How do I do that?"

"And you say there is no sound in the vision?"

"I could only hear the beast."

"Interesting. Why don't we see what Edward has to say about all this?"

"Really? Because I called him three times today, and he still hasn't answered."

"He is on a mission. He leaves behind all devices susceptible to tracking."

"So then how do you plan to—"

"We use this." He patted his pocket but came up empty. "Oh my." He made a movement in the other pocket, the one with his hand stuffed in. "Well, Belle, I am going to let you in on a secret of mine." His face had reddened considerably.

Belle had that *okaaay*-look.

"If Edward trusts you, then suffice it to say, I can trust you with this slightly embarrassing tidbit about myself."

He pulled the hand out of his pocket.

Belle stifled a screech, and she would pat herself later on the back for her restraint, because...there was no hand. Only a flat, electronic disk at the wrist.

"In the rush to get over here, I couldn't locate my bionic hand in the darkness fast enough, especially with Edward threatening bloody murder if I didn't move more quickly to get here. And you know he doesn't lie." His tone took on an annoyed edge.

"Oh." She cleared her throat. "It's, It's not noticeable at all when the hand is...on."

"Yes." He used his only hand to reach across his body into the opposite pocket and retrieve something from it. "Long story short, the Jäger Father found me with a grotesque hook attached to it," he held up the handless arm before shoving it back in his pocket, "and a confounding case of amnesia."

"You don't remember your past?"

"Not a stitch of it. The Jäger Father gave me a new purpose, and it is the hope that through my research, I can peel away the layers to my past."

"Right, because you are a child of a Fae acolyte, like me. What are your powers then?"

"We are only aware of one. I should have two: an offense and a defense."

Belle's eyebrows shot up. "I didn't know it was like that." She thought about her own powers. Her electricity-wielding must be for defense, while the dream-walking must be for offense, like for intelligence-gathering.

Dr. Helsing continued, "I hope to unveil my second power somehow. I am actively working on it."

"So what power do you have now?"

"I am a lie-detector. Once I touch someone's skin, I know whether they're lying, and I will always understand the truth behind their words."

"Wow, that is handy."

Dr. Helsing chuckled. "It sure is. It almost makes up for the missing one."

Her eyes went wide. "What? No, I didn't mean it like that. Gosh, I'm sorry."

"It is quite alright. Extra credit for being punny." He waved his hand around. There was a smooth black stone with a sheen in his palm. "Shall we?" At her questioning look, he explained. "We are going to use this communication stone to contact Edward. He has the other one."

She held her hand out for it. It weighed as much as she expected a stone this size would weigh. It was cool to the touch, smooth, oval, and the size of her palm. Peering more closely at the stone, she traced the faint lines of gold ingrained in it.

Dr. Helsing answered what she was thinking. "It's made of Neverland volcanic rock. The veins of gold you see are naturally occurring pixie dust."

She oohed at that. "How does it work?" She handed it back to him.

"You give it a kiss." He planted one on the rock and set it on the floor. He stepped back and motioned for Belle to join him at his side. "Edward will have to answer on his end."

"Does it ring or something?"

He smiled at that. "No. The last person to hold the rock receives an image in their mind of the Fae who constructed the pair of calling stones. In this case, the Fae's name is Petros."

"How would you know it's not just your imagination?"

"Petros has shining silver hair. You would know when he pops into your mind."

At that moment, a scene outlined in a mix of glittery gold and black erupted before them. It was Eddie in Jäger form, and his back was to them as he fought three creatures at once.

Belle stepped in closer to her teacher's side. She whisper-squeaked, "What are those?!"

"Wendigos," he replied calmly, as if he were simply naming a breed of dog.

But to Belle, they were the stuff of nightmares.

The monsters towered over Eddie and had heads of deer skulls with larger-than-life antlers. Their chest cavities were exposed and missing flesh, but the rest of the skin on their bodies looked like deer hide. They swiped at Eddie with their freakishly long arms like tree branches tipped with black talons.

Belle held her breath as she watched Eddie ninja-dodge each attack and wield a long, skinny sword, slicing off a pair of hands, and driving the sword straight through one of the monsters' chests. It released a high-pitched screech of pain that chilled her blood.

"James!" Eddie shouted over his shoulder as he dropped low and took out another wendigo, at the knees this time. "For the love of God, please tell me Belle is safe!"

Before Dr. Helsing could answer, Belle cried out, "Eddie! I'm right here!"

He whirled about. "Siren?" He looked like a shadow holding the long sword out at his side.

"What are you doing?!" She wanted to reach through and yank him back to this side of safety.

"Getting your pixie dust." He said it with the air of someone making a quick stop at the grocery store. He cocked his head as the golden orbs in that dark mask trailed over her. Right over her pink long-sleeved shirt and pants pajama set, and fuzzy socks with cupcakes on them. "Sweet," he murmured.

Dr. Helsing cleared his throat. "Where is the third wendigo?"

Eddie's attention snapped to his uncle. "I thought I—"

Belle screamed as the monster rushed at him from behind, its rakish hand closing over his entire face and the other long, sinewy arm clamping over his chest. Eddie went flying backward.

The creature stood in their view with its back to them. A long tail like a lion's swished from side to side. The wendigo flexed its long arms out and let out an ear-piercing shriek that vibrated the windows in her house. But the sound was cut short by a flash of steel and then the antler-head falling forward while the body crumpled over sideways.

Eddie stepped over the monstrous heap. After one look around, he planted the sword's tip into the ground and took a knee.

Belle watched as he bowed his head. "What's he doing?" she whispered.

"His priestly duties," Dr. Helsing answered. "Offering a prayer for the souls of the humans these creatures once were."

Eddie crossed himself. As he stood, the Jäger suit slowly snaked back into the leather wrist wrap, leaving him in a beaded moccasin shirt and dark jeans. He swung the sword once before sheathing it at his side. "Silver," he said, "the wendigo's kryptonite. The katana's coated with it."

"So those monsters have pixie dust?" Belle asked.

Eddie sat on the carcass's hip. "There's an Algonquin reservation here in Ontario where the wendigo bloodline is strong. The Jäger have kept a watchful eye on them. As long as they don't give in to their urges to consume human flesh, they're left in peace. But eventually, one of them always turns, gives in to just a taste, and then goes full wendigo. One cannibalistic rampage later, and the tribe members themselves call us to take it down. In this case, they waited too long. Three of them had turned by the time I got here."

"Is that why you were summoned?"

"Not entirely, but it is tied to my mission in Elmridge. In exchange for eliminating the wendigos, the tribe will give me a teaspoon of pixie dust. It should be just enough for restoring your mother after I've exorcised Violet."

That little bird called Hope fluttered its wings in her chest again. "Thank you, Eddie. I can't tell you how grateful I am."

He stood suddenly to his feet and approached them. He crooked a finger at her, beckoning her to come closer. She obliged. It was strange standing so close to this version of Eddie. It was like looking at an uncolored page out of a coloring book, only the page was black and the lines in shimmering gold.

"Do we look the same to you as you do to us?" she asked.

He nodded, his gaze holding hers. She outlined his jaw with one finger, but the line dispersed and reformed. "Amazing," she murmured.

"Indeed." His eyes tracked over her face and came to rest on her lips.

"Do you feel that?" She trailed a finger down his chest, watching the shimmering trail in its wake.

Eddie licked his bottom lip. "I feel everything in here." He palmed his chest, over his heart.

She wanted to kiss him. That juju was so darn strong. She leaned in, as did Eddie, but a loud impatient sigh from behind her made them pause.

"Good grief, Edward. It is close to 3:30 in the morning, and if I do say so myself, I am the one being subjected to a nightmare. I would like to wrap this up now before some naysayer discovers my vehicle outside this house at this ungodly hour, and I am fired from my teaching post."

Eddie looked as if he'd been struck with an epiphany. "My dear uncle, I've discovered your hidden power."

Surprise overtook his uncle's features. "What is it?"

"Mood-killer."

Belle laughed, and Eddie immediately pivoted to watch her.

Dr. Helsing scowled. "Bad form, nephew."

"Wait a minute," Belle said, arching an eyebrow at Eddie. "I thought you couldn't lie."

"But I can tell jokes, thank God."

"As well as resort to an aggravating cache of sarcasm," Dr. Helsing said. "Now, the reason we called you, Edward, is because, as you can see, there is no fire, but my trip here and my ensuing mortification—" He waved his stubby wrist.

"Oh, so she knows," Eddie said.

"She knows." Dr. Helsing continued as if he hadn't been interrupted, "—has thankfully not been wasted because Belle has had a telling nightmare when she attempted to connect with her mother."

Belle recounted the nightmare to Eddie. "So your uncle thinks I need to overcome each of my mother's fears in order to reach her."

"Sounds about right."

"I only recognized Jonas Black because of how he was described in my mother's diary. But how would I overcome him if my mother already killed him with a lightning blast?"

"Perhaps," Dr. Helsing said, "it is not Jonas Black you must defeat, but the girl who led you to him."

"Violet Wickeby," Eddie said solemnly.

Belle was stunned. "Th-That's Violet?"

"From how you described her, that's what she was wearing when she died."

"How do you know that, Eddie? And don't tell me *research*."

"*Hunger Games.*"

She blinked once. Twice. "Meaning?"

"I'm done with my annotations. You'll find some answers in there."

"Like how you knew about Violet's dress?"

He gave a slight nod and looked away, scratching the back of his neck. "Among other things."

Hmm, he was nervous about those answers. She wondered what those "other things" were.

He turned to his uncle. "Would you give her the book, please? It's in my apartment."

"Of course." Dr. Helsing put an index finger on the tip of his nose, as if in thought. "The fairy flying overhead in her dream is—"

"The Jäger Father," Eddie answered.

"Yes, I thought so. The prowling beast is the very same one in Elmridge that Belle seems to have a mental connection with. But the butcher she first encounters in the dream, whom may that be?"

"I have no idea," Eddie admitted. "Siren, does Abigail's diary mention anyone described as that man?"

She racked her memory. "No." But something else was bothering her. "I want to know why my mother feared this Jäger Father, and why he had two pairs of bloody fairy wings in his hands."

The two men exchanged knowing looks.

"What? Tell me," she demanded.

A yodeling sound came from a distance. Eddie's attention snapped to it. "That's the signal from the tribe. They're coming in."

"Edward?" Dr. Helsing prompted.

"Yes?"

"When do you expect to convene with Ernesto Panzinski?"

"Tomorrow."

"Will you be interrogating Violet's assistant then?"

"Hagar," Belle supplied. "I just remembered her name from my dream."

Eddie nodded. "We need to know what potions Violet ordered from her." He stooped as if picking something up, and his face suddenly took up the entire view. "I'll return soon." His face leaned in, and there was a second there where he stared into her eyes, and then the mirage dissipated in a shower of golden glitter.

"Does 'the call' have to be ended the same way it's started?" she asked.

"Yes," Dr. Helsing replied.

More to herself, she said under her breath, "So Eddie's allowed to kiss rocks. How nice."

"Do I detect jealousy, Ms. Montague? Of rocks?" He looked the kind of serious that thinly masked pure amusement.

"You detect nothing."

"As you say." Dr. Helsing pocketed the calling stone with a heavy sigh. "Good night, Ms. Montague."

"At least tell me about those fairy wings before you go, please."

He turned to face her at the door, an air of exhaustion about him. "Very well. When a human touches a Neverland meteorite, as your mother and aunt both did, they are transformed into a Fae with the lifespan, powers, and knowledge of the Fae."

Her jaw dropped. "I thought you said—"

"But," he continued, "the true Fae did not desire for the newly turned Fae to be equal to them. There is a sense of pride in the Fae heritage among the true Fae. Thus, it was decided that these turned-Fae would have their wings ripped from them"—Belle gasped—"so that they could not resume miniature Fae-form and fly off. It was a way to keep these now termed 'Fae acolytes' in check here on Earth. What's more, their memories were altered so they thought the fairy wings shriveled away into nothing over time."

Belle was stunned. "Having their wings ripped out must have been excruciating."

"Absolutely," he answered matter-of-factly.

She thought of her mother and aunt going through that experience, how it must have been like. Maybe like having your arms ripped right out of their sockets. A cold, dreadful shiver ran down her spine.

"Who did the wing-ripping?" She hoped hard that Eddie had nothing to do with it. It was too callous an act. She'd never be able to look at him the same way again.

"The Jäger Father."

"That's why he had the—"

"Two pairs of wings in his hands," he finished for her, a touch of impatience in his voice. "Your mother has a suppressed memory of the event, and probably witnessed Emily's as well." He unlocked the door and turned the doorknob. "Sleep well."

And he was gone.

| 23 |

Chemical Romance

When Belle answered the front door the next morning, she expected to find her usual ride to school, which was Candy, not Liam Rawlins.

Drinking in the sight standing on her front porch, only Liam could make a school uniform of khaki slacks and a white dress shirt look good enough for a Giorgio Armani photoshoot. He had a few of the top buttons undone with a pair of aviator glasses tucked into the opening of the shirt. His short hair was neatly combed over and back, and she detected the scent of an enticing fresh cologne.

And he wasn't empty-handed.

He held out a bouquet of bright red roses. "Forgive me? Please?"

"For which offense? Your disappearing act, or siccing your goons on my friend?"

His jaw tightened. "Your friend attacked my guys, and now two of them are out for the next game." He paused and exhaled. "But that's not why I'm here."

She crossed her arms defiantly over her chest, and when she opened her mouth to say something that matched her current mood, he rushed on, "I'm here to tell you the reason why I stayed away."

Her arms fell to her sides. "Oh. Well, go on then."

He held the flowers out to her again. "Please?"

Hesitantly, she took them, cradling their momentary truce in her arms.

"I signed Rawlins Enterprises over to Mr. Ellerson—he was my father's best friend and business partner—so I could focus on a new venture. I'm partnering with a company, RejuveNew Med. They've advanced the field of medicine and treatments for spinal injuries. It's a top-secret project for many reasons that I won't get into, but they were serious enough that I had to completely detach from my normal, everyday life and focus on this for some time."

"And a simple phone call was not allowed?"

He shook his head.

"But it was okay for you to pick up a call from Vasilisa?"

He hesitated, and Belle knew she'd caught him in a lie. She thrust the roses against his chest.

"No, Belle, listen, please—"

"I can't believe I even for one second—"

"Her mom's on the board of this company! Lisa's mom is one of the people I had to keep in touch with, and that meant if Lisa called, I had to pick up."

She stared at him in disbelief. "Then, why am I finding all this so hard to swallow?"

"Let me show you." His mint green eyes pleaded with hers.

She sighed, caving in. Those eyes in that face attached to that body that was now standing so close, his expensive cologne filling her lungs…. He was a chink in her armor, a crack in the dam of her resolve that he blew wide open with one puppy-eyed apology. "What exactly are you going to show me?"

"Not 'what,' but whom."

Her eyebrows quirked in confusion. He smiled and placed the rose bouquet decidedly in her arms before grabbing her hand and leading her toward a shiny, sleek sports car. She spotted a full name spelled out on its trunk. "Who's Aston Martin?"

He grinned as if he found something funny. "One of my ladies."

She frowned darkly.

"But you're my number one lady," he added, the dimple deepening in his chin.

"Amongst a slew of them, I imagine."

"All of them sitting in a row and waiting for me at home in the garage."

"We *are* still using car metaphors, right?"

He barked out a laugh, and before she could react, he tugged her to him and kissed her squarely on the mouth. She tasted mint. It was a hard pop kiss that sounded with a smack when he pulled away.

"I missed you," he said huskily, his eyes sweeping over her face.

Once recovered from that luscious ambush, she whispered, "You can't...just...kiss me whenever you want. I'm not your girlfriend."

His response was to peer at her lips again and wet his own as if he were thinking about saying hello to them again.

She took a step back, and before she could pull her hand away from his, he straightened with an air of resignation. He led her towards the car again, to the passenger side. He pulled the door open and a gorgeous redhead with long flowing hair and wide baby blue eyes blinked back at her.

"Marissa?"

"Hi, Belle." She looked up at both of them with a friendly, albeit embarrassed, smile. Her voice sounded hoarse, though. "I'm hoping Liam has explained by now." She looked meaningfully over at him with the smile tightening on her face.

Belle was so confused. Seeing Marissa in Liam's car, and not Jared's, was like an alternate reality scene. It looked wrong. That car/women metaphor Belle and Liam were joking over just seconds ago was grating against her nerves now.

"Belle," Liam gestured toward Mari with a flourish, "meet the new face of RejuveNew Med."

A pink flush invaded Mari's cheeks, from embarrassment, excitement, both…Belle wasn't sure, but when Mari lifted a leg out of the car and gingerly placed it on the ground, and then proceeded to lift herself out of the seat, Belle's jaw hit the floor.

"Mari! This is, oh my, this is a miracle!"

Liam beamed with pride.

Mari wobbled on her feet as she stood, and Belle grabbed her by one elbow to steady her. Mari grimaced as if in pain before forcing another smile.

"What's wrong, Mari? Does something hurt?"

"Just my feet, when I put my weight on them," she said hoarsely. "But I can't complain, right? I mean, I haven't been able to do this since the car accident when I was a little girl."

"We're still working on alleviating some of the side effects," Liam supplied, helping Mari ease back into the car. A look of staunch relief crossed her features when she leaned back against the seat. "The pins and needles at the feet and losing her voice."

"Oh," Belle said, unable to keep the pity out of her voice.

"But worth it," Mari rasped.

"Your parents and Jared, they must all be so excited for you."

Mari pursed her lips, while Liam answered, "They don't know. Mari's still using her wheelchair. She only walks when she's in treatment. No one knows about her progress outside the company, except you now."

"So, you've been hiding this from them?" Belle asked her.

Mari diverted her eyes, but Belle caught the sheen in them.

Belle turned on Liam. "Why am *I* allowed to know, but not her own family?"

He pressed his lips into a thin line and said to Mari, "Just a minute?" She nodded, and he gently shut the passenger door.

Liam moved into Belle's space, and when she stepped away, the hurt flashed in his eyes. "The secrecy is necessary, but everyone will know about it soon enough. We're getting her ready for a big reveal, and just imagine how many others with spinal injuries will be able to benefit from the treatment."

"That *was* pretty miraculous." She bit her bottom lip. "It's just…the pain you caused me, and the pain that Mari's obviously going through, it all still nags at me a lot."

Liam grabbed the battered bouquet of roses she'd been cradling in one arm and laid them on the roof of the car. Squeezing her hands in his, he drew her in closer so she had to look up into his face. Those yellow flecks in his crystal green eyes seemed to glow. "I will make it up to you. Just *let* me, please." She dipped her chin a fraction and that was enough of a yes for him. "Will you be my date for the Halloween party next weekend?"

Her heart fluttered with the same excitement as that last night between them on her porch. Her lips split into a shy smile. "Okay."

He pressed the backs of her hands to his lips, his eyes holding hers with a promise of more to come.

Candy pulled up at that moment in the Cadillac. Belle knew from her balked expression that she would have some explaining to do.

"I was hoping I could take you to school." Liam was still running the back of one of her hands slowly across his lips, his warm breath ratcheting up the sensation.

"Um, I think I'll keep Candy company." She gently pulled her hand away. "I'll see you in class today?"

He nodded, still not moving from his spot. He was staring at her lips again.

Almost tripping over her feet as she moved to the passenger side window, she tapped on it, and it slid down. Mari smiled up at her.

Belle offered her the bouquet of roses. "To one of the toughest women I know."

A genuine grin lit up Mari's face, and her round blue eyes shone with warmth. She took the flowers. "Thanks."

~*~

Belle was floating on the proverbial cloud nine. Things felt like they were finally moving in the right direction in her life. Yes, a werewolf was still loose in Elmridge, but her uncle had a team of animal specialists working on it, and she was planning to ask Q at lunch if he could use his computer magic to generate a list of tall, muscular blonde men from Elmridge.

And she was going to see Dr. Helsing today in literature class and get Eddie's book from him. She was excited about that, especially the 'answers' he said he'd left for her in the book. Eddie must already be in possession of the pixie dust by now, and as soon as he returns to Elmridge, they can kickstart their plan to get rid of Violet and free her mom.

Things were definitely looking up. Ernesto was coming back this weekend, and after school today, she was meeting up with Cindy, Candy, and hopefully, Millie, at the castle to formulate their game plan for winning the Homecoming crown. And with Liam at her side on that princess court, she might as well start preparing her acceptance speech now.

Liam could definitely help her win that crown, and then Eddie could help her defeat Violet.

But Belle should've known, though. With her rotten luck, anything too good to be true, most definitely was. She just knew the Fae had to be watching. Probably rewinding and replaying all the muddy twists of her day.

That *it's-a-wonderful-world*-high she was riding came to a screeching halt in chemistry class.

When Belle slid into her seat next to Jared Prince, she expected his usual, "Hey, Beauty, how's it going?" followed by his dazzling, dimpled grin.

Instead, she found him slouched down in his chair, eyebrows pinched together, staring stormily at the lab set of beakers and small test tube trays set before them. He was tapping his stylus pen against the tabletop so fast, it was almost a blur.

"This is a rare look for you," she said by way of greeting.

He instantly sat up in his chair and mumbled, "Sorry. Just got a lot on my mind."

Dr. Battersby began his lecture before she could prod further. Soon, they were in the midst of a delicate chemistry experiment that would've gone kaboom in their faces, if Belle hadn't constantly been diverting each of Jared's steps from disaster.

"Why don't you just let me conduct this part, and you can write up the lab notes?" She grabbed a test tube from his fingers that was threatening to bubble over and rushed it to the sink. She took the longer way about the room to avoid Kat and her minions, who were currently wafting away a noxious cloud spewing from one of their beakers.

Kat had tried to trip her in the hallway earlier that day, but thanks to her freakishly heightened reflexes, she'd sidestepped her, and Kat had ended up tripping one of her own clones, who'd then dominoed into another one of their own. Belle had fled the scene when the neon clique self-imploded into a screeching round of finger-pointing.

When Belle returned to the lab table, Jared sat absently twirling the pen between his fingers, staring at the lab notes on the tablet like he was contemplating murder.

She touched his hand and the pen-twirling instantly stopped. "Wanna tell me what's wrong?"

The pen clattered on the desk as he shoved his hands clear through his non-gelled hair. Strange, in fact, his black hair hanging loosely above his ears instead of cemented into an artful swirl. Even his rockstar accessories were missing. He looked like a simple gorgeous schoolboy, who if he were shy enough, could fade into the background as a wallflower, instead of going down in history as a pop music legend, permanently featured in teen fantasies.

"It's Mari. She's…she's acting differently. And I know it's because of," he glanced swiftly at her before looking away, "because of *some-*

body." He squeezed the edge of the table like he wanted to choke this somebody.

"Who is it? Do I know them?"

Jared faced her fully now, turning those ocean blue eyes on her. "Mari's running for Homecoming court, and I want to help her. She's my best friend."

"I think Mari's got a really great chance of winning," Belle said. "I'm pretty sure everyone likes her." Even though Mari carried a Princess Posse membership card, Belle had checked out her Peacock Profile, and she seemed to be friends with everyone and loved by everyone. She sighed as she realized something else. "And she really is the most beautiful girl I've ever seen."

Deep dimples appeared in his cheeks. "I guess you've never looked in a mirror."

Belle blushed tomato red and waved off his compliment. But the flirty smile slipped off his face when his mind went back to whatever was bothering him.

"So who is this 'somebody' affecting Mari?" she pressed. "You never said."

"I asked Mari to Homecoming. She said someone else had already asked, and then she told me I could take her to the Halloween party instead." He pushed the lab notes away from him and sat back in his chair with a huff, arms crossed over his chest. "Can you believe that? *I'm* the consolation prize."

Belle was starting to realize this was a case of bruised-ego syndrome. "Well, Jared, I mean, if another guy likes Mari, then she has the right to—"

"Ha. You don't get it." He leaned in again, his eyes pinning hers. "Liam Rawlins is taking her to Homecoming."

She heard the record scratch of her *zippity-doo-dah-wonderful-day* song coming to an abrupt halt. "What?!"

Everyone turned to stare.

"Ms. Montague!" Dr. Battersby barked. "Care to share why you've decided to interrupt everyone's four-grade lab assignment?"

"Four grades!" Jared whispered next to her. "Holy sh—"

Belle shot to her feet, holding a full beaker in one hand and a foamy test tube in the other. "Oh, it's just that I was amazed by this reaction." She lifted the items in her hands for emphasis. "This experiment is so cool; I looove chemistry."

"You're overselling it," Jared warned quietly.

Just when she thought he might be right, Dr. Battersby stood straighter and smoothed down the lapels of his lab coat. "Of course you do. Your top rank in this class confirms it."

A loud snort came from a certain corner of the room. "Nerd."

Belle shot back down in her seat when the teacher moved toward Kat's corner.

"I can't fail chemistry," Jared said, panic in his eyes.

"You won't," she assured him. "I'm your lab partner, remember?"

He grinned at that and scooted closer to her, his thigh pressed against hers. "So if Liam's taking Mari to Homecoming, wouldn't it make sense if I took you?"

"It would actually," she responded automatically, and then felt herself immediately lock up. She really tripped and fell into that one.

But the more she thought about it, the more it did make sense. Yes, she was currently restraining a raging, green-eyed monster inside her that wanted to lash out at Liam, but she was tempted to think that he was only taking Mari to Homecoming because, what if the 'big reveal' that Liam mentioned that morning was supposed to take place at Homecoming? Maybe Mari was going to finally show everyone there that she could walk. That made sense, even if Belle was still going to give Liam a verbal thrashing. But then again, didn't she keep telling him that she wasn't his girlfriend? Showing Liam that she wasn't mad about him taking Mari to the dance would surely make that clearer to him. *Was* she mad, though? That sharp sting on her conscience when she thought of Liam and Mari at Homecoming together proved she was. But was she actually jealous, or just suffering from a petty case of bruised-ego syndrome herself?

She needed her besties for this one.

"So," Jared traced a line up her forearm to her elbow, "you'll be my date for Homecoming then?"

She had to keep her main objective in mind. She needed to win that Homecoming crown. And if Liam wasn't going to be her date for that event, then one of the most popular boys in the world could surely help with that.

"Yes, I'll be your date."

The smirk and dazzling grin combo he gave her complete with dimples was notorious for knocking the girls off their feet. While it didn't have quite that effect on Belle, her heart did do a fluttery dance.

She smiled back, but when his eyes lingered a little too long on her lips, and he raked in his bottom lip between his teeth, she added quickly, "But just as friends, okay?"

He pursed his lips and groaned. "You got it, Beauty."

"I know you said you want to help Mari win the crown, but I, um, actually really want to win."

"Fatimah said your friends had to beg you to stay in the running."

Right, the lunchroom incident. But the memory of Eddie offering to teach her a magic act momentarily derailed her focus. She felt her core heat up and fan outward until her skin tingled with goosebumps all over her body.

"Cold?" Jared asked, running a hand along her goosepimply forearm. "You feel warm, though."

What in tarnation? She'd have to analyze later that very physical reaction to the mere thought of Eddie. She had to stay focused now.

"I do want to win. I think winning will, uh," she racked her brains, "help me feel accepted, and like I finally belong here."

And the Oscar for Best Actress goes to....

"I can feel that. How about this? I'll help Mari by taking her to the Halloween dance, and then...nah, I don't think you'll go for it."

"What? Tell me. I really do want to win."

"I know a sure-fire way of you walking off the stage with that crown." The excitement on her face was too obvious. He laughed, but then quickly sobered. "After the Halloween dance, and up to Home-coming, you'd have to be my girlfriend."

Her jaw dropped in outrage.

"Pretend to be," he clarified.

She snapped her mouth shut. "So, I'd be Miss November?" she asked in an agonized whisper.

"Psh, that's just gossip. Don't listen to that."

But it was widely believed as fact amongst the female population. Jared had a notorious habit of dating a different girl each month. Just last month, when Belle had shown up in Elmridge, and Jared was pay-ing her attention, the rumor that she was Miss September had spread like wildfire, only to be squashed when Liam had started spending time with her.

"But what about Mari? I don't want to hurt her."

"Why would she be hurt?"

Wow, he really was clueless. That comment proved he didn't see how in love Mari was with him.

"Besides," he added, "she's going with Liam to Homecoming. I'm the one that's hurt. First, he gets you, and then he moves in on my best friend." The pen in his hand snapped in half.

"First of all, he never *got* me. And second, I think you should give Mari some credit that she knows what she's doing. For the record, Liam is taking me to the Halloween dance; he asked me this morn-ing." She ignored the way his lips curled into a scowl. "So, maybe this is all part of Mari's strategy for winning. I would know, since I'm do-ing the same thing. Me and Mari are each taking you and Liam to a Homecoming event."

She waited for Jared to understand. "Wow, that's just *not* like her. Mari doesn't scheme."

"I do, apparently. See? I really do want to win that crown."

"So then you'll be my pretend-girlfriend after Halloween?"

"Of course." Her eyes widened as she locked up again. Another one she tripped and fell into. Mari may not be a natural schemer, but Jared sure was.

"Pretend," she emphasized.

"Of course," he echoed her. "But after a few pretend-dates with me, you may not want to pretend anymore." He winked at her, and her breath hitched at his audacity, and she definitely ignored that low curl in her stomach. "Besides, the only real contenders for the crown are you, Mari, and Nieves, especially with Lisa in the hospital—"

"Wait, what do you mean Lisa's in the hospital?"

He blinked. "What? You don't know? Everybody knows."

"Know what exactly?"

He lowered his voice when Dr. Battersby's watchful eyes swept over them. "Lisa's in a coma. The doctors can't explain it. It's like she's asleep, but just won't wake up."

"How-How did that—"

"She was found unconscious in a backroom of her store."

Briar Rose, the store Lisa owned and where Belle had purchased all her new clothes on her second day in Elmridge.

"And no one knows why she won't wake up?"

Jared leaned in closer, his warm breath tickling her ear. "I found this part out from Mari: Lisa's parents wanted to tell everyone in Elmridge what they think caused her coma, but Mayor Markham and the police had the DA put a legal gag on them so as not to," he finger-quoted, "'panic the public.' So, yeah, it's all very hush-hush. I mean, no one's even allowed to see Lisa in the hospital. It's messed up, if you ask me."

"Oh my."

"Yeah. Something's up in Elmridge. Everyone knows it." Jared leaned away as Dr. Battersby approached and pretended to peer studiously at the reaction in the beaker.

A molten brick settled in her stomach. She just knew the Violet Wickeby nightmare was spilling over into the town's radar. Somehow, Violet had to be involved with whatever happened to Lisa. And she wondered if it would be safe to wait all the way to Homecoming to execute the rid-the-world-of-the-wicked-witch plan.

If only Eddie was already here with the pixie dust....

| **24** |

Tinker Soldier Spy

A new sense of urgency compelled Belle to beg Q at lunch to give her a list of the strong, blonde men in town for a "project" she was working on, but she was rebuffed.

"I'd have to access the Internet channels that the CIA is monitoring me on." Q shook his ruddy hair out of his eyes and pushed his tortoiseshell glasses up the bridge of his nose.

Belle blinked back at him, momentarily thrown off. "CIA?"

"I declassified all the Area 51 files for the public," he said, all nonchalance as he bit into his cheese sandwich.

"I thought the government released those files," Cindy said over a mouthful of tuna salad.

Q rolled his eyes. "Governments and their cover-ups."

"So, can you do it?" Belle pressed.

"He'd get in trouble," Cindy reminded her.

She bit her lip. "You're right. I'm sorry. I guess I'll figure something out myself."

"I never said *no*," Q said. The bubble of hope inflating in her chest popped, when he added with a Cheshire cat smile, "I will do it if you beat me at our D&D game tonight. It will be your prize."

She groaned.

Belle thought seeing Dr. Helsing in literature class next would cheer her up, but the sight of a Principal Steifshwester look-alike, probably a close relative, sitting behind his desk instead, stopped her cold at the door, followed by the sting of disappointment that she wouldn't be getting Eddie's book from Dr. Helsing that day.

The slightly shorter, more overweight, and completely gray-haired version of the former principal narrowed her eyes at Belle. "I know who you are."

She swallowed hard. Crud. Belle had practically gotten Cindy's evil stepmother fired from the principal's post. Fired and jailed for child abuse and attempted murder, actually. Remembering that made Belle narrow her own eyes back at her before sailing past the glowering matron.

As the students filled their seats, Belle spotted His Hotness already sitting at his desk in the back. Right behind hers. And Liam was still a vision that made her mouth go dry. He was leaning back in his desk, turned at an angle to accommodate his long form.

Everyone was staring at them, waiting to see how this second encounter would play out. Two days ago, she'd ignored him in class, pretended he didn't exist. And now...she thought that would make a great plan again.

For the few seconds that his gaze had held hers—his, hopeful, until it turned into confusion at her indignant stare—her shoulder angels battled it out, and for some reason, they looked like Millie and Candy in school uniforms with respective demon-horns and angel-halo headbands.

Bad Angel/Millie: If you're supposed to be his girlfriend, shouldn't he be taking you to *both* parties, especially the one that really matters?

Good Angel/Candy: Girl, please. You heard the man this morning, right after he laid a juicy kiss on you—he's giving Mari back her legs and letting the world know on Homecoming so other people that need the same help, know where to find it. The man's a hero! And smoking hot, too. Don't forget that, Belle.

Bad Angel/Millie: And *when* exactly did he say that Homecoming was supposed to be the big reveal for Mari? You're just assuming that's it.

Good Angel/Candy: (Pouting.) Mmm. She's got a point, hon'. But do you see the way that shirt hugs his muscles?

Belle paled. She was assuming. And yes. Yes, she did see. She was looking at them right now. Even across the classroom, she could see the sleeves straining against the swells on those arms.

A tiny smirk crossed Liam's lips, as if he knew she was checking him out.

Focus! Bad Angel/Millie whisper-shouted.

Right, assuming things. He never said Homecoming would be Mari's big reveal. She couldn't just assume like that. Liam was taking Mari to Homecoming, and not Belle, his supposed girlfriend. Well then. She'd have to use this to reinforce what she'd told him earlier: she was *not* his girlfriend.

Her lips pressed into a deep frown.

Thattagirl.

No wonder you ain't got a man, Good Angel/Candy grumbled at Bad Angel/Millie.

Belle ignored her two angel-besties duking it out in the back of her mind, especially since Liam was now beckoning for her to come sit in front of him.

"Can you move?" A Kat-clone with a long, dark ponytail and neon accessories scowled at her, waiting for Belle to move from her petrified stance in the desk aisle.

"Uh, sorry," she mumbled, and slid into Lisa's vacant desk, towards the front, away from Liam.

She could definitely feel his questioning, hurt expression boring into her back. Soon enough, her hearing picked up on some suspicious whispering between Liam and his friend across the aisle, Shawn.

"Uh, Ms. Stiff—I mean, Steifshwester?" Shawn called out. The monstrous scowl on the teacher's face silenced the titter that had erupted from the class. "Belle's not sitting in her assigned seat."

A slow, triumphant smile crept across the old woman's face as she turned her beady eyes on Belle, who promptly made herself smaller in her seat.

Great, I just got handed over on a silver platter.

"Since you think you are above the rules, Belle Montague, you will serve detention this afternoon."

Belle's jaw dropped as indignation flushed her cheeks.

Shawn piped up, "She already has detention this afternoon."

Her head whipped around to face him. "What?"

Shawn looked pointedly back at her and pantomimed a punch to his own chin, as if that was an answer.

Oh. The brawl with Eddie and the football team by the Peacock Fountain. She and Eddie had ditched the meeting in the principal's office, and she definitely hadn't checked the dozen messages on her phone from the school office.

She refused to meet Liam's eyes before whipping back around. If he hadn't sicced the football team on Eddie, there wouldn't have been any such trouble to begin with.

"Tomorrow then," Ms. Steifshwester amended.

"It's for two weeks," Shawn added.

An irritated Liam interrupted, "Will you please just let her go to her seat?"

Belle's eyes widened. She'd never heard a student speak to a teacher that way.

Ms. Steifshwester indeed looked rumpled. But if Liam Rawlins pulled any weight in this town, it was evident right then.

When she first moved here, Belle learned that Aunt Emily was the wealthiest resident, who practically owned the town, while the Rawlins family was the second wealthiest. But with her aunt out of public sight for the past few years, and her uncle-the-sheriff busy in Europe, the protection her status should have offered her felt downright null and void at the moment. But with Liam Rawlins, not even the suspicion of familial homicide hanging over him like a black cloud detracted an ounce from his authority.

Ms. Steifshwester gave him a tight smile. "Of course, Mr. Rawlins. We wouldn't want to hold up today's lesson. But, do mind your tone."

Liam said nothing, holding the old woman's stare as if still waiting for his request to be met.

The teacher turned sharply to Belle. "Move to your seat."

Mortified, she gathered her things and shuffled down the aisle to the back.

Once the teacher turned toward the interactive whiteboard, she felt Liam's hand sweep back one side of her hair. "Are you angry with me?" he whispered by her ear.

Goosebumps erupted on that side of her neck. Proving that he noticed the reaction his breath had on her skin, he trailed a finger over that responsive area.

She flinched away.

He drew close again and murmured, "I don't remember you being this ticklish."

She heard Shawn snort, and her cheeks flamed. They still had an audience.

"I'm in enough trouble as it is," she muttered back.

"Got it." And mercifully, he leaned away, taking that crisp evergreen musk with him that reminded her too much of the warmth of being in his arms.

Halfway through Ms. Steifshwester's butchered interpretation of Long John Silver's antithetical character, something crinkly tickled her ear. Her hand snatched at a long-stemmed rose origammied from white notebook paper. It had the words penned on a single leaf, *Please don't be mad at me.*

Boy, was she a sucker. She threw a little smile over her shoulder at Liam.

The last twenty minutes of class consisted of group work, which meant Liam quickly pulled hers and Shawn's desks in to form the group.

"Groups of four!" the teacher reminded.

One student remained. A quiet, slightly heavyset girl in front of Shawn with skin so pale, the array of blue veins was visible on the backs of her hands. Hannah, if she remembered correctly. Her ice-blue eyes were encircled in black coal and drawn out at the corners like Cleopatra, and her shoulder-length hair was a raven black, but Belle knew from when Hannah periodically flipped her hair over her shoulder, that the underside hair was bright rainbow-patterned. Belle thought it was the prettiest hair dye job she'd ever seen.

"Would you like to join us?" Belle asked her.

Hannah still sat looking forward. The only response was a flick of her eyeballs in Belle's direction.

Shawn tapped Hannah lightly on the shoulder. "Emo-girl."

"You're so rude," Belle whisper-snapped at him, just as Liam chuckled and then coughed to hide it.

Shawn ignored her, and spoke as if Hannah were slow, "You. Need. To. Join. Our. Group."

Hannah withdrew a black marker from a pocket, and in clear view, proceeded to write inside her hand:

Make a Shawn voodoo doll. Use extra-long pins.

Shawn shrank back in fear, rambling about "chicks trying to pose as witches and vampires."

Hannah did join after being told to by Ms. Steifshwester, but refused to say a word to them, except sport a permanent scowl. The only way the assignment worked for them was to divide up the eight questions posted on the whiteboard equally amongst them.

Liam pushed his two questions toward his friend with a meaning-ful look.

"Dude," Shawn muttered, "you're gonna have to pay me more. And that Helsing family report you made me do was no joke. Make it dou-ble this time, and I'll throw in the midterm, too."

All the color drained from Belle's face as she felt herself go cold. "You did his family report? The one that included mine? With the very personal history?"

Dr. Helsing had paired Belle and Liam together to write a report on how their ancestral family histories were tied together. They'd read family diaries, discussed and taken notes on the histories, and Liam had volunteered to have their notes typed up into the final re-port. But when he'd said those words, "I'll have it typed up," Belle thought he would relegate the task to a trusted confidante like his but-ler, Jacques, not a busybody like Shawn.

Liam stiffened in his seat while Shawn waved her off. "Nothing to be embarrassed about. You're famous! Your ancestors were the myth-ical Prynn sisters. Beast here, on the other hand," he jutted his thumb at Liam, "is infamous. His fam' burned your fam' at the stake." He stroked his chin, thinking. "But one of them had to have gotten away, otherwise how would you be here. Hmm, I wonder how much of the legend is true. The bit about them turning into fairies can't be true, but how *did* they get away?"

Belle felt her throat constrict while Liam growled at him, "You talk too much."

Ms. Steifshwester walked over, and Belle had to bite back her out-rage. The teacher hovered close by, peering over their shoulders at their lack of progress on the assignment, and gave them a beady look. "Not much to see here so far," she said snidely.

They put pencil to paper. Normally, the students worked on tablets, but the teacher said they were completing the assignment "the old-fashioned way" and had passed out pencils and worksheets.

Soon enough, Liam let out a frustrated sigh as he rubbed the spot between his eyebrows. He touched her elbow. "Belle, let me explain, please."

She paused writing mid-sentence and didn't even look at him as she said, "I don't want to talk about it here." She resumed writing, hoping he'd listen. She was not happy with him right now. In fact, she was furious. Cold, cold fury!

She drew a long breath in through her nostrils and exhaled slowly through her mouth. If she didn't calm down, a light show was going to erupt from her hands. Not even the feel of Eddie's rosary against her skin would prevent at least a few noticeable sparks.

A crinkly sound drew her attention towards Shawn's desk. He was busy folding a notebook paper into a bird. A look at Liam's desk showed no paper in sight.

Her insides felt like ice now. "Hey, Shawn," Belle said casually. "How many roses did Liam tell you to buy the other day?"

He responded automatically, "A dozen, why?" Liam groaned as he sunk his forehead into his palm, and Shawn's eyes went wide. "Whoops."

Belle plastered on a huge, fake smile, anything to mask the rage flashing in her eyes. "Well, thank you for the roses, Shawn." She stood abruptly and hitched her bag over her shoulder.

"Belle," Liam started.

She dropped the origami rose onto Shawn's desk. "And thank you for that one, too. It was beautifully done."

Shawn beamed. "Thanks."

Liam cast a dark scowl at him.

Belle suddenly swiped everything off of Shawn's desk, tablet and all, and ignored the brief flash of sparks from her hands as the stuff clattered to the floor, drawing eyes and shocked gasps in their direction. "And that's for sucker-punching my friend."

"Belle Montague!" the teacher hollered.

With Shawn holding his hands out in outrage, and Liam whispering for her to calm down, she grabbed her things off her desk and stuffed them into her bag. She grabbed the black marker sticking out of Hannah's pocket and plopped it onto her desk. "Why don't you add Liam's name to your list? Extra, *extra*-long pins."

Hannah's pursed lips slowly stretched into a smile as she nodded, like she was looking at a new kindred spirit before her.

Belle jutted her pointer finger at her. "And your hair is awesome." She realized she sounded angry when she said it, but she was barely containing her rage at the moment.

Belle had to get out of there before she turned into a Roman candle. She headed down the aisle, ignoring Liam's pleas and the teacher's threats. She burst out the door and didn't even realize she was running down the hall until a hand clamped down on her arm and spun her around.

"Liam! Let me be!" She cast her eyes around, frantically searching for an escape. "I need to get out of here."

"I need to talk to you, please, just give me a chance." He peered inside the window slit of a classroom door. "It's empty. C'mon, we can talk in here."

Knowing she was going to regret this, she allowed Liam to pull her inside and shut the door behind them.

Liam flicked on the lights. Rows of easels and stools stretched out before them. Paintings in various stages of completion arrested her attention for a moment.

At the sound of the door lock clicking, Belle spun around.

Liam showed his palms. "I'm just guaranteeing us some privacy."

"You." She dug her finger into his chest. "You're a fake!"

"My feelings for you are real." He reached for her hands, but she pulled away.

"As real as the paper rose you tried to pass off as yours. Or the roses you had someone else get, or the very personal report you had Shawn write about us!"

"He only sees it as the Prynn legend everybody else already knows about."

"Did you hear him in class? 'How did they get away?' If he keeps putting two and two together, he could figure out that Abigail and Emily Prynn never died, and the legend is actually real! Maybe, he'll even figure out that Abigail is my mom possessed by a demon named Violet Wickeby who shoots lightning out of her hands!"

The sound of snapping and crackling and Belle's heavy breathing filled the gap of silence that followed.

"What?" she demanded, when Liam just stood there, watching her, his face unreadable.

He looked pointedly at her hands. "I think you should stop shouting."

She lifted her hands, white sparks sizzling from them, and plopped down onto a nearby stool. "You're right," she said, slumping in defeat. "I can't let myself get worked up. I might go supernova and blow a crater in Elmridge." Again, she was grateful for the weight of Eddie's rosary tucked into her bosom. It was becoming her security blanket.

Liam pulled up another stool and joined her. After a spell of glum silence, he exhaled a heavy breath. "I'm...sorry I couldn't be there for you when you needed me."

"Yes. I did need you. We went through something together that no one else has probably ever gone through: standing up to a demonic witch who took both our mothers away. That should have brought us closer, and it did that night...and you were supposed to come back like you promised."

"Belle, believe me, I understand. But *you* have to understand, that when I got home, I got a business call that was too important to ignore. It took me in an unexpected direction for a while, and I know you can agree with me, but working on a cause to cure people of paralysis is pretty important. I mean, you saw Mari this morning. It's working."

"That. That right there."

"What?"

"It-It just doesn't make sense."

"It makes perfect sense."

"Just…explain exactly what happened. Regale me with the details. Here, I'll start you off: you left my house that night, drove home, and then what?"

He stared at her as if his mind was working to remember. "I-I got a call, and…that was it."

Belle shook her head, dumbfounded. "'That was it'?"

"I honestly don't remember. It all happened so fast. The next thing I knew, I was in Europe, fully immersed in the deal."

"And it was impossible to make just *one* phone call to the girl that you were supposedly crazy about? One call to ask how her comatose aunt was doing, one call to see whether Violet had struck again?"

He pressed his lips into a grim line and shook his head.

"You know her minions? The twins?" When he only stared and didn't respond, she continued, "Well, they attacked me. They used your cell phone to set a trap for me. Texted me to meet you outside Ridge Rats." Her eyes stung with hot tears at the memory. "They *attacked* me. One of them stomped down on my foot and crushed it. The other twin took out brass knuckles and was coming for me."

When he still sat, simply staring stonily at her, an icy chill crawled down her spine. She stepped toward him. "Why aren't you responding?" The tears slipped in warm trails down her cheeks. "H-How are you not caring right now?"

Liam cleared his throat gruffly and glanced down at her feet before meeting her eyes again. "Your foot looks fine."

Her heart felt like it had been dipped in liquid nitrogen. "I-I can't believe what's happening right now." She started to back away slowly. "If-If the Jäger hadn't saved me from them—"

Liam leapt to his feet so fast, she froze, clutching at her chest. "Did you say 'Jäger'? There's a Jäger in town?"

His sudden alertness and the slight panic in his voice jarred her. "He…left town."

Liam stalked toward her, and she found herself not wanting to be in the same breathing space as him. And she definitely didn't want to be in a locked room with him. His Mr. Hyde vibes were giving her the creepy-crawlies.

The backs of her legs crashed against a table and a stack of paint trays clattered onto the floor.

Liam stepped into the space between her feet and pinched her chin so she had to look up at him. He gave her a small smile that didn't match the vigilance in his eyes. "Why didn't the Jäger try to kill you?"

"Why would he?" She never told Liam about the Hammerson brothers….

He looked pointedly at her as if he knew she was playing dumb. "You're a supernatural creature who killed three men."

Her breath stalled in her lungs. *He does know.*

It took a moment for that implication to finish exploding in her brain. She swallowed hard. "The Jäger learned that I had done it accidentally and in self-defense."

He touched her bottom lip with his index finger and ran it slowly from one corner to the other. "So, if he's not here for you, who is he here for?"

When she didn't answer, he returned to pinching her chin with more force as he waited.

She licked her dry lips and flinched at the quiver in her voice. "I told you. He left town."

"You didn't see his face?"

The instinct to protect Eddie felt like a sharp sting. She shook her head, releasing her chin from his grip.

He stepped back and slid his hands into his pockets. "You'll tell me if you see the Jäger again?"

She nodded, feeling like her head was disconnected from the rest of her body. "Does this mean…we're back to working together?"

His face cracked into a wide grin. He looked relieved. "Yes. This is exactly what I want. You on my side." He added almost robotically, "And to see Mari win that Homecoming crown on her own two feet. I mean, I know you're in the running too, and I'll support you, but I hope you understand how big of a deal this is for her and the company."

"Y-You should take her to Homecoming then. We're already going to the Halloween party together, so Mari has a better shot of winning if you take her to the main event." She forced as genuine a smile as possible and hoped she didn't come off like a mannequin.

"God, this is what I love about you." He swept her into a hug, and Belle allowed her body to mold into his as naturally as possible. "You're so selfless and understanding." He pulled away, and she swiped the tears from her eyes before he saw.

She jumped when the bell sounded the end of class.

"Cindy told me you're coming over later?"

She nodded.

He leaned in to kiss her, but when she turned her cheek, he stopped and straightened. "Right. We'll take it slow." He winked.

She attempted her brightest grin. "Go on. I'm going to stay for a minute and pick up this mess." She motioned behind her at the paint trays scattered on the floor.

At the sound of the door shutting behind him, Belle collapsed into a sitting position on the floor, hugging her knees to her chest. She heaved out the great, big sob she'd been holding in this entire time and let the tears flow freely.

She knew without a shadow of a doubt Violet had gotten to Liam. She was using him, and possibly Mari, to get the Homecoming crown into her own wicked hands. And that taffeite gem would take Violet another step closer to completing her Jade Blade wish spell.

But Belle needed to get herself together right now. Students could come pouring into the art room at any minute. After she quickly gathered the paint trays back onto the table, she fled the room.

In the farthest corner of the room, behind an extra-large easel, Millie carefully slid off her stool. To steady her trembling legs, she grabbed onto the nearby table for support and then pressed *Stop* on her phone's recording.

| 25 |

Legends of Evil

The only bright spot that emerged again in Belle's day after that frightening encounter with Liam was seeing Grace Darling take a seat across from her in Study Hall/Work Experience. It was her last period, a class in which she alternated every other day between tutoring other students and going home early to "work" at the Elmridge Museum.

On Work Experience days, she was hard at work napping in her bed. But today, instead of the gangly eighth-grade boy who needed help with Pre-Algebra for the past month, a sixth-grade girl with long, blonde curls pinned with butterfly clips eased into the seat.

"Grace! Hey, I'm so glad to see you!"

"Hi," Grace replied glumly, barely meeting her eyes. She laid her tablet on the desk and switched it on. A poem filled up the screen.

"Everything okay?"

"No. But I'm not allowed to talk about anything but school. My mom already has me on house arrest. I can't go anywhere, except to school, and she says she'll have me homeschooled if I 'step out of line' one more time. And guess who my teacher will be then?"

"Mom?"

She nodded, her lower lip jutting out.

Grace Darling had a habit of disappearing for days on end, which always spurred a missing person's hunt with the police and the whole public looking for her. But then she'd always been found in Wych-black Forest or in Stoney Peaks. She always claimed she'd taken off on a solo adventure, but Belle knew she'd been out gallivanting with Peter in God-knows-where each time. Grace had told her that, and Belle had been the only one to believe her.

Belle had recently learned that her Aunt Emily and Ernesto's first-born child, Peter Panzinski, had been taken by the fairies when he was just twelve years old. The mermaid poem in the Elmridge book of fairy tales had explained it as the fulfillment of the Fae deal: immortality and powers in exchange for the acolyte's first-born child. The Fae had been looking for a champion to defeat a "bearded enemy" who was slaughtering them, so they were testing out this first-born in hopes of finding a savior. She didn't know if the Fae had succeeded yet. But Peter, her cousin, seemed to be allowed to travel back to Earth (or to this reality) and visit Grace Darling and listen to her stories. When Belle found a photograph of Peter with Emily, she was able to enlist Grace's help in reuniting Peter with his mother. Belle gave Grace the photo, and then Grace showed it to Peter on one of his visits, and that had sent him directly to Emily.

Belle's eyes watered as she reminisced over Emily's reunion with her long-lost son. Her mentally fractured aunt had seemed to heal in that instant and become whole again at the sight of her returned son. Peter whisked her away out the open window then. Yeah, he could fly. And with a pinch of pixie dust that he'd showered over Emily, she'd flown right out along with him.

"Sooo, what does that stanza mean?" Grace asked.

"What stanza?" Belle shook her head, snapping herself out of the reverie.

"I guess I'll read it out loud again." A hint of irritation crossed Grace's features.

After half an hour of dissecting "The Highwayman" with a moody adolescent, Belle couldn't keep the questions at bay anymore. "Grace?" she whispered.

Grace knew from her tone that she wanted to broach the forbidden topic. "I'm not allowed to," she whispered back. But after a moment, she looked up from idly dragging her pen stylus around on the tablet and asked, "Have *you* seen Peter lately?"

Belle bit back a hopeful smile at Grace's surrender. She shook her head to say that she hadn't.

Grace stabbed at the spacebar button. "I haven't seen him since that day I showed him the picture. He just took off without saying good-bye. Do you know if he...if he found his mother?"

Belle bit her lip and slowly nodded her head.

A light of excitement widened Grace's eyes. "So you saw him? And he really found his mom?"

Belle nodded again, chewing on the inside of her cheek, obviously hesitating to elaborate.

Grace seemed to understand. "You can tell me. No one would believe me even if I told them. I've tried. I've lost a bunch of friends over it, so I never spill about Peter to anyone anymore." She plunked her cheek into her palm. "I don't think I even have any friends anymore. Evie told me she couldn't hang out with me because her parents think my 'lying ways and runaway tendencies' will rub off on her." Her bottom lip began quivering and her eyes glistened. "Anything about Peter is the only thing that makes me happy right now. I miss him."

Belle caved. She told her about the night Peter came and took Emily away.

Grace wiped the tears from her eyes. "So he's really found his mom. I'm happy for him." She straightened in her chair as if pinched from behind. "Wait, so if Emily is his mom, and she is your aunt, that makes Peter your cousin!"

"Shh! Not so loud, but yes."

"Oh my God, are you magical, too?"

Belle's heart hammered in her chest, and she felt that at any second now, men in black would swing and crash in through the room's windows to grab her and haul her away.

"No. Absolutely not," Belle lied a bit too forcefully. She could feel herself sweating, and the room felt way too small now, the walls beginning to press in.

Grace watched her with wide eyes, forming conclusions in her mind that Belle thought a twelve-year-old shouldn't be wise enough to form yet.

Belle peered at the wall clock. Ten more minutes to go.

"Hey, can you tell me what else you know about Peter?" Belle wiped the sweat off her forehead with the sleeve of her cardigan.

"Um, sure." Grace blinked rapidly, trying to focus on the new direction in topic. "Well, it's Peter Pan, which now I know is short for his real last name Panzinski." She mesmerized Belle with the details of how Peter first visited her great-grandmother Wendy Darling, taking her and her two brothers, Michael and John, on adventures to Neverland. He didn't return again after Wendy had grown up, that is until Grace was born. He waited until she was ten years old before introducing himself. But by then, her own mother didn't believe her about Peter, thinking Grace was just hijacking her great-grandmother's stories and playing pretend and using them as excuses for her acts of disobedience.

Grace sighed. "Peter loves stories. I wasn't good at making up stories, so I showed him Youtube and AFV, and he just got hooked. He would take me to this little cabin out in Stoney Peaks, and we would just sit and watch funny reels and videos for hours." She tilted her head as if in thought. "I bet that's where I left my Twitch."

"What's that?"

"A handheld gaming device. He was starting to get good at Zario Carts, but not enough to beat me." She grinned with pride.

"Did Peter ever tell you any stories about himself or Neverland?"

Their conversation took them all the way to Grace's private school bus, up to the moment she climbed on, and then reluctantly waved goodbye and thanked her for listening after finishing her last sentence.

Belle walked back in a daze towards the school. She had detention to attend, but her mind was stuck on a certain part of Grace's story. It wasn't the mermaids, natives, pixies, or the Lost Boys who'd entranced her. It was the bit about Peter's arch-nemesis, Captain Hook.

Captain Hook and his crew of pirates terrorized Neverland. And when the fairies recruited Peter, he trained with Chief River Wolf, unlocked his powers, and earned the loyalty of the Lost Boys. Over time, they defeated Captain Hook and his men in an extravagant battle for the ages, one that involved a Jurassic-sized crocodile that had allied with Peter for a chance at a taste of Captain Hook. At last, with the pirate captain hanging by his boots over the side of the ship's plank, dangling right over the crocodile's open, razor-laced mouth, Peter extended a hand of mercy and preserved the captain's life. Instead of death, Captain Hook was banished from Neverland, forever. The High Fae took the pirate then, dematerializing him into a shimmering puff of pixie dust, never to be seen or heard from again.

Belle headed back towards Study Hall. She bypassed Mr. Chet again at his desk with his sneaker-clad feet propped up in its usual perch, thirty-something-year-old self hidden behind a too-large cell phone that was more gaming device than phone.

He looked up and jeered, "Well, look what the cat dragged back in. Detention for Ms. Goody-Too-Much-Hair?"

She stopped herself from rolling her eyes. He had a derogatory nickname for every student who had to put up with him. As the former principal's nephew, the mean-streak was probably hereditary.

"You're late by the way," he tacked on.

Belle looked around at the empty desks in Study Hall. "Shouldn't half the football team be here, too?"

He snorted. "Coach cleared them with Dr. Earheart. They're supposedly running more laps as punishment. Welp, looks like it's just you, me, and," he peered down at a list on his desk, "Millicent Kwan-Yin." He looked past Belle's shoulder. "Also, late."

"Sorry," Millie mumbled, emerging from the doorway to stand apart from Belle.

"Lucky for you," Mr. Chet continued, "your mother made sure you got another week's worth of detention just to make sure you really learned your lesson."

"I'm surprised she didn't try to get me a month," Millie grumbled.

"Oh, she tried. I just didn't want to see your face for a whole month." He plugged a charger into his phone. "So, like I said, lucky you."

"Lucky me." The frames of her glasses turned a dark gray.

Mr. Chet looked past them. "What are you doing here? Coach cleared you."

Belle and Millie turned to see Thiago standing there in a clean football jersey. "I wish." He turned a scowl upon Millie. "Your mother threatened to press charges on me for physical assault if I didn't serve the punishment with you."

"But *I* assaulted *you*," Millie said.

Thiago threw his hands up. "That's exactly what I told Coach! And Dr. Earheart has the video to prove it, but he wouldn't hear it. Said he wanted your mother off his back."

But something else was bothering Belle. "You said Dr. Earheart has video of what happened by the fountain?" *Of when Eddie ninja-handled four guys in the blink of an eye?*

"Uh, yeah." Thiago walked into the room and looked around. "Where's that Jason Bourne kid anyways?"

Mr. Chet answered, "There's no one else on my list."

Thiago muttered as he dropped his book bag on a desk, "Must be nice when your uncle's dating the principal."

"Enough jabbering," Mr. Chet snapped. "Park your butts."

As they headed to opposite sides of the room as directed by Mr. Chet, Belle tried to catch Millie's eye to smile at her, but Millie refused to look at her. Even during their mind-numbing hour of silence (they weren't allowed to do anything but contemplate, as Mr. Chet put it, "their pitiful existence"), and with him hardly looking up from his game, Millie kept her eyes trained out the window, which only had a subpar view of the main road in front of the school.

Man, she must really be mad about this Eddie-thing, Belle thought. *The conversation with Candy must not have gone well. Maybe Millie's upset because I wasn't the one to speak with her about it?*

"Hey, Millie, wait up!"

Detention was over, and Millie had practically dashed out. She slowed down to face Belle. Her glasses were white. Was that fear? What was Millie afraid of?

"Hey." Millie was looking anywhere but at her. "Make it quick. My mom's waiting."

Rude. "Um, ok. Look, I'm sorry about, you know, Eddie. I don't want it to affect our friendship."

"Eddie?" Her eyebrows shot up in surprise, but she recovered quickly. "Oh, yeah, Eddie."

Belle was confused. "Isn't that why you've been ignoring me in there? Again, I'm really sorry. He's kind of become my friend too."

Millie's eyes narrowed, glasses turning pitch black, nonchalance all gone. "You knew I liked Eddie, and yet, you were flirting with him." Belle opened her mouth to protest, but Millie held up a hand. "While you and Eddie ditched—yeah, I saw you two—the meeting in Dr. Earheart's office, we watched a playback of the security footage. It looked innocent enough at first, I mean, okay you two are friends, and Eddie is even hotter than ever now because he Rock Lee'd the meatheads in less than five seconds, and I was thinking so far, okay, I'm not mad at you, but then the way you were leaning against him afterward and holding hands, and then you two disappeared together..." She shook her head and pursed her lips.

Belle spread her hands. "I was practically hypothermic, so he just dropped me off at home so I could change." Half-lie. She'd left a voicemail for Dr. Helsing about Eddie being summoned by the Fae and his Jeep still sitting by the side of the road. Dr. Helsing must have received the message because a tow truck showed up, and the driver kindly took her home before towing Eddie's car away to Dr. Helsing's residence.

Millie's glasses slowly faded into gray. "You're...lying."

Belle felt like she'd been slapped. "Why would I lie?" But her voice cracked midway.

Millie crossed her arms over her chest. "You tell me." Belle had no response. "I Googled you, and nothing. So I used my dad's company computer to run a background check on you."

Belle gasped.

"Yeah, that's what *I* said. You didn't exist until you moved to Elmridge. At least, not officially." Millie waited for an explanation.

Belle swallowed past the bitter ball of dread and fear in her throat. "My dad—we lived off the grid. He was a chemist, uh, pharmacist, and paranoid about authorities coming after his products."

"Holy crap," Millie whispered, "your dad's Walter White."

"No, his name's Enzo Montague."

"Right, right." Millie waved off her confusion.

A shiny, white Bentley pulled up alongside them, the silver tinted windows disguising the passengers until the back window slid down revealing a twin-version of Millie, but with an impressive glow-up of long, wavy black hair, immaculate make-up, and a fierce stare that belonged on a fashion runway.

Millie grumbled. "My mom's here."

Belle's jaw was already on the floor. "*That's* your mom? She looks like your sister!"

"Don't tell her that. She's insulted we're even related."

Mrs. Kwan-Yin uttered one clipped word as sharp as the edges of her sleek, black bob. "Millicent."

Belle blurted out before Millie turned away, "You're not going to meet up with us at the castle? You know, to come up with our Homecoming game plan?"

Millie looked at her feet and shook her head. She climbed into the car, and Mrs. Kwan-Yin slid the window up, her piercing stare never wavering from Belle's face in a clear verdict of disapproval.

As Belle watched the car drive off, she felt like this was only the beginning of the price she would pay for leading a double life.

"Too expensive," she whispered to herself, a lone tear sliding down her cheek.

| 26 |

Operation Homecoming

Belle stared at the massive door of Rawlins Castle, feeling like Dorothy about to knock on the door to Oz. It definitely looked like a castle door with its lacework of black iron over dark, ancient wood. There was no knocker, so she rapped lightly on the door.

No response. She pounded her fist on it.

Still no one.

A restlessness invaded her. She was finally back at the place she'd been staring wistfully at through her telescope for the past two months, after only having ever visited twice. Grandmere, her beloved wisteria tree in the fairy-tale-like rose garden, was calling to her. And that grand library! She couldn't wait to curl up in its lap with a book from its shelves and escape her own nightmare. And with Cindy promising that Liam wasn't home, she wouldn't have to worry about another harrowing run-in with him any time soon.

She called Cindy on her phone, and at the same time, pressed what looked like an inconspicuous white doorbell button to the right of the door.

"Hey! I'm at the front door," she said when Cindy picked up.

At that moment, a loud gong sounded inside followed by two long, drawn-out gongs.

"Oh no, you pressed the doorbell," Cindy whined.

"I'm sorry?"

"It's just Beatrix will probably get there now before me. I was hoping to spare you from her."

As if on cue, the castle door creaked open with a heavy sound she felt rumble right through her.

"That's her," Cindy said. "Don't worry. I'll be right there to rescue you in seconds."

"I'll be waiting, fair knight," Belle muttered back. She slipped her phone into her bag and clutched it closer.

An Agatha Trunchbull stood before her. The villainous principal from *Matilda*, but a blonde, less homely version. The high, tight bun and starchy knee-length skirt and blazer were the same, though.

"Hi, I'm Belle. Here to see Cindy."

The woman slowly stepped closer, her eyes never leaving Belle's face. Her lips a sneer.

Belle waited for her to return the pleasantries, but the woman just stood there, her eyes snaking over her with that fixed smile on her face.

"Y-You must be Beatrix," Belle tried again. Anything to break this unsettling moment. In fact, she'd much rather be greeted by Jacques's semi-friendly face. Why wasn't *he* answering the door? "Is Jacques around?"

Beatrix narrowed her eyes to slits. "He is no longer with us."

Belle was about to ask, *Why not?* Jacques had been with the Rawlins family since before Liam was in diapers, and not even the parents' murders had driven Jacques away, so what in the world could have done it now?

But Beatrix's unnaturally slow blink arrested Belle. The woman tilted her head sideways. "You're different," she said. Her thickly, accented voice felt like a slither across Belle's ears. "Hmm, what could it be?" She touched her chin in thought as she scrutinized Belle again, that smile still frozen on her face.

There was something eerily familiar about Beatrix's manner. So familiar her senses fired up like a switch had been thrown on. She could suddenly make out the makeup-caked pores on this woman's face; she could hear the padding of feet like elephants coming toward the door; the ocean breeze, a physical caress along her exposed skin; and her nose filled with the stench of rot.

Belle gagged, and she pinched her nose.

"You smell it, too." Beatrix's lips finally twitched. Was that worry?

"Ugh, what is that?"

"I wonder…" Beatrix reached out a finger and trailed it along Belle's hand.

The contact felt like fire. Belle snatched her hand away and hid both behind her back. She could hear the electricity snap-crackling from them.

What the heck?

Beatrix's eyes narrowed at Belle's collar. "May I see your necklace? It looks like one I've seen before once. On a Jesuit priest."

Is that the kind of priest Eddie is? How would she know anything about it?

As she reached a hand out toward her neck, Belle stepped away and protectively clutched at the rosary. It was official. This woman was a she-devil, and like an animal could sense evil, her powers were probably sensing it, too.

"Belle!" An out-of-breath Cindy burst through the door past Beatrix, who simply turned away with an annoyed scowl and brushed off the arm sleeve that Cindy had grazed as if it were dirty.

Without another word, and to Belle's immense relief, Cindy grabbed her hands and rushed her into the castle, away from the devilish Dutch Trunchbull staring after them.

~~*~~

"Cindy, this is amazing! You are a true fashion genius!"

Belle held up the tablet with the picture of a dress Cindy had designed. She'd taken Belle's dimensions with a measuring tape, plugged the numbers into the program, and chosen an avatar that had her features, and now Belle was staring at a cartoon version of herself wearing a ballroom dress that she could never have dreamed up.

"Besides the dress, you created this design program?"

Cindy stuck the pen stylus behind her ear and toyed with the ends of the measuring tape that hung around her shoulders like a boa. "Yeah, it's just an app. Q did all the coding for me, though." She mumbled, "I'm not a genius."

"You are to me." Belle was in raptures over the dress. Cindy explained that the Homecoming pageant dress would represent her ancestry with the Prynn legend. At first, Belle had gone as white as a sheet, but when her friend talked about how the dress would transform her into the Fairy Prynn statue with special effects included, Belle fell in love.

"I'm glad you like it." Cindy took the tablet from her and cocked her head as she looked at the design again. "There's no way this dress can't win. And with you in it, a Prynn descendant of Elmridge's own original fairy tale, there's no way you don't win the pageant category."

Belle clapped her hands together. "That's what I wanna hear!" She was one step closer now to that Homecoming crown.

Cindy beamed back at her. She laid the tablet on her work desk, which was strewn with sample fabrics, accessories, and a hefty platter of fancy dessert bites. She had a massive bedroom: part dress workshop and part living space. It was bigger than Belle's entire Littleton house.

"Liam says my fabric and materials—" Cindy cut off and glanced nervously at Belle.

Belle had also paused, stopping short of picking up another fabric sample to feel. Did Cindy think it still bothered her that she regularly spoke with Liam? At first, it really did. Belle had waited more than a month for a word from Liam, and then hearing that Cindy may have had contact with him…yeah, it had bothered her. But now, Belle had reached a place with Liam that she was still trying to figure out. Liam made it clear with his affections that he wanted her, but also that the company project was just as, or more, important than her. And Belle wasn't that self-important to think that she had to be top priority in his life.

And then there was that conundrum: whether Liam was under Violet's influence or not. She was leaning heavily towards the former.

Belle urged her to finish her sentence. "What did Liam say?"

"All the materials ship in next week, so I can make your dress then."

"I'm going to pay you."

"Not happening. You helped me escape Mommy Dearest. I knew she'd been hurting Daddy somehow, making him sick. I just could never catch her in the act." Her eyes were brimming when she turned them upon Belle. "I am your friend forever. It wasn't until you caught her in the hospital," she swallowed hard, "poisoning him, and then you did something about it, telling Q…" She let go of a heavy sigh. "I wouldn't ever tell Q this because he'll wrongly think I'm trying to marry him or something, but he really is my best friend. Even if he isn't the greatest conversationist. I know he listens when I talk."

"Q's the real reason your stepmom's in jail. I give him all the credit."

"Teamwork," Cindy said, reaching over to give her arm a squeeze.

Belle bit her lip. She wanted to ask Cindy if she'd noticed anything strange going on with Liam but was unsure how to open that can of worms. She decided to lead with a natural question. "So, how's it been living in this castle?"

Cindy worked the tablet as she spoke, tweeking details of the dress. "I was excited to get a new start with Daddy; our house had too many memories of She-Who-Must-Not-Be-Named. And it was pretty exciting at first, hiring some staff, redecorating a bit, and we even got Arturo back, but, um…well…."

Belle leaned in. "What?"

"What do you think of the gold shimmer along the edges now?" She showed off the new image.

Belle thought it appropriate in representing the pixie dust in the legend, or more like her *factual* family history. "I like. You were saying about the staff, though?"

"Uh, the staff started eventually quitting, one by one. Not even raising their pay would retain them."

"Castle's haunted, isn't it?" Belle reached for the dessert platter.

Maybe Jacques did quit, then?

"Yep. A regular horror show. But it's only one part of the castle. The West Wing."

Belle choked on a bite of petit four.

Cindy patted her back as she coughed. "Are you alright? Here, have some water."

After Belle could breathe again, she asked, "How is the West Wing haunted?"

Cindy opened a drawer full of rolls of shimmering ribbons and began pulling out the gold and copper-toned ones. "I personally haven't seen anything. Then again, I haven't been to that part of the castle, nor do I even want to go to that part. But everyone who's visited that wing has quit. They all said they saw," she paused her business with the ribbons and pinned a frightened gaze on Belle, "dark spirits like, like shadows."

What Eddie told her the night he came over repeated in her mind, *"...these shadows spawn from dark supernatural events."*

The West Wing was where Violet had murdered Liam's parents with lightning bolts. That place must be infested with Shadow Spawn now. A wild urge to check it out arrested her. Perhaps, she could put her newfound shadow-zapping skills to the test.

"And get this," Cindy continued, "when Liam got back, and Daddy told him why the staff had quit, Liam told Beatrix to 'take care of it.'"

"So what did she do?"

"I don't know. Bring in a priest, maybe? I try to keep my distance from her."

"Yeah, for some reason, she makes my skin crawl." Her conscience was hit. "I mean, I know I don't know her, and I guess I shouldn't say stuff like that, but—"

"No, no. You're justified, trust me. Even Liam told her, in front of me, to stay out of sight. Did she even blink when you met her outside?"

"Once. Why would Liam say that?"

She blushed. "She kind of ambushed me with questions, and then Liam saw how uncomfortable she was making me, so…."

Since they were talking about Liam now, she wanted to ask about whether she'd noticed any strange behavior from him, but her mouth shut at the sound of the bedroom door opening and Beatrix emerging into view.

"Speak of the devil," Cindy muttered.

"Another guest has arrived for you," Beatrix drawled, her hands unnaturally tented together before her. She stepped aside and an ashen-looking Candy squeaked, "Hi."

Only after staring fixedly at Belle for a moment, a little secretive smile pasted on her face, did Beatrix exit the room, closing the door so softly behind her, the click sounded more like a hiss.

As if a paralysis spell was lifted, Candy threw herself at the girls.

"Goodness, Candy, what's wrong?" Belle embraced her trembling friend.

"Beatrix, right?" Cindy guessed. "I'm so sorry. She's Liam's work assistant and unofficial, self-appointed house manager."

Candy's lower lip trembled as she pulled away from Belle and sank onto a small ottoman. "She-She told me something."

The other two girls drew closer. "What did she say?" Belle asked in a hushed voice bordering on outrage. How dare this woman offend her friend?

"She said the man I love will betray me."

"Dmitri?" Belle gasped.

"Th-That's exactly what I said. And then she said, 'You don't love him.'"

"Who does she think she is?" Cindy said, indignant. "I'll have Daddy talk to her. Shoot, he's out of town today on business, though." She reddened. "I'd do it, but I'm not good at forming sentences in front of her."

This Beatrix was proving too weird to be normal, and anything not normal in Elmridge, Belle quickly learned, fell into the unnatural category. And just how unnatural, she planned to find out.

After Candy's scare wore off, the girls got down to planning Belle's Homecoming victory.

"Now, Cindy, honey, you must know the inside scoop on how exactly this whole process works, since you were on the dream team last year for Homecoming."

Belle turned to Cindy. "What does she mean?"

Cindy bit her lip. "I was on Lisa's team to help her win Homecoming. I did her dress."

"Wow, okay, um, so what should I expect?"

"Homecoming is different here than how a typical high school does it. It's actually super sexist because it's all about the princesses. The guys don't have to do anything but show up on the arms of the princesses for each event, while the girls have to do all the hoop-jumping." She made a noise of disgust. "The students vote on their favorite guy and girl for each grade level, and then finally pick one couple as Homecoming King and Queen."

"So, it's okay that I'm going to the Halloween dance with Liam, and then Homecoming with Jared?"

Both girls perfected the cartoon jaw-drop just then. "What?!" squeaked Candy. "Since when are you going with Jared?"

Belle cringed. "Since chemistry class today?"

"Wow," Cindy breathed out. "And you have Eddie in your talent act...." She met Candy's wide eyes. "I think she's got it in the bag."

"Dang, woman, that is a major G.O.A.T. move—greatest of all time," Candy clarified when she saw Belle's confusion. "Let me get this straight, Liam asked you this morning—"

"To the Halloween dance," Belle injected.

"And Jared asked you this afternoon to the Homecoming dance."

"Only because Jared told me that Liam was taking Mari to the Halloween dance, so he suggested that he take me to Homecoming."

"And you're okay with Liam taking Mari to Homecoming?" Poor Cindy looked perfectly confused. "I mean, he really likes you. He's always asking me about you. I told him he needs to talk to *you*. And then he started asking me about Eddie. Hates Eddie, by the way."

"Yes, Eddie." Candy crossed her arms over her chest and looked pointedly at Belle. "What is going on between you and that fine-looking emo stud?"

Yes, Eddie, Belle thought with a pang. There was so much she had to tell him, and he was the only person who could really understand and help her do something about all the weird in her life. She felt warm all over when that resting-smolder look and knowing half-smile, he seemed to reserve especially for her, flashed into her mind.

"You're blushing," Candy said dryly. "Ok, so *that's* what's going on between you two."

"What about Liam?" Cindy asked in a hushed voice.

What *about* Liam? She couldn't tell them her suspicions about him. When she thought of him as the old Liam—pre-Europe Liam—the feelings fluttered throughout her like butterflies, and she felt like she was his. But this Liam, the one who'd clenched her chin and demanded to know about the Jäger, the Liam who knew that she killed the Hammerson brothers...*that* Liam she was afraid of. Especially when she suspected him to be Violet's werewolf-minion.

Nevertheless, she knew without a doubt, that Liam, pre-Europe or not, needed her help. He would never in a million years willingly help the woman who murdered his parents.

"I-I do like him," she told Cindy, before turning to Candy, "And I'm drawn to Eddie...." It was true. Eddie's presence was magnetic. Even now, she felt his absence down to the cold cells in her body that craved his nearness. The level of physical attraction to him was unnatural.

But whoever said she had to have a boyfriend? She had no time for one right now, that is until she had to keep her promise to Jared.

Jeesh, she went from zero social life in Littleton to a complicated love knot in Elmridge.

Above all though, keeping the taaffeite crown out of Violet's hands was her sole purpose now, and that meant winning Homecoming Queen. At any cost that her conscience could live with. And becoming Jared's pretend-girlfriend soon was already stretching it.

Belle threw her hands up and repeated her Oscars speech. "I'm just trying to win Homecoming. Something I really want to do for myself, something I never imagined I would even have the opportunity to do."

Candy slowly nodded her head. "This is a one-eighty from the wallflower-status you begged for when you first came here. Homecoming Queen? Are you sure? You know that means you'll be front-and-center Elmridge news, even national news? Magazines will come calling, all kinds of people are going to want to interview you. You'll have to hire a publicist."

"Belle, are you okay?" Cindy grabbed her frozen friend's shoulders and squeezed.

The blood had drained from Belle's face, and she was deathly cold.

"Make up your mind, honey, because once we go all in, and with Lisa out of the race, you've got a really solid chance of winning, and then you *will* be famous."

Oh, holy mother of all that is holy…. Belle was on billboards, Times Square, on the entertainment news, on Kelly's interview couch, on the cover of magazines (with Jared just a small blurb in the corners now), but then a breaking news segment showed Belle surrounded by paparazzi snapping away at the electrical orbs growing in her hands. Their tone changed. They weren't calling out compliments anymore. It was all the names she'd endured in Littleton. And then she heard Violet's wicked laughter and saw her raise a green blade in the air encrusted with gems. Her lips moved, and the world's population all took to their knees and bent their faces to the ground in Violet's direction.

"Belle?!" Candy gave her a hard shake, snapping her from her daymare.

"I have to do this," Belle blurted out. "I-I have to win Homecoming." Her hands were gripping Cindy's, and by the pain on her friend's face, she knew she was hurting her. She let go. "Sorry." She wiped her clammy hands on her pants. "Will you two help me?"

The two girls nodded, and Candy said, "That's why we're here. I just wanted to make sure you understood all that you'd be getting with that crown."

Belle nodded. "I'll cross each bridge as I get to them." And hopefully not fall through and drown.

Candy clucked her tongue. "I'll talk to Millie again. She pretends like it doesn't bother her anymore, but I know she's still crushing hard on Eddie."

Belle sighed, deflated. "I had detention with her after school today. She hates me."

Candy flinched. "It may be tougher than I thought then to get her to come around. We need her editing skills for your campaign video."

"The what-video?" Belle asked at the new terror this Homecoming business was throwing her way.

Turned out, Homecoming court candidates usually had camera crews following them around, chronicling their every moment, and then posting choice-snippets on their Peacock Profile every day. Right before the Homecoming event, the final campaign video was made and released online. Belle thought she would faint, but then Cindy said that Lisa once opted to use her own self-made videos and selfie-posts without a camera crew shadowing her, and that she still won that year. So Belle decided *that* was going to be the way to go.

The girls were practicing selfie-shots with Belle, and pretty much training her in the art of the selfie—who knew lighting and posture and angles could transform how you looked in a photograph?—when Cindy received an incoming text from Liam.

Cindy frowned when she read it.

"What?" Candy asked, curious.

"He wasn't supposed to be here today." She locked penitent eyes with Belle. "I'm sorry. I know I told you he wouldn't be here."

Belle tried to shrug off the discomfort gripping her. "It's okay. What did he want?"

What Liam wanted was for the girls to join him and "some friends" in the castle's indoor heated pool.

"When did Liam suddenly get friends?" Candy asked dryly, while checking an incoming text on her phone.

"He's playing quarterback again for the football team," Cindy answered.

"Go to the pool with the same guys who attacked me and Eddie? No thanks."

"Yes," Candy piped up. "Dmitri's down there!" She waved her phone and her hips around.

The other two groaned.

Candy pressed her hands together. "We could just go say hi. We don't have to get in the pool." When Belle crossed her arms over chest, Candy grabbed her hands and playfully twirled her. "Think of this as a photo-op for your campaign."

Belle looked to Cindy for backup, but Cindy looked like she hated to agree with Candy on this one. "A few snapshots with these guys *would* help."

Belle conceded. "Fine." She crossed her arms over her chest. "But we're not done planning. I'm up against Kat, and we need to knock her out of the race."

"I like the 'knocking her out' part," Candy said, smiling darkly.

Cindy led the way to the pool, but Belle sidetracked them twice. The first time was to see the library again, where she found the Rawlins family diary just sitting on the table where she and Liam had once studied. She bagged the book, hoping Liam wouldn't mind.

The second detour was the rose garden. She just had to say hello to Grandmere. But when they stepped outside, her branches were bare, and the rose bushes reduced to thorny brambles. Belle had teared up at the sight. Cindy said it was the oncoming winter temperatures that had robbed the garden, but Belle had seen the effects of a snowy winter in Littleton, and the trees had not been gnarled black to their roots the way this one had. Whatever was affecting the castle, casting its suffocating gloom over it, had stolen all the life from this garden. She wondered if the Shadow Spawn she was sure was haunting the West Wing was responsible for this devastation.

After one hasty run-in with Beatrix, in which she handed Cindy a tray of snacks she'd prepared for her to deliver to the boys, they finally made it to the indoor pool space. The room transported her to a massive ancient Roman bath, complete with replica marble statues of the Roman gods free-standing around the pool. Gold-infused, deep blue mosaic tiles covered the floor and walls, interrupted by tall, arched windows filtering in the sunlight.

"See something you like?"

"Yes," Belle answered, turning toward the male voice, "this room is—whoa Mylanta!"

A very muscular, glistening wet chest absorbed her view. Her jaw dropped and her eyes followed the droplets trailing down washboard abs and disappearing beneath low-slung board shorts. The hand by his side reached up and pushed back the wet, blonde hair from his forehead.

"Liam," she breathed out.

He was smirking, knowing exactly where her thoughts, and eyes, had gone.

Not fair. He ambushed me. "Y-You should put on a shirt."

"Actually," he reached for the hem of her shirt, "you should take yours off."

She brushed his hand away. "In your dreams."

"Sweetheart, if you only knew."

Annnd buh-bye Hyde-Liam, hello Casanova-Liam.

"We're not going in the pool," Cindy announced. She offered the tray of snacks to Liam. "Beatrix made these for you guys."

He took it and promptly tossed it into the nearby trash bin, fancy tray and all. "You know better," he muttered to Cindy.

She huffed out an exasperated breath and muttered right back, "Then why do you keep her around if you clearly distrust her?"

Good question.

But Liam avoided her question with one of his own. "You're not coming in for a swim?"

"I'd rather dive off the cliff than get in the water with you lot of apes."

Go spunky Cindy!

Liam chuckled. "You know, there is a perfectly safe spot nearby for cliff-diving into the ocean."

"Really?" Interest replaced the snark in Cindy's voice.

"I'll take you there one day. We'll go for a swim, without the apes."

Cindy pressed her lips together into a small smile and shrugged one shoulder.

Wait, are they flirting? Belle exchanged a look with Candy sharing the same thought.

There was loud guffawing in the background. Five more guys splashed around in the pool. One, Belle was surprised to see, was Thiago, but her dread evaporated upon noticing his friend G wasn't present. Red-headed Dmitri was hard to miss, especially since he was headed toward them with a much shorter friend in tow.

"Hey, boo!" Dmitri called out.

"Heeey, handsome!" Candy called back.

Dmitri's face suddenly clouded with concern. "Quick, call the vet."

"Why, hon'?"

He puffed his chest out and flexed his biceps. "'Cause these puppies are sick."

Candy melted into a puddle of giggles, while Belle rolled her eyes.

Hans tilted his chin and nodded at them. "'Sup ladies."

Besides Candy, Hans was the first friend Belle had made at the school. He'd insisted on walking her to the main office that very first day.

Hans looked at Cindy and opened his mouth as if to say something but changed his mind when she visibly stiffened and turned her head away. Liam noticed the exchange and frowned darkly.

A mischievous grin crossed Hans's face and he shook out his brown hair like a wet dog. The girls recoiled, squealing out complaints.

"Ugh, I'm gonna get you back, just you wait." Candy scowled at him as she patted her shoulder-length afro of corkscrew curls. She and Cindy were in cute Fall sweater-weather outfits, while Belle was still in her school uniform and cardigan. She still hadn't mastered the art of multiple wardrobe changes throughout the day that these Elmridge girls had perfected.

"You're not coming in?" Dmitri had to bend to grab Candy by the hips and look her in the eyes.

She trailed a finger down his wet chest. "We're working on a school project."

He pouted. "You can't play now and work later?"

"Millie didn't come?" Thiago asked, leaning half out of the pool, his own guns on display. "Ain't she always with you two?"

"Why do *you* care?" Candy popped her hip as she stared him down.

"Hey," he raised his hands, retreating back into the water. "I'm just tryin' to see if she wants to play tackle again."

Candy launched herself in Thiago's direction. "Boy, don't you even try to disrespect—" Dmitri grabbed her by the hand and swung her back into a wet hug. She protested with a squeal and pushed him away.

"Jeez, come *on*." Cindy grabbed her girlfriends' hands and dragged them both away.

Liam reached out and squeezed Belle's free hand before she walked off. He winked at her, and the way he held her gaze made her cheeks flush, but instead of smiling shyly back as she would have done months ago, she averted her eyes.

Not happening, Liam. Not until we get you sorted out.

~~*~~

"So, let's talk the competition here," Candy said. The girls had settled onto a lounge sectional off the side of the pool's bar. "We can already predict who will end up on the final court."

Cindy nodded, setting down cold cans of fruity sodas before them. "Rapunzel's little cousin, Ezra, for the freshman spot."

"But you don't have to worry about her," Candy popped open a watermelon soda. "She's a total snob."

"I'm up against Kat for the sophomore spot," Belle reminded. She couldn't decide between the cherry or strawberry soda.

"Kat's prospects aren't too good right now," Cindy replied. She nudged the cherry one toward Belle.

Candy grinned and threw an arm around Belle. "No one's prospects are good against *this* queen."

Belle murmured her thanks and took a long draw of cherry soda. An unholy burp ripped from her, making them all giggle.

Candy threw a napkin at Belle. "Okay, so maybe the other girls do stand a chance."

Belle wiped the sticky soda mustache off. "I thought so."

Dmitri jogged over to them, his wet feet plopping against the tiles, and just as he dropped a kiss on an elated Candy's forehead, Belle cried out, "Hey, no boys allowed over here!"

He grabbed an armful of soda cans from the bar fridge and grinned back. "No boy here. I'm all *man*, sugar." And he promptly dropped a kiss on Belle's forehead too before rushing back.

The girls watched, grinning, as Dmitri tossed the cans into the pool and cannon-balled in after. When he broke the surface again, Liam was waiting for him, and Belle's keen ears picked up a few swear words mixed in with the following, "You're gonna pay for putting your lips on my girl." And then a wrestling match between the two hunky behemoths ensued in the water with the rest forming a shouting spectator ring.

"Good Lord," Belle complained, "I feel like my own body is about to push out some chest hair with the amount of testosterone energy in the room."

Candy stared comically at her. "Girl, you are so silly."

But Cindy looked uncomfortable, chewing her lip and fiddling with the hem of her sweater.

"What's wrong?" Belle asked.

"Um, well..." Cindy glanced at Candy, and then away. "It's just something I can't put out of my mind now."

"What is it?"

"Well, I *know* Kat. We used to hang out."

"Right, annnd?" Candy prompted.

Cindy finally looked point-blank at Candy, sympathy in every syllable of her words. "You do know that Kat and Dmitri are engaged, right?"

Belle's jaw dropped.

Candy shrunk into herself. "I know. Everyone and their mama know their parents have set them up since they were babies to tie their fortunes together. But Dmitri doesn't care about that. He says he's going to do whatever he wants. He and Kat aren't even together anymore."

Cindy bit her bottom lip and looked down. She looked like she wanted to say more.

"What is it?" Belle urged gently.

"Kat does this whenever she wants attention. She pushes him away or breaks up with him, so when they do get together again, it's news all over again and everyone's talking about it."

"Like Rachel and Ross," Belle whispered, "but mean-girl version?"

Cindy nodded. "I suspect she might try to get back together with him right before Homecoming. She might try next week."

Belle expected outrage from Candy but felt her heart crack when she saw her friend's bottom lip tremble instead.

"He swears he's done with her," Candy whispered.

Cindy smiled sadly. "I really hope you're right."

Candy stared at Dmitri splashing around in the pool, her eyes watering.

Even Belle, with her romance-knowledge mainly limited to books, knew that Dmitri and Candy's ever-after did not bode well.

After the girls had drained their sodas in silence, Candy crunched her empty can between her hands. "So…" She plastered on a huge grin, even though her eyes still shone. "Operation Homecoming Crown for our girl here: kickass campaign video, date a different hottie for each event, and one-of-a-kind pageant dress by Cindy."

Belle cringed. "Sounds shameless."

Cindy shrugged apologetically. "Unfortunately, it's the minimum standard for a Homecoming victory in Elmridge."

A one-time deal in the spotlight, Belle negotiated with herself, *and then back to obscurity for me. Whatever it takes to stop Violet.*

| 27 |

Secrets in the Night

Belle had died and gone to Heaven. She was sitting in a velvety wingback chair by a roaring fireplace, an old quilt spread over her legs and Edward Rawlins's diary open in her lap. She was in a room like Cindy's, only this one hadn't been renovated and still had the centuries-old style furnishings that she only ever fantasized about. A bowl of M&M's at her reach on a little antique table was the proverbial cherry on top of this Victorian bedtime hour.

She was staying over at Rawlins Castle for the night. Candy had gone home after Jo told her that Millie wanted to meet about an important "family" issue, while Cindy had practically begged Belle to stay the night. Knowing she wasn't invited to Millie's drama at Candy's place, Belle decided it would be best to stay at the castle. She wasn't about to stay home alone anymore with a werewolf on the prowl either. And she did want to sneak into the West Wing at some point in the night; she couldn't get rid of the itch to zap some Shadow Spawn.

She just had to wait until it was late enough that she could safely assume everyone had gone to sleep.

The day had been quite the roller coaster ride. Liam winning her over in the morning and telling her his truth, although she was still skeptical, and then having that rose-colored bubble pop in chemistry class later but walking out with a promising date to Homecoming...only to hit rock bottom in her day when Liam's creepy alter-ego cornered her in the art room, and she'd realized then that Violet had sunk her hooks into him somehow.

Seeing Grace had lifted her spirits though, especially when she learned more about Peter Pan's rivalry with the pernicious Captain Hook, and then it was down the roller coaster again when Millie had made it clear she hated her. But it was a steady climb since then...planning a Homecoming victory with her two friends and recording a piece for her campaign video with the guys at the pool.

It had been Hans's idea. The guys would each jump into the pool in some fancy flip as they tossed the basketball to one another, with the final act being a slam dunk into the hoop attached at the pool's edge. All Belle had to do, while standing outside the pool, was be the first to toss the ball to Liam, who jumped in first. Thiago made the slam dunk at the end. It had taken them a few tries to get it right, and the final attempt was capped with roaring approval. Liam had lifted himself out of the pool (an image that had slowed to a crawl in her mind), swung Belle around in a bearhug, and then kissed her before she could even screech about being soaked. It was still up for debate with the girls about whether that kiss would be edited out or not.

Liam and his kisses. He apparently had selective hearing when she'd told him just this morning to stop kissing her because she wasn't his girlfriend. Her mind was outraged, but dang it, her body wasn't putting up too much of a fuss about it.

And then there was Dungeons & Dragons. She had completely forgotten about it until Cindy told her to read the message that Q had emailed her because she had to help get her costume ready. Q was to the point: because the Highlander Cleric was unavailable to join the

Questing Table that night, Belle had to be a cleric, although she could choose what kind. Q provided a list of choices and links to study up on her chosen character. She'd chosen the Fairy Cleric.

Long story short, Belle was a D&D-er for life now. This was a missing piece to her existence. After a few mishaps and disapproving grunts from Q, by the end of the three-hour quest, she'd helped her team to survive the mission and end with a stalemate by killing the Elf Ranger (who happened to be Hannah from literature class, small world). Through a convoluted storyline involving noble bloodlines and clemencies, she chose to marry the imprisoned Highlander Cleric to spare him a morning execution.

So, at the next quest, Eddie was going to be in for a shock, being tied down to Belle in the game now. She'd also siphoned half his powers to make the marriage spell work and adopted a talking boar on his behalf. His life was now tied to the magical boar's health in the next quest.

She giggled at the reaction she imagined him having.

It was only yesterday that she saw Eddie. They'd had a few "moments" throughout the day. Moments of closeness that made her feel like fire when she thought of them. And that selfie he'd sent her that morning? She was tempted to retrieve her phone from the night table and look at the pic again, something she hadn't done since he'd first sent it. But with a deep and ragged exhale, she thought better of it. No need to delve into that den of sensations just thinking about the man.

No boyfriends, she reminded herself firmly with a painful pinch on the arm. *The fate of the world rests on my shoulders. If Violet completes the Jade Blade spell, she'll rule the world.*

Everything in her froze at the thought. Reminding herself had been a mistake. She could feel a full-fledged panic attack coming on. She sat up straight, the blanket and book tumbling to the floor. She tried to get her lungs to work.

Happy thoughts, happy thoughts, she chanted over and over in her mind, trying to drown out the screams of people caught up in the fiery chaos that Violet Wickeby caused, perched on a floating throne, cackling with glee as she shot lightning bolts from her hand at the fleeing hordes.

Belle tugged out Eddie's rosary from her shirt and clenched it in her hands, pleading silently to be able to just breathe.

Just when she thought she would black out with the strain, her lungs dragged in a deep gulp of air. She sat there, gripping the sides of the chair and just breathing, drinking in the air.

When she was finally steady enough, she reached down and picked up the diary, resettling back into the chair with the quilt. She was tempted to analyze that split-second fall and rise from what felt like the brink of death, but unless she wanted to experience another panic-episode, she buried her mind in the pages of the Rawlins diary instead.

This Edward was a doodler. He drew his little sister, Lucy, and his mother. Only faces, though. His cousin William's agonized expression was captured in the margins of the entry after learning of his father's schemes to murder his fiancée at the stake. The hawkish profile of the Reverend Judge Jonas Rawlins bordered the next entry about his death.

Belle gasped at the next picture. It was a pretty face framed by a ringlet of curls. Violet Wickeby. The same face from her nightmare. The same girl who kept leading Belle to the stake, just as she had led her mother and aunt to theirs. But instead of the smug expression Belle expected, this face was drawn with utter despair in its tear-rimmed eyes.

Belle read on, and almost dropped the diary as she brought her hand to her mouth in shock.

"Today was rough. Violet paid me a visit today. With William gone, searching for Abigail in the good Lord knows where, an utterly distraught Violet beseeched me, on her knees, to talk "sense" into William and force him to return and marry her. I could only profess to her that William indeed loves her, but it will never—cannot ever—be in the way that she so desires. I turned her over to Mother, then. I cannot bear a woman's tears. They reduce me to rubble.

"If Violet only knew the secret that my dear cousin burdened me with all these years ago, a secret I promised him I'd never utter to another living soul, Violet would speedily cast away her passions for William. If this truth ever saw the light of day, two whole families would be ruined, beginning with Violet's mother and William's father.

"(Like the other ones, I'm burning this diary as soon as the pages are filled.)"

The chime of an incoming text sucked her back into the present. Her mind still reeling from the revelation, she padded over to the phone.

Liam: **Still awake?**

Belle's eyes widened. It was 1:30 in the morning. And, yes, she was very awake, but did she want to start this back-and-forth with Liam now? What was their official status again? She'd said "not dating" while Liam thinks they're "taking it slow."

But she did need to investigate him while figuring out how to help him, and she *did* need his help with scoring Homecoming points at the Halloween party next weekend.

Belle: **Yes.**

A light knock at her door made her jump.

Liam: **It's me.**

She automatically fluffed her hair and smoothed down her pj's. Cindy had let her borrow a honey-colored, velour long-sleeved shirt and pants set. She would never admit it, but the color reminded her of Eddie's eyes.

When she cracked open the door, her heart jumped into her throat. While she was fully clothed like a sane person on a drafty night in the castle, Liam was literally half-naked. He was leaning one arm against the doorpost, in nothing but gray sweatpants. Long planes of curvy muscles from his shoulders, down to that v-indent were shamelessly on display. She dragged her eyes back up to more appropriate territory, which may have actually been worse. He was giving her the come-hither eyes.

She shut the door in his face.

That was *not* "taking it slow."

"Belle?" His deep voice was a mix of pleading and exasperation. "Please, open the door. Just for a minute. I want to say goodnight."

"Goodnight!" she called through the door.

He answered with a gruff sigh. "Please?"

She faked a loud yawn. "I'm really sleepy. I'll see you in the morning." He's not coming in here looking like that. The whole situation right now felt like a recipe for regret later.

After a beat of silence, he said, "I'll tell you a secret about the room you're in." Such an obvious lure he was dangling before her nose, but dang it, he knew the right ones.

"What secret?—No! You can tell me in the morning."

"That room has a hidden door to a secret passageway."

She swung the door open and stuck her pointer finger in his face. "Not fair."

Hands in pockets, he was all smirks as he walked in past her. His slow perusal of her from head to toe made her shift uncomfortably.

He reached out and felt the material of her sleeve. "Is this velvet?"

"It's velour, if you must know."

"I must." He sucked in his bottom lip as his eyes raked over her again. "You look like a plush doll I need to squeeze tight to my body all night."

The shock of that inappropriate comment felt like a slap. On the butt.

"Liam Rawlins!" He snapped his hand away from her sleeve at her outraged matronly tone. "You do not come in here in the dead of night, half-naked, trying to seduce me or something!"

His mint-green eyes seared hers. "But I haven't even tried to seduce you yet."

Holy shiskabob, she felt like she was in an episode of *Teen Hearts in Paradise,* the show she and Candy watched as a guilty pleasure. He wasn't being respectfully romantic; he was being blatantly provocative. But with the sketchiness surrounding him, there was none of the pleasure right now, just the shamefulness.

She crossed her arms over her chest. "Get out."

Hurt flashed in his eyes. "Why are you being so mean?"

Her ire evaporated. One thing she hated almost more than anything was hurting people she cared about. "Fine, then, show me the hidden door," she said in a softer tone.

He nodded. She followed as he crossed over to the fireplace, pressed the sun in the carved forest scene of the wooden mantle, and the edge of a door jutted out from the wall on the right.

"I think you've got some drool right there." Liam pointed toward her mouth, laughter in his eyes.

Normally, she'd snark back, but she was too busy staring at the object of her fascination. "I bet," was all she said. She wiped her mouth, just in case, and followed Liam to the new door. The door's outline had perfectly blended in before with the lines of the wood-paneled walls.

"Does each room have a secret door? Where does it lead to? The dungeon?"

Liam dug his fingers into the solitary crevice on the side of the door meant for pulling it open. "Dungeon's off-limits. Beatrix says there's a rat infestation down there. She's got someone coming in soon to take care of the problem." He grunted in an effort to open the door, but it wouldn't budge.

"But aren't the rats part of the dungeon's charm?" She still wanted to see the place. A real-live dungeon. She bet she could arrange a D&D game down there. Q would sure love that.

Liam gave her a knowing smile over his shoulder that made the dimple appear in his chin. "We'll get our dungeon picnic, don't worry."

He continued pulling at the door, his muscles pulling taut with the effort, but it only groaned open half an inch. "Not even the Hulk could get that open," he complained, shaking his hands out.

"Let me try."

He snorted. "If *I* can't open it, then…." He trailed off to let her finish the offensive assumption.

As annoying as that was, it was a good thing he'd discouraged her just then because she'd have to explain her new super-strength power to him, and she realized with a certainty now that she didn't trust him with any more of her secrets. Not until she got to the bottom of this Liam-doppelgänger problem from Europe.

Noticing the stark disappointment on her face, he offered, "How about I show you another secret door tomorrow?"

"Like right before school in the morning?"

"And then I'll take you to school after, or wherever else you want to go. We don't need to go to school."

"I *am* going to school," she said firmly, making all the nerds of the world proud. "And I'm going with Cindy."

"Great," he smiled broadly. "We can all go together."

Belle rubbed her eyebrow, more out of annoyance than an itch. "Okay." She walked him to the bedroom door. "Goodnight."

"May I *please* say goodnight?"

Belle was befuddled. It wasn't like she was preventing him from saying the words.

In one move, he stepped into her space and cradled her cheeks as he brought his face closer to hers.

Oh.

"Liam," she chastised softly.

He paused, his lips just a hairsbreadth away from hers. "I've been dying to kiss you all day."

"I thought we were taking this slow, remember?"

He dipped and brushed his lips against her cheek. "This is slow." He gently turned her face and kissed her other cheek. "Very slow."

This didn't feel...right. This isn't the Liam from that magical night on her front porch. Too many doubts and suspicions clouded the once pure connection that'd existed between them. Maybe Liam didn't feel it, but she sure did. And there was something else, something she couldn't quite figure out just yet that was subtly, but definitively, pulling her away from him.

She gently peeled his palms from her face. "Goodnight, Liam."

He brought her hand to his lips and pressed a kiss to her knuckles. "Sweet dreams, angel."

| 28 |

Shadowzord

One super-strength pull was all Belle needed to get the jammed secret door open.

Ha! Take that, jocks of the world!

But she wasn't ready for the blast of nose-assaulting stench: wet dog mixed with week-old garbage. It was also ten times chillier in there.

She stepped away from the pitch blackness framed by the newly opened doorway. Yes, she wanted to go in there. It's a secret passageway inside a castle! This was the stuff of fantasies for her. But, no, she did not want to go in there *alone*.

She shook her head. She had to put her big girl pants on. She had powers for goodness sake! It was time to start putting a little more faith in herself.

Once she hyped herself up to the task, she made preparations. Finding no other clothing in any of the drawers or closets (her day clothes were still being laundered), she shook one of the long pillows out from its pillowcase and wrapped the thick pillowcase around her shoulders like a shawl for extra warmth. Next, she armed herself with her cell phone flashlight and poured the bowl of M&Ms into her pants pocket.

The beam of light from her phone carved a path into the gaping blackness. It was a straight path ahead, wide enough to fit only three people standing shoulder-to-shoulder. The walls and floor were the same gray stone that comprised the outer walls of the castle. She chased the light before her, leaving a breadcrumb trail of candy behind.

Doors began appearing on her left-hand side, every minute or so. They were all locked. She was tempted to break into one, but the horror of it being Beatrix's room prevented her. She checked the time on her phone. Only twenty minutes had gone by, but it'd felt like hours.

Normally, given a setting like this, a *Phantom of the Opera* scene would cue up right about now for her to pretend in. But her senses were keyed-up, waiting in the trenches to counterattack at a second's notice.

As soon as I'm out of candy, I'm doubling back. She felt her almost-empty pocket. *Soon.*

New patterns appeared on the walls, deep parallel lines in rows of five. Belle stretched her hand out, each finger tracing a line in a downward swipe. Claw marks. What animal could claw into stone?

The beast, that's what. Violet's beast.

Or maybe not? Maybe the marks are ancient, and a wild animal like a bear may have been smuggled through here?

She froze when her ears picked up on sounds coming from a distance behind her. She strained to listen and suddenly felt her hearing amplified as if the volume had been turned up ten notches. There was a click, and then another click, like a door in the passage being opened and then closed. A shuffling sound came, and then another shuffle, and another...it was the rhythm of heavy feet slowly shuffling along.

Belle tore off. She had to keep going forward if she didn't want to run into whatever was back there. She ignored the barrage of frightening possibilities, each more terrifying than the last. Imagining a ghost wrapped in chains made her kick-up the most speed. The path had been straight, but she now ran into a T-intersection. She had to turn either right or left.

She borrowed one of Liam's swear words now. She was going to be lost in the belly of a castle! She could picture it now: a *Ghost Adventures* crew finding her skeletal remains years from now.

She stopped to listen for the creepy shuffling noise. An almost impossible task when her heart was pounding in her ears.

Nothing.

It was time to try a door. She walked back to the last one she'd just passed, gripped its cold iron handle, and gave it a great tug.

Dirt and debris rained down from the frame of the door as it opened. She gave her eyes a second to adjust to the darkness inside. Cracks of dusty moonlight filtered through closed window drapes, allowing her to decipher the outlines of cloth-draped furniture.

She heard the shuffle again at a distance behind her. Whatever it was, it was closing in.

She entered the room and shut the door behind her. Leaning back against it, she exhaled a giant sigh of relief and hugged herself, rubbing her shivering arms. The pillowcase-shawl had fallen victim to the secret passageway and its phantom inhabitant.

A brief search turned up an uninhabited bedroom, but a mighty dusty one. Apparently, only some of the guest rooms in the castle had been prepared by the staff before they quit. She had to get back to her own room, but there was no way she was going back the way she came.

What a waste of M&Ms....

She exited the bedroom and found herself in a massive dimly lit hallway. Lights glowed from medieval-like sconces in between a row of paintings along the wall. One particular painting made her stop in her tracks. It was of a large family sitting like a tableau of 18th-century aristocracy in an ornate living room.

But that wasn't what made her eyes pop. She recognized two of the men. The Reverend Judge Jonas Rawlins looked exactly like the one from her nightmare. In the painting, he sat at the center on a raised dais in front of the biggest open fireplace she'd ever seen. The blonde matronly woman reclining on a lower chair against his knee, Belle assumed, was his wife. To his other side, stood the second man, a gorgeous, black-haired doppelgänger of Liam. She stared, open-mouthed. This had to be William Rawlins! He matched the image of the man who'd revived Belle from death in that lost memory, which made it even more real.

A few children were sprawled about in the painting. A little girl clung to a doll, a boy chased after a fluffy white dog, and a raven-haired toddler in a blue dress lay against another handsome man's chest who was seated off to the side on a plush green couch. This man also had black hair, long and layered to his chin like Liam used to have it, but she couldn't see much of his face because he was looking down at the sleeping child curled up against his chest. The distinct Rawlins square jawline was evident, and his smile was pulled up on one side.

Her stomach did a flip. This must be Edward Rawlins. In the diary, he spoke of the little raven-haired girl as his sister. So then she was looking at Lucy. And the older woman with the big, light brown eyes on the other end of the couch must be his mother. She loved that she could put faces now to the people in his diary...even if they were all dead. A grim sadness filled her at that realization.

When she came upon the next set of doors, her heart banged against her chest. Two giant, ornate doors with a forgotten bit of yellow caution tape stuck on a bottom corner. The West Wing.

On her first visit, Liam had forbidden her from entering this room, but she'd gone in anyway. And she was going in again. This was the place that required some Shadow Spawn ghostbusting.

She marveled at this newfound reckless bravery of hers. No, she didn't want to face the Secret Passage Monster, but her instincts were raring a go at zapping away supernatural shadows. Maybe this was a new ability? Like she was *meant* to be a Shadow Spawn Hunter?

Eager to test out her theory, she slowly pulled the doors open.

It was the same as before. Living room furniture covered in dusty, white sheets; walls lined with smashed-in, glass-paneled bookcases; two tarp-covered holes in the roof that the moonlight filtered through; and a giant, gaping fireplace at the back—the biggest one she'd ever seen. In fact, it was the same fireplace from the painting.

She rushed over to lift the corner of a sheet on a particular lump of furniture. It was a matted green plush couch, the same one Edward Rawlins lounged on for the painting. This very room was the setting for that painting.

She ventured into the middle, morbidly enthralled by the history of the place, but a sudden movement from the corner of her eye cast her primary reason for being here back in her face.

Drawing in a deep breath, she clenched and unclenched her hands at her sides, willing for the electricity to spark in them. She felt her hands go warm, but that was it.

A long shadowy man extricated itself from the natural shadows in the back of the room. It stood there as if watching, waiting for her move.

Belle gulped and felt the breath stall in her lungs. She shook her hands, muttering frantically, "C'mon, sparkies, get to work."

Her palms got sweaty, but no sparks.

Maybe this was a bad idea. A very, very bad idea.

But a sudden *good* idea had her removing Eddie's rosary from around her neck and depositing it into her pocket. It was like having an invisible pair of rubber gloves removed from her hands: they fired up, each encased in an electrical orb.

"Yeah!" she whooped.

At that, the shadow man, retreated a step, and several other smaller shadows erupted from behind him and merged with the other natural shadows cast along the wall.

"Oh no."

Shoot, she thought, *there's a bunch of them.*

"A bunch of what, siren?"

Belle screamed.

"Shhh. It's just me."

"Eddie? Are you…inside my HEAD?"

"You took off the rosary, didn't you?"

"Yes. Wait a minute, so this whole time, all I had to do to talk to you was take off the rosary?"

"Miss me, siren?"

"NO. Is this, is this rosary like a tracker? Are you keeping tabs on me? You know what, this is epic-level stalking. You have really out-done yourself this time, Jäger. I should have a restraining order put on you. Yes, I'll have Ernesto do that."

He chuckled. *"What reason will you give? 'I can't get this devilishly handsome man out of my mind?' They'll probably give me the restraining order to put on you."*

"Are you…in my mind then?"

"Honestly, siren, I'm not sure why. My theory is that when we made that, erm, connection underneath the staircase at school, the mental connection remained somehow. Perhaps, without the rosary to dampen your powers, this connection can remain…accessible. Where are you, siren? I'm sensing a great deal of anxiety on your end."

"Well, voices in my head can be quite unnerving."

"Before I announced my presence, I felt your distress. What's going on?"

Belle bit her lip. "I'm in the West Wing of Rawlins Castle, hunting for Shadow Spawn."

There was a pause. *"Why the West Wing?"*

For some reason, she expected to be berated for attempting such a feat. It must be residual anxiety left over from her Littleton days when she was expected to live within the small confines of Papa's rules. Anytime she felt like she was doing something considered "risky," she felt deep reservations. Just being here on her spontaneous night mission was a giant leap outside her safety box.

Belle drew in a long breath and filled Eddie in on the deaths that occurred in the room and what Cindy had said about the staff quitting over the hauntings.

"I have more questions, but I have a feeling our time is short. Would you like my help, siren?"

"Like pep-talk help?"

"I want to try something with this connection. Do you trust me?"

"Not entirely." There was a pause. "But enough to let you try your thing. This will help me zap the Shadow Spawn?"

"I think so. Give me a second."

This was so weird. Weirder than fighting shadows. Anyone looking in would think she was nuts, talking to herself so animatedly. She was so engaged in this connection, though, that she was somewhat oblivious to the shadows flitting about at the far end of the room.

The sensation of Eddie's presence suddenly overwhelmed her everywhere at once, like a heightened awareness that was tangible. It was how her body always reacted to his close proximity. Whenever he was around, her body felt like it was on edge, but in a pleasantly warm, excited way. She felt like that now, like he was *here*.

She gasped. "Eddie, what are you doing?"

"Whoa. I can see what you're seeing."

"Are you, like, possessing me?!"

"Absolutely not. I'm following instinct here, based on an old Jäger legend. I guess the way to explain it would be I pulled on the connection to get closer. I can see the Shadow Spawn trying to hide inside the fireplace."

"Yes, that's what I'm looking at right now. How many of them are there?" She felt like she'd been squeezed in a warm hug. "What was that?"

"I'm trying to extend my senses through you and count the suckers. You ready for this?"

"For what?"

"There's about a hundred in there."

"What?! I'm out." She turned toward the double doors.

"I thought you were braver than that."

She stopped in her tracks. "That's an *army* of Shadow Spawn and just one of me."

"Two of us. And they're more scared of you than you are of them. You can do this, siren."

"*We* can do this."

"You're right. We can do this. I'll guide you. I'm starting to get a handle on this ying-yang connection."

She turned back. "Ok, Jedi Master, instruct me." She felt a warm, involuntary shiver run through her. "Care to explain that reaction?"

"I'd rather not." There was a pause. *"Ok, I need you to get closer to the fireplace."*

"Mmm, how about we see if my electrical blast can make it from here instead?"

"It probably could. But with the force you'd need to send it across the room, I can't guarantee you won't take out the entire back wall. Might be a little difficult to explain that one away. You need to get as close as possible."

As if sensing their plan, the Shadow Spawn began jumping towards each other, until a single mass grew like a bubble rising from the surface and threatening to pop. More shadows from around the room shot toward the mass as if being sucked in.

"Do you see that?" she whispered, jaw unhinged and ready to bolt from the room.

"They're forming a Shadow Spawn Megazord. It has to be taken out now. There's no going back. We can't let it escape. Others will see it, especially if it gets out into the town."

The dark, shadowy mass stood up on trunk-like legs and flexed its massive arms outward.

Belle spluttered, "I did NOT sign up for this. I just wanted to zap one tiny, lonesome shadow—not a Godzilla one."

Eddie chuckled.

"Y-You're laughing right now?"

"Just wait here. We're going to let it come closer."

At that, Belle backtracked and looked behind her at the inviting safety of the exit.

"*Siren,*" he said softly. "*I have faith in you. We're going to do this...to-gether. The Shadowzord won't know what hit it.*"

Big girl pants, Belle reminded herself. She stepped forward again and nodded.

"*Excellent. Put your two hands out in front of you like you're holding a ball.*"

She did so. "Okay."

"*Now, imagine creating a basketball-sized electrical orb in your hands.*"

"That's very specific."

"*I think that should be enough power to launch at it and destroy it with-out consuming anything else. Picture the orb in your mind.*"

Imagining for Belle was as easy as breathing. After just a few sec-onds, the very same orb she pictured manifested around her hands, crackling and popping. Despite the Shadowzord silently trudging to-ward her, she laughed out, "I did it!"

The Shadowzord growled in disapproval.

The orb flickered out.

"*Hold that picture in your mind. Don't let it go.*"

She pictured again, and the orb reformed, but it wasn't as bright as before. "That thing is almost right on top of me!" She began to cower while trying to keep the orb steady before her.

"*Bring it close to your chest, and then push the orb out with both hands. You can do it.*"

"Aghhh!" She shot the orb at the Shadowzord, striking it in the face. It stumbled back, arms flailing as the electricity snaked all over its form. The monster dimmed out as if about to disappear, but when the electricity dissipated, it darkened back to its full strength.

"It didn't work!"

"*Again. Concentrate. You'll get it this time. Just don't be afraid.*"

The monster rumbled out in a deep voice that shook her bones, **"You'll wish for death soon."**

"*Concentrate, siren. Hands out!*"

A wave of nausea overcame her, draining all her energy. All she could think about now was the immense pain and suffering in the world. When was it all going to end?

"I don't feel so good...I don't have the strength to stand anymore."

"Belle, no, listen to me—"

"A nap right now would be perfect." She sunk to her knees, tears of hopelessness blurring her vision. She didn't care anymore about the monster slowly making its way toward her, even slower than last time, relishing its hold on her and feeding off her anguish now.

"It's projecting misery onto you! Forget what I said about basketball-sized—make the orb as big as you can and launch it!"

"I'm too sad to care..." she whispered. She let herself droop sideways onto the floor, her arm cushioning her head.

"This is bad," he muttered. An idea came to him then. *"Darling?"*

"Mm?"

"Would you like to hear a story?"

After a few seconds, she responded, "Mm-hmm."

"Then, you have to sit up first."

She frowned. "No."

"When the Jäger call took hold of me, I had to cross the Atlantic Ocean in order to follow this pull. I booked passage on an English ship, but it was soon captured by pirates." He paused. *"Would you like to hear more?"*

At this, Belle pulled herself up onto her knees and faced the monster. It was almost upon her.

"In the scuffle, I fell overboard. My leg was entangled with rope attached to a cannon. I was sinking fast. I knew I was a dead man. Do you want to know what happened next?"

She nodded. The picture of Eddie sinking into the depths of the black ocean crowded out the soul-sucking, gloom-and-doom thoughts.

"Put your hands out."

She did.

The Shadowzord growled.

"The depth of the water was crushing me and there was no light; it was utter darkness. I knew I wasn't dead yet, though, because my lungs felt like they were being squeezed in and lit on fire. And then suddenly, I felt a jerk on my leg and the dead weight of the cannon was gone." He paused.

"What happened next?"

"Get that orb going first."

She thought about an electrical orb the size of a beachball. It was now or never. The Shadowzord was only a few feet away, and the miserable thoughts were quickly eating its way in at the edges of the scene Eddie had painted in her mind. That nap was becoming more and more enticing again.

"Can you still see what I'm seeing?"

"Yes. You need to launch it now."

"What happens if it gets me?"

"This one will put you in a weeklong coma—do it, now!"

She launched it with all her might. The orb blasted right through its chest, leaving a giant hole in the middle.

"That was different." She watched as it stumbled all the way back again. Her eyes widened as more shadows filled in the hole but was relieved that the size of the monster had at least been reduced to half.

"Well done, darling. You took out a solid number of them."

"What's with this darling-business?"

"I know you like it."

"I do."

"But I'll only use it for very special occasions."

"So me slaying a Shadowzord is a very special occasion?" Even though the very monster was slowly gaining on her again, she smiled at his banter.

"If you focus here, darling, I can finish telling you about my last kiss."

"Oh my, do go on."

"Orb ready, first."

She squeezed her eyes tight and pictured an orb the size of an exercise ball, but it kept flickering in and out.

"So my leg was suddenly free, and I was no longer being dragged to the bottom of the ocean. Nonetheless, I had reached my end. My lungs were about to explode, and I could no longer fight the instinct to breathe in, which I knew would be instant drowning. Just then, I felt something cover my mouth, and what I knew was a hand grab the back of my head and press me forward. I felt air pushed into my mouth, and I sucked it in. I truly thought I had died, and this was how the Afterlife was welcoming me. I didn't know we had been ascending until enough light allowed me to see my savior.... You need to blast it now, siren."

"Sorry, I was distracted." She pressed her lips together in concentration and with a loud grunt, she pushed out with all the energy she could muster. The giant orb soared toward the faceless monster, which paused in its step with its hands up, surprised by the size of the onslaught. The orb smashed into it, the electrical sparks and puffs of black shadow scattering outward and dissipating together at once.

"That was perfect, darling."

She fell back on her bottom and lay back on the cold, hard floor. She spread out her arms to the sides and stared up at the castle-high roof with the two holes in it. She smiled and exhaled in joyous relief. The room felt as light as a sunroom on an idyllic day. "Are there any more left?"

"Not a one. How does it feel being a certifiable Shadow Spawn Hunter now?"

"Like I want my own costume and cape."

"We'll get you one."

Belle laughed. She felt that pressure of warmth leaving and being replaced by the chilliness of the room. She gasped, "Eddie, are you trying to leave?"

"Your mission is completed, siren. I have to get on with mine."

She spluttered, "You can't just leave me on a cliffhanger like that! Who was the savior?"

"Think about it. What, in the depths of the ocean, has human hands, can breathe into my mouth, and swim us to the surface?"

Belle thought she was going to faint. "A m-mermaid?!"

"Her name was Jolie. She had long hair that changed colors with the waters and eyes like the starry night sky."

Belle felt like she was in a dream. She was lying on the floor, so maybe she had fallen asleep and was currently in a dream being narrated by Eddie.

But she knew better than that. "What happened after she brought you to the surface?"

"After I got my breath, I was just in shock at what I was seeing, even if she wasn't the first supernatural creature I'd seen by then. The Jäger recruiters had made sure of that."

"The Jäger recruiters?"

"That's another story for another day. She pointed at herself and whispered, 'Jolie,' in a very raspy voice. She had flinched as if it hurt her to even speak. I told her my name and thanked her for saving my life."

"There's an illustration of the mermaid you just described in the *Elmridge Book of Fairy Tales*. Right next to the poem about the Jade Blade Wish. But who cares? What happened next?"

"Jolie kissed me."

Belle sucked in a breath. "How was it like to kiss a mermaid?"

"Frightening. She had sharp teeth and kissed like a Hoover."

"A what?"

"A vacuum cleaner. I was starting to feel like her prey."

"Oh my."

"If there hadn't been a shout from my shipmates in an oar boat nearby...."

"She let you go and disappeared?"

"Yes."

"So your last kiss was with a mermaid?" she teased, but couldn't keep the awe out of her voice.

"Does a recent half-kiss on the lips from a certain naughty girl count?"

She blushed. "I thought Drix had made you disappear before you felt that."

"Nope. I felt it everywhere. I still do."

Her heart went thump-thump. "Still?" she whispered.

He didn't respond right away. The silence lengthened, pregnant with a crackling energy that made her feel even warmer everywhere herself.

His voice was a bit rougher when he spoke again. *"Can I show you something, darling?"*

Goodness, the *darlings* in that British accent of his were giving her waves of goosebumps.

"A-ha! What's the special occasion now?" she asked playfully. "And yes, of course."

"The 'special occasion' is you single-handedly slaying a Shadowzord. I'm...proud of you."

Tears welled in her eyes. Only Papa ever told her he was proud of her. "There was nothing *single-handed* about it. I couldn't have done it without you." She sniffled. "What did you want to show me?"

"You know how I can see what you're seeing? The roof right now, for example."

"Uh-huh."

"Well, I think if you pull on our connection the way I did, you'll be able to see through me."

"Yes, let's do it!"

"Alright, luv, then I want you to close your eyes and imagine me standing in front of you. There's a rope extending between us—"

"Like a tightrope?"

"What worked for me was a rope around your waist that I pulled to get myself to you."

"Oh, okay...done. I just pull myself toward you now?"

"Yes."

"I'm pulling myself, and—oh! I can feel the resistance."

"You're doing it."

"I'm picturing you in a clown suit, by the way, and we're in a circus act."

"Liar. You have me without a shirt, standing right there in the room with you."

"You do have a shirt on," she grumbled at his almost spot-on assessment. *Just the tight, black sleeveless one. And you're flexing, thank you very much.* "Wait, you can't hear my thoughts, right?" She failed to disguise the horror in her voice.

His response was to crack up.

"Right?" she persisted.

"Right. Have you reached me yet?"

"One more step...." She inhaled sharply. "I can see...a wide, stone staircase leading up to a dark, two-story structure. Everything's covered in snow." She gasped when she looked to the side. "That view! Those mountains, oh, how beautiful! Where are we, Eddie?"

She could hear the smile in his voice. *"Nepal. This is the Jäger Temple."*

"Wow," she breathed out, as she stared at the sloping roof and the two massive entrance doors. It reminded her of a mystical Tibetan monastery.

"I have to go in now. The Jäger Father's expecting me."

"Will you be back soon?" *Jeez, I sound so clingy.* "Because, you know, we have a lot of work to do here with the werewolf and Violet and all that. I kind of have a plan. Want to hear really quick?"

"I'm all ears."

She told him quickly about how she and Ernesto had figured out their theory that Violet was going to try and manipulate the taffeite tiara out of the Homecoming Queen's hands, so Belle was going to try and win the crown to bring Violet straight to her.

She waited with bated breath for his response. "So what do you think?"

"That," he began slowly, *"sounds like a plan you can pull off. Because each Jade Blade gem needs to be gifted—"*

"And because Elmridge is the hub of Fae magic. I overheard Violet say that in the first Beast-nightmare I had."

He was quiet for a moment, mulling it over. *"This is good intel, siren. Then, yes, it does appear that she will try to have that taffeite crown gifted to her. By 'one pure and sage,' wasn't it?"*

"Yes."

"I think you fit that bill."

"I highly doubt it."

"I do think so. And you'll need to figure out which of the other Homecoming candidates might fit that bill, too. Violet may try to, uh, boost that girl's chances of winning."

"Oh my gosh, you're right!" Her mind immediately ran through the possible candidates. Only Mari and Nieves stood out to her.

"The other gem she needs is the fire opal, right? What was the requirement again?"

"Vengeful rage."

"Ok, so then from what we know so far, the taffeite is the one she's going after next. Do you know if she has a blade made of jade, yet?"

She racked her mind. "No."

"Well, erm, I saw your uncle earlier in Amsterdam."

"A.k.a. your 'best bud?' I'm still mad at you about that, by the way."

"We can tussle over it later, siren, and work your anger out," he suggested, with a wicked tone that both annoyed and pleased her at once. But before she could retort, he continued, *"Ernesto showed me the ingredients list that they got off of Hagar. Three recipes for the three potions Violet ordered from her. I'm going to show the recipes to the Jäger Father, so he can tell me what the potions were for."*

"Did you see Hagar?"

"No. They let her go before I got there. As expected, she dropped off the grid then." He sighed in exasperation at that. *"But that's okay because I'm going to get answers now anyway."* He added ominously, *"I'll find the potions witch another time."*

"So, tomorrow, I'll take off the rosary and reach out to you." She added quickly, "I-I'd like to know what the Jäger Father tells you about the potions."

"That shouldn't be a problem. Have you told James about what you've discovered concerning Violet?"

"I would have liked to have told him today, but he was absent. There was a sub in class, instead. I couldn't even get your book from him; I was really looking forward to that." There was a silence on his end that went on a little too long. "Eddie?"

"I told him to give you the book. I told him to stay put. And he didn't answer my hail earlier either."

"With the rocks? But so what? Maybe he wasn't feeling well today and stayed home. And you sound very bossy. What do you mean you *told* him this and *told* him that? He's your uncle. Doesn't he have more bossing authority than you?"

"Belle, stop. Something's wrong."

Her indignation froze into fear. He'd used her name. This was serious. "How so?" she whispered.

"I need to see the Jäger Father, now. Ernesto said he was getting back to you this Saturday. I figured you stayed over at Rawlins Castle because the D&D game ran late."

"We're married in the game now, by the way. It was the only way to save your hide."

The sound of his breath hitching was clear. *"No time for that right now,"* he said more to himself. *"Belle, please, stay at Jo's from now on until Ernesto returns. Do not go out at night, no more Shadow Spawn hunting until I return, and, in fact, do not go anywhere alone."*

"Eddie, you're scaring me."

"I'm sorry, but, please, trust me. I'm going to get to the bottom of this."

"Ow, ow." She was trying to get on her feet again, especially after she realized she could barely feel her body. The cold from the floor she'd been stretched out on had seeped through her clothing and into her very bones.

"What's wrong, luv?"

"I'm frozen stiff, and I need to get back to my room in this place, but I'm not even sure how to get back."

"You're in the West Wing; I can tell from the fireplace. Step outside, go left all the way until you see a hallway on your right that opens up to the foyer's grand staircase. From there, you should be able to orient yourself better."

"Okay."

"Is there still a mirror in this room you can go to?"

"Um," she looked around and spotted the moonlight striking one long glass panel of a bookcase that hadn't been smashed in. "Kind of."

"Go there."

"Why do—"

"Please."

She sighed. "Okay." She moved to stand in front of the glass panel. "It's not a mirror, but I can see my reflection."

She felt a deep, warm squeeze that thawed some of the ice in her veins, and then heard his sharp intake of breath. He murmured a few words that she knew was in Fae language.

"You getting sappy on me, Jäger?"

"Keep the rosary on, siren, and remember what I told you." And then he was gone.

The severance of the connection was jarring, like when pulling on a rope and the other end suddenly goes slack. It was an inward feeling of spiraling backward into emptiness.

Sleep, that's what she needed. While following Eddie's map-directions, she halted in her tracks in the hallway when the realization struck her like a lightning bolt: how in the world does he know his way around this castle?

| 29 |

Two Truths and a Dare

Liam exhaled roughly. "Ice cold shower. Again."

Every encounter with Belle left him frustrated. He *wanted* her. In the past, with others, he'd never *not* gotten his way. And her wanting to take things slow? It was torture.

And now with that comment he let slip out of his mouth a few moments ago about using her as a body pillow.... He ran his fingers through his short hair and tugged painfully on it. Now she'll want to take things sloth-slow.

He made it to the kitchen and downed a cold glass of water. His insides always felt like they were on fire too, which was why he preferred to be shirtless at home. Hell, he'd walk around naked if he could. But then his creepy personal assistant, Beatrix, might lap up the view, and she totally gave off that fatal-attraction vibe. The only reason he kept her around was because of her expertise with the new company's first successful RejuveNew trial with Mari—a project that was giving him a new type of much-needed fulfillment in his life, like his hero, Bruce Wayne, using his wealth to give back to the community.

And there was also the reason of keeping Beatrix on as a temporary replacement for Jacques, his house butler and surrogate guardian. It gutted Liam when he returned from Europe and Beatrix found Jacques's resignation letter on the castle foyer's table. The letter stated that an emergency had arisen with his family that needed his immediate, long-time attention, and Jacques didn't know when he'd be back, if ever.

Liam had to admit, his time in Europe was a fuzzy memory, but he could never forget his faithful butler's lifetime of service. Even now, thinking about it, his heart felt like a knot. He promised himself, as soon as Mari's new legs were unveiled at the Homecoming Pageant and she won that crown, he'd search for Jacques and bring him home. He'd triple his salary, give him his favorite Rolls Royce, whatever it took.

"Mirror, mirror on the wall."

All thought fled from his mind, and his body locked up as he turned in the direction of the enchanted voice.

Beatrix stood on the other side of the island counter, her expression smug. "Who's your master, above them all?" she finished.

Liam answered in a toneless voice, "You are, Violet."

"That's right, I am." She slid a small, glass potion bottle across the counter to him. "Drink up."

He caught the bottle and downed the purple liquid. He made a disgusted face and shivered, and then went neutral again.

"Marissa will call you soon to pick her up from a party. I ensured that her original ride abandoned her. She will have Nieves Blanco with her as well. You will drop Marissa off at home first, and then you will take Nieves and—" She picked a large red apple out of the fruit bowl in the middle of the counter and tossed it to Liam. "Catch."

He caught it.

"Have the beast inject his venom into it. Now."

He looked at the apple in his hand. He pressed his lips together as if concentrating. His thumb elongated and sprouted blonde, wolfish hair. The nail lengthened into a black claw, and with it, he pierced the bottom of the apple.

"Very good."

Still holding the apple aloft, Liam's thumb receded into its human version, and he looked blankly back at her.

She placed both palms down on the counter and leaned in. "Now, listen very closely to the rest of my instructions."

"Yes, Violet."

~~*~~

"Liam, you're such a sweetie," Nieves gushed when he returned to the driver's seat. He'd just wheeled Mari to her front door.

"Shh, don't tell anyone; you'll ruin my reputation." He flashed her a heartbreaker grin, shifted the car's gears into place, and pulled out of the long driveway.

He'd thrown on a thick hoodie over the sweatpants. Nieves had on a tight ensemble hidden beneath a jacket overflowing with faux fur. She tossed a large sausage curl over her shoulder. "Sooo, you and Mari, huh?"

"Just friends."

"And 'just friends' who picks her up at three in the morning from a party to take her home?"

Enchanted words repeated themselves in the back of his mind, *"Get Nieves to take a bite out of that apple. The whole situation must look as natural as possible. When she goes to sleep tonight, nothing but your true love's kiss will ever wake her up."*

He smiled. "I'm taking you home too, aren't I?"

She rolled her red lips together before spreading them into a knowing smile. "Mari's playing the innocent card about it, but Jared told me you're taking her to Homecoming."

Liam clenched the steering wheel and muttered, "That little prick. No one's supposed to know." An animalistic sound rumbled in his chest.

"You will not use the beast tonight; your encounter with Vasilisa was far too messy. But after tonight, perhaps I'll allow the beast to come out and play with the final Homecoming princess who's threatening our chances of victory."

"It's alright, sweetie," Nieves purred. "All's fair in love and war. The way I see it, Mari really wants to win this year. Make Jared suffer a bit too, so he'll wise up to what he's been missing right under his nose. I think he's already starting to feel it. I mean, he's taking her to the Halloween dance and was all-out bummed when she turned him down for Homecoming." She bit her lip and glanced over at him. "Who are *you* taking to the Halloween dance?"

"Belle." His insides warmed immediately at the thought.

"Hmm, what a small world then." She popped her lips.

"What do you mean?" He knew she was baiting him. But about what?

"It's supposed to be a secret. I promised Jared I wouldn't tell. He let it slip tonight when he had a bit too much of the mystery punch."

The fuzzies quickly iced over. "Tell me."

"Uh, hello? It's a secret between besties. No can do."

He white-knuckled the steering wheel. Belle and Jared in the same sentence made him want to break things, maybe even human things, like a few guitar-strumming fingers off a certain punk.

"Get Nieves to take a bite out of that apple. The whole situation must look as natural as possible."

He pulled the apple out of his front hoodie pouch and casually put it in the cupholder. "Remember that time we played Truth or Dare in your den? It was you, me—"

"And my seven brothers?"

Liam laughed. "Yeah. The youngest one, what's his name?"

She giggled. "Donny. You dared him to bring in any creature from outside—"

"Hey, I was trying to go easy on him. I figured he'd bring in a bug or something."

"My mother almost had a heart attack when he let that peacock loose into the house."

He grinned in challenge. "You feel like a quick game of Truth or Dare?" They were almost at her house. It was now or never.

She turned wide eyes on him, her lips forming a perfect 'o.' "Beast Boy, are you—?" She lowered her voice to a hush, "You remember how that night turned out...."

He cocked an eyebrow. "I do. So are we playing or not?"

She bit her lip and smiled. "Two truths and a dare, then."

"Ladies first."

"Is it true that Cindy and her father are living with you now at the castle?"

Dammit. He'd forgotten what an insufferable gossip she was. "Yes."

"Hmm. Your turn."

He exhaled. He only had two questions to fish the information out of her. From how he knew she played this game, he had to frame his questions carefully. "This secret you mentioned...does it have to do with Belle and Jared having some sort of arrangement for Homecoming?"

Her eyes flashed with approval. "Oh, you are good. Yes."

He felt stabbing pain at the tips of his fingers, which he knew would soon be accompanied by a knifelike twist in his stomach and then blacking out. He'd wake up in bed to Beatrix giving him his medicine, the one they'd picked up in Europe after the episodes had started. The doctor, an associate of Beatrix's who promised secrecy, diagnosed him with a rare and extreme form of PTSD. No one else knew about this problem of his; he didn't want any more of his weaknesses on public display, or anyone's pity, especially Belle's, not when he had such a world-changing medical project in the works about to come to light.

"You will not use the beast tonight...."

He sucked in a sharp breath, and then another more calming one.

"Are you okay?" Nieves asked, concerned.

He pulled into her long driveway and put the car in park. He pinched his lips together and forced a smile as he turned to her. "What's your second question?"

She turned toward him, grinning like a kid in a candy store. She was having choice-gossip handed to her for free. "Is Belle your actual girlfriend?"

He ground his molars together. She sure knew how to punch his buttons. "Not yet."

"Huh."

"My turn again." He steeled himself mentally against reacting poorly to her answer to his final question. Just in case. "Is Jared taking Belle to Homecoming?"

Both her brows flew up like this was exciting, while her lips pouted in sympathy for him. Only Nieves could pull off that expression. "Yes."

He decided holding his breath and remaining very still was the next best course of action.

"Ready for the dare?" she asked.

He nodded a fraction as he stared at her, refusing to replay the new revelation over in his mind. He had to remain in control.

"I dare you to tell me what secret project you and Mari are working on."

His brows slammed down as he glared at her. Of course she'd use her dare to pry for more information.

She continued as if defending her nosiness, "She's my best friend, and she won't even tell me or Jared, so we're legitimately concerned, I mean, curious. That's all." She pointed at him. "And I dared you. You can't back out now. The Truth-or-Dare gods will curse you with bad luck forever if you do."

A dark chuckle escaped him. "Even worse luck than I have now?"

Nieves's face fell. "I-I'm sorry. I know you've been through a lot...oh, just forget it. Thanks for the ride."

Just as she pulled on the door handle, the lock clicked into place. She looked back at him, confused. "What are you doing?"

"You dared me, remember?" He was smiling, but the light that usually accompanied it was gone from his eyes.

She settled back uneasily into her seat. "Okay. I'm listening."

"I own majority share of a new medical company that is working on healing Mari's spine."

Her face lit up. "What?!" she squealed. "Like, so she can walk again?"

"Yeah," he grinned genuinely now. "And it's working."

"Oh my God!" She threw her arms around him.

This. This right here was why he was willing to put up with Beatrix and the secrecy and the Europe-fiasco that cost him Belle's trust. This RejuveNew treatment was going to help so many people.

Nieves pulled away with tears in her eyes and frowned. "But why is it such a secret?"

"It's a business-thing." He gave her a stern look. "You cannot tell anyone."

She pouted. "Can I at least talk to Mari about it, since I know now?"

"Fine."

She beamed, and then she bit her lip and glanced away.

"What?"

"Um, well, I think you deserve to know a little more about what I said, you know, about Jared and Belle."

He felt that clench in his stomach. "Go on."

"I thought he was lying at first, but he swore on his fans that he was telling the truth. And that's like his ultimate oath."

"What did he say?" Impatience hardened his tone.

She lowered her voice as if paparazzi could overhear, "Jared told me that Belle agreed to be his girlfriend after the Halloween dance. Like, legit girlfriend."

The floor cracked open like he was falling through ice. He shoved his hands into his hoodie pocket, balling them into tight fists to choke off the slicing pain in his fingers. The fire erupted in his belly. He had only seconds now.

"Liam?"

He swallowed hard, willing his gravelly throat to work.

Nieves cleared her throat. "I-I'll just be going now. Goodnight." She pulled on the door handle, but the door wouldn't budge. She looked back at him, fear, worry, uncertainty churning in her eyes. "Um, unlock, please?"

"What about my dare?" he whispered.

"Oh," she sat back again, stiff as a board, one hand still on the door handle. "Sure thing. G-Give me an easy one, though, okay?" She giggled nervously.

"Of course." He gestured his chin toward the cupholder and smiled. "I dare you to take a big bite out of that apple."

| 30 |

Nom de Guerre

In what felt like only yesterday, Ernesto was standing in the same spot Belle was in now, waiting for her to arrive by train. Now their roles were reversed. She rubbed her hands in excitement together. Finally, something good was happening after the last three days of disappointment.

The morning after her stay at the castle, Liam was nowhere to be found, and she and Cindy had taken themselves to school, which had been fine with them, but she couldn't understand the cold shoulder Liam had started giving her afterward. In literature class, he'd ignored her. And when she'd wanted to talk to him about the shocking news of Nieves being hospitalized in a coma, he'd glared at her and told her to go talk to her "other boyfriend" about it.

"What other boyfriend?" she'd countered.

"Jared. After the Halloween dance." When her mouth fell open in surprise and she couldn't deny it, he'd stalked off.

She had a mind to forget the deal with big-mouth Jared, but she needed to win that crown. And yes, she was feeling rather icky about her scheming ways. She was *using* people to get her way. But…it was the lesser evil. It was either that or allow an unsuspecting, powerless girl to become ensnared in Violet's clutches.

So, she made up her mind to apologize to Liam and Jared later. After she got that crown.

Ugh, again, that ickiness.

A sleek black train slowed to a stop at the platform as an electronic voice boomed its arrival. A flurry of people departed down its steps, unlike the last time when she'd been the sole passenger.

Ernesto emerged, and Belle practically fell into his arms.

"Well, this is a greeting," he chuckled.

She squeezed him and buried her face in his starchy coat. She breathed in that Ernesto-scent, a mix of strong coffee and busy day.

She pulled back, surprised to feel her eyes wet with warmth. "It's just so good to have you back."

He gave her a crinkly smile and patted her head. "Then, let's go home. There's much to debrief."

"You mean talk about." Once a cop, always a cop.

"Same thing." He put an arm around her shoulders and gave her a squeeze as they walked off the platform together towards the covered parking lot, where his car had sat the whole time he was away.

"Our talk has to wait until after lunch. Sergio and Trina are meeting us at the house soon. I invited them over for a three-course meal that I am personally preparing."

He grunted in disapproval.

"Hey, it's the least I could do for the way they looked after me."

"Fine. Any chance you learned to prepare Jo's gumbo?"

~~*~~

After the last of the dishes had been stowed into the dishwasher and the table cleared away, Belle and Ernesto sat down to the kitchen table for "the talk."

Sergio and Trina had left half an hour ago, the lunch being a disaster, but the conversation and camaraderie more than making up for it. Apparently, Belle had mistakenly used sugar instead of salt—the dispensers being the same—and the result was a cake-tasting meatloaf.

Ernesto pulled a file from his briefcase and laid it open on the table. He pointed at the mug shot of a scowling woman with disheveled curly brown hair wrapped up in a scarf. The tell-tale mole on the long, pointy nose gave it away for Belle.

"That's Hagar!"

He nodded, handing her the photo so she could look more closely at it.

"I saw her when I dreamt as the beast in the Amsterdam hotel. Do you know what potions she gave Violet?"

He shook his head and pressed his lips into a grim line. "A friend's working on that right now."

Eddie. Three days now since she last spoke with him through that bizarre connection they'd shared in the West Wing. Admittedly, she'd tried every night since then to contact him. She slept without the rosary on now, hoping to leave herself reachable to him. But nothing. She'd tried talking to him in her mind, calling for him, even hurling insults at him, and then, just once, describing what she was wearing that night. Not even a mind-whisper of a response in return.

She hated to admit it, but she missed her stalker/friend.

Ernesto slid Hagar's mug shot to the side, revealing another photo. It looked like a small hotel bedroom that had been raided, all marked up like a crime scene. He pointed at the distinct scarf lying on the floor and the drops of blood beside it. "When we looked for Hagar again for further questioning, she was nowhere to be found. We figured she was just laying low, trying to evade arrest again, but then the hotel called this in."

"What happened?"

"This is the scene of a struggle, and then a disappearance. We believe Hagar was taken against her will."

"You think Violet had something to do with it?"

"More than likely, but the forensic evidence points to a man being involved here."

Could Eddie have finally caught up to Hagar like he'd threatened? Dragged her off to interrogate her? She bit her lip, feeling disturbed. Even if Hagar was a witch of sorts, she couldn't imagine Eddie being physically violent with her...or killing her.

"W-When was she taken?"

"Just yesterday."

Her heart sunk.

"The team I left behind is looking into it." He dragged a hand down his face. "I have to turn my attention to here."

"It's bad, isn't it?"

He nodded heavily. "I-I need just one day of rest, though, and then I'm heading back into the station and taking the reins again." As if on cue, his cell phone trilled. He looked at the caller ID and silenced it.

"Do you know yet what happened to Nieves? Everyone at school was talking about it today; they said her parents couldn't wake her up this morning. She's in a coma in the hospital right now."

"Not enough yet, but...." He stayed looking at her, brows furrowed, suddenly deep in thought.

"What is it?"

He nodded once to himself as if reaching a conclusion. He started rifling through his briefcase. "I wasn't going to show you this because I know I've told you not to worry about such matters and to focus on being a teen. But..." he lifted two 8 x 10 photos out and spread them on the table before her, "we're a team. So it's best we share everything we know with each other about anything concerning Violet."

"Yes," she whispered in agreement, her eyes widening at the images. One showed a room that looked like it had been ransacked with clothing strewn everywhere, a chair overturned before a large sewing machine, and—

She gasped, a hand over her mouth.

Ernesto cleared his throat. "Those are mannequin parts."

"Oh, thank God," she breathed out with relief. There were limbs everywhere, and clothed torsos and decapitated heads with great hair. Mannequins. Now that she knew she was just looking at a messy tailor shop, the next picture became the most disturbing. It was the side of someone's leg, an exposed thigh, with three bloody lines scraped through like claw marks.

"This was the main injury found on Vasilisa Shveya."

Her skin pimpled over like frost. "She was *attacked?*"

He nodded solemnly. "When she didn't come home after work, her parents' personal security guards found her unconscious in that room in the back of her store, The Briar Rose. All security footage wiped. She was sewing some clothing when she was surprised upon and an altercation took place. She fought back, and she fought hard. No other human DNA underneath her fingernails, so she was mostly hurling objects at the assailant, which explains the mess in the room. Other than some minor bumps and bruises, the only injury were the lacerations on her thigh and a pinpoint on her index finger. There was a spot of her blood on the sewing needle; she must have stuck herself by accident."

Belle was in shock. "Poor Lisa." Actual genuine sympathy sprung up in her for her schoolyard nemesis. "And the police can't tell what caused those cuts on her leg?"

"They're consistent with animal claw marks."

"The beast...."

"I think so. Only a few of us have been privy to the information that allows those dots to be connected. Mayor Markham is one of them, but he's adamant about no one finding out. He's afraid of negative press during one of Elmridge's most marketable media events." Ernesto reached across the table and covered her clammy hand with his warm one. "Speaking of Homecoming, I think it best you lay low. With Nieves in a coma now too...it's better to be safe than sorry."

"You think the Homecoming princesses are being targeted? Was Nieves attacked, too?"

"No." He sat back and crossed his arms over his chest in thought. "At least, not from what we can ascertain. She just hasn't woken up from last night's sleep. There's no sign of injury. The only connections to Vasilisa are that they're both in the same coma and both on the Homecoming court, and they both have the same circle of friends."

She couldn't stop thinking of Liam as the main suspect.

"When was Lisa attacked?"

"Five days ago."

She swallowed. Liam showed up five days ago. But Liam was with her just last night, and there seemed to be no evidence of foul play in Nieves's case. Yet.

She knew she really should bring up Liam's name now, but she found that she just couldn't do it. She couldn't bring herself to instigate the Elmridge police force into breathing down his neck again. Not after all Liam suffered in losing his parents and then being falsely accused of their murder. She couldn't do that to him. Not yet.

"What are we going to do?" she asked instead.

He extricated his hand from hers. She didn't realize she'd been gripping them so tightly. "I am going to amp up the wildlife taskforce that's been searching for this creature, as well as interview the Blanco family, and deal with the dozen other cases I know are waiting for me at my desk." He got up as if that were the end of the conversation.

"It's a werewolf."

He paused, pinning her with a look. "A what?"

"Werewolf."

"How do you know this?"

Eddie told her. "I dreamt it," she half-lied instead. She didn't want to tell him about Eddie. It would just raise more questions and unnecessary worries. "When I saw through the beast in the dream, I figured out later from what Violet and Hagar were saying that the beast was capable of turning back into a man."

"Ave Maria." Ernesto sat back down again with an uncharacteristic plop, his face blanched. "And did you see what this man looks like?" His voice had raised to a high pitch.

She bit her lip and looked down, shaking her head. "But the man has to be tall, strong, and have blonde hair since the beast's fur is all blonde."

"And Liam Rawlins did not cross your mind as this werewolf?"

"Whoa. Why do you jump so quickly to that conclusion?" She was trying to spare Liam the witch hunt, but Ernesto was already jumping on that bandwagon.

He narrowed his eyes slightly. "Liam fits the physical profile you just mentioned, he was in Europe around the same time Violet was, and she does have motive for using him to get back at us."

It was hard to swallow around the lump in her throat. Liam really was the prime suspect, and it was all Violet's fault. The witch was hurting him all over again.

"We have to do something, but I don't want to put Liam through that ringer again with the police. He's been through so much. If Violet is using him, then I don't think he's even aware of it. Can we look into this—just you and me—and not get the police involved with him?"

"I will personally look into him. If Liam really is this werewolf," he paused and shook his head, stark disbelief at this latest development, "then I don't want you alone with him. Agreed?"

"Agreed, but I'm helping."

Ernesto sighed heavily. "Of course." He lifted from the table.

"What are you going to do now?"

"Honestly? Order silver bullets."

"What?! You might be shooting Liam! I mean, it's still a man in there."

"Fine. Silver tranquilizer darts."

"O-Okay. That silver ammunition trick might just be a myth, though." She bet Dr. Helsing would know for sure, but he was still absent from work. Eddie's concern over his uncle's absence prompted her to ask, "Hey, do you know if there's anything going on with Dr. Helsing?"

"What do you mean?"

"He's been out this whole week."

"Maybe he's ill."

She nodded, uncertain. She made up her mind to ask someone in the school's office on Monday.

"I'm going to lie down for a little bit. I'll order us some dinner later."

She smiled innocently. "But we still have some meatloaf left over."

He visibly cringed, and she giggled. "Eh, I'll bring it to the station tomorrow," he said. "I'm sure they'll appreciate it." He paused, something catching his eye on the floor. He peered more closely and moved along as if following a trail. He straightened and pointed. "Why is there black dog hair all over the floor?"

"Cat hair. Her name's Lady Catherine Debourgh. 'Lady' for short."

"And just when did we get a cat?"

"Um, when it zoomed in through the front door about a week ago and decided to move in with us. She's pretty independent. I just leave a bowl of water out front. I tried giving her cat food, but she wouldn't touch it. She likes meat. I'll leave some of the meatloaf for her." Belle got up and started calling for the cat. "Lady! Lady!"

Ernesto recovered from his shock. "You are completely in charge of this animal. What about a litter box? How do you know it hasn't been going all over the furniture?"

"I think she's been going outside. Like I said, Lady's very independent." Belle pouted, giving up on waiting for the cat to show. "She never comes when I call her."

"Get a litter box," he grunted and then disappeared into his bedroom.

Belle saluted his closed door. "Yessir."

"Oh, it almost slipped my mind," he called through the door, the sound of drawers opening and closing. "There's a book, a novel, in the large front pocket of my briefcase, if you want it. Someone left it behind on the train. No one claimed it, and I figured you'd appreciate it."

Before he even finished speaking, she was already at the kitchen table, sliding the glossy-covered book out of the pocket of the briefcase.

It was Eddie's book! *Hunger Games!* She flipped through the pages, her heart somersaulting at the scribbles and doodles meant just for her.

Wasn't Dr. Helsing supposed to give it to her? How did it end up abandoned on the train? Did he take the train out of here and then just carelessly leave it behind on the seat? And for the book to find its way back into her hands...it was preternatural. Possibly the work of the Fae?

In any case, she had it now. Like unwrapping a long-awaited birthday present, she lifted the cover and was immediately glad her uncle had not apparently opened the book because there were life-like pictures of Belle's face everywhere. Every emotion she exhibited on her face seemed to have been penned in photographic detail.

She continued flipping through, entranced by the incredibly realistic drawings. Her expressions at first were all sad—her lips arcing downward, and her eyes glassy and blank. Then, there were plenty of her smiling, and then an incredibly detailed one of her laughing, with shading and the illusion of light in her eyes, and every curl on her head expertly captured. The last ones were of her angry, annoyed, and then a few that made her flush: she had that come-hither look in her eyes, and it seemed then that even more careful attention was paid to her lips in making them look real enough to kiss.

She figured she should be alarmed by how obsessively he'd need to watch her to capture this level of detail, like he'd memorized her every pore, every twitch. But the last illustration stole her very breath...it was a full-figured one of her the day Vigo took her photograph on Maple Tree Trail. She bet Eddie's graphite portrait could rival the color photo itself, but Eddie must have exaggerated the roundness of her curves because there was no way she looked like that. She blushed. It was way too flattering.

She snapped the book shut. The man was clearly obsessed with her. This was evidence of his activation toward her. That was all. And of that Jäger juju that neither of them could deny—something he said he would ask the Jäger Father about.

She sighed deeply and opened the book again, this time focusing on his scribbles. The handwriting struck her right away as oddly familiar.

"Like Katniss here in the District 12 woods, I was in the forest when the Jäger found me."

Whoa. He'd confessed right away to being a Jäger.

"I was out chopping wood in Wychblack. We'd just lost my cousin, Will, and so the mantle had fallen to me now to keep the castle running. With Uncle Jonas having squandered the entire estate with his failed speculations before his death, it was all hands on deck with this Rawlins family, of which I was now the head.

"(So now you know, siren.)"

Her blood ran cold at the revelation. No way. It couldn't be.

She rushed to her room with the book and laid it side by side with the old Rawlins journal. Her hand flew to her mouth. The handwriting—the high crossing of the t's, the exaggerated loops of the tails of some of the lowercase letters—like a mix of cursive and print, a fusion of ancient, elegant script with modern, minimalist print...the kind of handwriting a man who's lived for three-hundred years might develop.

In shock, she lifted her head and blurted out to the room, "Edward Helsing is Edward Rawlins."

She collapsed into her desk chair. The handsome guy lounging on the couch in that Rawlins family portrait, with the little girl on his chest...that, that was Eddie. Eddie was a Rawlins. He was related to Liam. The same jaw, same lips.... He was Liam's great-great-great-something and William's direct cousin.

Great Scott...Eddie had personally known her mom and aunt before they'd transformed! How could he have kept something like this from her? She should be furious, but her curiosity was stronger. She wanted every detail. What was her mother like as a teenager? Did she also like to read? How did she and William fall in love? And Emily, did she live in her sister's shadow, or was she her own force to be reckoned with in the family?

She practically ripped Eddie's rosary off over her head and tossed it onto her night table. She needed to speak with him, now. Squeezing her eyes shut and clenching her fists, she focused on his face. Like the catalogue of expressions he'd drawn of her, she went through her own she'd memorized of him. Suspicious, angry, amused, enthralled...she held on to that last look, the one he'd captivated her with when they last spoke face-to-face using the stones.

Eddie! she called out silently.

No response.

She tried again and again. Over and over.

Still no response.

Tears burned in her eyes. She hated not being able to reach him. Edward Helsing, Rawlins, or Nobody, whatever it was. Next time she saw him, she was going to demand her own set of calling stones.

Her inner life-coach voice whispered right then, *It's not like he's your boyfriend and has to answer to you.*

She snapped back, "No, but he is my partner in crime now."

A rap on the door, followed by Ernesto's loud question, made her shriek.

"Everything alright?" he called through the door. "You said something about crime?"

Clutching her jackhammering heart, she answered, "Yes. I-I'm talking about a friend."

"In crime?"

"No, I mean, he's helping me solve a problem. For school. It was just a figure of speech."

A pause. "Goodnight, Belle."

"Night, Uncle."

Taking a deep breath, she whispered aloud, "One more time." She focused on repeating what Eddie had shown her in the West Wing about reaching him. She tried to just focus on seeing a rope tied around his waist.

Maybe if she used his real name.... "Edward Rawlins," she whispered. "Edward Rawlins."

After a moment, her mind cleared into a smoky blackness, and she saw the edge of a brown braided rope appear. Jubilation flooded her. She picked up the end of the rope and gave it a tug. Something solid was at the end of it, but she couldn't see it. The darkness was thick and obscured the other end. She followed the rope, one hand over the other, the anticipation of seeing Eddie mounting with each step forward.

She collided with a solid wall. She tugged at the rope, but it disappeared into this wall obscured by the smoky darkness. Shivering at the icy coldness of the air, she slid her hands over the wall, its surface perfectly smooth and cool to the touch.

She banged the side of her fist on it. *Eddie!* She banged twice more. Harder.

An invisible force expulsed her whole body backward. She flew back like a rag doll until another black void swallowed her whole.

| 31 |

Hellcat

Loud scratching noises woke her up from sleep. Just in time, too. She'd been burning at the stake in her dream again. Another failed attempt to reach her mother. She'd tried to disguise herself as a villager with a hooded cloak and then approach from the fringes, but Violet had shrieked wordless accusations while pointing her out, and then pitchforks had surrounded Belle in an instant.

Scratch. Scratch.

Her bleary eyes focused on the ceiling. Why does it look wrong? She sat up and realized she had fallen asleep on the wrong end of the bed and hadn't bothered to get under the covers—she looked down at herself—or change into pj's. A heavy daze lay over her and the sense that something was off. She glanced at the time on her phone: 1:02 a.m.

A loud hiss came from the other side of her door followed by more scratching.

She slid out of bed and answered the door. Just as expected. Lady sat there, blinking up at her.

"We need to work on your knocking," Belle said.

Instead of dashing in as usual and curling up at the foot of Belle's bed to sleep, Lady's response was to saunter away into the living room and then sit back on her haunches again, watching Belle.

"What in the world...." Her head still shrouded in sleep, Belle grabbed her shawl off her desk chair and wrapped herself with it. It was criminally cold outside of her toasty bed.

Her gaze landed on the two open books on her desk: *Hunger Games* and Edward Rawlins's journal.

The recollection slammed into her, just like whatever had knocked her out of there, straight into that nightmare in old Elmridge. Her thoughts raced back down that track, recovering what she couldn't believe had just slipped her mind. Eddie was Edward Rawlins, and when she'd tried to reach him, he'd been completely walled off. Was he in danger? Imprisoned?

A loud hiss came from the living room.

Feeling like a basketcase with worry over Eddie's safety now, she met Lady in the living room, and the cat did the same thing again—walked away and stopped at the door to the stairs. Belle opened it, and Lady sped down the stairs, stopping and waiting at the landing.

"I guess you've got an emergency, huh? You've never needed my help before." She descended the steps and was surprised Lady didn't shoot for the door, but, instead, disappeared into the museum space. "Wait, so you don't want to be let out?"

Belle followed, tightening the shawl around her shoulders to fend off the shivers from the cold or this strange situation, or probably both. She found Lady sitting in front of an old desk with a leather top and small drawers galore. She knew from the history plaque affixed on top that it belonged to "the Prynn sisters, most notably Abigail, the more prolific writer of the two."

She wagged her finger at the cat. "You are not allowed to do your business in here."

Lady narrowed her eyes, and if Belle didn't know any better, she'd say that was a glare. The cat retreated into the leg space of the desk and scratched upward.

"What do you want? Do you want to sleep here? That's fine. You can sleep here, but not pee. Got it?"

Lady stood on her back haunches and scratched furiously at the bottom of the long drawer.

"Hey, stop that! That's my mom's desk." Thinking there must be a fossilized mouse or something in there, Belle pulled the drawer out. She looked at Lady. "There's nothing here."

Lady narrowed her eyes into slits and pounced upward with her front feet against the bottom of the drawer. It popped up.

"Why, you—" But Belle stopped just short of swatting the cat when she saw that the bottom of the drawer was now askew, revealing another bottom. A secret false bottom. And there were papers in there. She could see the yellowed corners peeking out.

Excitement prickled at her skin at this Nancy Drew turn of events, she reached in and pulled out the top bottom of the drawer and lifted four very familiar-looking pages. They were in her mother's handwriting.

"The missing pages from my mom's dairy!" She held them aloft like a prize. "Good job, Lady!"

But when she looked at Lady, intent to scoop it into her arms and give it a grateful squeeze, or at least a hardy scratch behind the ears, the cat sprung toward her hand and snatched the papers with its teeth. It dashed out of sight, and just as Belle's reflexes overcame her shock and she moved to give it chase, she heard the window with the broken latch creak up and then slam shut.

"No." She sank to her knees, feeling utterly stupefied. "I just got robbed by a cat."

This was all very unnatural. She was being blocked, purposely kept in the dark. She finally found missing answers from her mother's diary, and they were snatched right out of her hand. And just before that, she'd managed to reach Eddie—she was sure of it—and then she'd been thoroughly expelled.

This had to be the work of the Fae. They were twisting her path, adding stumbling blocks for their entertainment, imprisoning Eddie, even manipulating poor cats to do their bidding, allowing all manner of violence in the name of money-grubbing stories....

She climbed slowly to her feet, feeling the rage churning in waves beneath her skin. Pinpricks of electricity snapped from every pore, joining together in a web of blue crackling light that expanded the more her thoughts fell over the edge into fury.

And then, in what felt like three cool drops of water hitting her fevered mind, she heard three chimes. Somehow, her brain interpreted them as words.

Look behind you.

So she did. And there on the floor, at the spot where the hoodlum-cat had bereft her, was one page. A corner torn off, but intact, nonetheless.

And just like that, the storm passed. Cool air washed over the lightning heat on her skin, and curiosity swallowed her anger.

Gingerly, she picked up the ancient page and pored over it. It looked like the last page and only about half-a-page long.

"...made sure he paid for what he did to me. To my friends. In the little time I spent in Whitechapel, burying my misery in the squalor of this place, drinking myself into oblivion to numb the pain of my dead William, I discovered another life. A seedy, dark underbelly of where I hid myself, immersed myself, and found glimmers of goodness in this filth worth fighting for. My dear friends, Polly and Annie, were each a light in this darkness that is the East End of London, until they were both slaughtered by that butcher. It took me too long to shake off the drunken haze, too long for me to do anything about the others...but when he finally got to me, I was the last one. I was caught unawares. Too weak in my state to defend myself. But when I felt the cold blade of the knife slice deep into my skin, I came alive. My senses ex-

ploded, and I could feel everything clearly for the first time in a long time. Including the cold steel buried in my body.

I surprised him then. I fried him. Fried him senseless.

Last I heard, he was rotting away in a mental asylum. And the butcher of Whitechapel still undiscovered. I must keep it that way...a secret forever. My son must never know his father was a monster."

The page fluttered to the floor from Belle's hands. To the shocked silence that held like bated breath, she whispered, "Oh no...James's father was Jack the Ripper."

Beauty and the Beast

Belle pounced on the mass of brilliant plumage. One quick tear with her razor-teethed mouth and the peacock's terrified squawk was silenced. She spat out the mound of flesh and feathers. With the rest of the peafowls frightened off, she moved unimpeded now at a brisk trot, only the full moon's watchful eye on her back.

She was on a mission, the enchanted words repeating in her mind like a haunting jingle stuck in a loop.

Before long, gravel crunched beneath her paws, and she slowed her pace to a silent stalk as she passed by the Historical Society of Elmridge signage-post. At the foot of the front porch's steps, she went still, gazing up at the dark windows, listening for any sounds of movement inside.

She sniffed. There was a strange scent of another creature, of feline fur and human sweat. Odd. Cat-like, but not.

No matter. The enchantment drove her forward, and she crept up the steps, her talons clicking against the wood. The next part was easy. The window to the left of the door, she knew, had a broken latch. She stood up to her full height and with a snarling grunt slid the window up. It had made a long, creaking whine, and after pushing aside the bookcase that stood in its way, she quickly climbed inside and crouched in the shadows, listening and waiting for any response from the humans in the home.

Her instincts were correct. Lights flicked on, flooding the museum space, but not the wide shadow of the bookcase she was in. She remained motionless. Through a long, antique mirror, she could see the man standing by the light switch halfway down the stairs. How she had missed the sounds of his approach, she could not fathom.

She heard a tell-tale click, and her suspicion was confirmed by the sight of the raised black barrel gleaming in his hand.

They both waited. As long as that gun remained in the man's hand, he was the hunter and she merely the prey. So, she waited.

Finally, finally, the lights switched off, and she heard the sounds of steps receding on the staircase. She waited to hear the door close at the top of the stairs, but it never came. Had the man left it open then? Prudence told her to wait it out some more, but the enchantment propelled her to step out and finish her mission.

She padded as slowly, as quietly as ever, not even letting the tips of her talons touch the floor. She emerged from the furniture space, and just as she reached the foot of the stairs, the lights flew on and she found herself staring at the end of a barrel, pointed right at her face. In that nanosecond of shock, she froze, eyes wide.

The man's own eyes mirrored her surprise, and he lowered the gun a fraction. "Your eyes..." he murmured.

That was her chance.

With a snarl, she launched herself at him, and the deafening shot pierced through her.

~~*~~

Belle awoke with a shout of agony, gripping the front of her shoulder. She looked at her hand, her shoulder, but there was no blood, no injury. Her mind reeled from the scene she had just dreamt. She didn't know what it was about this night, but the nightmares just kept coming.

"Oh, Jesus! Ernesto!" She tore the bedspread off and raced out of her room to her uncle's.

I have to warn him! Her mind raced on as fast as her feet. *First, the revelations about Eddie and my mom, and now this?!*

She banged on the door. "Ernesto! The beast is coming here! We have to hurry!" She took a grain of comfort in the fact that she dreamt these sorts of events before they happened.

A gunshot rang out downstairs. Belle instinctively cowered with her hands over her ears. Horrified, she turned towards the staircase door. It was open, and the lights were on downstairs. She'd had more time the last time something like this had happened, but it was happening much sooner, almost in real-time.

"Belle, stay there!" came Ernesto's warning cry.

A cacophonous crash erupted, mixed with ferocious snarls and her uncle's grunts. The long, rolling smashes and cracks told her the museum was being torn apart.

And possibly Ernesto!

With that, she scrambled for the stairs.

Belle halted on the last step. There was an eerie quiet now. A path of destruction carved through the museum displays, leading toward the back.

A human moan of pain reached her ears. She ran toward the sound, scattering through the debris.

Ernesto lay at an odd angle on his back. A bookcase she knew to be solid oak lay crushing his legs.

"No!" She flew to his side, flipping the bookcase off him like a cardboard box.

His eyes flew wide at the act. "H-How?"

"Something new." Her hands hovered frantically over him. "Are you hurt? Where does it hurt? Tell me how to help."

"G-Get my phone. On my night table."

"I don't want to leave you."

"Hurry, please. I can't feel anything beneath my chest." He coughed and blood trickled out of the corner of his mouth.

In a mad scramble that felt like forever, she returned with the phone. She pointed the screen at his face and unlocked it. "Who do I call?"

"Dr. X."

"Okay." She opened his contacts list and searched. "Is he the same one who came here and helped Emily?"

He nodded, grimacing from the pain.

"Found it. It's going to be okay, Uncle." She tapped the contact button.

On the second ring, the call was connected, but no hello came from the other end.

"Hello?" Belle called into it. "Hello? My uncle, Ernesto, needs help. He's been hurt. He told me to call you."

"Password," the voice whispered.

"He wants a password," she told her uncle.

Ernesto nodded, and when he opened his mouth to speak, Belle brought the phone closer to his mouth. "Comenzó en Tunguska."

When he'd turned his face toward the phone, she noticed a long, bloody scratch along the side of his neck.

"Hurry," she said into the phone. "He's getting pale, and he's not looking too good." She dropped it after ending the call and grabbed Ernesto's hand, pressing it to her face. Not too long ago, she was in this very situation with her dying father.

She couldn't believe the universe was doing this to her again.

"You're going to be okay. Just stay with me. Help is coming."

"M-My gun. Take it." He had tried to reach for the barrel, lying just inches from his fingers.

"No." She shook her head feverishly. "No. I don't need it."

"I heard something when you went upstairs for my phone."

"What was it?"

He exhaled a ragged breath. "It never left."

"The beast?"

Any remaining color fled his face, and just before his features went slack, one word left his mouth, "Liam."

"Uncle?" She grabbed his shoulders and gave him a shake. "Ernesto?!" But it was like shaking a bag of flour. He remained unconscious, eyes closed. "Oh God, please don't be dead." She lowered her ear to his chest. A strong heart beat steadily.

Coma. Like the others. Her mind chased the dots, stringing them together. Lisa had the bloody scratches on her thigh similar to Ernesto's scratch on his neck. Maybe Nieves also had a scratch, but an inconspicuous one. And they're all comatose right now.

And Liam. Ernesto implied it was Liam who'd attacked him. Violet was using Liam to sideline the competition for the Homecoming crown...and he was still here.

Liam had come for me. *Ernesto had just gotten in the way.*

Her senses fired to life on their own. The danger felt tangible, like an icy, cold caress making her hairs stand on end. She rose slowly to her feet, her keen ears dissecting the various sounds: the chittering insects in the walls, the ticking of the grandfather clock upstairs, the wailing squawks of the peafowls in the nearby field, Ernesto's beating heart and shallow breathing, and there was another beating heart close by....

She forced herself to take a deep breath, and she caught the heavy musk of a large animal. There was another scent in the mix, very faint. Evergreen and spice. Liam's cologne.

"Liam?" she called out in a shaky voice.

There was a creak, as if a pause in step on the floorboards.

"You don't have to do this." She moved slowly, silently away from Ernesto, hopefully drawing any danger away from her uncle. "You're stronger than this, Liam. Don't let Violet control you. Don't let her keep hurting you."

Dr. X was on his way. Maybe if she kept talking, stalling, Liam would run off before another witness showed up. Or maybe, come to his human senses.

There was a low growl.

She paused. She was right next to the desk that Lady had led her to. The growl had come from somewhere by the bookcase next to the open window. She could dive for the staircase and lock herself upstairs, but she wasn't going to leave Ernesto alone with the beast.

Electricity flared in her palms. She was going to have to keep it busy. Just long enough for Dr. X to get here.

The beast emerged slowly from the shadows on all fours. It looked like a cross between a starved, blonde bear and a lanky wolf on steroids. It stalked toward her, its head low to the ground, eyes pinned on her. They were the stark, unblinking eyes of a predator.

Belle gasped. But the eyes...they were unmistakable. The clear green with yellow flecks.

The sparks in her hands extinguished.

"Liam?" she whispered.

He paused, a fraction of recognition, like a dog familiar with its own name.

Belle's heart cracked in two. This was Liam. *Her* Liam. Violet had cursed him into submission. She knew he would sooner kill himself than let Violet use him this way. Then why...

"Why?" Her voice trembled. "Why did you give her permission to do this to you?"

He snapped at her, and she banged her hip against the desk in jumping behind it. With the desk between them now, the slow, circling around it began as she tried again. "Violet c-couldn't have done this to you unless you allowed her. How did she get you to agree to this?"

He pinned her with such a look, it was almost, almost, as if he understood.

"Blackmail? Did she threaten to hurt someone you care about?" Belle knew that Liam was aware that Violet couldn't physically hurt her, not unless she wanted Abigail to emerge and pay some swift and bloody retribution. Unless... "Did she threaten to harm my loved ones? Or your friends?"

A paw slammed against the desk's leather top, making Belle jump. The beast raked its claws down the top in such a way that the electricity in her hands flared up defensively.

"L-Liam, please, stop. You're scaring me. This isn't who you are. You've got to fight it. Don't let her win." She noticed a patch of deep red over his shoulder, trailing down the length of his forearm. "You're hurt." The gunshot in her dream when she'd been seeing through the beast. Ernesto shot him. "Liam, you've been shot! You need medical attention!"

With a growl, the beast placed one paw, and then the other, on the edge of the desk, and Belle could only watch, her mouth falling open wider, as the creature slowly raised itself to its full height.

She fell back a few steps, colliding with a dresser. The beast towered over her as Liam had, its imposing bulk on display. He grabbed the desk between them, raised it in the air, and launched it aside. With a great crash, the old rocking chair with the doll was demolished.

Frantically, she looked for an escape but there was none. The beast could see that, too. It swiped away obstructions in its path, and then slowed to a stalk as if salivating the moment before the pounce.

He paused, like a tiger ensnaring its prey with its eyes, and then lunged.

She jumped away, but he caught her by the foot. She fell to her hands and tried to pull her leg away, but he dragged one claw down her calf, tearing through cloth and skin. She screamed. Still gripping her injured leg, he tugged her roughly toward him, making her t-shirt ride up, and he promptly gouged her exposed stomach. Again, she screamed. But when he tore his claws away, she still had the sense to kick him in the face with all her might.

The beast let go with a short whimper, and she scrambled away from him. Her leg and stomach were on fire, and she felt a numbness spreading outward from the injuries. Holding her bleeding stomach, she used her other hand on the edge of a heavy armchair to drag herself up onto her good leg. She quickly turned her attention back to the beast and found it standing still, down on all fours, watching her with those predator-eyes, waiting.

Panting in fear and with tremors racking her body, she shuffled backward away from it. What was he waiting for? A minute must have passed as they stared at one another across the space. Belle was too frightened and shocked to do anything in the moment.

She became aware of the wet warmth her hand was pressing against. She held her hand out; it was covered in blood. She lifted her shirt, dreading the sight of her insides poking through the gouges. But to her surprise and relief, there was only blood and no deep scratches.

As if also noticing, the beast grunted, and its ears tipped forward.

She lifted the flap of her torn pajama pant and, lo and behold, only blood, no injury. She'd healed! She'd forgotten about that new ability.

The beast roared.

Belle dodged behind the armchair and stood her ground.

The beast charged at her.

"No! Liam, don't!"

He swiped the armchair aside, and she just caught him by his massive forearms before they could close around her. His eyes widened as if surprised by her strength.

"Liam, please!" she grunted. "Stop!"

He snapped at her face, but she turned her head just in time and felt his spittle slime her cheek. He roared in her ear, the hot breath blasting her hair back and making her very bones rattle.

She cried out in a sob. "God, please."

As soon as the blue sparks ignited in her hands, the beast, with a short whine, went flying backward, crashing into a display case. The shatter of glass and splintering of wood was followed by a heavy silence.

From where she stood, she could only see the beast's taloned feet. But when she saw the long, blonde fur recede into itself, so only human feet with ten toes could be seen, she rushed to his side.

A very naked Liam lay there with eyes closed and mouth slightly parted.

Belle almost choked on her gasp. She grabbed the nearest item that could suitably cover him. It was Abigail's childhood doll, previously ejected from its seat on the rocking chair. She laid it over his private area, ignoring the steaming heat in her cheeks.

Two spidery black marks, the size of her own hands, were imprinted on his forearms. She patted his chest. "Liam? Liam, wake up." He didn't stir. She shook him by the shoulders.

Nothing.

And then horror slammed into her. His chest wasn't rising. She pressed her ear against his left pec. Not a sound.

A terror worse than anything she'd ever experienced, worse than her run-in with the Hammerson brothers, worse than losing her father, consumed her.

She'd killed Liam. She didn't care that Eddie would probably have to kill her now, she just couldn't stand the idea that she'd murdered her own friend.

A sob escaped her. *What do I do?!* She tried shaking him again, harder, but his head lolled to the side. His golden color was fading fast.

CPR! She pumped his chest fifteen times, breathed into his mouth while holding his nose so his chest rose and fell, and then repeated the routine.

Tears splashed onto his chest. She repeated and repeated, but now his skin was turning a ghastly gray and his lips were bluish. She would have to stop and call for help on Ernesto's phone.

She screamed out in frustration, grief, and her fists pounded once on his chest. But at that contact, a burst of electricity popped from her hands and Liam's eyes flew open as his chest contracted.

"Liam!"

He sucked in a breath, his eyes looking about wildly, trying to orient himself. Finally, they landed on the girl crying and laughing at his side.

"Belle?" he croaked.

"Liam! Oh thank God, you're okay!" She threw her arms around his neck and squeezed. "I thought I lost you!"

At his sharp grunt of pain, she pulled away. There was still a bleeding hole in his shoulder. She quickly pulled off her pajama top, leaving her in the sports bra, and started tying the shirt around the shoulder. When she tightened the knot, he gritted his teeth in pain.

"Belle, is this really happening, or am I dreaming? Because it feels like I got hit by a truck, and then woke up in Heaven."

"This is real. And how can you even say you're in Heaven right now?"

"Because that's what opening my eyes and seeing you feels like."

Her mouth dropped as her heart melted. "I...can't believe you're flirting with me right now."

"Before I find out what's going on and feel like I'm back in hell again, will you please kiss me now?"

Before she let herself think or object, her lips covered his. She poured all her gratitude for his life into it, and when she pulled away, he groaned, "Remind me again why you want to take things slow?"

"Liam, do you remember what happened just a few minutes ago?"

A deep shiver came over him. "Why am I so cold?" He tried to sit up, grimacing at the pain in his shoulder.

"Careful, you've been shot."

He froze as he pinned her with a look. "I've been *what*?" This time, he scrambled harder to sit up. Belle helped him. He looked down at himself and then back at her. "I'm naked." He pointed down at himself. "And there's just a doll covering the goods."

She opened her mouth to explain, but he cut her off as he surveyed the destruction. "What. The hell. Happened. Here?" She followed his gaze at what made his eyes pop even wider. It was Ernesto lying on the floor by the staircase. "Is he...is he dead?"

"Unconscious."

"Did-Did someone break in? And fight with him?" His hand flew to his injured shoulder. "Was it…me?" She gently drew his face back to hers. His eyes looked like a lost child's. "It was me, wasn't it? He shot me. Pan shot me."

"Liam." She gave his cheeks a gentle squeeze, trying to get him to focus on her. "What do you remember before you woke up just now?"

It took him a moment. Like he was fighting through the haze, trying to anchor himself in reality. Finally, he said, "I've…I've been sleepwalking at night. Some nights. With no memory of what happens. I wake up in the strangest places, no clothes, totally in the buff. At least, that's what I think has been happening. It's the only thing that can explain the blackouts." He exhaled raggedly and tugged at his hair. "But it doesn't explain the stomach pains right before the blackouts." He glanced at her nervously. "And…"

"And?" she encouraged.

"And the voices." He closed his eyes in defeat. "I need help, Belle. I know I've cracked. Even now, I can still hear them…singing."

"You can?"

He peered cautiously at her, surprised to find an earnestness there. "You believe me? I thought, I mean, I think I've finally gone crazy."

"What's this song you're hearing?"

He stared at her. "You *do* believe me." His eyes softened as they tracked over her face. "I knew you were perfect for me."

"The song, Liam. Are there words to it?"

He nodded. "I don't understand them, though. It's another language. I've checked through every language on that online translator and none of them are familiar."

"And the melody?"

"It's haunting as f—I mean, it's what you might hear in one of those slow haunted house rides."

"And you hear it now?"

"Like in the back of my mind." He suddenly gripped his stomach and grimaced. "It's happening." His pained eyes went to hers, searching her face. "M-Maybe you could take care of me? Like make sure I just stay here and not wander out—" His next words were replaced with a loud groan as he doubled over in pain, clutching his stomach.

Belle shot to her feet, backing away. "No, Liam. You don't understand. It's Violet. She's using you."

At that, his wild eyes arrested hers.

"She keeps turning you into a—"

His guttural cry cut her off. He was suddenly on all fours, back arching upwards, head low to the ground.

Belle continued backing away, heart rending in two at the anguished cries of her dear friend—her first boyfriend—and the mounting terror at facing the primal beast again. What could she even do? She'd barely shocked Liam, and she'd almost killed him. No, actually killed him, until she restarted his heart. If she had to defend herself again, she was terrified she'd lose total control this time and really end him in a no-second-chances way.

Her back stopped against a full-length wardrobe. What if, what if she simply hid? His back was still to her, the transformation really taking him over now with the fur and limbs elongating.

It was worth a try. She climbed into the empty wardrobe and shut the doors before her.

Within seconds, Liam's cries had ceased. There was a silence, and then a low growl, followed by sniffing.

Belle covered her mouth with her hand, trying to reign in her rattled breathing. She heard the clicks along the floor getting closer, the claws that would try to tear through her again.

She couldn't believe this was happening again. Why won't the beast stop coming after her?

The answer came to her from some tiny part of her brain that hadn't yet bunkered down in panic mode. Maybe, just maybe, beast-Liam would change back into human-Liam once he completed the command Violet gave him?

That had to be it. *She* was the mission. Belle was the other Homecoming princess that needed to be put out of commission. And so the beast wouldn't stop until she ended up like Lisa and Nieves. The toxin that causes the coma must be in his claws, only Belle had healed quickly, and so the numbness hadn't consumed her.

She could pretend—yes, that's it. If he clawed her again, she would stay down this time.

There was an eerie quiet outside. And then the doors cracked open.

Belle slammed them back shut and a great bellow of rage shook the room. The strength in her legs left her and she collapsed, just barely keeping her strong grip on the doors. The wardrobe began to shake violently, and she screamed in terror.

The electricity erupted in her hands.

"No!" She didn't want to kill him. "No powers." She tried to do what Eddie had suggested; she imagined her hands free of the blue energy. Just her hands with their pastel-yellow nail colors, a shade Candy had said was sunny, and if she ever felt sad, to look at her nails as a reminder that there's always a bright side.

It worked. The small electrical cages around her hands fizzled out.

One of the doors ripped off, and a punch of terror had her flattening herself against the back of the wardrobe.

"No powers, no powers," she chanted in a ragged whisper. But the energy, not finding an outlet in her hands, began building beneath her skin, all over her body.

"No, no, no, no!" It was the moment before she killed the three Hammerson brothers. If the power exploded out of her now, Liam was a dead man. And Ernesto, too.

The other door ripped off. The terrifying beast framed her view now. She crouched down into the farthest corner, trying to make herself as small as possible. *No powers, no powers!*

The beast roared into the closeted space, and the very sound assaulted her every fiber. She squeezed her eyes shut, tears streaming out.

Belle had made up her mind. She would die before she killed her loved ones.

She heard the click-click of the claws entering the wardrobe, but she also felt the energy roiling beneath her skin, prickling outward, on the verge of bursting out of her. Soon, she would pass out and then awaken to the carnage.

A rippling growl filled her ears and hot breath fanned her face. She could feel her strength leaving her.

This was it.

Her eyes peeled open, and she found herself looking into minty green, yellow-flecked eyes devoid of emotion, framed by blonde fur.

"Hurry," she whispered.

Just like in her nightmare, he opened his razor-teethed mouth wide and latched onto her shoulder.

Darkness consumed her.

~~*~~

Belle's eyes fluttered open and shut, open and shut. The world appeared sideways. The floor of the wrecked museum appeared to be a wall now, and the beast was walking along it, away from her.

That couldn't be right. No one can break the laws of physics like that.

Her attention snagged on a pool of red expanding away from her along this wall. Shouldn't it be moving downward? Like how gravity dictates?

She was so sleepy.

A feral warning growl drew her from the darkness, and the sideways world, somewhat blurry, filled her view again. The beast's back was to her, and it was staring at the open window.

Hey, it was Lady! Perched on the windowsill on all fours, staring with eyes narrowed, right back at the beast. But then, something not right was happening again. Lady was changing.

Was *no* one following science today?

The beast backed away slowly, still snarling its warnings as Lady placed one nimble paw on the floor. But that paw fluffed into a leg as wide as the cat's whole body, and when the other paw met the ground, the same thing happened.

Lady and the beast started circling each other, all while the cat kept changing, growing bigger and fluffier until she stood up on her own hind legs.

Hey! Lady was a bear now! A huge, black bear! Wow, that cat was sure a bag of surprises.

The beast quickly stood to his full height.

They were both evenly matched. Both let loose a roar that rattled the house and then launched themselves at one another like two freight trains colliding head-on.

But Belle hadn't been able to see the rest because she was sucked into the black void of slumber once again, convinced, at least, that she could now dream proper dreams that weren't just products of her weird mind-melds.

Dreams like a death match between a magical bear and a beast.

| 33 |

The Jäger Temple

Eddie placed a hand over his racing heart, willing it to calm. Not even a fight with a monster got it going like this. Belle had only to smile or sigh or just turn those hazel eyes on him, and his heart took off like a Diomedean horse.

And now this telepathic link with her. What James claimed was soul symmetry. Something of legend that the Jäger Father had once mentioned happened in an alternate timeline, in another reality. Otherwise, nothing else Eddie understood explained this phenomenon.

He smiled, pride swelling in him. She'd just blasted a Shadowzord to oblivion a moment ago, with a bit of guidance from him. He liked this. He really liked that she needed him for help. Or for anything. Her needing him, period.

He shook his head. It'd been too long since he let any emotion govern his actions. Duty. The Jäger Brotherhood. The good of the many over the few, over his own self. These were the driving forces of his life for so long, but now...Belle was upsetting that balance.

He had too many questions. And too many lives hung in the balance for him to deviate from his prophetic path. Even with Dommedag on the horizon, the significance of everything he had worked for these hundreds of years, every mission completed, every monster slain, was paling in comparison to the weight of the pull Belle had on him. She was the sun, and he was slowly, irrevocably falling into her.

But to his destruction? Or salvation?

Eddie whispered the words that would open the doors to the temple. They shuddered and then creaked wide, the powdery snow blasting past him. He walked through the long, narrow hall illuminated by soft electric lights. On his right were the sleeping quarters, on his left, the dojo, a martial arts training space. Only a handful of Jäger were present, practicing a lethal form of martial arts lost to previous generations.

They stood at attention, right fists over their hearts, and inclined their heads when he passed. "Ehrenjäger."

He nodded back, making the same gesture. The Secret Ehrenjäger. The secret honorary hunter. And because of this, he was considered elite and the only one in the Jäger Father's inner circle.

Only one other Jäger, besides Ernesto, had a title given to them by their prophecy: Verfluchterjäger. The Cursed Hunter. That unfortunate title had gone to his former best friend, Owen Douglass. Already fulfilling his prophecy when he went rogue and dropped off the Jägerhood's radar.

But Eddie didn't blame him. Not when Owen was cursed to have his best friend kill his girlfriend.

Eddie reached the spiral staircase in the back, the only way to the second floor, to the Jäger Father.

The ancient Fae sat on his cushion in the middle of the expansive stone room, lined wall to wall with books and artifacts, each with a prized story behind it. The ultimate antique hall.

Entering the room was like bathing in the tangible mystique of a carnival funhouse, excitement and mystery lacing the air. One entire wall glowed with the light of a myriad of changing scenes of real people and creatures and different places and times. Like a magical television automatically flipping through channels, it showed dizzying scenes from alternate universes and timelines.

Eddie stopped before the old Fae. He knelt on one knee, fist over heart, and inclined his head. "Jäger Father."

The legend of the old wise man on the mountain began with this Fae sitting before him. The Jäger Father resembled a Nepalese elder in the traditional pants, long shirt, and Topi hat. The long flowing mustache and white beard were braided with flowers. A Fae eccentricity. Only his eyes gave away that he wasn't human: the whites of his eyes were normal, but there were no pupils—only the irises which were black like the night sky and dotted with star-like twinkles.

And those hypnotic eyes were turned on Eddie now.

The Jäger Father's lips spread into a Joker-esque smile. He inclined his head, and still without a word, looked expectantly at his visitor. Waiting.

Words were extremely valuable to the Fae. They were the building blocks of the stories that served as currency in their realm. So any word from the Jäger Father's mouth had to be paid for at a hefty price.

Eddie dropped a small black leather sack of "monster gold" between them. A quarter-sized pixie coin for each story behind every monster-kill. Centuries' worth. It was his entire Fae fortune.

He had a lot of serious questions right now.

Jäger Father raised his bushy eyebrows at the sight of the pouch but still waited.

Eddie pulled out the lock of hair from Belle—his breath involuntarily hitching at the feel of it—and laid it next to the pouch. This was the conversation-starter, the mandatory memento.

The excitement that lit up the Jäger Father's eyes was unmistakable. And surprising. Eddie had never seen such euphoria on the ancient Fae's face. His long, sinewy fingers gently cradled the lock of hair as if it were glass. The other hand reached into a pocket and produced a corked, cylindrical vial like a test tube. He uncorked it and promptly captured the stray, shimmery tear that had trailed down his cheek. Fae tears glittered and had medicinal properties.

It wasn't something Eddie was going to ask, but now he just had to, and he had to do it carefully. From what Owen had once told him, the answers he'd gotten from the Jäger Father were confusing and misleading because he hadn't chosen his words carefully.

"Why does Belle's lock of hair bring you such joy?"

The old Fae laid it back down on the wooden floor. He lifted the bag of monster gold into his other palm, and Eddie knew he was weighing it, calculating its value. Finally, he gestured for Eddie to sit. This conversation was going to take a while.

A cushion materialized beneath Eddie, and he sat cross-legged like the Jäger Father.

The old Fae pointed to himself. "Me. Go home."

The answers were never more than three words. The Jäger Father's words were rare like diamonds, or in this case, monster gold. The clinking of three coins falling into a glass jar was heard from somewhere in the room, and Eddie knew his pouch had just gotten lighter.

But the answer had been worth it. Belle is the reason the Jäger Father can go home, back to Neverland? The old Fae had arrived with the original meteors, the Neverites, all those hundreds of years ago to kickstart the search for their savior and oversee the balance between the emerging Jäger and the Unnaturals.

"Is Belle Montague Neverland's savior?"

He shook his head. One coin clinked elsewhere. Yes or no questions were worth one coin.

"Who is the savior then?"

He smiled dreamily, and a pair of tears escaped from his eyes; he captured both of them in the vial. "Peter Pan."

The name was familiar, something he'd investigate later. But if the Fae had found their savior, then Dommedag was imminent. The sound of three coins leaving the pouch renewed his focus on the original reason for this visit.

"Belle Montague. Who is she to me?"

"A friend." *Clink, clink, clink.*

"In the Fae's eyes," Eddie corrected, "who is she to me?"

"A plot twist." *Clink, clink, clink.*

"How is she a plot twist?"

"Not what's expected." *Clink, clink, clink.*

"How is she not what is expected?"

"She still lives." *Clink, clink, clink.*

Eddie swallowed. "Was I...supposed to kill her?" Even saying it was difficult.

"Yes." *Clink.*

He dreaded the Jäger Father's answer to his next question, even though he already knew what his own answer was. "Should I kill her?"

The Jäger Father smiled. "No." *Clink.*

Eddie's relief was profound. The answer agreed with his own. He felt a giant weight lift off his shoulders. He didn't want to kill Belle, and now he knew he didn't need to kill her. But then why...?

"The day Belle killed the Hammerson brothers, I was activated to hunt her. But this hasn't gone to plan as it should when a Jäger acquires his prime target. I don't *want* to kill her, at all. It is the opposite, in fact: I would kill *for* her." He breathed in and exhaled a shaky breath. "I-I feel like she owns me. And it's different than just love because this is—I never thought I'd ever say this—more undeniable than what I felt for Marianne. So my question is...what is this hold that Belle has over me?"

The Jäger Father raised his right hand and closed his fingers into a fist. The gesture for, *I will answer, but not yet.*

Clink, clink, clink.

Eddie looked wearily at the pouch, feeling as deflated as it looked. The Jäger Father could take up to years to provide a promised answer. And that was one he wanted, no, *needed* right away.

He took a deep breath and began again. "Belle is the second child of a Fae acolyte, so she should only have two powers. Yet, besides dream-walking and wielding electricity, she has super strength, speed, and healing. She's immune to my mindfluence, and yet, she can communicate telepathically with me. So my question is, what sort of Unnatural is she?"

"One of kind."

"One of a kind," Eddie repeated.

The old Fae's lips lifted a fraction at the corners. That's a *yes*, then.

But that still didn't tell him enough. He rolled his lips, his frustration simmering. Three resounding clinks reminded him he now had two open-ended questions and two yes-or-no questions left.

"My prophecy. I suspect mine is the one that is switched with Ernesto Panzinski's." At the name, interest lit up the old Fae's face, and Eddie proceeded carefully, daring to hope. "Does...my true prophecy involve *me* stopping Dommedag?"

The Jäger Father did not respond.

"Of course, my apologies. You won't answer questions about Jäger prophecies." Eddie squeezed his eyes shut and thought to himself, *Concentrate. What do you need to know that you can't figure out on your own?* His eyes popped open. He couldn't believe he'd almost forgotten. "Through a dream, Belle saw Violet Wickeby obtain three potions. What does each potion do?"

"Obedience, resistance, masking."

Eddie could figure out pretty well who Violet was forcing to obey her and then masking that magic's smell: two potions were being used on this beast then. Could the resistance potion perhaps be the antidote? Maybe Violet wanted it as leverage. Whatever the case, it was something he knew he could find out without having to ask now.

"How will—no, wait." He needed to save his final open-ended question. "Will Violet Wickeby play a significant part in Dommedag?"

"Yes." *Clink.*

The hairs on his forearms rose. When he returned to Elmridge, Violet Wickeby was going to be his prime target. And because he couldn't ask enough to fully understand the anomaly that Belle was, he had to at least ask the most important question: "Will Belle play a significant part in Dommedag?"

"Yes." *Clink.*

"How?" he shot off.

"She'll start it."

The warmth left his body, invaded by icy realization as he strung all the Jäger Father's answers together into a fuller picture. Belle was going to start Dommedag, a planetary purge of the Unnaturals, which would kill millions, if not billions, of innocents in the process. He was supposed to kill Belle, but wouldn't, and according to the Jäger Father, *shouldn't* kill her.

Rage entered him. The Fae want Dommedag. Just as that demon that he'd exorcised from Belle had said. It was their ticket home. The Jäger Father's ticket home. He'd even admitted it when he saw Belle's lock of hair.

That's why they don't want me to kill Belle, he thought, a sour bitterness churning his stomach. His eyes blurred with heat as he met the Jäger Father's sympathetic stare. The conclusion he'd reached sank its bloody claws into his heart and ripped it right out.

Eddie had to kill Belle to stop Dommedag.

Eddie's voice quavered, and he worked really hard to not reach for a weapon and attack. "So, this whole time…Owen was right. We really are pawns in the High Fae's elaborate story-game. A real-life *Dungeons & Dragons* game. Only in this one, the players are getting rich off of our suffering and plot twists." He practically spat out the last word.

The Jäger Father picked up the empty pouch and offered it back to him.

The message was clear: Eddie was out of money, so no more answers could be purchased. He looked at the pouch with disgust, not touching it. "All's right in the universe as long as your pockets are being lined, am I right?"

Never had Eddie directed such venom at the person who'd he respected and admired for so long, at the being who'd given him a greater purpose in life, a sure compass to guide him through this long, immortal life.

But never had Eddie thought the Jäger Father would allow the slaughter of innocents, just so he could get home. It was ingrained in the Jäger to protect the innocent humans from any murderous Unnaturals.

So this...this was a betrayal.

A hot tear slipped down his cheek, and the Jäger Father watched, fascinated.

"That's right," Eddie hissed. "Mine aren't worth anything. I don't need a precious vial to bottle them up." He slowly stood to his feet. The Jäger Father, wearily watching his movements now, stood as well. "You have taught us, every single Jäger brother, to cut down those Unnaturals who shed human blood. Are you not an Unnatural then planning the slaughter of hordes of innocent people?"

The old Fae simply shook the empty bag at him, reminding him: no money, no answers.

Eddie pressed his lips into a hard line. He held his palm out beneath the raised pouch, a small gold fire erupting. Eddie held the Jäger Father's stare as the pouch disintegrated into embers that floated away.

The old Fae frowned and dusted the ashes from his fingers as if they were mere cookie crumbs.

"What do I do, Jäger Father," Eddie began to circle him, "if I know of an Unnatural who will soon have an ocean of innocent blood on his hands?" A long dagger shimmered into his hand. "You taught us not to strike unless the Unnatural drew blood first. A bit convenient, don't you think? After *you* strike, there will be no one left to strike back."

Eddie stopped before him, the old Fae's face remaining impassive, but the stars in his eyes held a sharpness that wasn't there before. "If I hold to Jäger creed, isn't it only right that I strike you down?" He pointed the dagger at the old Fae's chin.

Eddie tried to be resolute, but his whole arm trembled. Flashes went off in his mind of all the kindness and wisdom his mentor had shown him these past centuries. From his initiation to his training, to his guidance through the heartbreak over his best friend's abandonment, and then the loss of his first love, Marianne. Each time, the Jäger Father's purchased words had brought comfort and guidance, and then the old Fae would freely gift him tokens that spoke volumes to his situation. Like the trademark Jäger wrist-wrap Owen had discarded and left behind. The Jäger Father had gifted it to Eddie, as a sign that Owen would one day return to the fold, and Eddie would be able to present it to him again.

But that was all in the past.

Eddie stared into the old Fae's face, the latter not moving, even while a dagger dug into his chin, waiting for the young pupil to decide his move.

And the thought of what lay now in the future, imagining having to drive a dagger into Belle's heart, cemented Eddie's decision. With an anguished shout, Eddie drove the dagger in. But instead of flesh, the blade pierced through a cloud of shimmery gold.

Eddie whipped around, heart hammering wildly.

The Jäger Father had disappeared and reappeared at the far end of the room, head inclined with sorrow at the choice his pupil had made.

"You coward!" Eddie screamed. "Fight me!"

The Jäger Father waved his hand, and a confused Jäger, who Eddie recognized had been training on the first floor, appeared before him.

"Get out of my way," Eddie growled.

The Jäger stumbled back a step, put off by this sudden hostility from the revered Ehrenjäger. The newcomer swung his head around to the Jäger Father, who promptly crossed his fists over his chest and pulled them apart. The sign for "fight."

Understanding, the Jäger faced Eddie, but before the newcomer could even set a stance, he was promptly knocked out by a side kick. Just as quickly, though, another confused Jäger appeared before Eddie.

"So this is how it's going to be," Eddie muttered, knowing full well the Jäger Father could hear him. "Fight my way through every Jäger in the place to get to you. So be it."

The second Jäger was quicker on the uptake than the first, and smoothly defended against Eddie's strike.

Eddie had gotten rid of the dagger. He knew his fellow Jäger were being used as pawns, too. One after the other—six brief martial arts dances that would have made Bruce Lee proud—each of the six Jäger disappeared after a knock-out or submission until only the Jäger Father was left.

Eddie, panting heavily, his bruised eye and bloody lip already healing, stared down at the old Fae. "Fight me." Twice in the past, the Jäger Father had made him fight everyone in the dojo—to fight out his anger over losing Owen, and then Marianne. But this time, it wasn't enough. "I *need* to fight you."

The old Fae held up his right fist and slowly opened it toward him, palm up, as if releasing something to Eddie. There had been one answer the Jäger Father had been holding on to, the one he most wanted to know.

"You'll tell me now?" Eddie's anger promptly diluted into a mix of anxiety and hope. "What hold Belle has over me?"

The only hold Eddie felt he could learn to resist was an unnatural, sinister one. "Siren" was his pet name for her, but if it was real, and she really was some form of siren…then, maybe that would make it easier to do what his mind already knew he had to do, no matter how impossible his heart and soul felt it would be. He would just have to picture the horde of innocent people suffering and dying because of his weakness, and how he couldn't allow that. The good of the many had to outweigh the good of the very few. And he and Belle were that very few.

The Jäger Father held up a finger, silencing him, and then motioned for him to follow.

Eddie did, keeping close and watching as the old Fae crossed the room, stooped to pick up the lock of hair, and then crossed to a wall lined with scrapbooks. One scrapbook for each Jäger, filled with the mementos each Jäger brought from their missions, and which the

Jäger Father kept record of. A physical record of each Jäger's life-story. Eddie's own scrapbook was bursting at the seams with mementos.

So imagine his astonishment when the Jäger Father waved his hand, and a new Jäger's scrapbook appeared on the small crafting table before him. He opened the book to the first page, spat a glob on it, and glued the lock of hair to it. He then closed it and squeezed it onto the end of the shelf. The shelf of Jäger scrapbooks.

Eddie sputtered, "Are you telling me Belle is a Jäger? B-But she's a girl." He thought about it out loud some more because the Jäger Father couldn't answer. "There never has been any rule against female Jäger." He nodded to himself. "So, because we were all male, we assumed only males could be Jäger." He started rambling, trying to keep up with his fast-working mind. "Her extra superpowers...they are *Jäger* powers. And she's able to take out the Shadow Spawn, too. Is this connection between us because we're Jäger? Would she have the same connection with other Jäger?" Hot jealousy stoked inside him, and he suddenly felt fiercely about keeping this particular Jäger to himself.

The Jäger Father held a finger up for silence again.

Eddie held his tongue. He continued following and watching, his mind reeling.

The old Fae paused in front of a shelf of collectible boxes, reached into an old Cracker Jack box and withdrew a crystal vial, the same used for stopping up Fae tears. He pushed aside old soda bottles and rummaged around until he withdrew a flat square box. The box was opalescent and dotted with tiny spots of gold pixie dust. He moved to another shelf and picked out two small black leather sacks from a cracked fishbowl. With the items in his hands, he shuffled over to the large viewing screen, which was flicking through various scenes of realities at a dizzying, incoherent pace.

The Jäger Father looked at Eddie and motioned for him to follow as he stepped through the screen and disappeared.

Eddie's breath stalled in his lungs at the sight. Tentatively, he pushed a hand towards the screen, and it went right through. The other side was slightly cooler. The promised answer had to be waiting for him just through there. Wherever *there* was. He took a deep breath, held it, and stepped through.

He found himself inside a small room with seamless walls and a domed ceiling made up of a patchwork of mini-screen versions of the larger one outside, all flickering their silent hectic images. The floor was the same wood-paneled one as outside, and behind him was the same larger screen.

"I will face a tribunal for this."

Eddie's eyebrows flew up as he focused on the Jäger Father, standing in the center of the room, a solemn smile on his face.

"You've just said more than three words. And I haven't paid for any of them."

"No one can overhear in this room. Out there, our every move, every word is recorded."

"Why then—"

"I was losing you. My Lieblingsjäger."

"Your *favorite* Jäger? I thought I was the Ehrenjäger. The honorary hunter. You just told me my true title from my true prophecy, didn't you?"

The old Fae nodded.

Free answers! Where would he begin? "Can you tell me my true prophecy?"

The old Fae shook his head. "You must read it for yourself."

"I may never have the chance. Emily Prynn has it, and from what James and I have discovered, she's in Neverland."

"Emily will return for her husband."

When Eddie opened his mouth to fire off another question, the Jäger Father raised a hand to stop him.

"Forgive me," Eddie said instead. "I-I just feel so lost. I came here for guidance, and from what you've told me, I am going to leave more wretched than before. I know now I need to kill Belle, but I cannot bring myself to do it."

"Now, you are on the right path." The Jäger Father stepped closer and touched Eddie's forehead. "You are using this, as you should, but you are in doubt, so now you are using this," he pointed to his heart, "as you should. Continue to lead with your mind, and double-check with your heart, and you will not go wrong."

Suddenly resolved, Eddie said, "Belle will not die by my hand, nor by anyone else's, if I can help it."

The Jäger Father gripped him by the shoulders and squeezed. "Good."

Eddie looked down at the old Fae. He'd wanted to kill him just a minute ago. Repentance washed over him, and he hung his head. "Do you forgive me, Jäger Father, for losing my temper on you?"

"Only if you forgive me for the price you are paying for being in this room." Eddie's head jerked up. "It was the only way to give you more clarity and not be overheard."

"What do you mean?" Alarm prickled at Eddie's senses. "What price?"

"We don't have much time. The High Fae will soon send their Inquisitors to find out why I have blipped you out of their radar. I am the only one sanctioned to come into this room."

"What is this place then?"

"It is not important for you to know." The Jäger Father presented him with the items in his hands. "Take these gifts. Put the vial and the box in one of the pouches. Make sure to give it to Belle. The other pouch is for you, since you saw fit to incinerate your last one."

Eddie did as instructed, and then pocketed both pouches. "Only a Fae needs a tear-catcher...."

"Belle is one of a kind. She became both Jäger and Fae when she was resurrected at your cousin's hands. It was the only way to reverse the demon's possession and restructure the timeline so Dommedag would happen at its appointed time."

Eddie clenched his fists. "Why are you allowing Dommedag to happen? How could you want this? So many innocent—"

"YOU misunderstand Dommedag!" The room shook with the force of his words.

Eddie stumbled back. The whole mountain must have shaken.

The vehemence of the Jäger Father's tone lightened with each word uttered. "Which is why you have fallen into wrath. You will need to relearn the true meaning of Dommedag." The Jäger Father stroked his beard once, a self-soothing gesture, and then pointed to Belle's pouch in Eddie's pocket. "Give her the contents. Explain the use of the vial. Feel free to tell her all I have told you. And most importantly," tears glistened in the old Fae's eyes now and a dreamy smile spread on his lips, "you must give her the box in the presence of two witnesses. Only Belle can open it, and then you must help her put it on."

"What's in the box?" Eddie asked slowly, suspicious of the cloud-nine look on his face.

"That will be for you both to discover." The Jäger Father stepped closer to him. "Are you ready?"

"I am ready for the answer that I'm owed." *What hold does Belle have over me?* He was starting to suspect, though, that he already knew the answer.

The Jäger Father nodded and pulled a folded paper from his pocket. He handed it to Eddie, who gingerly unfolded it, the yellowed paper crackling as if about to disintegrate in his hands.

"What is it?" Eddie asked.

It was a hand-drawn poem beneath a small, faded painting of a beautiful woman standing in a field, and a figure in black, glowing blade in hand, lurking behind her. A blue sky held cherubs sitting on puffs of clouds looking impishly down at the pair.

"It is your destiny," the Jäger Father answered. "Foretold by the Prynn sisters long ago."

Eddie's brows pinched together. The girl in the picture had long, curly hair like Belle. He pored over the poem.

> *For those gifted and empowered*
> *From the immortal Fae's bower,*
> *Let no human blood spill from your kill.*
> *Let no human life be cost of your strife.*

For soon as their blood seeps into the Earth,
Your Jäger—your death—will be given birth.
But the Fae love twists and polar opposites,
The cure for the death then is a love truly pure.

The Jäger, the hunted—one match of true love,
Passionate soul symmetry ordained from Above.
Only one switched prophecy in Jäger history.
Only one doomed kiss for Dommedag bliss.

Eddie looked to the Jäger Father, heart pounding in his ears, "This is about me and Belle, isn't it?"

He nodded.

"James mentioned 'soul symmetry.' Is that the hold she has over me?"

He nodded again. "The hold over both of you."

"She…she feels it, too?" Unease quickly replaced his thrill. "But isn't this all unnatural? This connection then…it's not real."

"You misunderstand soul symmetry like you misunderstand Dommedag. Soul symmetry is one of a kind. The legends of it whispered amongst our kind…they are all of you and Belle."

"I-I don't understand. How can there be legends of us, if we have no history? I've just met Belle."

"You are wrong again."

At that, the Jäger Father snapped his fingers, and all the flickering images stopped, each settling on a different episode of what looked like the *Eddie and Belle* show.

Eddie spun in a slow circle, his mouth falling, eyes growing wider. He and Belle were together in some form, in every single viewscreen. Seeing her again, right before his eyes—laughing, crying, wrinkling her nose in that adorable, confused look—made his heart feel like it was seizing.

His eyes bulged at one screen. She was beheading a gorgon, and then tossing her long curls over her shoulder and throwing a long-haired version of himself a smug smile. But it was the next sight that stole his breath and made him drop to his knees: they were engaged in the most intimate act, on piles of fur rugs before a roaring fireplace.

He couldn't breathe.

The Jäger Father snapped his fingers again, and the images returned to their chaotic flickering. "I hope now you understand. In any timeline, alternate reality, or universe, a person's soul is the same. But you two...the only pair of beings with soul symmetry...share a soul. Belle is, in every sense of the word, your soulmate."

Overwhelmed, Eddie dropped his head into his hands.

The old Fae stepped closer and his deep sigh ruffled Eddie's hair. "There is more, but I cannot divulge any further." His hand came to rest on Eddie's head. "I sense a greater upheaval in your soul than before, my Lieblingsjäger."

Slowly, Eddie stood to his feet, his eyes casting a tortured glance once more at the viewscreen that had stolen the strength from his legs, but the screen was a mere chaotic blur now. He took a deep breath and attempted to verbalize his turmoil. "Since this mission with Belle began, many of the feelings I'd buried so long ago...they've resurfaced. And they all feel so magnified."

"Feelings such as?"

"Anger, fear..."

"Love and desire?" The old Fae added.

Eddie tugged at his hair. "I don't know. It-It feels different than with Marianne. With Belle, it's like I don't have a choice, and I guess I know why now." Disappointment tinged his tone.

"You feel shackled, then."

"Yes. No. I mean, I don't know."

Bang!

Their attention snapped toward the noise.

BANG! BANG!

It was coming from outside one of the walls.

"What is that?" Eddie asked, a dagger already shimmering in one hand.

The Jäger Father briefly closed his eyes as if concentrating. He opened them again and smiled serenely. "Nothing to worry about. Yet."

"That wasn't cryptic," Eddie said snidely, still eyeing the direction of the abated noise.

"Do you trust me, my Lieblingsjäger?"

It took Eddie longer than usual to answer, but he nodded finally, the dagger shimmering away into nothing. "Yes, Jäger Father."

The old Fae tented his fingers together beneath his chin and proceeded to walk slowly around the small room. "So...you are worried your connection to Belle is a product of Fae magic and therefore not real by human standards."

He sighed. "Precisely."

"Then, tell her nothing of soul symmetry and your entwined destinies, and let her be free to make her life choices without the burden of this truth."

Eddie felt a painful squeeze in his chest. "Even if it means..."

"She chooses someone else," the old Fae finished for him. "So, whoever she does choose to be with, it will be entirely of her own free will, unabetted by Fae magic. Isn't this what you want?"

"What I want?" Eddie repeated, his eyes taking on a faraway look as he gazed past the Jäger Father's shoulder. He remembered Belle's lightning smile lighting up the green-gold skies of her eyes. Her laugh igniting the sunrise in his soul, every single time, versus that blank, lifeless look in her eyes and grim line to her mouth from when he'd first met her, a haunting look he swore he would always work to keep from dimming her light ever again. "What I want...is her happiness."

"Even if it's with another?"

Eddie hung his head again. "Yes," he whispered.

"A wise path, my Lieblingsjäger, and one barely trodden on, for only the pure of heart could make such a choice."

A bolt of sheer terror and despair rocked through Eddie's body, nearly knocking him off his feet. The Jäger Father caught him by the shoulders.

"Belle's in trouble," Eddie gasped out. The only other time he'd felt anything close to this magnitude was when she'd dreamt she was being burned alive.

"I hope you will forgive me," the Jäger Father said, all chagrin. "I told you that there would be a price to pay for bringing you in here."

Eddie grabbed him roughly by the collar. "The price can*not* be Belle."

The Jäger Father patiently pried his fingers off. "Time. The price is time."

Panic stabbed at him. "What do you mean?"

"Time moves differently in this room. A minute here is a day out there."

"Oh God."

"We have been here seven minutes and 35 seconds."

"Seven days? I've lost a week!"

"Yes, and Belle *is* in mortal danger; Violet Wickeby has possessed her."

The color leeched from Eddie's face.

"I will send you directly to her, but first—"

"Now," Eddie said hoarsely. "You send me right now."

"A warning—"

"NOW!" he exploded. An aura of gold dust escaped his body, causing the room to rumble, the screens all freezing on still images.

The Jäger Father leveled him with a firm look. "Beware of Hook."

"I don't care about any hook! Send me now, or so help me God, I will—"

Just as Eddie was about to close his hands over the old Fae's neck and commit murder, he disappeared.

The Jäger Father stared forlornly at the space before him, the last of the shimmering pixie fading from Eddie's outline. "Goodbye my Lieblingsjäger. I fear this is the last you have seen of me."

A chorus of chimes and tinkles from afar grew louder and louder. "For the Inquisitors are here."

THE END

SNEAK PEEK: NIGHTMARE KISS

Belle was in a realm of wool pressing in on all sides, a smothering darkness. Her senses useless, save for the heavy pressure against her skin and a pinching sensation on one hand.

Light finally dragged in. The blurred image took a minute to sharpen, and a heavenly voice reached her ears.

"Baby girl?"

"Jo?" Belle rasped, and then winced. Her throat felt like it was stuffed with cotton balls dipped in acid.

"Oh, baby girl." Tears glistened in Jo's kind eyes as she pushed the damp hair away from Belle's forehead. "I shoulda known you was special, too. You being Abigail's daughter and all."

"H-How did you—?" she tried to sit up, but she was under a mound of heavy blankets in her own bed. Jo peeled them back for her, and she leaned up against the headboard, feeling dizzy from the effort. An IV line was plugged into the back of her hand.

A familiar male voice spoke up, "I called her."

"Dr. Helsing?"

He stepped into view, a contrite look on his face. "I needed help with you." He pointed to what she was wearing. She'd been changed from what should have been blood-soaked clothes into fresh pajamas.

"Ernesto! Is he—?!"

"He's stable. Sleeping in his room right now."

(Visit www.ileenmartin.com and sign up to request the rest of the Sneak Peek of *Nightmare Kiss: Chapter 1*!)

ACKNOWLEDGEMENTS

I want to thank my Life Team: God (*Philippians 4:13)*, my husband, son, parents, brothers, and extended family for their never-ending love and support. Thank you from the bottom of my heart to:

My second family: my students a.k.a. "my kids" and my school co-workers.

My teen beta-readers in the *A Nightmare in Elmridge* Book Club for their enthusiasm over the story which kept me motivated in writing this second book, and Sienna, for reading the entire 500+ page manuscript in a week and providing amazing feedback.

The readers—You!—who made it all the way to the end of the book to this very point and will hopefully love Belle's world enough to continue reading what happens in the next book!

If you can, it would mean the world to me for you to leave a review wherever you can of my books; I appreciate every single one.

ABOUT THE AUTHOR

Ileen Martin lives in the vibrant city of Miami, FL with her husband, son, and two dogs, embraced by her large and lively Cuban family. A language arts teacher by day, she spends her free time writing in her zen spots around the city, salsa dancing, enjoying funny viral videos, and indulging in paranormal and mystery romances. *Nightmare Beauty* is her debut novel, launching *A Nightmare in Elmridge* series, which promises to thrill and enchant readers. Visit her website www.ileenmartin.com for all the latest updates on her books.